Also by Helen Flint

Return Journey
In Full Possession

Making the Angels Weep

Making the Angels Weep

HELEN FLINT

HEINEMANN : LONDON

William Heinemann Ltd
Michelin House, 81 Fulham Road, London SW3 6RB
LONDON MELBOURNE AUCKLAND

First published 1992

ISBN 0 434 26703 1

A CIP catalogue record for this book
is available from the British Library

The author has asserted her moral rights

Printed in Great Britain by
St Edmundsbury Press Ltd, Bury St Edmunds, Suffolk

To Alex Rees
there is no substitute for a good friend

Contents

PART ONE **SATURDAY**

1 What Road?   3
2 Interruptions   14
3 Melanie   22
4 Original Sin   25
5 Edible Rainbows   30
6 Bridget   37
7 Precautions   45
8 Did Didn't   57
9 Time Out   62
10 Invasion of the TinCan Family   72
11 Democracy   82
12 Neil & Zina & Fred   87
13 The Potting Shed Man   90
14 The Importance of Fred   93
15 Seldom So Simple   101
16 Banquet in the Kruldom   106
17 Mankind in General, Toby in Particular   112
18 Sorry   119
19 The Written Word   125
20 A Good Night's Sleep   129
21 The Purport of his Thoughts   134
22 An End is Put   142
23 Dear Faces   144
24 The Bank Holiday Condom Conundrum   146
25 Taking Advantage   148
26 From the Feet Upwards   150

vii

PART TWO **SUNDAY**

27 The Contest Begins   157
28 Apartheid   168
29 The Wizard of Godnet   177
30 Snake in Paradise   182
31 A Missionary   186
32 Dressing Down   195
33 Predictions   201
34 Insurrection   204
35 The Storming   208
36 Krul's Game   212
37 Exposure   257
38 Altar Cation   262
39 St Boddi's Road   265

PART THREE **MONDAY**

40 Close Call   275
41 Human Lighthouse   279
42 Waking Dream   286
43 Catapult   291
44 Heart Full of Fur   294
45 Wyndcombe Manor Farm   296
46 Vision of St Boddi   303

My thanks to the K. Blundell Trust
for their generous financial help
during the writing of this book.
Also to Lesley Collington,
whose mixture of research
and imagination produced the two maps.

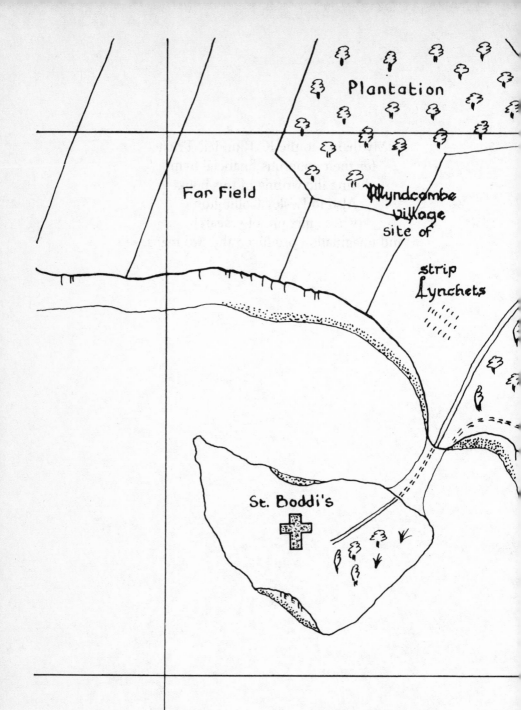

Plantation

Far Field

Wyndcombe
Village
site of

strip
Lynchets

St. Boddi's

ENGLISH CHANNEL

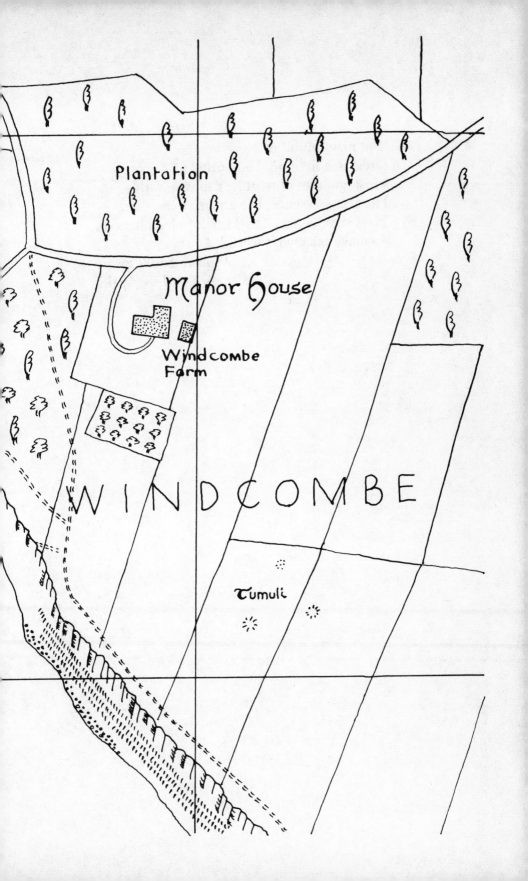

Plantation

Manor House

Windcombe
Farm

WINDCOMBE

Tumuli

'But man, proud man,
Drest in a little brief authority,
Most ignorant of what he's most assur'd
His glassy essence, like an angry ape,
Plays such fantastic tricks before high heaven,
As make the angels weep.'

William Shakespeare
Measure for Measure, II:ii

PART ONE

Saturday

What Road?

Tyrants don't have two neat cystic protuberances on their foreheads; they don't have charred barbed wire for hair; they don't have quivering extensions of flesh at the base of the spine; nor does smoke escape from their cracked, black lips when they are not smoking cigars. So it can be quite difficult to spot them. It can take a whole lifetime. Or ten minutes, depending on your sensitivity.

Krul was even what you would call handsome.

His three-page-long set of directions was about as straightforward as an Income Tax form in Mandarin handwritten by someone suffering from a severe tremor of the hand. Nevertheless, Bernard had studied it minutely and this, together with his own fondness for geography, was serving him well on the south coast of Dorset.

He had turned east at Windmouth and, throwing a dry yellow dust-screen into his wake, negotiated the increasingly narrow road towards Windcombe, knowing there was no longer any such place, except in the memories of the locals. Now he turned sharply down an unlabelled zigzag cliff road towards the sea, jerked round a hairpin and stopped at the bottom.

'Typical,' he said to his companion. 'How typical of Krul,' for in front of them was a small stone and cement road, perhaps eight feet wide and two hundred yards long, down at sea level, just lapped at the edges by wavelets. The road ran out to a piece of land on which stood a small Gothic church.

'I knew it used to be a church,' said his companion. 'Doubtless Krul's not-so-latent desire to be God.'

'No, I mean the tidal road.' 'Arrive before ten and no later than ten-thirty' on the laser printout of Krul's. Now Bernard could see why: not for his own safety, but so that he would drive over and ten minutes later the road would disappear, and Krul could say 'What road?' As if all your experiences were just hoaxes arranged by him.

Bernard considered leaving the car at the beach by the 'Danger – Tidal Road' sign, and walking over, just to frustrate Krul's joke, but decided against it. Why stoop to that and perhaps living here had wrought changes?

Disconcertingly, as he began the slow drive along the damp road, a mirage lifted the growing church slightly, so that it seemed to be floating on the sea.

Over on the sometimes island of St Boddi's things had been hotting up all morning. Literally. All over the Kruldom, blinds, curtains and shutters were shut against the light, the inner air gasping for a two degree drop in temperature or humidity. Either would do. On this greenhouse-hot day, the grass white, the sky white, the sea green with poached seaweed and boiled plankton, when every atom of everything melts into its neighbour, when even dolphins dive for the cold deeps of the seabed, Krul had been waiting. Waiting for Bernard.

With Krul nothing is passive. Even his waiting is an action. Today it involved inspecting both floors of his once ecclesiastical dwelling, testing the water level in the tank, the valve on the cesspit, the spare bed. Addie had done her duty in the fridge. Bowls of food chilled quietly in there under the slight ripple of clouded clingfilm. He wasn't quite sure what lurked within. Knowing her, it would all be colour co-ordinated, if not strictly nutritious. He sometimes wondered that his children were growing up so robust without Carcass to eat, and that their skin was not rainbow.

Krul couldn't abide dust, especially in hot weather. Clogs the pores of the mind. All surfaces must shine to attention. They did. The pile of each berber must kneel towards Mecca awaiting his down tread. It did.

So his waiting was walking, was noisy and deliberate.

Addie couldn't bear to wait with him, so she shifted in and out of the cool corners of the house, avoiding him. The heat said to her body, 'Hey, why don't you lie down and die?' and her body replied, its will robbed by the sheer centigrade of it all, 'Okay, I will.'

So, dreaming of damp crypts, and despite wanting to spread herself naked on the stone flags of the darkest room of the house, to be one with some delicious and final Cold, Addie braced herself and went into the fierce oven of her seaside garden towards the treehouse and told the children there:

'He is waiting' because they deserved to know. They had been loyal troops, here in the desert on Full Alert, even though it meant braising themselves in the upper (and hot air rises) reaches of the tree.

'Oh no,' said Sophie, a cloud passing briefly across the sun of her face. She was only ten, and yet the sun rose and set behind her eyes. Ask Krul. Wasn't she the epitome of Aryan girlhood, of red-blond green-eyed beauty budding into adolescence? She uncrossed her legs on the wooden plank and instantly looked military. Like a girl guide on the brink of a salute in her khaki shorts. She would be ready for whatever Krul came up with in the storm of his Waiting. That was her strength: being able to live up to Krul's expectations without giving any sign of the effort involved. As if it came naturally never to look flustered. Nothing untucked, nothing astray or wispy or crumpled. Always crisp. Even as the edges of the world melt into greenhouse lava, she glows white-blue of skin. Her brother Toby sees her in the dappled light as an Angel on Earth: one who could please the Father with the minimum of visible effort. Unlike him, she was never never caught unawares doing Wrong.

'He was all right until just now, when the Interfacing

stopped,' said Addie. 'Interfacing' used to be a sewing term; to Addie it had simply meant that strip of loosely woven white fabric she placed behind the embroidery to hold it rigid. Now she knows better.

'He has put them all in prison, the Nerds.' Sophie offers this as commentary on the vortex of the war zone.

It is not an indictable offence, being a Nerd, except for Great Wolf or Yogi or No Big Dealer or Sugardaddy or SantaKlaws – all players in Godnet, the interfacing Krul does up in his study in the tower of St Boddi's. There he plays (though you must never call it so) on his dished white keyboard in front of his amber screen. Toby and Sophie wish they would put up a better fight, those Nerds. Father swipes them so easily. Or, as Toby thinks of it, he swashes and they buckle. In they go behind the bars for forty-eight hours, all weekend, and Father is loose and free. On the prowl for victims.

'So now he is waiting,' Addie repeated.

Father is waiting. In Kruldom such things ought not to happen: they are not allowed. Toby shudders. He is all at sea now, thoroughly unhinged, frayed, bobbing up and down on the brittle plank of the treehouse, remembering.

That pane of glass *seems* to be broken, those pieces there as evidence, and that ball *was* in his hand still, but it was nothing to do with him.

Nothing! You know that. But Father is waiting. His waiting is like a hand grenade with the pin inching out millimetre by millimetre. Not just one. The whole garden is now littered with hand grenades whose pins are rising like spring bulbs. He is waiting. While those short white fuses of hotdrops prick up through the sand.

There is no such thing as Not My Fault in the Kruldom. Innocence is nowhere to be had. You *know*, don't you, what you have done?

Why doesn't God drop whatever He's doing, rend open the sky and swoop down to savage Father like a mad Rottweiler?

6

How can He let this unfairness go on? Can't He see His beloved world is on a short fuse?

And Father is waiting.

But we haven't done anything, their eyes say to Addie. Sophie's eyes – Toby's eyes. Two sets of her own eyes, green as the sea, soft and terrified. We aren't to blame.

Bernard is eight minutes late, is all.

'It would be wise, Sophie, if you sent him a little note.' Of course Addie doesn't know about the notes. It is *their* secret. In every family there are such secrets, which they all share, but which still remain secret.

'Saying what?'

Many Notes has Addie designed – spontaneous outbursts of affection laboured over to assume an innocence not possible in the Kruldom.

'We are waiting with you, or something like that. Or just I love you.'

Without warning, Krul is amongst them, by the treehouse, saying, 'Would I be justified in assuming that an engineer requires, both from himself and his associates, a finer sense of timing than this? The swinging into place of a girder must presuppose exigencies of space *and* time. Or does one merely *hope* that the workers on the other side of the river have affixed the necessary supports, rather than gone off to watch television?'

'I'm sure he'll be here soon,' said Addie, standing in front of Sophie so she could hide the piece of paper, and thinking, charitably, how awful it must be for Krul that normality has to freeze into a hiatus whenever he arrives.

'On what do you base this certainty, Adeline?' He only called her that when he was angry. Toby called people nothing to their faces, but inside him were many nicknames. His nickname for his mother, Sykik Sosij, based on her uncanny ability to find even tiny lost things immediately you asked her, by merely thinking, though nothing would induce him to say anything out loud in front of his father. To invite him to do so would be like inviting someone to fall on their sword.

So, Krul said, 'Is Toby of the same mind? Is Toby of any mind at all, that is the question. Grace us with your opinion, Toby. Will he be here soon?'

Being so right all the time has made Father very tall. He has been stretched out tight by all that correctness. Standing on the ground, he can look straight into the treehouse, which is just two hotswelling planks between a pear tree and an apple. Mummy thinks he didn't see Sophie hide the notelet. He did. He sees everything. Knows everything. I am only seven: halfway to a beard. I watched him shave in the round bathroom in the tower this morning. He uses his Fearsome Blade, a dart in its own sheath, scything dead each innocent little stub of hair on his sharp jaw with exact and deadly scrapes. Never anywhere else. Sosij shaves her legs and armpits with a small buzzing shaver, a friendly gobbler of fuzz. Imagine Father shaving his legs! Easier to think of him in a dress.

The thought of this makes him shiver. He has no intention of replying. They will speak for him. No need to mumblejumbo anything.

He is right. Both Addie and Sophie informed Krul, together, and therefore incomprehensibly, that Toby was hoping Bernard would arrive soon.

'In that case, I shall now go and halt the phases of the Moon, for the convenience of Bernard's brakes.'

Been tried before of course. King Canute proving that, unlike Krul, he was not all-powerful. Krul is only joking. Probably. You never know, though. Never completely know what is a joke, and what not. Just as you never know, since his wrath and his humour share the same vocabulary, when his illogical anger might fall like lightning out of a clear sky.

At the moment Krul went to stop the tide, his guest, now ten whole minutes late, and an univited companion, drew up on his beach. They were in the sort of car which takes your breath away. A hand-built white Morgan.

Hearing the car pull up, Toby slid gracefully down from the tree, saying 'Burn – ing – Ber – nard – burning – up'. The

8

words were simply coming untucked from his tongue despite his desire to be neat and invisible.

'Shhh,' said Sophie, sliding after him.

Krul had invited Bernard and Fleur. For Fleur there is no happy phrase in English. In German there is *lebensfreundin*, there might even be a lovely word in Swahili. In English we are reduced to such clumsinesses as Live-in Lover, or Cohabitee. But Fleur had not come. Everyone knew she wouldn't. She never did, even when they were only an inch away on a map of Central London. In fact no member of the Boyd family had ever met her. Or him? Or it? Krul went on inviting her because it was the proper thing to do. The Done Thing.

Perhaps somewhere in Krul's magnificent Library on the curved walls of his office in the tower of St Boddi's, is a book called The Bible of Done Things. It would contain instructions about the exact nature of such delicate topics as the sexual relations between married couples (there being no other type), instructions about the rearing of children, the discreet duties of mothers and fathers. But most of all, there would be a section on Friends: How to Keep Them. Obviously it was important to Keep Them. More important than anything else. Not because friends are essential to your spiritual well-being or anything as airy-fairy as that; because they are a Possession and should be guarded closely as such.

For all they knew, and Bernard was vague on the topic, Fleur may have been a Martian, or a large dog.

Bernard didn't *mean* to be secretive. He was simply bewildered as to why anyone should be interested in his personal arrangements. Like someone given bad news a week ago, who can't yet believe it, he had on his face always a mixture of worry and enquiry which suddenly gives way to anxious laughter. This uncertainty informs his appearance, for his clothes are all indeterminate shades of grey, his hair a shiny mixture of grey and brown, his eyes are colourless, and the features around them melt into one another. The only definite thing about him is that he looks slightly hungry all the time.

But his is an intellectual hunger. He is a Man with a Mission. He catches fire when asked for a bridge. And he is often asked for one. He is one of the world's experts on reinforced concrete. There aren't many. In his working world, bridges are planned, worlds spanned, peoples introduced to each other and to the twentieth century.

Children notice, foreshortened as he is to those at ground level, that he is bent like a bridge himself. As if building bridges has unhinged his parts.

It's like looking up the Empire State or the Eiffel Tower: he blurs above, his face fading. His eyes are filmy and insubstantial. They slip away under a thick lock of hair which swings like a silk girder over the span of his forehead. He is always lapsing into a dream, or coming to, having lapsed. So he is negligent of the Bridgeless World, and should Addie ask after Fleur in a Direct and Meaningful way, meaning 'Will you marry now?', she finds he is soon lost in thought, and will digress about marriage in general, or life in general. Until she has lost the thread entirely and, as usual, Bernard has suspended between himself and others some wondrously impossible structure along which they, and the whole world, will hang in the balance for ever.

Bernard rose from the low-slung car, stepped over the door, flicked back his lock of hair, and shook hands with Krul. A smile passed between them. A formal smile such as diplomats perfect. Bernard knows better than to try to excuse his lateness. Krul would find loopholes and drive trucks through them. Addie hugged him and greeted his companion, now struggling with his door. It was not Fleur but her own brother, James.

No sooner were they seated at the garden table (for Krul's punishment for their lateness was that they must endure a lecture on the history of St Boddi's before entering its welcoming coolth – either a joke, or not one) than James blurted out his excuses for being there, and Addie knew it was all lies because she had known her brother since she was three years and he was two days old. When his first political cartoon had appeared in a newspaper, she hadn't needed to read the caption.

To Addie, it went something like this:

James' story: Hearing that Bernard was about to be the first guest ever at St Boddi's, felt jealous. Rushed over to his house and asked for a lift. Also seized by sudden Bunburying desire to be by the sea. Paper on strike, so no deadline this Sunday.

The Counter argument: The comicbook simplicity of this did not fool his sister: he was too good at encapsulating reality. Never known to feel jealous in his life, hates countryside, seaside, wildernesses and travel. Only the strike sounds plausible. An outrageous and unstable lie, if not.

'Come into the kitchen, James,' Addie said. (Where I will winkle out the truth.)

'What, and miss the lecture?' (What, and be winkled?)

'Obey your sister.' Krul made as if to punch him and he made as if to swerve. It was one of their rituals. Toby flinched. Addie hated it.

James gave Krul his Cheshire-cat smile – the one which disappears as soon as it's served its purpose – and then followed Addie into the house. He was a short person in short shorts with a slight red fur on his very white legs, and a sleeveless T-shirt with a doomed whale on the chest. Time was enlarging his freckled turnip-nose and his bushy copper eyebrows. He was becoming one of his own cartoons. Lovably grotesque. Short and fiery and purposeful, he was, to look at, the most unsuitable companion for Bernard. At least he couldn't possibly be Fleur.

'I'm sorry to hear about Fleur,' said Addie.

'Oh it's nothing serious – just an upset tummy I think.' If James were a woman, Addie could have moved her eyebrows up her forehead at this point and the simple gesture would have meant 'Pregnant?' But he wasn't, so she didn't.

Instead, she quizzed him. Shamelessly. The unspoken deal was: tell me the truth about Fleur and I'll try to find your other lies plausible.

'So you must have met Fleur then, at Bernard's.'

'Of course, she lives there.' He used the female pronoun at least. Thank God for that. Krul reserved the death penalty for child molesters and homosexuals. He still used words like 'pervert' which Addie had long since excised from her own vocabulary, along with 'nigger' and 'dyke'.

'What is she like?'

'Very nice.'

'That's the best a cartoonist can do is it?'

'I could draw her for you.'

'No. I don't want one of your jokes.' If Addie had known how elucidating a picture would have been, she would have found pen and paper there and then. 'Is she like Bernard?'

He laughed. How could a woman be anything like Bernard?

'You mean is she huge and vague and baggy and really into bridges? No.'

'You know what I mean – are they *suited*?'

'Well, they both giggle a lot. Oh, and they must suit each other to have stayed together so long.' Either this was meant to be evasive, or he was really that naive, being a bachelor himself. Or, and this was true at least, he had never met Krul's parents. Two more unsuitable people the world did not contain and yet they had recently celebrated forty-five years together. Time for some parole, Addie had thought.

'Perhaps Bernard will marry soon.'

'Her you mean?'

'Yes, not the girl next door. Her.'

'Maybe not.' James took the tray out of the kitchen door, and across the dining room and into the nave. It seemed dark indoors, even though, and this was a problem they hadn't foreseen when drawing up plans for the conversion, there could be no corridors in a church. Addie ran after him.

'Why not?'

'I don't know. Ask him.'

'You don't know. I thought you knew everything!'

'No, that's Krul.' Now they were in the morning room, flooded with gold through the open french windows. The light outside was blinding for a moment.

'What luck awaits you,' said Krul. 'I refused to start without you.'

'That was kind of you, Krul.' Cheshiring another fleeting grin.

Addie was in luck too, for at that moment her telephone rang, and she missed the whole explanation answering it.

2

Interruptions

The men sat in a formal triangular arrangement on what was left of the grass, in the shade of the pear tree. The drought above and the sand below the ground had wreaked a double vengeance on the plant, so that only small sad tufts of yellow spikes, memorials to grass, remained. Stretches of lone sand, the precursor of deserts, spread sufficiently to house the bottoms of Sophie and Toby, in the middle of the triangle consisting of six legs and three garden chairs.

Toby counted those limbs, just to make sure. Of what? Of their number or suitability? Father's were straight out like giant Iraqi gunbarrels because to cross them could distort the circulation; Bernard's moved about, crossing and uncrossing, restlessly; Uncle James's were short and furry and he kept them so tightly crossed that he must shortly be feeling pins and needles. But knowing him, he'd like that. He often said things like 'Isn't it a strange and lovely feeling when your eyelid suddenly starts popping on its own, in a spasm of winking?'

Must concentrate on Father's story. Might be called upon to applaud. Can't always rely on Sophie's nudgings.

Father must not be interrupted. Sophie hoped they realised that. Sometimes people didn't. But they soon learned. They only needed to stop the flow a few times and be met by the glare of Those Eyes, and it was enough to instruct them. You don't interrupt. It isn't Done. (In a dire emergency, like the need to wee, you put up your hand or catch Mama's eye. She hoped they'd been.)

What Sophie didn't, couldn't realise, was that James intended to interrupt as much as possible and as annoyingly as possible, suspecting already that Krul would elaborate on the truth and that Bernard also intended to halt the flow because he was still cross about the tidal road not having been mentioned in his instructions.

All in all, Krul's lecture was doomed.

The sky, dry for six weeks, said to the pear tree, 'Hey, why don't you lie down and die?' and the tree, tired and virtually sapless, replied, 'Okay, I will,' and dropped its first, unripe pear. It fell on Bernard's head. Wap!

Sophie laughed out loud. James yelled, 'Gravity!' and Toby looked aghast at his father, alone with the knowledge that Krul had made this happen. Listen careful or I will kill you with pears.

He began. The pears stayed put in the dying tree. The listeners listened in the rising heat. Only the slight murmur of Addie talking inside the house and the lap of a tired sea around them broke the quiet as Krul's voice, melodious, strong and Oxbridge-rich, filled the garden.

'The Victorians made no artificial separation between their beliefs, odd though they often were, and their activities. Hence they incorporated into architecture ideas about the Noble Savage, the Incarnation and the Virgin Birth.'

'And Gravity,' said James.

Krul stared at him, and continued.

'Naturally gravity did have an inevitable effect on architectural design.'

Bernard giggled.

'So, they were always on the look-out for unusual places to build churches, places where the Glory of God would startle and inform. Up mountains, in jungles, on islands. This spur of land we now sit on is just such a place: totally unsuitable from every point of view. The land is infertile and crumbling because it is sandstone, the area is only accessible at low tide, and there is no village to *use* it: there wasn't one even at the time of building. Despite this, they were not deterred. That's what I admire. Isn't every mollusc, every atom of nature a piece of His Infinite Jigsaw?'

'No. Not at all,' said James.

'It was meant as irony.'

Bernard giggled again.

Krul stared at him, and continued.

'You can see their thinking. Doesn't a church attract a congregation like a hive bees? Don't even the the darkies flock into such havens when they sprout in the jungle, singing their hearts out?'

Now something really took hold of Bernard and he began to splutter.

'What is it?' asked Krul.

It's just ... your saying ... darkies,' he spluttered back, 'reminded me of something.'

'*What?*'

So Bernard took hold of himself, gathered himself up, and told it.

'The early missionaries in Nigeria translated "Onward Christian Soldiers", and many other hymns, for the native converts to sing. Once a week, on Sundays, they sang them lustily, all the more so because the missionaries didn't realise that the language they were translating into was *tonal*. The converts were singing such ripe things as "Jesus ...'' here he stopped and noticed the two moonwhite faces of Sophie and Toby looking up at him, expectantly, smiling.

'Go on,' said James, 'Jesus what?' Krul's eyes narrowed onto Bernard as if to say, 'Don't you dare,' knowing what was coming.

' "Jesus does some naughty things with my mother on Fridays and twice at weekends" ' – here he took breath, feeling another cackle welling up, and said, 'all because of the *tune* and unknown to the innocent Jesuits who thought they were praising God.'

'Wonderful! The Love of God redefined! Can you imagine

their joyous faces?' James could. He could see a perfect cartoon of them in their Sunday-best loincloths, taking the piss!

Krul stared up at the tree for a moment. No pear fell. He continued.

'For the design of the church, Messrs Richmond and Sons, who had built the Pavilion at Windmouth, took as their guiding consideration, the current fashion for the medieval. It would be stone, and covered in gargoyles. So the edifice rose up, stone block by block on our windswept little peninsula in the cruciform shape of a Romanesque apse-ended basilica with an intersecting transept. The walls were thick and the arches rounded and a Gothic spire crowned the Tower at the apse end. It was all designed to inspire awe and wonder in the as yet nonexistent inhabitants of Windcombe.'

'Especially if they knew no Latin, poor buggers,' said James.

Krul stared at him, and continued.

'Of course they exercised *some* restraint, and the whole church was not on a grand scale like a cathedral – as you'll see, the nave area is no more than thirty feet long, the rood-screen only six feet high and the vestry a mere ten feet square. There are, alas, no cloisters, no lychgate to rest a coffin on at the entrance to the graveyard – just a large stone like a mounting block for a giant. Also the minuscule buttresses serve only cosmetic purposes, and the steeple contains only a small belfry with a clockwork bell inside. Addie and the children like the story about the hitchhiker hearing this bell on a windy day.'

Sophie's heart froze. Mama wasn't here, so it fell on her. She'd rather have a hard pear whack her on the bonce. She realised now that he had rehearsed it with her last night, at bedtime. He was staring at her, though with a slight softening of his steely eyes. She launched herself into the abyss:

'A few years ago a tourist – we call them Grockles – was walking from Christchurch Priory – where there is the Miraculous Beam to see – towards St Catherine's Hill – where they have the Bonfire Night – and he passed St Boddi's – all empty then – and heard the bell. He phoned the Coast Guard – who rescue people – to say he was sure a fire-engine had lost its way on the coast road – that road up there – and was sinking in the sea. The coast guard ignored it, because they had heard so many stories – of ghostly bells and beached mermaids, and even floating churches.' Was there a punchline? A snappy ending? A clincher? She couldn't remember one. Father smiled at her. Uncle James was smiling too.

Indulgent adults can be when there is no punchline to a child's joke, no final chord to applaud. James thought her daring to have told it, and wondered at the need she obviously felt to qualify everything. Bernard was thinking that twenty men could build a spur-bridge in one day. Krul was stretching down over Toby to ruffle Sophie's hair. Everyone in the world hates to have their hair ruffled, but still there are people in the world who do it.

How Toby admired people who could climb Everest on one leg at the drop of a hat, like his sister. And then not mind having their haloes twiddled! His admiration was infinite.

Krul smiled, and continued.

'The masterpiece was to be a huge stained-glass window at the east end. But depicting what? Richmond the Younger strode out one day shortly before the stained glass was to be designed, to ask the nearest living inhabitants, probably a farmer on the mainland, whether there were any local saints. They told him of St Boddi.'

'That's a Cornish name,' said James.

'I know that,' said Krul. Stared, and continued.

'Apparently, St Boddi bore witness, and performed miracles including the wondrous extracting of his own "mylk whyte breastbone" in his home village of Wyndcombe in Dorset. His canonisation has always been obscure, shrouded in mists, like the church. Still, the locals worshipped him and he became the patron saint of the Dorset Oppressed. Not that there ever were any oppressed here – it's always been a prosperous area, but simple folk like to think they have a Champion.'

'A sort of shop steward in Heaven,' said James.

Krul stared and continued.

'So the Richmonds were able to embellish their new church with a fanciful picture of the suffering Boddi done in a mock-Gothic Victorian manner, on the long stained-glass window on the east side, substantiated by the medieval lore attending it. The window now enhances our sitting room and stretches up into our bedroom. It depicts the death of St Boddi.'

'Charming. Nothing like fanciful pictures of death to enhance a bedroom.'

Krul stared, and continued.

'But here concludes the happy part of the story, for the rood screen, constructed to separate the clergy from the congregation, never did so. There were never worshippers at St Boddi's.'

'Ah, cursed, then?' James asked.

'Meaning what?' said Bernard, to extend the interruption. Toby felt his skin prickle. James sat back, his legs now tingling, and let his mind float on St Boddi's:

'A cartoon strip: in the first frame we have God, much like a young girl stood up for her first date. He has bathed, done His hair, put on His most flattering vestments. Notes of music arise from His open mouth: He is singing a few scales to loosen His vocal chords, and standing waiting at the altar of His New Place, at the stained-glass end, watching for the Loved One. In the second frame, He checks his watch. No one comes. In the third frame, He opens a can of beer, lights a cigarette, rips off His best dress and declares that He Couldn't Care Less! Didn't want worshippers *anyway* – to Hell with them!' Bernard laughed.

'And then,' said James, 'in the fourth frame, he sends out his curses into the rafters of the church for all time.' Krul was not amused.

'No. Weightier reasons kept worshippers away, such as St Boddi's being too close to the seductions of a growing spa town, Windmouth, where there abounded lovely sandstone churches full of wealthy people. No, in spite of persistent evidence to the contrary, the locals did regard this place as divine, for they buried people here.'

Bernard and James both scanned the garden for gravestones, warily.

'Where?' said Bernard.

'Not *now*,' said Sophie, 'they've all been dug up.'

Bernard was once again surprised at how Matteroffact children could be about death. Last time he had seen these children, when they were much smaller, Sophie had referred to a hamburger he had offered her as 'dead cow between bread' but had eaten it none the less.

'No one needed to come here, except for funerals. Windmouth was so popular a place for dying, that the graveyards soon reached bursting point. So out they processed with their dead, over the tidal road. It must have had some attraction: there were so many graves. It proves that there is still, in the minds of simple folk, a corridor to Heaven open here.'

Toby knows where the corridor starts too. He spends much of his time avoiding it.

'Moreover, St Boddi's was seldom empty. Ecclesiastical purposes notwithstanding, it went through many phases of occupation: haybarn, youth hostel, gangsters' hideout, even once a look-out during the Second World War – a brilliantly disguised pill-box on the southernmost tip of Dorset. Windcombe's Home Guard.'

'But whatever happened to Wyndcombe village?' asked Bernard.

'If there ever *was* such a place, and I doubt it, rumour is that it never recovered from some disaster in the Middle Ages. A few people now live on the shifting rock and sand of the "Mainland", but they are far-flung, and always give "Nr Windmouth" as their addresses, sometimes leaving out Windcombe altogether. Only one farm, a ragged few fields on the cliff's edge mismanaged by a couple whose entire income derives from an Agricultural Edict made in Brussels, encouraging them not to grow things, still sports the name "Windcombe Farm". Until we moved here the church itself had no address at all.'

'The question is,' said James, 'has God finished with it?'

'The Church Commissioners decided so eighteen months ago when they sold it to me. Dorset is turning pagan again. All the churches will soon be libraries, pottery workshops, community centres, day centres and even mosques.'

'No, not mosques. Too drab for Muslims.'

'Was it habitable?' Bernard asked, thinking of Addie.

'Not by any civilised standards, though you could have camped out here. It was a solid stone shell with a graveyard attached. According to the search documents it had taken Messrs Richmond and Sons three years to build St Boddi's but it only took eight months to make most of it habitable. We ran electricity in waterproof conduits yards out to sea and a septic tank was built. The actual *bodies* upset Addie, though. "Must there be bodies at St Boddi's?" Didn't bother me of course. Still, the graves were emptied, the ground deconsecrated and we employed a man to fill in the open graves before we would exchange contracts. The person we employed was nervous, saw ghosts, beached mermaids, heard small bells, felt in danger of floating away towards France, and fell ill before completing the job. A Nerd of the first order. I quite like the open graves. It might be convenient, you never know, to have some graves ready dug in your garden.'

Entrances to the Corridor, thinks Toby. Should he let them know?

'Excellent,' said James, 'if one of you falls ill, why have the bother of summoning medical assistance? You could just bury them quickly. Wise in this heat, anyway.'

'As I said, the ground it deconsecrated.' Krul stared at James, and finished his discourse. 'Of course, I've yet to discover whether there ever was such a person as Boddi.'

3

Melanie

Look who's talking. Look who's telling her friend Melanie on the phone not to think of herself as a victim, not to put up with this abuse any longer, to just take her daughter and leave. Yes, it's Addie!

Adeline Boyd, repository of sound advice, in control of her own life, who has escaped the emotional warfare of living in London. Or so Melanie thinks.

Melanie has roamed about her empty flat, in the background the insistent drone of North London traffic, where she had always meant to start the unpacking or do some cleaning, Colin out, Bess out at ballet. She had wandered into the cardboard-box-filled bathroom to find enough aspirin, and then thought of phoning Addie

'I'm sorry, Addie.' Melanie is always sorry. She is sorry to be alive, sorry to be poor (a crime for which she is singularly responsible), to be a mother (when the world is so overpopulated), a wife (when marriage is obviously a trap), a tenant (when she could live with relatives and thereby free some accommodation for the homeless), consumer (the depletion of the planet's resources are entirely her fault), recipient of state benefits, female, human, socialist, to be wearing these awful dungarees all the time, and, most of all, sorry to be phoning, of course.

Being entirely responsible for all the ills in the world is only half Melanie's problem. Colin is the other half: he had come back to the flat drunk again, smashed the glass in the front door, committed several other atrocities, threatened Bess and herself, and stolen the rent money from the Flower Fairies satchel where she had hidden it. This was straightforward enough but, with the addition of so many Sorries, it took a while to relate.

Also, Addie had let her go. Since she no longer saw Melanie on an almost daily basis, there seemed no point in prolonging the sadness of losing touch by pretending to be still friends. The minute details of her day no longer held any fascination. The swapping of developmental and educational details of their children no longer held any relevance. It was sad, but not desperately so. You simply moved on, let some relationships drop, fostered new ones. So when Addie had said goodbye eighteen months ago, she had meant it.

Also, she had half an ear to the garden, to Bernard and James.

Bernard was here because Krul can't let people go. Possessive. Everyone who has come into his orbit is *his* for ever. Consoling that he will never leave her because of this. He can be relied on. But this also means that people who have long since lost their relevance must be kept in touch with. Relatives, of course. But also people he was at school with, their parents, their lodgers, their neighbours. What surprises Addie, who sees all relationships as fluid and apt to change, is that these people put up with it. She wonders that Bernard, for instance, who has absolutely nothing in common with Krul any more, still keeps in touch. Not literally though. Nothing would persuade Krul to *touch* him. When he and Bernard are together, they simply swap information about their lives. Interrogation rather than affection. They fill in forms about themselves. Though there is one area about which Bernard has no comment: Fleur. To Addie, this is not friendship; it is acquaintanceship, and pointless. She likes best the friendships the children forge and break daily: best friends one day, enemies the next, then friends again. It seems more human. Still, Krul regards it as her *duty* to entertain his nearlyfriends thus. It is the least she can do. So, to avoid

war, she does it. And with a good grace because life is too short
to do anything half-heartedly or grudgingly.

After ten minutes of tuning in to Melanie's distress, Addie
was able to advise her. She was surprised to hear herself
advising her to leave him. She could live on Child Benefit like
she does now. She could go wherever he couldn't find her. Any
other time Addie would say come here but she's got guests for
the Bank Holiday and . . .

'Oh no. Sorry. Aren't I awful? Ruining your weekend. I can
always take Bess in and lock the door. Sorry.'

'Melanie, it's just I've hardly said hello yet.'

'Oh God, go now. Say hello from me too.' Now Melanie had
in her voice that Ultimate Sorry, and Addie felt she was telling
a one-time best friend to delay feeling suicidal while she
entertained guests. What kind of priority was that?

'Melanie!' She had rung off.

She walked quickly through the nave and into the morning
room and out of the french doors towards the three deckchairs
under the pear tree, just in time to hear Krul question the
existence of St Boddi.

4

Original Sin

Most medieval saints were bishops by profession. The posthumous honour was political, a perk of the job. Not our Boddi, though. He was a saint by miracle: the best sort.

To look at, Boddi had a wonderfully wise and windswept look, even indoors, which he seldom was. His light blue 'eyen' twinkled under bushy dark brows. Living on the south coast of England, he was brown of skin since the sun was kind to folk thereabouts on farms like Boddi's, and gently cooked them as they hoiked turnips, scarified foxes from hogpens, weeded on hands and knees.

Boddi was unmarried, not because of any moral purity or higher spiritual ambitions but because one leg was shorter than the other. This meant he walked with a lilt: a sing-song way of moving. From a distance you could always spot him working in the field by this uneven, wavering movement together with the rich brown bush of his hair and beard which caught in the wind.

In Wyndcombe then, seven centuries ago, there were two sorts of work for honest men: farming or fishing. The two industries were interrelated, though only Sir Piers's Bailiff knew this. He sent women down to the beach to collect the guttings and debris left there, the rottingness of fish which stank so badly, the unsaltable entrails of cod and plaice and porpoise in wooden buckets. These he would have emptied over the crops because he had heard that the life-force still in them could invigorate the growth of anything. He was a mystic in farming matters, though a dull sort of man to know, otherwise. Also the fishermen themselves relied on Sir Piers's horses to carry their salt fish barrels inland, for which they paid him.

The farm workers fared worse because they worked His Lordship's land, not their own, and never had quite enough to eat. But they were safe. Unlike the fishermen who sailed out of the Bay onto the wide waters between Wyndcombe and France (so *they* claimed) who, though they owned their own boats, caught fish which belonged to no man, only to God, and sometimes, if the catch was good were in ale and food without stint for months, oftentimes failed to return, met their maker suddenly and too early in terrible storms. Boddi was no coward, and wanted to go to sea, but his unevenness of leg prevented him. No one would take him, so he would never earn even a share of a boat.

Often he would scramble down the steep zigzag of the path from the cliff's edge to stand on the spur: a jutting of land which formed the northern wall of Wyndcombe's little harbour. Here he would stand, gazing out to sea, on the spot where the women congregated to wish their menfolk home in bad weather, and then to keen parting songs when the time for return had long passed. This was a sacred place, invested as it was with all that longing, all that sadness. Boddi did not wish anyone back, he wished himself away.

Wyndcombe was not thriving at this time, the time when Boddi was scrabbling in the soil on the cliff's edge, in the Lower Field overlooking the Bay, for there had been months of drought and all along the coast people were suffering, even giving up and walking out on their homes to go and find kin elsewhere. This was nothing unusual, for the ordinary person living here at this time, a person like Boddi or his mother say, did not expect life to be easy or comfortable or rewarding. It was simply a question of enduring it as best you could.

So Boddi was bending a little lollopy sideways over some scrawny drought-spoilt crop in a field on this southernmost edge of England, when a travelling friar stopped by the hedge at the side of the field and asked the reeve for some food and ale. He said that the heat of the sun had dried all streams and he had supped no water for days. He was told to ask at the Manor, where no doubt he would be offered some hospitality, for not to offer it would be bad manners or worse.

Before he did so, the friar blessed the workers near him and exorted them to 'Sin No More'. Boddi (who knows why at that very moment and to that very person?) replied, though no reply was called for:

'I haf done no sin yet!' The friar stopped in his tracks and approached our Boddi, who straightened up, anxiously, aware that perhaps, without even knowing it (and wasn't this usually how it happened so that the Master could order a beating before you'd become aware of the nature of the transgression?), he had just *sinned*.

'My child,' said the friar, who would have had to have fathered Boddi at about the age of eight to qualify for this role, for his sandy beard-growth was scanty, 'there is not one person alive today, or who has lived in the history of the world, who has never sinned, save our Lord Jesu.'

Boddi, unaware that he was in any peril, for wasn't he in his own place of work, talking to an unarmed Man of God (not so much as a staff, though an irritable donkey stood behind him), surrounded by his friends, and the day sunny and boding well, pushed his point.

'Well, your Reverence, I remember nought sinning save when as a chil' I understood poorly. Which counts *not*.'

The Holy Man looked as if lightning had struck him then and there in the field. His brown hood shivering off his head, he jumped towards Boddi, grasped the collar of his shirt and wrenched it towards him.

'ORIGINAL SIN!' he shouted, and started dragging our poor Boddi towards the house at the top of the slope, 'HAVE YOU NEVER HEARD OF ORIGINAL SIN?'

Boddi hadn't – he had heard of sin, of course, and even of the Ten Commandments (this is why he could say with confidence that he had never transgressed any, though to be

27

honest he longed to commit at least one, obviously) in the church on St Catherine's Hill when an itinerant lay preacher had spoken before a court hearing held there. Also he had heard of Jesu, the Man Without Sin, and knew that monks and friars were his representatives on earth, that there were certain places dear to Him, as the spur was dear to the inhabitants of Wyndcombe. Places like the Priory. One Christmas Day, he and his mother had travelled many hours to Christchurch Priory to see the Miraculous Beam and hear Latin singing which might or might not have been on the subject of Original Sin. In fact because of its sad beauty Boddi assumed, as did most of the folk there, that it was a song about losing a loved one, possibly at sea, a sadness well understood in these parts.

All in all, it would probably have been fair to say that Boddi was, at this time, innocent of any notion of Original Sin whatsoever. Whether he was therefore innocent of Original Sin itself is a question of deeper theological significance than anyone then in Wyndcombe, save the friar himself, could even have discussed.

The reeve, to his credit, who had not heard of it either till then, did approach the friar and ask what he was doing, but was informed that this man was Possessed and needed to be dealt with.

It wasn't within the man's power to do more than make an objection. He was under the bailiff, who was under the steward who answered only to Sir Piers. On the other hand, he had been *elected* by the peasants working in this field, including Boddi, and thus felt himself in a special position, similar to that of a father.

'I am sure this lad meant no harm, your Reverence,' he panted, trotting along beside them.

'This is not your demesne, Reeve. Let it go.'

'Sir, please. The boy is simple minded.' That stopped the friar. He looked Boddi in the face.

'Is that true?' he asked him.

'No,' replied Boddi.

They continued. The reeve retired to the edge of the field and his workers. It had been worth a try.

Despite his bold 'no', Boddi was terrified. At the front steps of the Manor the splendidly attired Sir Piers himself stepped out to meet them, all glowing and clean. He had just been told of a commotion in the Lower Field by a woman carrying the bailiff's infernal fishrot tubs, and he was not pleased to be disturbed at one of his meals. The fact that Sir Piers and his family ate more than once a day was a subject of much speculation and rumour in the village.

The holy man up and spoke directly to him, nothing afeared, and said, in a very loud voice:

'It surprises me, my liege, that no man has yet noticed this limp for we deem it a Mark of Satan.'

5

Edible Rainbows

Like all polite people, Bernard pretended to understand Toby.

Sophie judged people on the basis of their attempts. Good people tried to keep from their faces any evidence of worry or concentration. Then they would make a good guess based on the situation and the sounds of the 'words'. Bad people frowned, grinned, and gave up. Then they made some stupid remark like, 'That's beyond me, I'm afraid', or, 'What language is that then?'

Father was attempting to persuade Bernard and Uncle James to follow him into the house for the Tour. Mama was trying to lay the table. Toby was failing to warn the guests about the open graves, which he believed led to another, horrible place from which you could not return.

Bernard was a good person. He was really trying, really attempting, really failing. He had heard 'my graves' and said, 'Microwave, do you mean?' For to him, this speech was just words issuing at top speed like half worked out acronyms spinning off a three-dimensional crossword onto the ground in front of him.

Of course Father pretends *not* to understand him, which is a whole other category of person. He has explained this to Sophie: he doesn't want Toby to realise that he can understand him because then his last incentive for speaking properly would evaporate. Sophie had been obliged to ask Mama what 'incentive' meant, to get at this truth. Fortunately Mama always knew his words, though she didn't use them.

Thus Father hated it when she translated for people. She held her peace. Toby didn't. He was determined to warn them.

In some ways Uncle James was the best of all, and the worst. He had always insisted that he *could* understand Toby, every word, because it was just 'surrealism not a speech defect'. Hence he would listen, laugh, and reply. But his replies were as eccentric as Toby's statements. However, Toby didn't seem to mind. At least James took him seriously and found him funny.

Krul interrupted the cascade of words and said, 'Toby is our intelligence test. You have to have an IQ of over a hundred and thirty to stay here and understanding one tenth of what this boy says is sufficient proof of that.'

'In that case, Sophie and I must have a combined IQ of two thousand six hundred since we understand it *all*,' said Addie, seeing that crumpled look creeping into Toby's face.

That was good, thought Toby, if only he could say the odd thing in his head now about 'hoisting petards'.

'I know what he's getting at,' lied Bernard.

'He's talking of the magic of this place,' said James. 'Probably only children can activate it.'

'James, just do the tour now,' said Addie. She didn't like the way he seemed to encourage Toby's worries. Perhaps he didn't realise they were worries.

The tour began. James was expecting to spend it wisecracking on one topic or another, finding the stained glass gruesome enough to warrant a caption. However, he was soon silenced by the spectacular beauty of the interior, despite Krul's marching them round it like those tubby women in acrylic blouses who take you round cathedrals for a donation to the Restoration Fund.

They entered through the morning room french windows. At first it seemed gloomy. Then a golden and pink light spread towards them along the polished oak floor, down a vast inner hall, once the nave. It was 'St Boddi and Oppressor' at the far end. Pure light. Pure colour.

Reeling, James let Krul usher him up a set of brand new spiral wooden stairs, across the second floor landing and into the tower. Bernard followed, bumping his head uncomplainingly partly because he had been brought up never to speak in churches, let alone say 'shit' at a bumped head. Bernard did in fact have some deep religious feelings which he seldom aired. He was rather embarrassed about them. Even Fleur may not have realised why he was always so ready to build bridges for poor people. She probably assumed, like his colleagues, that it was the challenge which attracted him, not the desire to Do Good, or to put his talents at the service of any higher being. Bernard was content to let people think what they liked, and to have a permanent bruise on his head.

At the top of St Boddi's in the tower beneath the belfry, up a stone staircase, a damp and spiral place, past the tower bathroom, was Krul's office. He worked here. James had once questioned Addie about his work and had decided he didn't really want to know. Knowing Krul had all this equipment and no morals, or none that he could approve of, he suspected it involved some sort of electronic espionage. The machines were all mounted on pivoting towers of black chrome, and the walls lined alternately with books and boxes of floppy disks. Two small slits provided a little natural light on opposing walls.

Below it the bathroom was also round, with a round, green bath in the middle of it. Someone had painted white shells and blue seahorses on the walls. He could guess: Addie.

She had been born decorating walls. No sooner had she encountered crayons than she had spied a wall. By the time she went to school, when James was two, both their bedrooms and the playroom had been completely covered with drawings. He remembers now, with a kind of incomprehension, their mother saying, with only the merest hint of regret, 'It was a good thing Adeline went to school when she did because we'd run out of walls.' How could they let a child do that? Had they never heard of paper? They had also let him destroy things for the sake of Art: he had once been allowed to paint his beautiful elm-wood bed black to 'embrace the nighttime colour' – some notion of his adolescence which took hold.

Back on the first floor, into the multicoloured main bedroom with the top half only of the forty-foot-high stained-glass window which stretched from behind their bed down to the floor below: a bedhead of mosaic light. The glass depicted a wealthy man in a long, jewelled robe. From here, they could only see the top edge of St Boddi's halo. He was below, in the sitting-room.

On this floor too, divided by thin new walls in which were set parts of an old trellis-work roodscreen, once brilliant with what Krul pointed out as 'Greek disportments', now ingrained with dust and rather sad, were the children's room (yes, one wall *covered* with a sylvan scene – Addie's handiwork) and the large 'boxroom', an area not reclaimed where dusty pews with puppet heads riddled with pinpricks were stored, and a wooden font, and the guest room where they had made up both beds, knowing that Fleur would not come. Bernard barely looked in here.

Downstairs was the outsize sitting room (originally the nave) where St Boddi lay beneath the jackboot of the splendidly attired fellow kicking him from the bedroom upstairs, looking not at all serene: a Saxon lad burdened with Christianity and looking, no wonder really in view of the boot on his chest, extremely worried.

Okay, thought James, rising to the occasion, I must not seem to be overwhelmed. The window was crying out for a caption.

'The man on top is saying "Any famous last words?" and the poor bloke on the bottom gasps, "Yes – get your foot off my neck!"'

'Pathetic,' said Krul, and James wished he hadn't bothered. 'It has always puzzled me that so many good cartoonists have to be freelance and live by their own merits while *you* are employed permanently.'

'One of his feet is the wrong way round,' Bernard said.

'I never noticed that. Trust you to spot the engineering fault.'

'You left the pulpit,' said James. Its lectern was a beautiful wooden bird, whose carved wings foamed around its own head, as if about to hide or take flight. He was hoping this was an oversight. The thought of Krul being prey to an oversight was almost overwhelming.

'Yes,' said Krul. He couldn't really explain this. He had felt strongly at the time that it should not be moved. Not that he wished to placate a God. Far from it. Rather, he left it there to enrage God, with whom he felt always in dispute for this house. If he ever felt the need to address God, this is where he would do it. But he doesn't. Until God goes Network, compatible with Krul, He can jolly well stay inscrutable. God's loss.

'It could be a talking point,' said Bernard. Some of his jokes were carefully thought out like this. Krul laughed.

'You can give us a sermon from it later on Bridges in the Third World.'

'I think I will.'

'With slides,' said James, 'we must have tedious slides.'

'That window will be the visual aid,' said Bernard.

The Vestry had become a kitchen, with wooden spoons, dried herbs, heavy orange saucepans strewn about the rafters and surfaces, and some machines. Addie made few concessions to modernity here. She had a toaster and a food processor but not a microwave and no freezer. Krul tried never to enter the kitchen. He had been brought up not to bother the Help. This thinking extended to Addie herself now, since the only 'help' they employed was a cleaning lady whom Addie insisted on calling her Domestic Maintenance Operative, to avoid the embarrassment of thinking of her as a servant. Krul called her 'our skivvy'.

The transept arms had become a dining room and a south-facing morning room. Here there were evidences that board games could be played, newspapers read, and embroidery done. Several of Addie's tapestries were folded on a shelf.

'And this is the one place in my house where, if you must smoke, you may do so.' He was showing them the porch, and speaking to James.

So, thought James, if the weather turns, I shall have to puff away here in the stone archway of the porch, an exposed, northerly place where an enthusiastic vicar, had there ever been one at St Boddi's, would have posted notices about the Spring Fayre or the Mother and Toddler Group, together with posters exhorting people to Come To Jesus Before It Is Too Late.

Above the door, in the stone, someone had scratched the words, 'Smyl on us now, Saint Boddi.'

Food outdoors always looks more plentiful. This explains why the picnics of our childhoods always seemed so lavish. So Addie had decided, having cooked for five and needing to feed six, to put lunch out on the picnic table. The children helped her, reluctantly. Sophie's job was to clear after the meal and she was calculating the *miles* extra she would have to walk to do so, through the morning room, nave, dining room, etc. Toby was worried that the food might attract wasps, which might sting someone who was 'allergenous' to wasp stings, and they might have a heart attack and die.

They laid on the cedar table in the semi-shade of the apple tree, a Catherine wheel of colour: a jug of lemon juice shot through with Grenadine, purple and green coleslaw in a white oval dish, carrot salad with coriander in a glass bowl, a white salver with rows of transparent, green-edged coins of cucumber, a silver plate with flakes of tuna with dill stalks, and cubes of beetroot in a pyramid of aspic on a bed of nasturtium leaves. Food fit for angels from a vestry. All Addie's meals were symphonies, tapestries. In the vestry waited a bowl of chilled raspberry and redcurrant snow with mint leaves suspended inside like curled cross-stitches.

'Too beautiful to *eat*,' said Sophie, who had yesterday night beaten the egg white until it was so dry it resembled feathers and had said, 'I see now. The yolk makes the body of the chicken and the white makes the wings!'

Toby could definitely now hear the wings beating hard on the front door, summoning attention. Could it be the ghost of St Boddi activated by Father's denial of his existence? He had just seen all three men walk through the house and out towards the table. Someone, or something, had paddled over the wet road to bang on the door.

It was now 90° Fahrenheit in the shade of the porch, and the heat said to the wiring of the doorbell, 'Hey, why don't you melt and cease to work?'

'Okay we will,' they replied.

Someone was having to pound at the door.

6

Bridget

It was Bridget.

The rucksack bowed her down. The mysterious twin bosomly swell beneath a thin T-shirt strained against its straps. The single black spiked ridge of her hair and the unkempt look of a serious traveller seriously exhausted contradicted the wonder of her lovely long shapely legs in tattered shorts. All the elements, in fact, which the male eye lights and dwells and speculates on, stood there in the sunlight at the door of St Boddi's, pounding.

Bridget has spent large swathes, whole passages, entire volumes of her life escaping from Fates Worse Than, and she has just done it again. Something about the contrast between her outspoken individuality and her delightful shape seems to excite the very attitudes she most desires to eradicate. No one flinches when plain girls take the veil; when chemistry students with the facial features of a cabbage-patch doll after a heavy drinking session – sweet natures behind mashed faces – declare that they will devote themselves to science and not 'settle down', the world sighs with relief. But beautiful people excite the Genetic Imperative (or is it just lust?) in men, and even in women. Surely this lissome creature must marry and deal into the world a whole pack of Bridgetlets while entertaining (in long gowns of exquisite lurex) the husband's irascible but ultimately seducible clients with splendid meals she has whipped up between breastfeeds.

It was perhaps this silent scenario, lurking in the background of life, like some insidious but irreversible condition, such as baldness, which so determined Bridget against settling down.

So strong was her resistance to it, at this turning point in her life (thirty-five years old) when even dedicated, career women can become unaccountably broody, that she had embarked on the series of events which had resulted in her being here, now, at this tidal road.

She was rehearsing the best way of presenting these events to Addie. It was one of those lightning rehearsals people do when they find themselves suddenly pressed to perform.

It was years since she had seen Addie, though their letters had been frank and often. At least, Bridget's had been frank to the point of confessional, and so she assumed Addie's had been too. Perhaps they had not. Perhaps when she had written, if you're ever in any trouble, you can count on me, she hadn't really meant it, hadn't imagined that Bridget would ever put it to the test? Would ever call in that number? Surely, Bridget thought, she had been too close a friend ever to be 'dropped'?

Her only whole qualification (she was half a teacher, a third of a nurse, a quarter of a reflexologist, and so on) was her driver's licence, so a driving job appealed to her, and Charlie, who ran the company American Sunset Tours, didn't even seem to notice she was female. In fact he seemed *grateful* that she was prepared to accept the job.

Bridget should have known better. She should have known it would be the second shittiest job on earth. In fact, as usual, only the beginning had been even barely acceptable: the flight to Paris before she had met the passengers or the vehicle. At least it was a real aeroplane with real food really going to Paris. This was becoming one of the truisms of Bridget's life, that the beginnings were always best. It was the continuings which turned out so sodding awful. This was, of course, not her fault. Her father was always accusing her of having 'no staying power'. He was wrong. She had. It was the world which shifted dangerously about beneath her trusting feet.

The minibus was not *impossible* to start. Not quite. Bridget would pump with the foot, and try to trick-twist the ignition on, to take the engine by surprise, to creep up on it electronically.

Sometimes it worked, sometimes not. And while she struggled thus, the Senior Zits would not 'talk among themselves' as she had hoped, but kept silent.

Absolutely quiet – as if holding their breath.

She knew they were praying. She just knew it. And the knowledge unnerved her. Because of this reverential hush, she could not grunt her accustomed 'fuckanayatolla' which she had found so effective in the past.

'Listen, chappies, you guys, folks,' she would shout at them in exasperation, 'would you chatter, gossip, rap, *speak to each other, please!*'

Then an infuriating four silent minutes later Elmer or some other spokesperson would come down to the front and explain to Bridget that she-all could do what she-all wanted to, but she-all could not expect to dictate what they-all could and could not do, especially as they-all were on the holiday of a lifetime for which they-all had worked very hard all their difficult, capitalist lives (eyes wandering obliquely where their hands longed to travel . . .)

Oh, weep, weep.

Such a conundrum: the frail old tough old eagles of people. Swoop – peck! Watch out! So easily offended, and yet so shallow, such dumb sods.

Budge up, Bridget, give me a turn. Women drivers! Don't mind my hand there, do you? Won't kill you, will it? All hot and bothered is your trouble. Unbutton a little, let yourself go a bit. Won't kill you, will it?

The multicoloured shorts and the screaming shirts and the winged sunglasses, the greenbacks and the exclamations of 'Jesus H. Christ!' to express amazement. Seeing them *en masse* in a narrow European alleyway and guessing their nationality, American would not be your last guess.

Everything here is so *quaint* and small and old and, to think, if it wasn't for the US of A, the Russkies would bomb you-all to bits. And you know what they say about older men, Bridget, men with *experience?* No, you can rely on us, sweetie-pie. No one's gonna bomb you out.

'Why should they do that?' asks Bridget. They look at each other; they laugh. They have heard of this indifference. They have been warned.

'Don't worry your pretty little head about it, Bridget.'

'No, really, why? Why should they want to? Perhaps you haven't heard about the Berlin Wall?'

'Well,' says Elmer, or Horace, or Donald, 'your communist mind is still bent on domination, walls or no walls, and they would be after the *Culture*. They haven't any of their own.'

The Russians – no culture of their own!

'Right, well let's get on and soak up some more culture, shall we, kids?'

'Go for it, Bridget.'

For a while Bridget went for it: she smiled diplomatically, drove, pointed out the window, interpreted when she could (a Scapegoat is a Fall Guy), sometimes made up stories about things she knew nothing about as coherently as Krul did about St Boddi (a little general knowledge going a long way down the road of the imagination and coming back gasping) just to hear their astonishment, their utter trusting naivety, their Jesus H. Christs. During a ten minute 'johnbreak', she invented a circular she could put about for the next group of Senior Zits: it read:

> Bridget is of Scottish descent. Only men wear kilts. Her family do have indoor plumbing, and she is an only child. She has never married, divorced, been engaged, or even 'going steady'. Yes, she is tall for her age (35) and well built in front (38) – confusing eh? and does not find the little pinchings and surreptitious pokings of elderly men at all interesting, ever, and the fact that it will not kill her does not enter into it.

So although Bridget fulfilled for them the roles of driver, mechanic, courier, historian, guide, booking clerk, interpreter, geographer, nurse, and priest, she still, *even then,* had to endure sexist remarks and the invasion of her personal space by elderly persons of low IQ.

'Why is a female driver like a pregnant panda in a zoo?'

'Don't know,' she would mutter, yearning to add, why is an ageing American man like an unemptied Porta-Potti?

'No good ever comes of it!'

Oh, ha ha. Did you make that up yourself, Horace, Elmer, Donald? Very good. Seat belts on now. Time to belt up now! Ha ha, just my little joke: I *know* you haven't got any. Off we go! Bridget felt absolutely sure that somewhere in the world there was a poor American girl going through the same agonies with a bunch of British geriatric turds.

Bridget drove carefully for all that; the bus veered to left on application of the brakes and she knew her papers were not *in Ordnung* at all, now fully realising what a conman Charlie must be. In the back they sang, played cards, and smoked so heavily that Bridget often activated the windscreen wipers before realising the fog was inside, and merged into each other. They became one loud, insufferably stupid old person, with loud check Bermuda shorts, straw hats, a deep voice telling her to stay away from its husband, relax it won't kill you, listen to me, and eat more red meat.

Once they had thus merged, and Bridget realised that she was no longer able to treat them as individual human beings, simply as The Enemy, she knew she would have to go.

There was, after all, nothing really helpless about these old buggers. On the contrary, if there was going to be a Third World War, reasoned Bridget, these arseholes would initiate and run it.

So, while they were gazing up at the oil paintings swinging dangerously from the roof of a small church in Brugge, next to a canal whose ordurous smell was enough to take your breath away, Bridget scribbled a note, put it on the driver's seat, fetched her rucksack from the boot, put the ignition keys in the ignition (let Horace or Elmer or Donald drive; they could now prove their much-boasted superiority not to mention Shine in the Emergency and thus refind their fading macho credibility) and shut the door. She jogged down the main road, found the station and was on a train to Ostend before they had sat down to their *Bier und Wurst*.

She had run out of money at Dover, and hitchhiked along the south coast until she arrived at Windmouth. With the aid of instructions from innocent bystanders (people who could not guess, just by looking at her, what she had just committed) and a surprisingly good ancient map of the south of England, Bridget was able to walk the five miles or so from Windmouth to St Boddi's, despite the fact that she had not slept well on the ferry and had been travelling for twenty-four hours.

Bridget could not go home to Edinburgh, even if she'd had the money, to tell her wee daddie that she had left twelve ancient Americans stranded without a word of French or German, let alone Flemish (German with a Scottish accent as she had discovered), simply with a note to say which hotel they were booked into. He wouldn't like it. He would weep. He would send her back. Her mother would inveigh against foreigners for hours on end. She needed refuge and Addie had once said, if you're ever in any bother, you can count on me. She had it in writing, somewhere in that damp flat in Edinburgh, the last place on earth she could now call home.

Fortunately it was not high tide yet. She had read the sign, like someone glancing at the index when they have finished the book as if to say, 'Surely I've read enough by now', and paddled through an inch of water. She was now so hot that steam rose from her wet trainers.

Bridget felt tired and incoherent and not at all the adventuress she had hoped to appear. As soon as Krul materialised in the arched stone doorway of the church, she remembered the one drawback about Addie – she was married to an Absolute Bastard. How could she have forgotten?

It's easy. How many times had she longed, from the safe distance of another country, for all the comforts of home (constant running hot water, cooked food, clean clothes) and her loving parents, only to realise moments after arriving home that they drove her up the wall? Bananas in moments, doolally in days.

'Ah, Krul. It's me. I've walked from Belgium. Well, not all the way. But.' It wasn't at all what she had meant to say. She felt like the child from down the road who is not really approved of but comes anyway every few minutes to ask whether your child can come out to play. Krul smiled though.

'Hello, Bridget,' he said, 'we got your postcard.'

'It's an emergency really. Is Addie in?' Krul led her through the church, which had obviously become a house (how typical, thought Bridget, supposing that Krul had finally come out as God) and out again the other side into a garden, where lots of people (oh shit, they must have guests already) were seated at a large picnic table, about to eat.

Bridget saw Addie and thought she might burst out crying. Not because there were guests and she was so obviously *de trop*, on the contrary, she felt overwhelmed by the sensation of having finally come home, of having reached the end of a Big Journey. Partly this sentimental rush of emotion was the result of *seeing* Addie for the first time in years and seeing that she had not changed much, so that Bridget felt she had arrived in their past, a safe and fixed place where they were both happy and in their early twenties.

That was fifteen years ago. People age so differently. Some retreat behind rills and baggy lumps of flesh, displaying fewer and fewer traits of themselves. But some emerge, their inner selves, their bones and shapes, clinging closer to the inside of their skin which stretches a little tauter every year. Addie was one of the latter. She had only just started to age at all. Her hair was still red gold and wispy, her eyes still bright and green, her skin tautening and her face emerging more definitely than it had. She was becoming less vague, less like other people. Bridget found something moving in her slight frame, her bright bead belt like a token around a small waist, her sky-blue cotton dress, her flat little leather sandals with blue buckles. She was still faultless, like a brand new tapestry where all the silks retained their brightness and their texture.

On the other hand, the last thing Bridget wanted to do was burst into tears, so she held them back, and Krul helped her by saying, 'Let me divest you' and removing her rucksack from her which made her feel dizzy so that she lost her balance for a moment, and staggered.

Addie saw Bridget a few moments before Bridget saw her and it was a shock. She saw only a dimly lit shape; a woman past her prime with an unflattering short black helmet of hair, spiked into a spear, long bare legs, stooping slightly under a large rucksack, with a peculiar gait, as one who is trying to throw off the foot from the ankle with every stride. But it was enough to identify her. As she came into the sunlight her hair went chestnut sunbrown, and her breasts, loose and large and wandering beneath the white T-shirt, caught the light as only Bridget's do.

7

Precautions

Is there ever a moment when it would be possible to turn away a friend at the door? Strangers, yes. We don't believe in Christian Aid, we're Jewish, we're Mormons, or even, my husband has gone for the shotgun. You can say all this to those members of the General Public who dare invade your porch with sudden financial requests or Good News, but a friend, however old, however distant, can never be turned away.

Unless, of course, you are about to emigrate, that moment. If you had sold your house and its contents and were actually walking out the door with your passport and vaccination certificates, you might get away with it. *So* sorry, just emigrating at the moment, can't entertain you.

Surely Addie and Krul could have said, but we already have two guests and only one spare room and not enough food to cover the Bank Holiday, and shouldn't you go home? They could even have offered her the train fare to Edinburgh. No, this too entails an implied insult. The insult is that the guests we have are *trouble* enough, so we can't bear any more: it is a denigration of guesthood, an error of hospitality you may not commit. One guest implies two, implies three, and so on.

So Addie kissed Bridget and introduced her to James and Bernard, almost as if she were a welcome guest. Almost. She didn't quite carry it off because she had forgotten that Bridget had met them both at their wedding, of course.

Bridget had not realised, until James told her, that it was a Bank Holiday, which somehow increased the nuisance value of her sudden visit, and could not believe Addie had invited two guests, remembering now (for she had thought of what she would say but had not really spared Addie a thought) a long letter from Addie last year, hinting at Krul's 'trouble'. She couldn't now exactly remember what this trouble was (though men you took on long-term were usually trouble, in her opinion) but knew that somehow it had precipitated the move into this isolation. And who or what was Fleur? Was she meant to know? Had she forgotten?

'Jeez, I'm so tired,' she said, hoping this would excuse everything; hoping to be offered a bed. 'I've been hitchhiking across Europe.' She was offered, instead, a few inches of space on a wooden bench squashed between James and Bernard.

'Why?' asked Sophie. Oh God, thought Bridget, this is what children are like, isn't it? She looked across the table to Addie but mis-aimed and caught Krul instead.

'I expect it's a long story,' he said, smiling. 'One in which the dastardly exploits of some male person of the species who unwittingly caused Bridget some gross gender distress figures largely.'

Bridget stared at him. She had forgotten how he spoke.

'Did someone open a door for you, or offer you a seat, or refer to a manhole cover without calling it a Metallic Service Access Indicator? Did someone dare compliment you on some aspect of your physical appearance in a gross and sexist way?'

'Krul!' implored Addie. There was tittering from Bernard, and James also giggled, though he was amused at his own inner thoughts, not Krul's comments, but Addie felt herself burning inside for Bridget, who was so astonished she could not eat and obviously too tired to frame a suitable reply, though in general people who were not even tired found it difficult to make any suitable reply to Krul either. Bernard came to her aid, and she was forever grateful.

'I referred to something as a manhole recently in Nigeria and you wouldn't believe the raucous laughter – they assumed I was referring to a man's anus.'

Bridget laughed, and her own tongue was loosened.

'I've heard they lead to sewers.'

'Not always,' he said, not looking at her.

No not always, she thought. Perhaps he was, after all, despite being a friend of Krul's (only an accident of birth, perhaps, like gender?) a reasonably all right man. Was that the slightest flicker of a spasm against her bare thigh (his in soft corduroy)? Or did she imagine it?

There seemed to be no way to indicate to these people that she was too tired to eat. So, wearily she munched her way through what seemed liked curried carrots and purple coleslaw, trying to join in with a conversation which slipped and slimed around her like ungrippably oiled seaweed. She could hear the sea and felt it hypnotising her to sleep. To stop herself slipping under she stood up to offer to wash up and found that the blood stayed at her feet so that her head felt alarmingly light and detached. She sat down suddenly.

'Thought better of something, Bridget?' said Krul.

'I was going to volunteer for the dishes.'

'I shouldn't,' he said, 'never volunteer for anything.'

'I'll do them,' said Bernard.

'No! You're the guest.' Addie couldn't stop herself, so she added, 'One of the guests, I mean.'

'See what talents Addie has at her command! One of her most charming ones, backpedalling,' said Krul. 'All that time squirming about on a bicycle seat in Oxford was not wasted after all!'

Bridget felt threatened, though this talk hardly concerned her, and she turned to Addie at the end of the table and looked enquiringly at her. She meant, where can I go and lie down? but Addie replied, out loud, 'We'll have to go shopping, I'm afraid. And before the tide turns.'

'Shopping? Here?'

'Food shopping. Windmouth. There are now five adults and two children to feed over a Bank Holiday . . .' at this mathematics, Addie paled and left her sentence to trail, thinking her own thoughts.

'No freezer?' said Bernard, helpfully, imagining that everyone had, as he and Fleur had, sufficient frozen food to withstand the first six weeks of a nuclear blast. Not that they hourly expected the holocaust as some couples do but because Fleur had convinced him that if you prepare sufficiently for a disaster, it won't happen.

'Ah, Addie doesn't believe in freezers,' said Krul, 'for all the vitamins dwelling in food turn blue and scarper, isn't that so, dear?'

'That's an exaggeration, but we haven't one.' Bridget was beginning to feel she would like nothing better than to be alone with Addie in a car going to Windmouth, except on a bed going to sleep, which seemed not to be an option.

'Yes, let's go then,' she said, rising this time with circumspection, that is, more slowly.

The children chose to show the Aruncles (James and Bernard having acquired a sort of consanguinity by virtue of having arrived together, though their almost opposite appearances made the joint term humorous) round the grounds. Toby insisted (to Sophie) that they first inspect the graves, those corridors to heaven, one of which germinated the little green frogs from hell in its damp bottom, and the treehouse and their place, the chalet on the south side. James was especially pleased at having this opportunity since he was planning a small series of cartoons entitled 'Life Chez Les Boyds' and needed some explanations from the mouths of babes.

Krul found himself alone with the dishes, or shortly to be. Bridget wondered about this. Wasn't this a sort of challenge to him?

'Will Krul deign to wash up?' she asked Addie as they unlocked the garage, a wooden structure beside the vestry.

'Only if no one is there to see,' she said, grinning. 'He hates a mess.'

*

Good God, there seemed to be a slight flood on the road over to the mainland but Bridget tried not to panic about this. After all they had lived here a while – they must have strategies for coping. She had once visited a church in Gloucester near a river with her parents and they had seen on one of the pillars alongside the nave an inscription saying, '1947 floodwater level' about waist height. Whatever was happening to this road must have happened for centuries; there was comfort in that. But then Addie said, 'Everything is going wrong. Have you noticed? First we had a live and frantic wasp on Christmas Day, then summer storms in February with lightning, then daffodils were over by March and the blackberries came and went in July, the frogs had a second season in August and the tides have become erratic.'

'Well, I've been abroad.'

'Yes.'

So Bridget told Addie about the Senior Zits and Addie didn't laugh or show any particular compassion for anyone involved – them or Bridget. In fact all she said was, 'How long do you think you'll need to stay?'

'I don't know. I haven't thought it through. Something wrong?'

'Everything.' Now they were turning onto the main road into Windmouth and picked up speed.

'Can't be that bad. Kids seem well. Krul seems – well, his own dear self, I suppose.'

'Oh yes, he's cheerful, and he'll get more and more cheerful as time goes on; then he'll get feverishly cheerful . . . I suppose so long as this is *all*.'

'You're not expecting anyone else are you?'

'I wasn't expecting you. Or James.' Addie tried not to imagine everyone she knew or had known, arriving at the front door, each with a battered suitcase and a lame excuse. All her 'dropped' friends bouncing back up.

'I see what you mean, but it's just coincidence. The fact that

James and I turned up at the same time doesn't mean that more people will.'

Addie just frowned.

'And I'll keep out of Krul's way. And when I've had a sleep I'll be a help. I'll look after the children for you or cook, or anything.'

'Oh, Bridget, I'm sorry. How could you understand?' So perhaps those letters had been less than honest?

They were approaching the outskirts of Windmouth, a dreary set of fields linked by roundabouts in which stood various large squat blue and chrome aeroplane hangars with their own car parks. Acres of glinting metal and hoardings, one of which proudly announced 'The Largest Shopping Complex in The South', rose out of the tarmac to welcome them.

To qualify for using the complex, you had to own a car, for there was an ocean of cars. It was like the forecourt of the Volkswagen factory she had seen from a train in Germany. She had looked away, bored, for five minutes, and when she glanced back again it was still rolling by. Addie toured round these cars for a good five minutes before finding a gap big enough to park in. It was admirable parking: what Elmer would have called 'on a dime'.

'Bridget, wake up!' Unsteadily, Bridget walked with Addie across the hot acres of cars and into an air-conditioned supermarket (cool enough to make your nipples harden) where acres of trolleys linked by coin-operated chains greeted them. Addie bent to free one.

Addie filled the trolley with cheese, chicken, tins of baked beans, rice, jam, dried milk, honey.

'Are you rich at the moment?' asked Bridget, realising for the first time since Dover that she was penniless. Charlie owed her hundreds of pounds.

'By your standards, yes.'

'Then could you lend me some money? I need a few supplies.' Bridget threw a tube of toothpaste and a three pack of condoms into the trolley. Addie frowned.

'I've run out,' she explained.

'Who are you thinking of?' Addie was having a delightfully precise vision of a nude Bridget rocking to and fro over the prone form of first Bernard, then James, and then Krul.

'No one. AIDS is what my mind is dwelling on, and unwanted pregnancy. You can't be too careful, can you? I suppose Krul buys monocled ones mail order by the dozen to be more efficient?' Bridget forgot she was in England and was speaking loudly as if not one of the women wheeling past them down the aisle were possessed of English. 'Everything has a disadvantage – the Pill made me fat, the cap was too slimy and spun off into the distance and got lost, with an IUD you might have an ectopic pregnancy, and even if a bloke says he's had a vasectomy, he could still have AIDS. I wouldn't have any sex life at all, if it weren't for my own precautions. It's down to me.'

'I'm not going into all that now, Bridget,' Addie whispered, pushing the trolley forwards to escape from the section, and, she hoped, the subject.

'Well, it's all very well for you, isn't it?'

Leaning over the delicatessen counter's glass top, Addie suddenly turned to Bridget and said, 'What did you tell Krul about the Americans?'

'Nothing. You won't tell him will you?'

Addie considered this, weighing up the benefits of Krul knowing and not knowing, while trying to imagine how much tricoloured vegetarian pâté seven people might eat.

It was a question of loyalty. With Krul loyalty was paramount, but family loyalty was absolute. Even old aunties he had never met had to receive, and send him, £1 tokens every Christmas. Should this elaborate ritual collapse, Addie felt sure that Krul felt sure that the world would cease to turn. Hence by interpolation she knew that should she ever have a secret from him (the thought of it!) he would not rest until it was out. For instance it had once crossed her mind, when extremely drunk, and not at all herself, that she might like to sleep with an Indian colleague of his they had met in New York once. The man had dark whirlpools for eyes and his skin was like black shot silk, and it was all too easy to imagine stroking and being stroked, an exotic oblivion so unlike Krul's own cool, Scandinavian passion. But, nanoseconds after this thought had crossed her mind, and of course, she could only allow it to traverse briefly for fear of inviting the reality, or allowing the thought to be projected in Panavision on her forehead, she realised that Krul would find out, kill her, kill her lover, and then set about razing New York to the ground.

On the other hand, she could argue to herself, knowing full well that whatever argument she employed it would not stand up to one single philosophical swipe of Krul's, Krul was not interested in Bridget in the least. He would not be at all concerned about the events which led to her being here. Would he? No. Of course not.

Also, Bridget was such a dear old friend, and didn't deserve to be sent home, which is *definitely* what Krul would do.

Addie then noticed that Bridget had fallen asleep on the glass foothills of the counter. The assistant serving her also noticed and he seemed angry.

'By rights, technically,' he said, 'customers aren't even allowed to *lean* on it, sleeping on it is definitely . . .'

'I know, she didn't *mean* to,' and Addie woke her, with difficulty.

Bridget was raving by the time they reached the car.

'I know,' she said, 'I will soon have passed the stage where I need actual sleep. I will become one of those rare people who do not need sleep ever. Perhaps I will be in the Guinness Book of Records as the woman who went without sleep the longest ever. How long? The rest of my natural life.'

'Calm down, Bridget. You can sleep as soon as we get home.' Addie shifted the bags from the trolley into the car.

'If we aren't washed away into the sea on the tidal road. I know something dreadful is going to happen to prevent me ever sleeping again. I know that now. And in that knowledge is a sort of liberation . . .'

'Just hang on, Bridget. I'm going for my trolley money now.'

Bridget couldn't think what she meant, but saw her reunite the trolley with its family in the distance and extract her coin again.

'Why don't you leave that bastard altogether? It's his fault,' she said when Addie had returned.

'What?'

'Everything. Not sleeping.' They set off. Addie couldn't tell whether Bridget was aware of what she was saying, or on the verges of unconsciousness.

'You don't understand, Bridget: I love him.'

'That doesn't make sense. Though I suppose even Saddam Hussein has a wife. Or wives! But how *can* you love such a total prick?'

'Bridget!'

'What? What did I say?'

'Something really horrible.'

'Oh like Krul does all the time you mean?'

'I don't see why you have the right!'

'I'm a friend of yours. Remember?'

Remember? Oh, yes. All men are turds. Especially aristocratic bullies with cruel, angular faces. Observe, mock, and leave well alone. All you need is friends. Women make better friends.

Despite all this, Addie is eighteen and longing for life to pin her down. On the towpath, two abreast, are the sort of folk you see in dramas about Oxford: nicely dressed and better spoken, blinkered and beautiful. Addie floats there joining in, though not joined on. She wears a filmy summer frock whose hem she has embroidered with swans, and a brimming straw hat with a wide blue ribbon but under one arm is her sketchpad, a sign of the Artisan in a world of Masters.

Perhaps she lost her marbles in the boathouse; not surprising in such a place. A *house* for boats! In winter, locked and damp and full of men's dripping things and the stale smell of beer; but now, for one week, a fourth wall falls away and the boathouse, open to the river, is for people and the warped oars that never made the grade. Somewhere here, in among the water-stretched oak slats of paddles which date their own antiquity ('New College 1892'), she sits sketching, until she loses her reason that is. Naturally enough, the loss of her reason prevents further sketching.

The Masters of the Earth are drinking, standing, swaying riverward and landward, catching this one's eye and that one's, all in finery of early summer, rowing between groups as between bullrushes, their tulle and calico and net. Lemonade and skewered strawberries and mint and paper umbrellas hoisted aloft the sour brown Pimms. High-pitched voices sling greetings over the room as men called Jeremy or Algernon or Jolyon enter and leave, randomly, unsteady with drink.

Addie was not drunk. That isn't why she lost her reason. There was never to be any such excuse.

This thought was the last one to pass through Addie's mind before it happened: the racing boats go almost unnoticed by the crowds, so it could be a tapestry in which the movement would be indicated by the ripples of cross stitch under the oars, and groups of people could be standing quite still with their backs to the river – a long silk picture like the Bayeux.

Then Krul entered. Someone next to Addie knew him and called out his name. He waved and left.

Just waved and left. That's all. He didn't even see Addie. But in that moment when he was framed by the golden light behind him, blond, upright, dressed in white shirt and white trousers and springy white plimsolls, Addie lost her reason so suddenly, that she could hardly breathe.

Afterwards she did wonder whether it had not been lust. It was a first. In the past, her loves had been gradual, slowly uprooting her from disinterest to interest, then to wondering, then giving in. Never this painful, overwhelming 'otherness'. And yet men might well feel it often, and Bridget was always saying there was no reason why a woman, freed from the constraints of repression, might not feel it too; not feel that excitement men feel at the sudden lifting of a skirt or the unplanned exposure of cleavage in the folds of a blouse. The

54

explanation might be just that scientific. Hormonal even. This explanation would of course have fitted with those theories of the world, a hasty cobbling together of Freud and Jung, to which Addie was so exposed then. Everything had its feet in Science – even dreams.

Then the gods stepped in. They threw them together and they found themselves in Port Meadow picnicking, wedged together, on punts Krul was poling, at parties he was co-hosting, and debates he was winning. And then, that night when Bridget was out, and they talked late, late into the night, they found themselves for the first time alone in Addie's room in the small hours of the morning with neither the desire to go nor the desire to ask him to leave.

Bridget inveighed, Addie assuaged, and she and Krul drew closer in the assuaging of Bridget, all the more determined to outwit her little wiles to separate them. It was a kind of courtship by conspiracy.

Addie didn't want to be like Bridget: manless, childless, homeless. She wanted to be stitched into the fabric of life; to be that person in the corner of the tapestry who is just getting on with some daily task like sowing, or tending a child, or carrying a bucket. Not *in* the main design, but a crucial part. Just getting on with some ordinary thing while the rest of the world fights the battle in the main picture – to be firmly embroidered in. And Krul was the sharp needle which could do the threading. Sharp Krul: straight and clever and in control. Krul sits on an armchair, and the armchair becomes simply the thing which Krul is sitting on. It has no separate function. Things cease to matter around Krul. They lose their identity. They become the means to his ends. He was the man on horseback at the front of the others, in the main picture: her precaution against isolation and old age and a lonely, meaning-less death.

'And for all his failings, he still is that, and I still love him. You don't stop loving someone because they hold some dubious opinions or are in pain or flawed, or struggling to find a place in the world. If you had ever loved someone in this way, Bridget, and had children with him, and everything, you would understand this. People are redeemable; there's good in everyone. Sometimes a turning, a change of heart is called for, that's all. I trust in the future. Confronting Krul like you do makes no difference. It hardens him against you. I suggest things and wait. This makes a difference. In his own time, he will even out.'

By this time Addie had turned onto the sandspur road and driven through two inches of sea water onto St Boddi's. Bridget was fast asleep.

It was Bernard and James who carried her up to Krul and Addie's double bed and laid her down. Addie supervised, removing, when they had gone, her outer clothes (she only seemed to be wearing outer clothes), and tucking her in.

'Died journeying,' said Toby, watching.

'No, she's just asleep.'

8

Did Didn't

Normally Krul would have criticised the food. Did she realise that chicken harboured salmonella, that beetroot from Poland was probably still radioactive, that pâté contained beef which might have Bovine Spongiform . . .? However, she found that Krul hardly watched her unpack the food. He was lost in thought.

He was standing at the sink. A first in itself. Addie was determined to make no comment about his having washed up the dishes, so she said, 'I think I'll take them all to the beach.' He turned round at this, astonished. He had not heard her call it that before, to him it was simply the southern edge of their island which happened to have a few yards of sand on it.

'To swim?' he asked.

'Yes, of course,' said Addie, 'it's so hot.' She knew this was a curious idea to Krul, to whom swimming was something undertaken in Public Baths, rigorously, with an underwater lap counter. Addie was looking for an opportunity to interrogate Bernard about Fleur while the children were busy.

'That's something normal people do, Krul. Just relax on the beach.'

'Ah, you're going to relax.' He smiled at her.

The telephone in the tower rang and Krul turned to run for it. This meant that he had put *his* phone on Answermode but wanted to get there before the four rings were up. He enjoyed the challenge. Addie thought it stupid. Why set the machine and then answer it yourself?

She didn't understand the technology: there was a reason.

So the Aruncles, and Addie and her children set off for the beach, a hundred yards from the morning room doors, without Krul or the sleeping Bridget, but with towels, swimsuits, deckchairs, a bottle of fizzy pop, everything in fact that you might collect together for a day's outing to Bognor Regis. The Aruncles carried everything and Toby and Sophie ran so that they were in the water by the time Addie and they arrived at the beach.

The sea and its beach had been there for the past eighteen months, been there during drought and storm, murmuring in the background of everything like traffic noise in daytime London. But somehow Addie had not deliberately visited it. Even ordinary people who live in houses with gardens often find there are parts of their property they don't really discover until they have guests.

'What's that in the bay?' asked James, peering out to sea, westward.

'An oil rig apparently.'

'No, it can't be that.'

'Then why ask me?' It had always been so as children. James asked; she replied; he denied her reply; she chastised him for this; he came up with a better idea ... it bored her. It bored her that to him nothing was ever, predictably, what it seemed.

'Toby thinks the husbands of the mermaids use it for cricket practice,' said Sophie.

'Mermen,' Toby corrected her. He loved odd words. Them he could say every time without mix-up. Words like ogre and chilblain and mermen, and, the best of all, Electrolux.

'How's that, James – sufficiently exotic for you?' At last James sensed that he was spare and went into the water with the children.

During the next half-hour, sitting cross-legged next to Bernard, Addie ascertained that Fleur did not like gardening, loved animals, worked shifts, was not pregnant, not engaged to him, and socialist. Bernard said many other things, but none of them interested Addie – she was becoming obsessed by the absent

Fleur. He had no photographs of her. He did have photographs of a floating bridge he had designed and built in Benin, Nigeria. Addie wondered if there was a question which, once asked, would really tell her all she needed to know. Was there one, crucial question? Bernard himself had once told her this very thing: that he had found the important thing is asking the right questions, not finding clever solutions. It was no good building a bridge where the local economy depended on ferrying goods over the river.

'I can hear something else,' said Bernard, just as Addie was framing a Big Question to ask him.

'What do you mean?' Was Fleur communicating with them telepathically?

'Other children, arguing.' Addie looked into the waves, where Sophie and Toby were jumping with James, and heard also behind her the insistent sound of 'Did. Didn't. Did. Didn't.' And it was not her children.

Krul replaced the receiver in his office, frowning. It had been a short conversation with a stranger, and he was perplexed and a little angry.

However, he had noticed, running up to the tower, Bridget, lying in his bed. It was usually dark by the time Krul and Addie retired to the large double bed beneath St Boddi's glass oppressor, so generally Krul never saw this vision – a woman in his bed under a thin white sheet but also under the marbled shafts of coloured light falling over her from the window above, streaming in from the backlighting of a high mid-afternoon summer sun, a steamy rainbow of mist about her.

Krul walked quietly down into his bedroom and stood by the bed.

The sheet looked like a wet white film sprayed on: as if she were naked, or near it. Addie had undressed her then because Sophie had told him the tall lady was asleep when they arrived. So Addie had undressed her. How had that been? He had often wondered about their two years together in the confusing time of late adolescence, perhaps they had been close in more ways than that? Certainly Bridget had been so jealous of him at first that she had tried to sabotage their affair, even leaving messages in his pigeonhole saying Addie was busy when she wasn't. She had called this 'protecting a friend'. Krul called it jealousy. Sexual jealousy perhaps?

Some men, he knew, delighted in that. Imagining breast on breast, a fumbling between same and same. A coming without outcome. Two sets of long hair, draped over similar curves, twin sets of fringed and empty abdominal slopes, arching. Sisters. Incest. Close to the wind. Nipple on nipple on nipple on nipple, a wondrous symmetry of sensation.

Not him. He had researched all that of course, been round the houses mentally, working it out. No woman was ever going to accuse him of being incompetent at anything, least of all sex. He would learn to do it right, to do it the best. Some people had orgasms in shoes; some molested children, animals, trees. To be pitied, not envied! But Krul: a straight up man – sure of himself. No need to dream dreams. Krul's fantasies were copy-book ones. The ones you could take home to mother (dressed and neatened up of course, but essentially apple-pie) and introduce into polite society. Nothing sideways about Krul. Nothing to hide.

Something about Bridget though. She's *not* a lesbian, said Addie firmly. Don't even think it. But how could you not think it when so many of her men friends were faggots, she swore like a trooper, her very bearing was that of the unattainable, hands . . . off? Not that he had ever ever ever wanted hands *on* of course. Not ever. Though a man is a man and it's only natural, of course.

And also, there *is* something about Bridget nevertheless: her curves and crevices under the rosy light. He could hear her breathing: she was deeply asleep. Bridget was by no means his favourite woman, in fact hadn't they once actually agreed to be enemies? But this was not Bridget, simply a delightful collection of flesh now turning towards him beneath the sheet, now revealing a large taut breast that rolled and pointed at him in her turning. She wouldn't even know. Not know it was him, if he should enter her and her dream? She stirred again, stretching out an arm towards him and he stirred too within and below and stretched back an arm across her thigh, thinking, who would ever know in this empty house with everyone a hundred yards away on the beach talking and swimming. Us here, in the heat of the sheets under the sunlight from this window and ... then he heard 'Did. Didn't. Did. Didn't' from directly below the window.

9

Time Out

Morris and Lottie and their four children had been lost in their Mobile Recreational Vehicle, or, more apt a description on account of its age and flirtation with rust, the TinCan, in more countries than most people have explored.

There were many reasons for this, and Morris and Lottie's hobby was finding new ones. Morris was searching the world for something, and Lottie relied on maps rather than instinct and neither of them had any sense of direction. Hence Lottie, always the navigator, had to hold the map in such a way that the direction they were heading in was always forwards, down her ample lap on its way to being capacious enough to seat all four children comfortably. Thus there were no absolutes such as north or south, only relative terms such as left and right, and should a road make an unexpected, or, as often happened abroad, uncartographed turn, the map was rendered useless.

This unusual relationship with geography had many times provided them, first as a couple, and then as a family, with unique experiences in Morocco, Oman, Iran, Tadjikistan, and even in Britain, but there were times when both adults wished simply to arrive swiftly at their destination. And this was one of them. For once, the nomadic spirit which restlessly informed all their endeavours, was flagging. It had started flagging in Gillingford at the motorway service area where Morris only agreed to stop so that Clare might empty her bladder and Lottie spread out the map and contemplate it.

While she was in the toilets with Clare, four, and Greta, eleven, Morris took the boys into the Gift Shop. This was a mistake. George, only eighteen months, nestled harmlessly enough on his back in a Kanga Pouch, happy to take in the gaudy surroundings at that height – the height of a whole human and so much more interesting than the twenty-four-inches-from-the-ground view the occupant of a pushchair is accustomed to.

But Hugo, who was seven, was a born scientist and to him the world was simply an elaborate laboratory bench waiting for him to make use of it in the right way, by designing the Right Experiment. The Right Experiment was for him always a mixture of circumstance and materials. Whatever was to hand would do. Having been itinerant for the whole of his seven years, he was accustomed to not having Lego Teknik, Straw City, Sticklebrix, Meccano, Duplo, Construx or any of the prefabricated elements most first world children conjure with. To him a Gift Shop was a design factory, a place where every device and object begged for investigation.

So Hugo was a rooter. He rooted through the world's technological undergrowth, trying to come up with Answers. Thus he had as equipment an enquiring mind, a snout of a nose (very sensitive, he could distinguish smells most humans gave up on), fidgety brown eyes flecked with metallic blue, and hands which never ceased to move. Even in sleep those tendrils would twitch and scrabble about, as if trying to catch hold of a fleeting dream-moment to interrogate it.

Daddy and George obligingly wandered off into the book-shelves at the back and Hugo set to work on the freezing compartments. Powered at the back by electricity, insulated, noisy, no doubt inefficient. A dial on one side indicated – what? The temperature reached or the temperature desired? Only one way to find out. Switch it down to Zero and come back in a few minutes. Soon done.

During those few minutes and before a man in a suit with a big frown on his face approached him, Hugo managed to disconnect the back of a set of earrings (no, not sprung properly), team greetings cards with envelopes which matched

them in colour rather than size, tested the ring-tabs on three
tins of (warm) Pepsi Cola, loosened the security tabs on two
videos (rendering them useless, but they were only *Rambo*
anyway which Mummy and Daddy said 'belonged in a dustbin'),
redesigned a jewellery stand, checked that the Real Dorset
Fudge hadn't melted (it hadn't), checked that the eyes of several
soft toys were unremovable by babies (they weren't), opened
some boxes of sanitary wear (tampons make good submarines,
but he then remembered that there was no water here), tasted a
Junior Aspirin (orange flavour, sugarfree) in a childproof con-
tainer (what child is it proof of then?), tested the colour of two
pens on the paper provided and also, to double-blind the
experiment, on a nearby comic. He was just about to test the
sunglasses and nailclippers for sturdiness, and thinking of
seeing whether you could open the Alice in Wonderland biscuit
tin without showering the world with crumbs, when the man
said: 'Where's your mummy, son?' Hugo didn't answer. He
wasn't allowed to talk to strangers, and in any case he had
nearly forgotten to check the freezing compartment, so he
hurried away.

Things were definitely melting in there. The man followed
him. This wasn't good. Men following you. He couldn't think
what it meant – it must mean that the indicator controlled the
temperature.

'Daddy!' he yelled, and Morris was there in under ten
seconds. 'I've found out all about this freezer.'

'Splendid!' said Morris. 'Perhaps you'll tell me about it later.'

'Is this your son?' said the Floor Walker (a barmy title, said
Lottie later, as if everyone else goes walkies on the walls or
ceilings), 'because he has been a little vandal, hasn't he?' He
bent down so close that Hugo could smell cigar on his breath.

'Oh no, Hugo isn't really destructive,' beamed Morris, proud
of his son's Independent Mind, despite noticing out of the
corner of his eye that Hugo was releasing a heart-shaped
helium-filled metallic balloon as they spoke, 'he just has an
insatiable curiosity – all children do. If properly fostered . . .'

'If you don't leave this shop within one minute,' interrupted the man very rudely (and Morris *hated* unpleasantness of any sort) 'I shall call the police.'

Morris was perplexed, but hurried out. There was no 'what on earth did you do in there?' to Hugo, and only a perfunctory explanation to Lottie when she emerged with the girls, and they went outside to the Dinosaur Picnic Area quietly, not at all like the family of a vandal.

The outside world (those unwise enough to travel on British motorways for pleasure and end up desperate for something at such a place) tutted over them. Tsk tsk. Four children is either carelessness or over-optimism. Two is quite enough. The baby is being abused by the older girl on the slide. Two of them have no shoes on. Okay it's hot, but there could be broken glass anywhere. Negligence. The parents aren't even *watching* them – they are looking at a map and smiling! The fat mother is not properly covered in front (that might even be a breast peeping out), and slovenly in the extreme. Her husband, if husband he be, is no better. Long greasy hair and jeans not deliberately tattered, just tattered.

Their crime against humanity is, of course, that they look *happy*. Happiness is something British people frown on.

They were all rather wild, though. It wasn't that Morris didn't believe in discipline; he did. But appropriate discipline only. Obviously it was never in order to *hit* a child, for this only taught them that Might Makes Right and could lead to real injury as they grow bigger. He and Lottie had heard of, and approved of, a system called Time Out, a system of child discipline which seemed both logical and humane.

It involved simply telling the child why their behaviour was unacceptable to society and then removing them, for a pre-arranged (voted on) time, from that society. The idea was that after a few such Times Out, perhaps shut in his room, the child would modify the unacceptable behaviour to avoid it, hence the words 'Time Out', uttered as a threat, would be enough to set in motion the elements of a moral education.

Fine. Only Morris and Lottie and Greta and Hugo and Clare and George (who was the only one without a vote) live in a van most of the time and there is *only one room*. How to isolate the child? How to provide Time Out? The only option, and it was one reached on the spur of the moment, was to eject the misbehaving child from the (stationary) van and make them stand outside. This seemed a very severe punishment when it was raining, and when the sun shone almost a reward. Difficult. However, they persevered, but the children soon realised that there was a system of punishment in place which could seldom be put into action. The need for a safe grassy verge outside the TinCan, clement weather, and a quorum, worked in their favour.

'Self discipline is what matters anyway,' said Morris, often, thinking, like Rousseau, that the essential goodness of human beings would triumph in the end. Human nature would shine out.

After all, it seemed to be triumphing now. Greta was taking George up the stairs inside an orange polystyrene Tyrannosaurus Rex in order to thrill him on the slide down. He would love it. Clare was following them. Hugo was staring into the bottom of a small pterodactyl on a large spring in cement, pushing it now and then. Morris had spread out the map in the sun, on a picnic table. Lottie touched his hand for a moment, and he squeezed hers. Moments like this when the whole world seems harmonious and you can't regret anything, even, or especially, being lost, are rare. Lottie hugs to her such times, and feeds on them. And she is fat. Ginormous. Gorged with content.

'I think we're only about twenty miles from them,' said Morris, peering down, and pointing at a grubby fold in the sheet.

George screamed on the way down.

'He loves it, Mumsie!' Obviously George is going to be the explorer of the family. He lived for new experiences. He has already started to wrap his three sneg-pegs around the nipple to feel her wince. Hard to do that, because you have to bite your own tongue in the process!

Lottie turned the map.

'Going south?'

'Must be. Isn't it the most south you can go without crossing the Channel? Where's Clare?'

The panic was brief but total. Lottie always thought that the moment she was really happy, tragedy would strike. It seemed that her satisfaction at being lost in a good place, all together, content, had invited the very thing all parents have nightmares about – the child gone missing. Clare had only wandered into the woods along the side of the motorway and Morris soon found her, while Lottie kept the others with her, for fear she would lose them looking for her.

However, it blighted a bright moment, threatening to blight the whole day, and both adults were suddenly tired of travel and while Lottie comforted the distraught Clare with the right tittie (Num-num) while feeding George with the left (Mer-mer) in the back of the van, Morris put on speed and headed, he thought, due south.

George's tiny fist floated towards Num-num to pummel it and Clare said, 'Mine!' and thumped him. He didn't cry. He was too busy.

By accident, it was south, but that last hour of travel, the last twenty miles or so, encompassed several repetitive tours of the New Forest and a fruitless safari around the one-way system of Windmouth's Complex's outskirts, enraged the children and exhausted their parents' patience.

Somewhere between Windmouth and St Boddi's Morris suddenly had misgivings. Lottie could always tell he was having misgivings when he scratched his beard and then bunched his long hair into a pony tail in one savage gesture.

'Do you really think this is all right, Lottie? Remember that time in Holland . . .' She only just heard him, buttoning herself up in the back and trying to shift her enormous bulk back onto a front seat.

'Of course it is. We have no alternative anyway.'

'But Addie will flip.'

'Diddums. Krul won't.'

'But for God's sake, there are *six* of us and we didn't even phone!'

'There are some things you can't explain on the blower.' Actually to Lottie all things fall into that category since she has an antipathy, almost a phobia about telephones. To her communication was ninety per cent nonverbal, being herself a very fluid and physical person and bulky in every way, so the limitations of the telephone rendered her often speechless at crucial moments.

'And they would be thrilled. Who do their kiddiewinks play with in this godforsaken spot?'

'Each other. They're a regular little nuclear family – that's what they like.'

'Well it's what Addie likes. No family is just one person.'

'Oh God, the road is flooded.'

'No it's not, it's only a splash. We drove through worse that time in Turkey.'

'So we did. Here goes.'

'Mumsie, Hugo hit me.'

'Hugo. Time Out. Honk the horn, Morris.'

'I didn't. Ouch! Let me out then.'

'In a minute, Hugo. Be patient. I can't honk, dear, it's a church! Now I've seen it all: they've got a Morgan, *and* two other cars!' said Morris, half anxiously, half admiringly.

'Not everyone's poor like us.' Lottie didn't say it at all enviously – in fact Morris knew that if anything when Lottie described someone as wealthy it was a term of abuse. Few women, thank God for Lottie, would put up with his patched jeans – comrades in legs – the old chums his trainers, his friend the Save the Rainforest T-shirt all day every day, but she liked it. You can't judge a jam by the label on the jar. The scruffier he became, the more she hugged him to her, in every way, even metaphorically. He still regarded her as beautiful, though her beauty was now seriously overblown, like a camellia gasped over when it first appeared, delicately pink in among the waxy dark leaves, which has crinkled and rusted and lost its shape, but still holds within its gentle complexity a memory of beauty.

As he slid open the passenger door of the TinCan, a tumble of children fell out, some of them shouting:

'Did.'

'Didn't.'

'Did.'

'Didn't.'

'Hello! Anyone at home?' Lottie had let herself into the church/house immediately. After a second or two Krul appeared on the staircase, an open tread modern one, beaming what Lottie had once called 'his delightfully wicked smile'.

'What have we just been up to?'

'I've no idea, Lottie, what have you just been up to?'

At the entrance to the nave stood lots of Lottie, even more of her than last time he had seen her. He remembered now that with the production of each child, Lottie's mountainous bulk had increased disproportionately. The first child had merely thickened her ankles and added a foot or so of long curly dark hair, but the second had doubled her neck and covered her torso with a duvet-sized layer of flesh, albeit hidden then by a yard of thick hair, the third had made of her a dirigible all over and perhaps a fourth . . . judging by her appearance alone, she must now be the mother of nineteen.

On the other hand fatherhood seemed to have wrought no physical change on Morris. He was still lithe, tattered, bright of eye. Mentally, he must be different, thought Krul, for he could now read Lottie's mind. Obviously these many children gave them no time to communicate verbally, so Lottie's every thought had to be transferred instantly, by telepathy. Like Russian astronauts caught in the flux of orbital pull, they spoke effortlessly without words. A big family was something he had always hoped for himself, though for reasons vastly different from theirs.

Behind Lottie, Morris must have heard a wish, for he bent back through the inner door to pick up the smallest of the children, a babe just out of arms.

As Krul stepped off the bottom of the stairs, Lottie hoiked up her shirt and released the flap of her left bra, revealing the full gleaming globe of her left breast. It had that distended look of a balloon full of water, heavy but dangerously tensile. Morris deftly swung the child he had just lifted into position in front of this breast and approached Krul, arms open.

Morris had forgotten that Krul never let a man kiss him, even on the cheek. This had puzzled him for a long time in the past until Lottie had explained it for him – kissing between men implied a female side in each man, admitting a female *aspect* and Krul was unable to admit this, or, put forward Lottie, in her most damning voice, he *has* no female aspect. That would of course be for Lottie the ultimate criticism she could make of a man – that he was *totally* male (the worst kind of inadequacy). Lottie had not forgotten this problem however and at the last minute afforded a deflection of the kiss, by saying 'Where's Addie and your sprogs?' so Krul was able to sidestep Morris, brushing against him by way of greeting to embrace Lottie herself, an easy thing to do since she presented such a huge target.

'At our beach. Was she expecting you then?'

'Well no, not quite,' said Lottie, tying the front tails of her enormous shirt into a hammock for the baby, thus making herself into a combination of mobile playground and fast food outlet, 'but we can explain everything.' Krul began to laugh, shading his forehead, and shaking.

'Why are you laughing, Krul?' asked Morris. 'Sorry about the breastfeeding. She does it anywhere. Once we found ourselves at the end of a reception line in Addis Ababa and I looked down and saw both her breasts hanging out like sea creatures and thought, she's done it again . . .'

'Morris! Don't be daft. Addie's sprogs had titty. Krul is all grown up now.'

Krul stopped chuckling and said, 'No, it's just that . . . soon we'll have enough for a small service in here.'

'Oh, loads of family staying?'

'Some are family, some aren't.' Morris paled. The possibility of being unwelcome somewhere always terrified him, and the more seasoned a traveller he became, the more terrifying seemed the possibility, as if the odds against his acceptability were narrowing with time.

'So it's not *your* Morgan,' he said.

'Alas no, it is Bernard's.'

'Super!' said Lottie. 'Party time! We love crowds and I've got tons of nosh on board the TinCan and we can even sleep there.'

Addie had just seen the TinCan, leading the group up the path round by the front of the house, and said to her brother, 'No, we mustn't have this many people. We can't.'

'In the first frame, Krul sends off dozens of invitations to a Bank Holiday Ball . . .'

'Why would he do that?'

James looked at her with those bushy brows, and his eyes said, well I can think of one reason, written crookedly in the thought-bubbles, and she said no more to him. She was engulfed, anyway, just then, in a flabby confusion of Lottie and baby which stank of sweet milk.

10

Invasion of the TinCan Family

A skirmish was underway. Krul can't stand a skirmish. He must organise it, disperse it. If only he could stand them all in categories, say by age or height. First he sent most of Morris's children on a childhunt as if to cut down the numbers.

'I have two children somewhere in this house. Drying the sea's effluent from their skin I assume.' Even Greta could scarcely comprehend this, but when he said 'Go and look,' she did understand. Also she felt an unspoken menace which she could not have put into words. She found herself deliberately putting her body between Krul and her younger siblings, like a shield, as they went.

'George?' said Clare as they ran up the stairs.

'Having boobies as usual,' Hugo replied. Lucky George. Excusable on account of his age. The childhunt was on. They soon stood around the large (could be bouncy?) bed beneath the window with a picture on (a man with hair as long as Daddy's but a much prettier outfit), looking at someone asleep. It was either a very big child or a lady.

'I don't know *you*!' said Greta, pulling the sheet off Bridget's top half.

'Boobies!' pavloffed Clare.

'What the hell?' Bridget woke from the nightmare in which she was being confronted by a policeman with her father's face who only spoke German with a Scottish accent.

'Whose kids are you?'

'Well,' said Greta, 'Lottie and Morris are our parents. But they don't own us. They have borrowed us.'

'Borrowed you from whom?'

'From ourselves.' She couldn't have made a better reply had Bridget asked her to *prove* her obnoxiousness.

'Are you going to play with us?' asked Hugo.

'No, definitely not,' said Bridget, pulling the sheet around her, pinning it between her breasts with the right hand while fishing about on the floor with her left for some clothes. 'There are few things in life,' she continued, 'about which modern children like you can be absolutely sure, but that is one of them. I will *not* be playing with you. Not ever.' She found clothes and started to put them on. To put the T-shirt on, she had to let go of the sheet.

The small one (Clare) could have been the silly girl out of the Sickening Seven in an Enid Blyton: that well-fed, waking-the-Nanny-at-midnight-for-a-glass-of-ginger-beer one. She had those bright 'adventurous' eyes, the livid red cheeks, the long plaits which someone might be paid to braid. This child looked longingly at her and said

'Booby.' It was, again, pure Pavlov.

'Vampire avaunt!' said Bridget and bared her teeth. They ran away. The words were foreign (Arabic no doubt) but the tone was clear.

When Bridget made it downstairs she found tea had been set out on the picnic table and a huge woman was cutting up a giant fruitcake on a giant chopping board with a small saw. James and Bernard were sitting by her, waiting for cake. Addie and Krul were nowhere to be seen. Behind this woman, only visible now and then in sections, like cartoon characters secreting and revealing themselves behind convenient but impossibly narrow tree-trunks, near a pair of fruit trees supporting a platform with ropes on it were five children, obviously introducing themselves.

'I've just met your delightful children,' said Bridget to the fat woman.

'Oh good,' she said, 'had a lovely nap?' What on earth was a 'lovely nap'? One in which you dreamt yourself wealthy beyond waking hopefulness, fucked everyone you'd ever fancied, or one after which you were allowed to come gradually to a civilised state of consciousness? The question ranked with all those stupid ones people unthinkingly greet you with. Once Bridget had suffered for six months with a serious illness. After the illness, it took her some time to recover the two stone in weight she had lost but when she had done so people kept saying to her, 'You do look better. How are you now?' At first she was pleased. People had been sad when she was ill, were complimenting her on her now healthy appearance. After all, people often died of that illness. But it went on and on. She began to think people were trying to tell her something: perhaps something about how *awful* she had looked when ill? After a while she came to dread the 'Hello, how are you now?' because it brought up between her and the person greeting her the spectre of her illness which she was trying to forget. They wouldn't let her forget it. She tried firing the bullet back sometimes – 'Fine, and how are you?' – but the reply was always, 'Okay. But you do look so much better, Bridget. How are you now?' The desire to say 'piss off' was almost overwhelming.

Bridget had started to avoid people who would greet her at all; she even crossed the street to avoid people she would quite like to see before she went abroad again. If only English had another greeting like the Swedish 'Hey!' or the French 'Bonjour!'

'Hi,' she replied to Lottie, 'and who the hell are you?' It sounded ruder that she had meant it to.

James took it upon himself to explain the TinCan family. Narrative was his strength; he was used, after all, to encapsulating a full story into three line drawings, or even one. On the other hand, his was a foreshortened and schematic view of reality because of this. He favoured the pithy caption over long exegesis.

He took as his main theme the link between Morris's sojourn in different states with various uprisings and revolutions. Morris left a country and civil war or revolution or a *coup d'état* happened. Morris always insisted that it wasn't his fault.

Also his version was a respectful one because he envied Morris his total disregard for money, though aware that many of their expeditions had been dubiously funded. Morris and his family wandered the world knowing that should they ever fall totally through the net, there were The Shares. Several members of Morris' family were apt to hand him cash in large quantities whenever they saw him, which was often in hard times.

Despite Lottie's interjections (no, that was in Kuwait), Bernard, fascinated that this family had spanned the world without ever entering a country possessing one of his bridges, noted that odd concurrence of Lottie and Morris's leaving a country with revolution. Insurgence seemed to spring up in their wake. He didn't realise this was a deliberate 'slant' of James's narrative.

While he was thus relating the comings and goings, Bridget examined the once-lovely, vast face of Lottie, the undone blouse, the wet flesh beneath wobbling visibly, the long unkempt hair, all the expressions of unashamed slovenliness and generosity of proportion which she associated with Women Who Let Themselves Go. And why shouldn't they, thought Bridget. Heaven knows, men do. But one day, she thought, I'll tell this poor woman all about birth control. No doubt it would be a revelation. Surely no one *wanted* that many children? A baby was wandering away from her over the grass. Bridget tried not to think of the open graves. Would it be such a loss? What a horrid thought. Children always brought out the worst in her. And geriatrics.

'Have some of this gooey cake. Addie and Krul are having a rest after welcoming us all. It was an eensy bit of a shock. My hubby, Morris, is seeing to the TinCan.'

'Seeing to it?' Bridget tried to ignore the babytalk. Perhaps all those children overwhelmed your organs of communication, not just your bladder, uterus etc.

'The road was a teeny bit wet when we sploshed in!'

'I'm sorry to say this but I think you might be the last straw.'

'Oh, we're used to that. We always are.' Then Lottie told them all how they had run out of dosh (again) and arranged to rent their home in Cornwall, which they had inherited and seldom lived in, to an aunty for the whole of August and live themselves in a cousin's empty house in Cambridge. Unfortunately the cousin had forgotten everything, he was a bit of a wally, and forgot to leave the key in the place where a key should be. Never mind, they thought, much worse things happen at sea, we'll vote on this and camp in the garden, in the TinCan. But a toffee-nosed neighbour, the sort of woman who ironed creases into her pale lilac velveteen tracksuit, you know the sort (Bridget did, and laughed), then accused them of being gypsies and threatened to have them moved on if they tried to set up home there. So they had to turn back, but could not go home. Bit of a pickle really.

While she was relating this, she managed to supply the men with cups of tea, and Bridget, and collected some nappy pins from the table and fastened them onto a chain hanging around her neck.

'Is that a fashion somewhere in the world then?' said Bridget.

'It's the only way I can be sure of laying hands on a pin in a jiff.' Lottie was surprised at her making a personal comment about her appearance. After all, she wouldn't dream of saying anything about the terrible accident which must have happened just now to Bridget's hair. An electric shock perhaps?

James and Bernard munched silently, James amused at what he took to be Bridget's obvious disapproval of Supreme Womanhood as manifested by these pendulous orbs drying in the sun (surely a gross cartoon in the making?) and Bernard, enjoying the way the sun, trembling through the leaves of the pear tree behind them, played and displayed on Bridget's long bare legs, giggling from time to time out of nervousness.

*

Addie and Krul were sitting in the vestry at the table, behind the temporary privacy of a closed pair of swinging louvred doors, opposite each other. They were not resting.

Krul could not agree with her that things were turning into a nightmare or that any terrible problems were now being courted with the arrival of so many unforeseen guests. But then he wouldn't, would he, thought Addie. He went on to say, and Addie to tremble on hearing it, that it felt like an enlargement of the spirit to be able to welcome so many into St Boddi's, that he was feeling *elated* at the presence in his domain of such a throng.

Since he was feeling so elated, Addie felt bold enough to ask him a question which had been worming away at her for the last hour.

'Krul, you didn't *invite* all these people, by any chance?' He laughed. That demonic out-of-control laugh which so chilled her.

'No. But I can still welcome the serendipity. Joyfully.'

'Why?' she asked. He stood, exasperated.

'As you are always telling me, it's no good examining happiness. You only destroy it. Peer too closely at the fleeting moments of joy and they evaporate. One of your wiser utterances.'

He came to her round the table and she could see a fizzing and sparkling in him, as if the skin of his face, always stretched tight, was lit from within. He kissed her on the lips but it wasn't that old marital kindness, that 'through thick and thinness' of fifteen years together, it was something more: an Invitation to a Dance. Then he left, saying, 'Morris fears wet brakes. I shall go now to reassure him.'

'I wish you could reassure me,' she said to the flapping doors when he had gone.

Krul went from the vestry through the dining room to the front door and onto the land between St Boddi's and the watersunk road where the TinCan was parked, near the wooden doors of the garage.

In a normal house, say a semi-detached 'villa' on a road of similar houses, on an estate of similar roads, in a town of similar estates, this would be the front garden. But at the end of this 'front garden' was moored a sixteen-foot rowing boat, for emergencies, a mooring which Krul had calculated, were it five miles up the coast at Windmouth, would fetch £900 a year.

Only Morris's feet were visible beneath the back of the van.

'Doing some archaeology, Morris?'

'Yes, Krul,' came the muffled reply. 'This reminds me of a time in Afghanistan when the alternator . . .'

A mist was coming down now, the five o'clock mist as Krul thought of it. In hot weather a cloud of heat would swirl in from the sea and settle around them. It sometimes looked, when he returned home in the car at that time of day, as if the church were floating.

He, too, was floating. At last his island was populous, multitudinous, a congregation gathered at St Boddi's. God would be pleased, wouldn't he? Posthumously pleased, as it were. Better late than never.

All those children hatching plots in the chalet he had built. He strained his ears to hear but although the open house's stone walls made sound fly swift and true, the distance was too great for anything but a slight alteration in the frequency of sound waves mixed with the tides swelling to reach him. But since the french windows were open he could hear china clicking, Lottie talking to Bridget, and James and Bernard talking, everyone laughing from time to time.

He could imagine it. Gossiping or talking of trivia. Once, at a dinner party, he had, by mistake presumably, been set down in amongst a group of women, Addie among them. They spoke of washing-up bowls for ten minutes! Later Addie denied that the talk had been *about* bowls at all, he hadn't understood: it was about eclecticism. One woman had said that when she was depressed or lonely, she went out to the market and bought plastic. Washing-up bowls, brushes, dustpans, cutlery drainers. Another woman admitted to the same weakness, and they spoke for some time of the changes in availability of colours, red being ubiquitous, blue impossible to get, beige sometimes available, and so on. Then Addie had said: why must it all match? Wouldn't it be more beautiful to have each thing different? She said she had seen an oval dining-room table somewhere with ten chairs around it, each one different. Wouldn't it be interesting to watch which guest chose which chair? They agreed. But in the end, it was a discussion about washing-up bowls really, and Krul could not see the point of it.

One really splendid thing about Morris was that you could talk with him about long wheel-based Landrovers till the cows came home. The man's knowledge about cars was phenomenal!

Perhaps Bridget and Lottie and Addie were even now discussing washing-up bowls. For some reason, the thought pleased him.

He looked into the mists now isolating St Boddi's and thought, let there come over this boundless ocean fleets of people, swarms, countless hordes of folk. May they teem over the beach in untold numbers, a vast mob so that my island might shake and shudder like bleachers at football matches where millions murmur as one, the masses become one endless high density drove, waiting for me to . . . to what?

Address them! Saying what? Krul frowned. He didn't know what he meant, just that he would enjoy that frisson, that surge of adrenalin that comes when there are people as far as the eye can see, blotting out the ground and the sky. An apprehension of danger: as if one ripple, growing in still water burst with a pebble, might spread throughout them and crack the earth, like troops not breaking step on bridges. The manifold of people, the possibility of giving the order to break step and averting a disaster, or letting them march on and standing by to watch with awe a river chasm yawn and split to swallow them.

Addie could never see this. Nervous when two or three are gathered. Constraining him, isolating him. For safety's sake.

Everything small scale and sure and safe. As if the soul itself might be outnumbered and die.

Peaks on the Underground, this fear. He had always to hold her hand. Going up. Nearly there. Read the posters, it will calm you. The anti-abortion literature repeated at intervals. Now you see it, now you don't.

> *Don't kill your baby.*
> *You deserve a break in the Seychelles.*
> *Don't kill your baby.*
> *Call in at Barclays.*
> *Don't kill.*
> *You deserve.*
> *Don't kill.*
> *Call in.*

The middle one, the down one, always seems to be stationary, broken. There is always a disconsolate commuter walking down it. Halfway up Addie asks him what he is thinking.

He wishes she wouldn't ask him this. Surely his thoughts are inviolate at least? And the mind goes into Ansaphone mode: all the compartments are suddenly Unavailable for Comment. He looks at the press of travellers with ashen faces ascending the escalator on the far side of the stationary one. Serried, they stand closer than they would queue, the eight-inch platform of each conferring sufficient private space. But some are trying to escalate their journey, to run up one side to get there quicker, to save a few milliseconds.

What if a bar clamped down at the top, or someone stood there and pushed the top man downwards? They would all fall like a row of dominoes, into a seething heap at the bottom. Gleefully he tells this to Addie. It will amuse and distract her.

It doesn't. She pales. He can see her willing him not to imagine it. They gain the top. You always do. They stand, recovering. Addie looks at the far side elevator. Then it happens.

The front half of a Labrador dog is sucked into the top step as it tries to disappear and there is a great hollow YOWL and all the passengers topple back as the escalator halts.

'Oh God, someone get an ambulance! Quick! Get an ambulance!'

'You can't get an ambulance for a dog!'

'Dogs aren't *allowed* – you stupid man! You've killed your dog!'

Addie thought he had done it, didn't she? She thought his thoughts had the power of command – that by willing something he could make it happen. Also she seemed to know that he hadn't *really* cared about the folk at the bottom and was quite grateful that she seemed to feel responsible and hurried them into a taxi, where she kept saying, 'How could you? Such a terrible thing! How could a dog understand that the stair it stood upon would disappear?' – and home. He had taken First Aid classes for the good of his children, to avoid that horror of helplessly watching the suffocating, choking, drowning child, not for the good of the General Public, after all. But the sound of that dog was a haunting one.

Even now when the road in front of him was waterlogged, submarine, and the sea mist thickening over it, the barking of a dog was so clear it cut straight through the mist like the howl of a dog whose front paws are caught in an escalator or of a demented wolf in a forest you thought empty.

11

Democracy

When Krul built the chalet, he had imagined six or seven children occupying it. Bolting together timber-framed Section A with the interface of section B's nodular ratchet as per the instructions which were in a form of English once well known to voluntary workers overseas when it appeared on the walls of their rooms as cryptic instructions to do with the Correct Maintaining of Kettles, Krul actually imagined his own six children making this their base. It would be a safe place with its own rules and access denied adults, something he had always wanted himself but never had, for no one builds a camp for an only child.

Addie had thought it an odd idea since it didn't seem to be based on their own children's personalities. Toby, for instance, never wanted until recently to be more than a few feet away from Addie for any reason, and Sophie was often watching children's television from the time she came home from school until it was dark, which, even so far south, wasn't long. Admittedly Krul had installed electric light in the chalet, but no heat.

Nevertheless Addie furnished the ten-foot-square room with jumble sale armchairs and a carpet, and some faded rose-coloured buckram curtains she had found in the vestry were put up. It had a genteel beauty of its own: dusty and comfortable, neither fully outdoors nor fully indoors. Sophie soon moved several dolls into it and posters appeared on the walls, of pop groups like The Frowning Bros and someone Toby called Mydonna Kylom. But they only really used it when the weather was warm but inclement, preferring always the roped platform of the pear tree, an open place, without facilities, knocked up by Addie in half an hour, but somehow preferable and which, annoyingly for Krul, they even dignified with the name 'Treehouse'.

Now Krul's dream was coming true. They were not his children entirely, but there were five of them, soon to be six when George had made it down the grass slope by the graves, and the place was obviously a magnet to a group of children. The Treehouse would not accommodate them all of course: it was too small. Hadn't thought of that, had you Addie? No, she had not.

Inside the chalet on a day like this there was little air and much heat, and that Mistery Foglet as Toby called it was coming down around it. Greta sat in the armchair, trying to fill it with her thin self, Sophie on a stool, thus seniority of age was established as Sophie explained to Greta the history and function of the chalet, while Hugo's busy fingers fidgeted their way down a row of tattered hardback books (were the spines integral with the cover or the pages?) and Clare sat at Greta's feet sucking her thumb. Toby followed Hugo's every move, fearing that he would somehow fiddle the entire unstable bookshelf to the floor: it wasn't the mess which worried him but he wondered whether the floor was strong enough to take such an impact, or would buckle, collapsing the whole flimsy (for Father was no builder) chalet which would then roll down the hill to the slope of the beach and over, drowning them all. He had to keep an eye on Hugo.

'Why do you live in a church?' asked Greta when Sophie's introduction was over. It was a good question coming from someone who usually lived in a van and was often asked, just as aggressively, why.

'I don't know,' she said, looking at Toby. Who would know, but could not say. 'At least, I think I did know once, but I've forgotten.'

'Bod needen quids for Saint Gollies,' he said to Sophie but

they all heard and burst out laughing, even Clare who thought he was speaking French or Arabic, the Other Languages there were.

'Is that how he *speaks*!' said Greta, splitting her sides (she was holding them dramatically as she had seen someone doing on a cartoon to indicate that laughing so hard might produce an organ overspill).

'He means God needed the money for Saint Boddi's, so we bought it,' said Sophie sternly. 'Only very clever people can understand Toby's dialect.' She had got this from the speech therapist in London who had told them to say this when *pushed* for an explanation.

Clare took out her thumb and said, 'Why?'

'You bought it from God?' asked Hugo, coming nearer. He was intrigued that someone might actually have scientific, or at least financial, proof of God.

'Toby is the best at school,' said Sophie, the laughter still ringing in her ears, like an awful siren which might mean an emergency.

'At what, handing out the pencils?' said Greta, whose attendance at schools had been sketchy in the extreme.

'No, the best in Maths and Writing and Projects. Just because you can't understand him doesn't mean I can't.'

This explains why Toby is under the impression that Sophie is a divine being: she interprets him to the world and as far as he knows, always will. With Sophie so articulate, there is really no need to whip those rebellious words which overwhelm him into order.

Then Greta did a horrible thing to them. She invented democracy and had a vote. They had to raise their hands, like at school, if they could not understand what Toby had said. Greta and Hugo put up their hands and then Clare removed her thumb and held it up. Greta said, 'three to two'. Thus it was somehow *proved* that Toby was an idiot.

'Why does that prove it?' asked Sophie.

'In our family, we always vote,' said Greta, smugly.

'In ours we don't.'

'How do you decide things then?'

'Father decides. At least, usually.'

'And what does he decide about Toby's talking?' Now Sophie felt hot and bothered and didn't want to go on with this. In their family Toby's speech problems were a taboo topic. Even the speech therapist said they were to *ignore* it in 'the context of the family'. This was such a context, wasn't it?

'Nothing, it's not important.'

Something huge and obviously very important blotted out all the light coming in through the half-glazed door of the chalet. Lottie knocked and, when Sophie had opened it, offered them George as one might offer a plate of biscuits.

'Would you mind having Georgey-porgey? He won't mess up your games I'm sure, but he so *wants* to be with you, my chippy chappolatas. He was trying to crawl here on his own but his leggies gave out.' She was looking at Greta. Toby was delighted to meet an adult with a speech impediment almost as bad as his. He had hoped they might vote on it and reject George. But this didn't happen: Greta simply stood and took the toddler's hand, leading him in.

'I hope you've done his nappy,' she said to her mother.

'I have. I've spared you all the jobbies.'

'Mer-mer booby?' asked Clare, rising.

'Not just now, my little fruitbat. At bed-byes time I promise. Dins in a jiffy.'

'I'm starving.' Clare sat down again and sighed.

'Well Sophie's mummy and I are busy cooking up a treat now!'

When Lottie had gone, Sophie and Toby both stared at Clare, astonished.

'How old is the little *fruitbat* then?' asked Sophie for them both. Greta went red.

'She's four. Too old to be still having the breast, aren't you, Clare?' So Greta did not defend her sister, but gave her instead a tiny cuff on the hand she was sucking so that it wobbled and fell out, but Clare was smiling behind her wet fist. Perhaps because she knew, as Greta did, that Lottie never refused a child the breast, it was Policy – so you could get comfort there even if you were ten, and why not?

Toby didn't want to say anything any more, not while these children were here, but when Lottie had opened the door, he had definitely heard something else, so he nudged Sophie and pointed first to his ear and then out of the door, down the grass towards the spur road. She listened.

'Barking,' she said. A very clear sound of barking. Toby smiled. Only one thing in the world could upstage his sister in his affections: a dog.

'At least, it *could* be barking, though it could be someone playing a joke on us.'

There was now the very definite sound of frantic barking.

12

Neil & Zina & Fred

There comes a point when a sane person has to admit it is not a ghost dog they are hearing, but a real one. At nearly half-past five, Krul, standing by the TinCan, did this, nudged Morris's feet with his own and shouted, 'Morris, come out!'

It only took Morris and Krul a few minutes to unbuckle the boat and launch it along the now totally submerged road towards the sounds.

Someone called 'Krul?' into the mist.

The boat needed stabilising: it was bobbing about on the small waves over the sandbar like a toy boat without a keel. In fact, it was without a keel, a flat-bottomed barely boat. Just an elongated coracle.

Morris had once witnessed the restoration of an oil painting in Italy. Gradually someone in a white dress had appeared where there had only been grass and a column. It was like that now because of the fog: two figures and two small lumps (children, luggage?) resolved themselves out of the surrounding mist. At first they were just grey shapes swaying at the water's edge, but gradually they became two bedraggled adults (she tall and elegant, he short and chubby) with a suitcase and a dog. At first Morris thought the dog had sunk in the sand (was there quicksand in England?) because it seemed to be an Alsatian with no legs. Then the fat spectacled one bent and lifted the dog into his arms, so it must be whole, for he didn't exclaim, where are your legs? or anything, simply, 'Hello, Krul.'

Krul jumped out of the boat (it nearly capsized) and seemed, as Lottie would have put it, to 'lose his marbles'.

'Caloo Calay! Rapturous to see you. Rapturous the day! Welcome aboard my ship. We don't inhabit a ship of course, but yon church, which is even now shrouded in mists. But you found your way here! Despite the fog! No doubt you Zina, cousin of my genes, were Navigatrex Superb and found the very spot of earth which is here, for I know old Four Eyes is a little hard of seeing, aren't you, Neil? New pair of specs, I see. Well done on the modernity front but can I just say, Neil, that they do nothing for you *qua* Neil – *qua* human being? No offence. Just a friendly pointer. May I introduce Morris here, traveller extraordinary, I never go anywhere without him, and father of millions, and, of interest now, superb oarsman?'

'Hello, Morris.'

'And you thought to bring your dog, Neil. How nice for the children. Personally I detest dogs, as you know, regarding them as little more than faecal processors. Polluters of the first order, but I know how sentimental the English are about canine companions, and being childless, you might well be excused falling prey to . . .'

'Krul, we're not.'

'Not what, Zina?'

'Not childless.' She opened the front of the fog-soaked beige trenchcoat she was wearing to reveal a definite bump. Having thought her marriage unwise in the extreme, Krul had silently congratulated her on never having reproduced. Surely one Neil was enough for the world?

'Does science back you up on this supposition?'

Zina laughed, and gave him a hug. 'Absolutely.'

'Ah, Zina, what a surprise. I thought you were above all that! Come aboard my trusty yacht and we shall ferry you, Morris and I, to the house,' said Krul.

The boat was small for four and a half people and a dog and a large suitcase, but they crammed themselves in and bobbed out to sea, towards the fuzzy lights of St Boddi's.

To Zina it seemed hours since they had sat in the car, surrounded by mist and Neil had said, we're here, and she had

said, they live in the sea then? and, due to their elation, they
had not rowed, but laughed lustily. Nowdays nothing could dent
their joy. Even Krul's cruel eloquence was washing over Neil,
she could tell. There had been a time when Neil had felt about
Krul as he felt about school inspectors: only a satanic mind
could have first invented them and then allowed them to
continue living. But all that was in the past.

13

The Potting Shed Man

For ten years Neil and Zina had been content to cultivate their own plot. They hadn't even bothered with Abroad.

Their own plot was a stretch of land fifty feet by thirty abutting Hardrick Crescent in Hunters Bar, Sheffield. All the houses on the road were roughly on the same level but their back gardens either rose steeply or fell away steeply, depending on which side of the street they were placed.

Neil's garden fell away. So steeply did it fall away that leaving the side door of the house entailed negotiating a step of some two feet before steadying yourself on the dry stone wall to slide down the (often icy) path to the garden.

Neil was heading for the shed at the end. He was a Potting Shed Man. Not that he didn't join in fully with the inside life of the house – life with Zina and Fred the dog. He did. But since Zina was a nurse, there were often, too often, times when he was alone with the dog. At such times the house never claimed him. He headed for the shed. The dog came with him.

In the shed, he did two things: he played games on his computer, which was at one end of the gardenwide shed, and he made people in the workshop at the other end. He had made Henry, and Arnold and Sheena and Jess and nine jointed figures, such as the Witch, the Wizard, the Devil, an Angel, and so on. Some of the people he made were just bags of fake fur material with faces and hand-holes, some were full-blown wooden people with their own faces and their own way of walking, their own set of near-invisible nylon string.

Zina said, sadly, that it was because they had no children of their own that Neil spent so many hours in the potting shed building wooden children, like the Father of Pinocchio.

No, said Neil, nothing is your fault. They are so useful for teaching purposes. Closed up, trapped children, even abused children, find they can talk to a puppet. They let down their guard. Puppets are an invaluable tool for him.

Nothing must ever be Zina's fault. That fact informs his love for her. She is perfect, flawless.

Neil's relationship with these inanimate objects in the shed didn't just sadden Zina, it frightened her. He was an affectionate man drying up. He was beginning to live in his head. Hours on end he sent imaginary warships into imaginary zones to defeat imaginary enemies on the screen. Further hours he sat crafting figures in wood and varnishing them minutely. People marvelled at his puppets. So lifelike! So convincing! But to her they were corpses, effigies of the babies she had conceived, carried for a few weeks and lost. Only she knew that the numbers of the puppets – thirteen – corresponded exactly to the numbers of her miscarriages. Even Neil had not realised this.

So they went, finally, to God's potting shed at the Northern Hospital where she worked. It was called a Fertility Clinic. There they both underwent humiliations for six months. Neil was peculiarly well adapted to suffer these humiliations, for who better than a chubby bald man to cope with it? He was so used to it at work – the children who didn't know him every year would scoff at his rotundness and myopia. Only Zina and his older students ever treated him with respect. Neil put this down solely to the length of their marriage. She had first known him with hair. She had fallen in love with a hairy, slim idealist. Now she was loyal to him. That was all Neil asked of life. All he could ever expect. Her pregnancy now was so advanced, and so established, that it was a bonus beyond his imagining. Every day was Christmas Eve. He had stopped making puppets.

Once a year Zina writes to her cousin Krul, an eccentric rich man who lives down south. He likes her to keep in touch, though Neil has often wondered why. He is their only contact with the exotic. Several months into their longed-for pregnancy, Neil and Zina need quite urgently to visit him.

14

The Importance of Fred

Zina is only too aware of the fact that her new beginnings will also be new endings. The future, here inside her, bulging, quickening, somersaulting, also bodes the end of something else.

In front of her was a triple-headed boatman, Krul and Morris and, between them, Fred, trembling. Neil held her hand, knowing her fear of water. It wasn't a debilitating fear, such as people have so badly they shake when bathing, it was actually a fear of instability, of rocking on a boat; and this boat was the epitome of rocking. Behind the triple heads grew a floating church, the conversion Krul had written of, which they had not yet seen.

Then Krul sounded a warning shot.

'If you remember, Addie is sometimes a little antisocial. Shall we say, she is apt to espouse Milton's view that "Solitude sometimes is best society".'

'We should have phoned,' said Zina reproachfully to Neil.

'Yes, but that would have spoilt the surprise,' he replied. Krul admired, despite himself, the slight irony. He did not admire the way all Neil's utterances began with a 'yes' even when disagreeing with you. He had forgotten that.

'Quite right, Neil. The element of surprise is not an advantage to be sneezed at. But Achoo! Because, what you don't know is that Addie's dear brother, James, Addie's old friend Bridget, and Morris's entire family have all had the very same idea and are at present, I expect, awaiting us on the far shore.'

Zina gasped. She had assumed that this tatty and long-haired man was some sort of servant, an oarsman, living perhaps on the further reaches of the island, or a neighbour who owned the boat. Visitors they had – hundreds!

They weren't *all* thronging the shore as Krul had hoped. James and Bernard were. But back in the dining room at the large oak refectory table, Addie insisted on dishing out the Treat she and Lottie had scraped together for the children, as if that was all she would ever be required to do again in the world. She knew that the boat had been launched and someone was being brought over, but she was trying to ignore it, as if ignoring it might make it cease to happen.

'Some more people and a dog are coming, Mama,' said Sophie, sorrowfully, knowing instinctively that this would distress her. Also she was a person who clung to order and timetables and gloried in routine. 'Or one person and a dog.'

'Well, children,' said Addie, 'I don't care if the Vienna Boys' Choir and all their friends and relatives and pets arrive, or the entire population of Panama, I am just going to serve this meal and enjoy watching you eat it.' She dished out Lottie's contribution to the meal: portions of five-bean salad stored, dry, in the TinCan and rehydrated in Addie's pressure cooker, and pieces of bread and Marmite without which Lottie had assured her, her own children would eat nothing.

Bridget was helping, as she had promised.

'I'm beginning to think you're right,' Bridget was saying, 'there's something sinister now about the way people keep arriving. Perhaps we ought to start shipping them out, one by one, or just asking them to leave.'

It was not lost on Addie that Bridget now used the pronouns 'we' and 'them', encompassing herself fully into the family. She was even moderating her language in the children's earshot. No doubt all the others felt equally 'at home'. Wasn't Krul making everyone feel so very welcome?

Bernard had stood for nearly twenty minutes, with James, at the side of the flooded road, waiting for the visitors to be ferried across. Much of his life had been thus spent, thinking of ways to transform aquatic crossings, to obliterate an obstacle nature had provided to trade and cultural interchange. But also there was something spiritual about travel over water, even short distances. Often gods lived in the water, and, like alligators lurking below, they were jealous of their domain and ready to bite. They were always to be placated before bridge work could begin.

Then there was always the question of just who was coming. If there is a ferry, there is always the possibility of intrusion and attack. You are never safe from the possibility that a team of television reporters may hijack the boat and arrive, beaming and well dressed, to film you. Bernard had once been witness to a near massacre of television reporters, trying to make a 'candid' film about primitive peoples.

It was a pregnant woman, a bald man, a dog, and a suitcase which Morris and Krul had transported. Bernard and James helped them ashore, and were introduced to Krul's cousin and her husband. They weren't introduced to the dog, but Bernard looked it in the eye and an instant rapport was established. Bernard loved dogs. All dogs. He was of the opinion that dogs were Nature's saints because they never consciously did wrong, were loyal unto death, and loving. Even Rottweilers, handled properly, could be saints. He and Fleur were researching dogs at this moment, but he was so often abroad, and she so often at work, that it seemed they might have to settle, as some Americans do, for a Video Dog. Either that or hire a nanny to care for it when they were away.

They all trooped into the house, where the women were trying to feed the children.

Fred might have read Bernard's mind for so full of love was he, that no sooner did he see the people in the dining room than he burst in and tried to have sex with Bridget's right leg. Bridget was adept at fending off such attacks and danced backwards from Fred, landing him a hefty swipe on the forehead. The children cheered, except Toby.

Bernard tried to read Addie's face as she congratulated Zina on this pregnancy, apparently long awaited, given up on. Addie looked pale and rather weak. She continued to dish out food as if that took priority or as if she was preoccupied with higher matters.

Toby was dismayed at the blow Fred had received and asked Bernard if 'God wil recumber?' which Bernard took to be a worry about the dog, replying, yes, don't worry. The boy may not know how to ask, but he knew whom. Presumably, he had decided the extent to which dogs had higher feelings. In fact Toby had recently been assured by Addie that anchovies had no emotions but dolphins undoubtedly did. This creature seemed closer to the underwater fishmammal than the pizza decoration.

Fred's life so far had been a golden one. So was his fur. He was a golden Pembrokeshire corgi with a white 'shirt front'. Nestling among his two siblings in the cage in the window of a pet shop in Sheffield one spring, he caught Neil's eye at an auspicious moment. Neil fell in love. It was just as well Neil fell for Fred, for the remaining two of the litter later fell prey to a genetic trait common in the breed: madness.

If anyone had asked Zina and Neil what *sort* of dog they would have (eventually, when they were ready), they would have laughed outright at the notion of a corgi. Only queens and Welsh farmers have corgis. Everyone knows that. They are humorous dogs. The butt of jokes. Why? Because their heads are perfect copies of Alsatian heads, complete with pricked up ears and long snouts. Their necks are thick and fur-collared, their backs long, their tails full, their barrels deep. But underneath this perfect proportion, below this Alsatian top, are four very little legs. Shorter than a tall dachsund, they often stand so close to the ground that the white 'shirt' on their breastbones becomes grey with dirt from the ground, especially in old age as the back dishes.

Of course Neil didn't see this when he fell in love. In the shop they told him it would never be a large dog. This pleased him. Hadn't Zina said she didn't want a *big* dog which would eat a whole cow for dinner, need walking every ten minutes? The puppy was in perfect proportion, for its head had much growing to do and its legs hardly any.

Zina was soon in love also. They cosseted their dog. When the time came to dock his tail, they couldn't face it. Hence he became one of the very few pedigree corgis in the world with a tail.

Fred was intelligent. As a teacher, Neil had planned to devote a weekend to house-training him. It took an hour. Zina bought a Teach Yourself Book of Dog Management to train him in the simple commands. She had to speed read the chapters while Fred waited for the next command. They were the envy of neighbours when at the local shops they didn't need to tie him to lamp posts. The simple command 'Wait Fred' kept him rooted there, panting and smiling at passers-by until they returned. Similarly, he wouldn't accept biscuits or sweets from children. He *knew* it was bad for his teeth. At least it seemed as if he did.

Fred had one weakness. Don't we all? It was sheep. Fortunately the suburb where Neil and Zina lived didn't have many sheep. Only Dresden ones on mantelpieces. But sometimes they motored off into Derbyshire, into the Peak District, for fresh air. The first time they encountered sheep outside the car was during Fred's second year. They heard him gulp. This was a noise he made when excited. They looked round. Fred had flattened himself on the path, looking at the field of sheep.

'They won't hurt you, Fred,' said Zina, laughing. But no sooner had she spoken than their dog, who had never been on a farm in his life, never seen or smelt a sheep before, raced into the centre of the herd and did an extraordinary thing. He didn't worry them. He didn't chase them. He didn't nip their heels. But somehow, by barking and manoeuvring, he put them all in a straight line, a line one deep. Then, ooching forward on his stomach, swimming with his short legs through the long grass, he came towards his parents, asking with his eyes for approval.

It was his only weakness. A genetic fault. They avoided sheep.

Fred was not good for their social life, though. It wasn't that they minded leaving him alone for the evening – though to tell the truth they did worry about his being *bored* without them, and sometimes left the television running, for security. It was the fact that his staggering intelligence, his physical prowess, his affectionateness, became the main topic of their conversation. Parents bore their friends about their babies' progress. Neil and Zina had Fred. And his progress was always staggering.

Zina's pregnancy was the first event to challenge this obsession with Fred. It was going to be complicated.

Bridget had not thought such people as Zina existed any more. The effort which she had apparently put into her appearance spoke of an era which must now be itself an anachronism. Either that or the woman had a maid. Bridget imagined she had spent twenty minutes this morning finding unladdered dotted tights of a plum colour to tone with the gently wafting gathers of a silky maternity dress, tucked over the bosom to confuse the eye, another twenty minutes sweeping her glossy and hennaed hair into a French bun, ten minutes applying plum and pink make-up so delicately that even her features seemed nostalgically to speak of another, more finicky era, five minutes finding earrings to match the brooch, shoes to match the handbag (burgundy kid) and perhaps another five minutes gazing for long enough into the mirror to practise that bearing, that mincing gait, which despite the discreet but advanced bump at her waist, was perfect and seemed to indicate a spell in the Army.

One hour's work. Bridget gazed at it. You couldn't help admiring where you despised. It was a work of art. Interesting that her husband had made no effort at all, except presumably to wash once in a while. For whom does a married pregnant woman make this display? For herself? For other women?

Then Zina made the error, how could she know, of turning

to Bridget, and telling her that this pregnancy was the result of *years* of trying. It was meant to be a friendly comment. Bridget laughed out loud. How the gravest of people reported that they had been bonking away frantically for years without a flicker of embarrassment!

'How awful for you,' said Bridget, rather cruelly. She couldn't help wondering whether this prolonged rogering had ever been allowed to interfere with the hour's preparations she had just envisaged.

'Don't listen to her, dear,' said Lottie, who had not, she thought, ever met this woman, 'she's just jealous.'

'Jealous?' gasped Bridget.

Addie felt her grip on reality slipping away. Some children were asking for baked potatoes, citing the joys of microwaving (Addie had no microwave). Bridget had insulted Zina, who was finally pregnant but whose dog had attacked her, which surely excused her. Neil, her husband, slightly fatter, slightly shorter, slightly balder but otherwise no different, had come in and kissed her and patted his foetus and Krul had made everyone laugh deeply, even Bridget, by some remark which she didn't catch, and the table had been extended, stools brought in so that everyone could sit down to the meal which had only been meant for the children.

Krul then ordered James and Bernard, wet from standing in the mist, being what Krul called 'the welcoming party' for his cousin, to go and raid the larder, open tins, packets, bags, spread on plates all the reserve food Addie had so carefully stored: corned beef, corn, beetroot slices, peach slices, rice pudding, tinned plums, packets of raisins and flaked almonds, the lot. Feast now, exhorted Krul, for tomorrow is another day.

Yes, and a Sunday too, thought Addie, her head swimming.

Lottie, surprisingly assertive in someone else's house, encouraged Morris to fetch similarly extravagant provisions from the TinCan. Which he did, matching Buttered Space

Invaders Popcorn for Krul's Monster Munch Crisps, like magicians of old, offering surreal twists to each other.

Then the sides of the room were rippling like the sides of a tent and the corners of everything grew dark and vague, the heads of unrecognisable children were swimming above ranks of cutlery and a dog lying on the ceiling until . . .

'Addie, sit down, you look pale.' This might have been the professional voice of Zina, calming a patient. She would know about sitting down, and other things. Good, I must ask her about things. There is something I always meant to ask her, about Krul's family, about their state of . . .

Krul caught her as she went down, deftly, like someone who had been waiting for this faint for hours, sighed, and carried her upstairs before she even gained consciousness.

Before she went to sleep, she was aware of someone undressing her gently on what she knew was her own bed and humming a catchy tune which stayed with her through her dream.

It was

> Fif – teen in the bed
> And the little one said
> Roll over.

She dreamt of St Boddi.

15

Seldom So Simple

Boddi may have been uneducated and (as yet) innocent in the ways of the world, but he was not stupid. When Sir Piers Maldespeau and the friar, having partaken of ale together in the hospitality room as was proper, asked him whether he would rather be burned at the stake or renounce the Devil and give himself to Christ wholly, he found the choice an easy one.

To him it was simply a question of saying one thing and dying, or saying another and living. Life was seldom so simple.

He was obliged to hold a book, which he could not read, in his right hand, a cross in his left, and repeat some words of a spell in Latin which the friar murmured at him. This cleansed him sufficiently to escape death, it seemed, but Sir Piers, his bailiff (reluctantly), and the friar all agreed that some form of atonement must be done.

The atonement decided on was that he was obliged to travel with the friar onwards to Sussex (it might have been the land of the Saracen for all he knew) as a slave.

Sir Piers was not altogether sorry to lose this worker, since Boddi's lameness had meant he often had to be excused very heavy tasks at harvest time and the drought meant he would have to start laying men off soon anyway. Best to start with the bottom of the barrel and what could be lower than Boddi, a lame and illegitimate peasant with no Norman blood at all?

They departed just as the sun was at its highest, the friar having eaten well and supped much ale. Also the donkey had been attended to, and Boddi shown, by Harden, the stableman, how to tie bundles onto him.

Boddi was loath to dislike anyone, always finding excuses for the odd behaviour of his fellow men. For instance, he didn't even hold it against his mother that she had been unable to produce a father for him when asked: the poor woman had simply lost his father. Presumably the man had set off in a boat and never returned, as was often the way of things in Wyndcombe. So it wasn't difficult for Boddi soon to form a favourable opinion of the friar who had abducted him. Since he so wanted to, he did.

The man was after all only doing his duty. It was a rough world and terrible justice often meted out before you had time to blink, and Boddi was still alive and the day still sunny as he limped along leading the friar's donkey, wondering what slavery might entail.

Presumably it meant that he was no longer a free man; but what had being free meant to him? Free to work from sunrise to sunset and never have enough to eat, free to live in poor conditions, unable to gift the Wise Woman sufficiently to obtain ointments to quiet the raging in his hip? Free to stay in Wyndcombe and never leave it. On the other hand, no one beat him (often) or made him do foul things (like Awdlay the Mad had to do in the dark hours behind haystacks: Boddi couldn't imagine what things, but the screaming was awful, worse than his laughter afterwards) or –

'Your holiness, sorry to be bothering you, but what is it you will be wanting of me, as your slave?' he dared to ask when they were well out on the steep cliff road overlooking the sea. Below them to their right was the fishing cove and women with wooden buckets of silver fish leavings climbed up the Ziggerzagger, past the children climbing down to go wading in the shallow water, near the Spur where the drought at least meant few storms to wail about. His mother was down there somewhere. He would like to say goodbye to her, but didn't think he would be allowed. Travellers seldom pass by the same place twice, so he didn't expect ever to return.

The friar laughed, threw off his hood to look round at Boddi, and said, 'Let me see. First of all I require you to sing.'

'Sing?'

'Yes, like you do in church, surely you know what I mean. Maybe you sang in the fields as you worked?'

'No, your holiness, I were never allowed to sing. I would a spoiled it for sure.'

'Why?'

Now it was Boddi's turn to laugh. He pointed to his lame leg by way of explanation. The friar looked down too and stopped walking.

'Because you are a cripple?'

'Yes, course, your holiness!'

'Do stop calling me that. My name is Hew. Brother Hew.'

Then the friar did an extraordinary thing. He started to unload the donkey. Not everything, just enough to make room for a rider.

'Get thee up!' he said. Boddi had ridden a donkey once before at Wyndmouth Fayre for a bet and remembered that the uneven lengths of his legs was an advantage. He rocked sideways and launched himself at the animal, landing square on its back.

Brother Hew slapped the donkey on the buttocks and it moved forward sharply. He then picked up the bags from the ground and walked beside it.

'Now sing!' he said. Boddi looked down at him, at the little round bald patch he had not seen before and frowned.

'Now you aren't crippled, so you can sing!' It seemed logical to Boddi somehow, and he tried to think of a song.

'I don't know any, Brother Who, sorry.'

'Then I shall have to teach you. Listen carefully. Songs can be Amorous, Divine, Moral or Trivial. That is about Women, God, Right and Wrong or Ale.'

'And which do you prefer, Brother Who?'

'Amorous and Trivial.'

'So do I then.'

'Let us begin.' Brother Hew taught Boddi the words of an extremely silly song about bachelorhood. Boddi memorised it quickly as only illiterate people can:

> In all this warld nis a meriar life
> Than is a yong man withouten a wife;
> For he may liven withoughten strife,
> In every place where so he go!

While they were reciting it to and fro, Brother Hew was apt to shout for joy, meaningless phrases like 'a a a a yet I love where so I go' and 'ut hoy!' or 'terly terlow' which Boddi thought must be glorious prayers or evocations of holiness. Then the tune. Brother Hew was an indifferent singer, but confident. He droned out the tune and Boddi nodded, and then attempted it himself.

Hew had heard Brother Godric singing in the vestry at home mightily tuneful in a tender old voice, he had heard young girls crooning in the fields, giggling and stopping suddenly at the approach of boys, he had heard the dawn chorus twice, and he had once heard a choirboy practising in a market place, but he had never heard an angel sing. Till now.

So delightful were the sounds coming, surely via Heaven, from the rude peasant atop this humble donkey, that Hew was moved to tears by the time Boddi came to 'Thou berest thy love behind thy back, in every place where so he go.'

'How was that?' asked Boddi, for all the world as if he had just learnt to bind a sheaf, or something downright earthbound.

'You have the voice of an angel,' said Hew. Before they had reached Sussex two days later, Hew had taught Boddi to sing

> He cam also stille
> To his moderes bour,
> As dew in Aprille
> That falleth on the flour.

For it seemed somehow sacrilege not to teach him anything Divine, and 'The lif of this world ys reuled with wynd' for the sake of the exquisite tune, and many many more. Also, Hew had discovered that Boddi could sing in several ranges, including a completely natural falsetto, which he had never in his life heard before. If you weren't looking directly at him, you would swear it was a woman singing.

They approached the Friary of Bodiam in Sussex at the end of that week with such light steps (Hew found he now limped in sympathy) that a casual observer might have mistaken them for a young man leading his new bride home, or even a famous biblical pair with donkey.

16

Banquet in the Kruldom

While Addie slept, there was a riot of eating going on downstairs as fourteen human beings made a meal out of her food stores, for even George was being permitted to nibble crisps flown in like an aeroplane from the throne of Lottie's lap. His first ever Monster Munch. You've got to start somewhere.

Krul stopped halfway down the stairs and looked into the dining room, framed by the arc linking it with the nave he was now at one end of.

No one seemed to notice him. They were all too busy talking loudly and grabbing food, as if it might hop up and run away if not instantly apprehended.

On the nearside, the nearest to him, were Morris and Lottie's entire family. Lottie sat at the kitchen end with George on her lap, and Morris at the other end. In between them were Clare, Hugo and Greta. At the bottom end, Morris's end, were first Neil, and then Zina, who was bending towards her neighbour on the far side, Toby, desperately trying to understand him. How could she know it was no more plain English than the language her foetus might speak? On that side of the table were Toby, Sophie, Bridget, James, and finally, Bernard. Thus Bernard, the *real* guest, was next to the empty Head of the Table, waiting for Krul, as was Lottie on the other side. Heaven knows where Addie would have sat. Perhaps it was just as well she had been overwhelmed.

They presented a satisfying picture: a European gathering, such as they are rumoured to have in Italy when adults and children simply gather at harvest time and spontaneously banquet, there being surpluses of food. Krul felt a largesse rising in him. He had surpluses of food to give away, tables large enough to sit these people, even places for them to sleep, provided they did not want luxury. But also he felt a slight misgiving; the pitch of their voices, as it rose to compete, each with the conversation intersecting it, sounded dangerously near the edge of chaos. Chaos must not be allowed to happen.

He walked in to take charge.

Of course, they didn't stand or bow or gasp when Krul entered the room, or make salute or obeisance, nor did they straighten their backs or stop talking altogether, but his entrance shifted some vacuum hovering over the table, where perhaps a large crystalline chandelier might have swayed, onto himself so that absolute silence fell quite naturally when he raised his glass of wine and exhorted then to toast Neil and Zina's foetus.

'Better late than never' was the toast. Even the children lifted their Cokes. Then, seeing he had their attention, and concentration, he started a speech, unrehearsed, beginning low and quiet, the tone gently amusing, so that he endeared himself to them all, as they all remembered how very entertaining he could be.

'It is the privilege of a host to address his guests at dinner. I am sure you won't mind being addressed.' A sound of assent flowed round the room much like that sound groups make when someone asks whether they may switch on the television. No one really wants the television on, but everyone is too polite to say so.

'Well then, here we are. Here *you* are. And the odds against it might be a million to one. What, I wonder, are the odds now against one more turning up, or two more? Calculable even? With a sufficiently complex computer, you could input all the variables, which would take *years* and obtain odds. Meanwhile that extra person might well have traversed our lives long since. Proving my point – that the longer the odds, the closer we are. If something is reckoned to happen once in a million years, it will happen tomorrow. Tomorrow being the first day of the next million years. So I ought not to be surprised to see you here. I'm not. I am delighted. The long odds have come sailing home like boats called in.

'After all, aren't we all the products of outrageous odds? My parents meeting, their mating, me. There are trillions of people in the world and yet we are all unique. So if you say to me that the chances of a nuclear power station exploding are a million to one, I fear I know it could happen tomorrow. Kidnapped by destiny continually.

'So I stand here, and you sit there, at the intersection of a random set of possibilities, some of them good, some evil. You don't have to be a cynic to conclude that the world might be full of pitfalls, of evil forces bound by chance to frustrate us. So we must take precautions against the long odds coming home to roost. We must be fortified against disaster.'

Something about the seriousness of what he was saying, here at a banquet, made everyone laugh.

'What stands, then, between us and chaos?'

A set of open graves in the garden, thought Toby, but to himself.

'You can rest assured, I have it all taken care of. Think of this: even behind the now sieve-like iron curtain they're finding that freedom doesn't feed the children or keep the factories running, or make the air fit to breathe. Freedom doesn't make the sick well or the disabled able-bodied, or the poor wealthy. What use is it then? No use. Consider the organisations of youth – those comforting groups of people to which we all belong, which knew where they were going and why; the extended families and the schools, Girl Guides, Boy Scouts, the Churches, the Boys' Brigade, the Woodcraft Folk, even the gangs of boyhood in the shed by the canal. Here were rules and regulations and charters for success. You could do well, and do it by the book.'

Krul's audience found they were swept along and agreed with him, even Morris who had not had a haircut for seven years.

'There are a few rules here, you'll be glad to hear. To understand them is to *want* to follow them. First of all, smoking is only allowed outdoors, including pipes, Neil, loud radio music will not pollute the air inside either, no money shall be left lying around and then mourned over when lost, no group will foregather and leave St Boddi's without telling me, nor shall anyone leave without telling me for fire precaution reasons, nor shall any door be locked other than the bathroom, whatever rooms you are assigned shall be kept in order, so that single socks, etc, shall not go missing. And finally, I shall draw up a rota for the preparing and washing up of meals which you will find affixed to the kitchen wall tomorrow. Is that clear? Everyone happy?'

A laugh, and a sound of assent, a sort of atonal murmur filled the dining room. Krul smiled, and sat to eat. His tongue, which had a life of its own, made the transition with ease.

Hard to imagine that Toby's tongue could have any genetic link with Krul's, for Krul's never erred. Even slightly. It was as correct, or more so, than the OED, and grammatical constructs sat on it as naturally as taste buds. Surely, thought Toby, this tongue had sprung fully apprenticed at birth? Perhaps his father had turned to Granny moments after his own birth and said, sorry for the inconvenience – it won't happen again?

Later some of them, especially Bridget and James, wondered at their ready assent, for they had all joined in, especially when they saw, later, the (grossly unfair) rota itself. However, it is common for people to lose any real sense of selfhood in a Crowd Situation as sociologists call it, and each was able to excuse himself in some way afterwards. After all, it was Krul's house, Krul's food, Krul's rules. Addie wasn't there. Unfortunately.

Once Krul had sat down at the head of the table, James leaned forward towards the throne and asked, 'What's the matter with my sister?'

'Just overwhelmed, that's all. As you know, she is predisposed to anxiety and nerves,' he said, without looking at him. James didn't know any such thing.

Bridget had lipread this and saw that Lottie had too. Lottie mouthed the word 'pregnant?' to her across the table and Bridget mouthed back 'bollocks' but Lottie just frowned. For some reason conversations were now muted, not exactly whispered, but definitely quieter.

When the meal shuddered to a halt (with four types of cheese) Bernard volunteered for everything, but Krul prevented him, saying that Addie would be upset to wake up and find he had not been 'relaxing as a guest should'.

'Unlike me, she puts some faith in relaxation.'

James intended to draw a cartoon of the assembled multitude as a souvenir for Addie and the children, as his 'contribution to the festivities'.

First, though, he felt the need to smoke and went out to the porch and lit up. Even while he was standing there, he felt annoyed, despite the pleasure, that he was obeying a stupid rule of Krul's already, and the night was young. He was joined, shortly, by the short bald man with a pipe.

'Fellow conspirators in air pollution, eh?' said James.

'Yes. But I only smoke outdoors or in my shed at home too, because of my wife's pregnancy.' Then James told Neil about his plan. It was greeted with enthusiasm and Neil asked whether he could have a copy for a time capsule his class were assembling. James then made the error of saying, 'Oh, you're a teacher then are you?' and was treated to a resumé of the man's career in far greater detail than anyone could ever want, save a future employer. All James could remember about this man was that they had toasted his foetus during their meal and a picture began to evolve in his mind of Neil as a grown-up foetus – the bald egghead, the steel glasses, the slight pot belly, the blue blazer – another, slightly more acerbic cartoon.

Inside, Bridget felt she had done sufficient domestic duties previously with Addie, and rather liked the idea of relaxing with Bernard, especially if this might involve a drink or three.

However Lottie tried to prevent this by announcing that she would require her in the bathroom with six children for 'bathies' because, adding that sexism had nothing to do with it, Morris was simply hopeless with water (that he had nonetheless a magical effect on all children – calming them to the point of comatose, she did not say for her own reasons), and Zina too pregnant (and, it seemed, anyway, too tired) to undertake any lifting. Bridget refused but suspected she might weaken.

'Lottie, you may have guessed: I detest children.'

'Rubbish, you just don't know any.'

Krul instructed Zina to put her feet up for the sake of his nephew-to-be, and Morris to arrange three beds in the TinCan for his own children. Morris wanted to stage a vote for this but didn't dare contradict Krul.

It was obvious who remained and so Krul endeared himself unwittingly to James for the first time ever by opening the front door, mock-gagging at the fug, interrupting Neil's diatribe about the intelligence of his dog as compared with the average intelligence of 4D, and leading him unto the kitchen sink where he introduced him to the hot water system and a small plastic scourer. On his way out of the kitchen, he managed to trick the dog in question, Fred, into walking through the back door, and shut it on him.

17

Mankind in General, Toby in Particular

If that many children, six, were very quiet for a very long time, you would be anxious. What might they be up to? Was this a lull before some unthinkable storm? Of course Lottie was with them up in the bathroom, but she wasn't one to insist on silence. No noise, even of gentle splashing, floated down from the tower.

Bridget felt uneasy. She was sitting with the men, in the nave, for she didn't see why possessing a penis alone should qualify you for an intellectual discussion. Had Lottie gone mad and drowned them all? At least it was masquerading as an intellectual discussion: they were opining about Western Civilisation, as folk are wont to do after a large meal if they are not sleeping.

As Addie was doing up in the bedroom, and Zina in the morning room. In fact the sounds of Neil's clumsy washing up were the main background noise.

Could there be such a thing as mankind in general? Oh yes, said Bernard, he had observed the same general trends in society wherever he went – caring for the weak, attitudes to children, defending homeland and so on. Morris, diplomatically, agreed with him, adding that it reminded him of a time in Oman when . . .

'Don't, Hugo! Leave it *alone*!' came Lottie's voice from upstairs. So one of them was alive.

James had a more surreal view: he thought that those in power held a tenuous magnetism on flimsy structures, which you could draw as a cardhouse with Finance, Politics, Class, and so on, written on the individual cards, and should their grip loosen, the cardhouse would fall, and anarchy sweep in. Everything done by politicians, even those on the other side of the planet, had a direct effect on the lives of every one of us. No one led a sealed life. Each character drawn in a box has a foot or an elbow bleeding out from the frame. We are all jagged at the edges, and interlocked with each other. His was more of an image than a view. Morris agreed with him. It reminded him of a trip to Leicester Market, when . . .

'I mean it. You'll be *sorry*!'

But Krul's was a definite view. There was *no* such thing as mankind. It was just a notion.

'I'm going to *count to three*!' Oh God, the ultimate threat: she is going to count to three!

Bridget found it difficult to follow his train of thought because it was, as she had often found with phallocentric ideologies, Opinion rather than Argument. It seemed that Krul regarded the world as a threatening and dangerous place, as he had hinted during his speech, full of negative forces, where static ideas become ends rather than means and the whole world is divided into hollow bureaucratic schemes – fields of endeavour whose success can only be measured in their own terms.

'One!'

Life was just a colony to be properly administered.

'Two!'

There was no place in his world view for companionship or love or art – simply for hierarchical success: a sporting view of life, with penalty kick-offs to decide an overall winner, no matter how unfair or subject to chance.

'Two and a half!'

Morris said he would have to give this view 'some more thought' before agreeing. They were all waiting for three. They waited.

'Lottie's so good with children: she has a natural authority,' said Morris, as if to assuage their anxiety.

'About as natural as fishes riding bicycles,' said Bridget. Only James understood her, and laughed.

Ever since Bridget had been old enough to think such thoughts, she had vowed never to be one of those women for whom male company automatically took precedence over the requirements of female friends. The Supremacy of the Cock: Heaven knows she had been the victim of *that* often enough.

Upstairs Lottie was counting, on her own, enabling these men, two of whom were fathers, to chat away like old gossips downstairs. Was this right?

'Do you think Lottie needs some help?' she asked, of them all. Only Bernard shifted slightly. NO! Not him.

'That's kind of you, Bridget,' said Krul, 'I'm sure she'd appreciate it. Sounds as if she's half a point away from the end of her tether.' Bridget felt a hot rush come to her face, a mixture of anger and that helplessness you feel when dismissed by some person in charge before you've had your say, or come to the end of an interview.

Up yours, Krul. And went up, stomping defiantly on each wooden tread.

Upstairs she crept up on them, so that they didn't notice her standing in the bathroom door at first. It was a round room, which gave it the feeling of a pod. The bath was almost round too, and in it were Sophie, Greta, Clare, Toby and Baby George. Lottie sat on the toilet reading a book! Reading a book! It was a cartoon book for adults which Bridget had spotted in the bathroom earlier, called *How to Have Sex in Public Without Anyone Noticing*. She was chuckling to herself. Hugo was nude but outside the bath, busy testing taps, of which there were so many round the green acrylic edge of the tub that Bridget concluded they must have some sort of Jacuzzi within the bath.

The girls were quiet because they were intent. Intent on drowning George. Greta would push him under, head first, towards Sophie, who would scoop him out, let him take half a breath and send him, underwater, to Clare, who fished for him but usually missed. Toby would then lunge for him and pull him up. Then Greta would grab him and it would all start again. Bridget, watching this for a few seconds, felt like you do in a dream when you want to run but your legs won't move, because they are nothing but reinforced concrete.

'Oh, hello, Bridget. I thought you'd change your mind. Bored into submission? Inwards of cars was it? The chappolatas are teaching the baby to swim, isn't it a Good Idea?'

'Looks like drowning to me,' said Bridget.

'No, no. Babies automatically close the nog and hold the breath. He loves it.'

Bridget caught Toby's eyes. They expressed, absolutely no doubt about it, horror. He didn't want to be present for the drowning. She didn't blame him: she didn't either. She reached for a towel and pulled him out.

'Thanks, petal. One down, four to go. Hugo voted not to have bathies, which is his right.'

'Could be a wise decision.' Just then Hugo must have found the Jacuzzi 'on' switch, for a wet volcano started in the middle of the bath. George was nowhere to be seen. Bridget ran with Toby.

She shut the door of the bedroom and found that she was alone with a naked dripping boy and a towel and she had never dried anyone but herself so far in her life, so where to start?

She started with the feet. From the feet upwards, as she did with herself. He laughed. At least his laughter was standard. He stood very still. She began to feel herself warming to him. Perhaps Lottie was right: you had only to *know* a child. Hadn't she read his eyes as surely as if he'd spoken?

Turning to find pyjamas, she saw something startling. The whole of the long wall opposite the bed was a mural. There are places where you almost expect to see a mural now: Italian restaurants (out of perspective grape-treading damsels and a gondola with the gondolier on the wrong end), tiled Métro Stations (abstract frictionless tiles designed solely to deter graffiti, which Bridget loved), some fancy launderettes even (homely objects to dispel that suicidal urge which launderettes encourage), but in a small bedroom! There was no furniture against it, so the perspective it created (of a beach leading to a cliff, to a forest) was uninterrupted. In the distance stood an old woman in a shawl, wielding some garden tools, between two sets of trees. Beside her, spilling down the hillslope, was a flock of golden sheep. Dotted about the picture, and this was a clue to Bridget that Addie had designed at least part of it, were small objects and insects forming a frame, such as tapestries have.

She wanted to ask Toby about this mural but had noticed that no one ever asked him anything directly: only closed questions he could shake or nod to. She decided to break with the tradition.

'What is the story on this mural, Toby?' His eyes widened. 'I won't laugh at you, honest,' she added, reading his eyes again.

She had expected it to be difficult, but she was astonished that he put on (she assumed) a Dorset lilt in his voice to recite it. Although she was aware of making an imaginative effort to organise the fragments of his narrative together, Toby's story sounded, to Bridget, like this:

'When it was lot lot lots of ago happened this: a boy awakened up waking in his shinebright room. A written stick sway swayed on his bed-edge, saying MAGIC and ZOOM! Where shall I gowan? said the boy to his stick. "Off to the magic wood," it replyen. Trailing so alone lonely with noticing eyen he jollywell humf humf humfed up the cliffentoppen. Be jellyscope! Be clydoscope! No needen maps, wooden or roaden. He went and went and went. Up past the gods and down again down darkly green is getten the woods. Only Mrs God gardens gardening herbules herbies, amfibicides for her conclockshuns, and nova nova novelteas. Coloury shapes on your stick she say, it be a treasury-finding tease: mohair mules all glow gold: they be shag sheep of the mudfields, very bold. He went and went towards the lights in the olden muds sloppy where spiders hold slippery parties and sad all webnights. Insidespide is more than could be from outerinwards all because of the magic rod, feastingbuns and jewellery and a go go God! Here on my bed delightfully of me and nobody knowen the inroads outsailing, excepting that Bridge One here who scanners eyen.'

Bridget found she was shaking.

Toby edged towards her on the bed and put his surprisingly furry little arm on hers, and the gesture made her cry.

'I love your story. Every bit of it. *Especially* the bits I couldn't understand.'

They say crying is a great relief to those under stress, or those who have reason to grieve. Go on, have a good cry. As a nation, the English are bad at crying; in fact, English Men may be the world's very worst weepers. Where American politicians are expected to shed a tear or two, preferably on television, English ones might well fear incarceration in a mental home should they sob once. The Scots are a little better, but Bridget was not adept at it. She preferred never to let emotion get so imprisoned inside her as to need that sort of senseless outlet. She favoured swearing out loud. Also she was terrified, as so many English people are too, of ever being *seen* to cry.

Toby was seeing her now. He had noticed different sorts of crying in Sosij and Sophie and himself, though never never never in Father of course, and having a more complex friendship with language than most people, did not think of all these activities as simply 'crying'.

TOBY'S CATALOGUE OF TEARS

1. *Dreeping.* Slowly marching clear oniony globes of water from puffed eyes down the cheeks. Silent.
2. *Leeming.* Annoyingly low buzzing whinge followed by
3. *Honing.* Hone hone moaning.
4. *Wimpring.* Most hated by parents. Whimpering bleating animal noise when it has been *unfair*.
5. *Kreening.* Howling, wailing inconsolably for the unending unfairness of Everything.
6. *Yalping.* Parents run! Something suddenly bad like broken glass underfoot, you earsplittingly shriek with pain – the sort of pain you bleed to death from.
7. *Squarking.* Squealing of Sophie when a spider with long hair and one eye watching her comes in.

8. *Birsting Out*. A scream for any grown up but not necessarily because of dying.

9. *Sorring*. Lusty bawl for twenty mins minimum – a lament or wake for the self, so damaged by a smack, which was the result of your father hearing 1–8, now means more than the original subject of the Sorr.

10. *Blubbing*. Trying to control a sob, a bubbling hubbub of bubbles.

11. *Snazing*. Gasping back into yourself, the back-to-front sneezing of trying to stop.

Toby could see that Bridget was well into sorring, though no one had smacked her. When she had blubbed down into the hubbub and snazed five times, she said to him (or the mural, to be precise), 'I can see what a trap love is,' which must have been referring to that feeling about the unfairness of Everything which was not, it seemed, confined after all to children.

'Goodly it is to peck up chins,' he said to her, comfortingly.

But Bridget was finding it about as easy to peck up chins as she would have found it to lift a two-storey house with one hand. A sense of loss had hold of her. She had no idea what she had lost, which only made it worse.

18

Sorry

Inside Zina were not simply a foetus, but also Warring Selves. There was the Health Visitor, the Humanitarian and the Follower of Advice she was having to become on account of her first, late, pregnancy. So, although resting for the sake of the foetus, other worries assailed her when she woke: Addie had fainted, had not eaten, and might now be suffering from low blood sugar and/or various other things; so she went into the kitchen and made her a sweet drink and carried it upstairs, reassuring Neil, still struggling with more washing up than he could ever imagine there being (they had a dishwasher at home), that she was not overdoing it.

When she found Addie, she checked her pulse. Normal. Then she checked it again, to confirm the first result. This was one of her many safety devices like double-emptying the bladder to avoid cystitis.

'Zina, what are you doing?'

'Drink this. You're lucky I have no rectal thermometer here.'

While Addie sipped the tea, Zina related the surreal goings on she and Neil had been subjected to in the instigating of their baby.

Her story was made funnier and ruder by the clipped and clinical manner of its telling.

Of course she was one to dabble in other women. As midwife, you understand. Up to the elbows in vaginas. Many a time. All in the line of duty. Augmenting births. Came to regard the bod as a gateway for babes. Chin up! Breathe properly. Don't pant, that's only in books! Oh, books. Of course, she knew it all, didn't she? Who else has to read about 'locked twins' being decapitated in utero and then eat lunch? Thought nothing could embarrass her. Then Neil was asked for a sample. The thought of him wanking in that cubicle made her blush so deeply she thought her face would catch fire.

Then the questions, Addie. You can't imagine. When and how and how often and afterwards, do you? Oh God, the ins and outs of the bod. Her soul made nude on chest-high tables with sinister stirrups seen from the *other* end. Her thighs parted in front of the whole world. Two million men in white coats looking up her nether parts with telescopes.

Addie had to laugh. Surely these were exaggerations? Every indignity of the fertility clinic took on a double significance when she noticed how petite and well groomed Zina still was. Were such probings and advice to have been dished out to such as Lottie, their bawdiness would quite have been swamped. But to tell Zina to lie with her legs in the air after making love!

Neil's part in the proceedings seemed to have been minimal (though crucial of course) so far, though he was suggesting the idea that he might give up work when it was born instead of her! Zina didn't seem at all thrilled at this prospect, though her salary would be greater than his, because she was determined to breastfeed.

'If Neil could take pills and grow breasts, he would,' said Zina.

'Gosh! Neil must be one in a million.'

'Adopted. Hasn't recovered.'

'Perhaps he will now,' said Addie, 'though I hope he doesn't. It sounds like he might make the best father in the History of the World, with or without breasts,' Zina smiled at her. She remembered Krul as a child. Well, he never was really a child. Apprenticed adult.

'I know. I cherish him.'

How could Bridget have been so cruel to this poor woman, laughing at her *trying* for a baby, and her make-up? To try so assiduously, to go through all that humiliation, to have been raped by metal machines, screwed into position inside her, and all the other indignities, was probably worth it, if you ended up with a Sophie or a Toby of your own. Sophie who would one day be a film-star; Toby able to talk.

'And you've had all the tests known to man, and everything is fine, yes?'

Addie realised this was something she couldn't dare to agree to. Yes she had undergone even invasive tests at a risk to the baby. Yes, she had undergone blood tests and amniotic fluid tests and scans and all the paranoias of science, but still she could not dare to say that there inside her was a perfect human child without any monstrous features or abnormalities. Addie knew this superstition too: many times in her first pregnancy (by the second time she was too busy looking after the first to worry) had she thrown coins into wishing wells or dipped her finger into the holy water of a font to say to the spirit world, forgive me for asking, but please, please I don't care if it's a boy or a girl but let it be *normal*.

She wanted to hug Zina, smudging everything, and her longed-for foetus in there. But there was a piercing bell.

'What's that noise?' said Addie.

'Krul blames the belfry.'

'That's not the belfry. It's the front door.' Addie sat up in bed, handed the cup to Zina and swung her legs over the edge. Zina handed her back Krul's dressing-gown since she was naked, and watched her stagger giddily into the outsize garment.

'Who could it be?' said Zina, seeing the panic in her eyes. 'This late. Someone locked out?'

'But we never lock it,' said Addie.

'Never?' said Zina.'

'No, Krul is terrified of fire. He thinks the minute you might spend finding a key and unlocking the door might be the minute when you are overwhelmed by smoke. He says he'd rather be robbed than die of fire.'

'He's paranoid.'

'That's no more paranoid than locking burglars out, is it?'

Addie wanted to defend him because she knew that no burglar would really risk having to swim away in the night if the road was flooded, and Krul prowled the house nearly all night. They were safe. Krul made them safe. It was Krul's main strength.

Most people suffer palpitations when a policeman approaches them, no matter what they have or haven't done. With Krul you don't. Should an officer of the law approach them, say in a traffic jam, Addie can rest easy that it will only be for a consultation of some sort and the policeman will call Krul 'sir', and not 'you bloody idiot'.

'No. I know this isn't all yet. I know someone else is about to arrive. I can feel it.'

She wobbled out of the room and nearly bumped into Bridget who was fighting and pissoffing her way out of the bedroom, now full of dripping, tearful children.

'There's someone else here,' Addie said to her.

'Jesus wept! What now? Whoever it is had better have a brilliant excuse,' Bridget said to Zina, following.

Addie heard this as she started down the stairs and was reminded that she had been horrified to hear that political refugees fleeing from bullets in Albania had sought sanctuary in the Chinese Embassy only to be *handed back* to the Albanians the next day. And yet she had agreed with Krul only a few weeks before that the number of Hong Kong families allowed into Great Britain should be minimal because we are over-crowded, and their needs are only economic. To control immigration, or not to? And when is a refugee just a Machiavelli in a tattered coat? Now she felt like the Queen of a country about to make immigration qualifications: whoever was at her door had better have the best reason to be there in the world, or she might, yes, she who thought herself so humanitarian, turn the person out into the cold night, and good riddance. We are not a hotel. There are limits after all. Her rest had strengthened her. No matter how welcoming Krul might be, she would not.

She had reached the bottom of the stairs. Krul was standing

at the door gazing into the porch and turned up to her and said, 'You won't believe this.' Standing in the beam of the 200-watt outdoor halogen lamp in the porch was a woman in her mid-thirties, though looking older on account of the creases and worry of her existence, with crumpled greasy blond hair scraped back into a pony-tail, worried little eyes, one of them blackening, the sort of corduroy dungarees a jumble sale would reject and a pair of plimsolls which had died ten years ago. She had the most asymmetrical face you could ever hope to see. Of course her demeanour seemed to say, so sorry the two halves of my face don't match, even slightly, because that too must be her fault. Beside her was a large suitcase and an even larger child. The child had inherited nothing from her mother, to look at. She was beautiful, shining, and moved like a dancer, which she was.

'Sorry,' she said.

'Melanie? What's happened?'

'You said leave him, and I have!' There was triumph in her eyes, especially the bruised one.

'Argument with a door, Melanie?' said Krul. Melanie smiled at him. Either she hadn't understood, or chose not to. The latter would be like her.

'And the charming Elizabeth!' said Krul, smiling even more broadly. His emotional altimeter was flickering towards maximum. Only Addie knew this.

'The door was my father, whose name is Colin,' said the large girl, coming in and gazing at the multitude in the nave.

'Only daughter of a door! How interesting for you. Mix with the knobs do you, hinges well oiled, ajar unto the world?' Now Melanie frowned at him. This sounded like nonsense, and no mistake. On the other hand, the girl had spoken rudely and *out of turn* perhaps.

While Krul was saying this, and more, for he then went on to inform her that she had stumbled into a reading weekend – hence all these famous people I won't have to introduce – arranged in conjunction with the BBC who would start filming

in the morning, Melanie looked around her, trying to understand what she saw. Addie had said on the telephone that
morning that she had guests, but she had not given her any idea
of the numbers, for there were about five children dripping at
various levels on the stairs in front of her, a very fat woman with
a baby among them, Addie herself had stepped off the bottom
stair at the same time as a very masculine-looking tall woman
with a spiked hairdo and shorts. Behind whom was a pregnant
lady in a beautiful dress. At the far end of the large room she
was now in were two men who had stood when she entered,
one of whom she recognised as Addie's brother. The other was
a hippy. When Krul had finished talking, a short, bald man (a
servant?) came out of the left side of the building carrying a
stack of wet plates and asking where bowls lived.

She had lost count. Could this really be a reading weekend?
Or was Krul kidding her, trying to make her feel uneasy
because of her lack of education? Could such a cascade of wet
people and children really be famous readers?

Not that sheer numbers frightened her, they didn't. Only she
and Addie had shared a very private time in the era of
Toddlerdom when their children were so small, and then just
starting school, so that they had a few hours, mornings only
perhaps, to swap anecdotes, to unite against Colin, whom Addie
had never actually *met*, or against Krul, whom Melanie had met
once. Now she was here, in the longed-for freedom of her first
ever flight from Colin, and she was beginning to regret it. There
would be no opportunity for those leisurely long chats with
Addie, to explain everything, to re-establish the closeness they
had, to recover enough to think of the next step. And where
was this place, some sort of abbey, or friary?

19

The Written Word

They arrived at the Friary in Bodiam late at night, but the moon was full and Boddi was pleased to see that it was such an odd stone building, leaning higgledy-piggledy into a hillside with so many ramshackle wooden huts and workshops leaning into it at its base, that he felt instantly at home – it was a sideways-on place falling to pieces, like himself. He had expected to feel in awe of it, but he didn't.

Hew led the donkey straight into the Great Hall and started to unload it – no servant scuttled forward to help him. But an old, old man came out of an arch to one side and stepped forward to embrace Hew.

'Have you done it?' he asked, looking at Boddi.

'Yes, Brother. This is young Boddi – an untutored man with a mind of his own. It has taken me seven weeks to find such a one.'

'Not long. I thought you would be gone a year.' At this the elder put an arm out towards Boddi and made the sign of the cross on his forehead.

'I bless you,' he said, and Boddi smiled back. Shouldn't he have said 'God bless you'?

Soon Boddi became accustomed to living in a Friary – it was not difficult, for he had never had the opportunity to become accustomed to any luxuries or to any leisure. All day he studied under the tutelage of the four patient Brothers: Godric, Godfre, Godwhen and Godwiy, who seemed to regard it as a privilege to be allowed to teach him.

He learnt how to read and write, the basic Laws of England,

how to sew leather, how to mend fences, the basic Laws of Agriculture, how to ride a horse, how to protect a village from drought, the basic Laws of Philosophy, how to sing in Latin, conduct a debate, argue effectively, the basic Laws of the Church and of God. He learnt fast and never questioned the usefulness of anything he was given to master – for he was given few Answers, merely ways of questioning.

When he was not learning, he would wander into the suburbs of the Friary where rows upon rows of shacks leant into the hillside, and it was here that he made a particular friend of a cobbler named Jankin. One day Jankin offered to make Boddi a pair of fine rabbit shoes, if he would bring him the skins. Boddi replied that he did not think wanting shoes was a good reason for killing two rabbits.

Jankin laughed. That was what he liked about Boddi – his odd ideas! As if rabbits were put on earth for their own pleasure! Boddi was sitting on a seat near his workbench, swinging his uneven legs backwards and forwards, and humming. Watching him, Jankin had an idea.

Then and there, he jumped up and measured each foot – then he measured the distance between each knee and its ankle, and then the ankle to heel measurement. He asked Boddi to write down some numbers, which he did, in the dust on the bench, with a wet finger.

'Now tell me the difference,' said Jankin, who unlike Boddi was both illiterate and virtually innumerate since, despite having a string with equidistant knots on it (invented by Brother Godwhen), most of his customers made an impression of their feet in soft clay for him.

'What is this, geometry?' said Boddi. 'You sound like Brother Godwhen,' but he bent over it and said, 'about four knots.'

Two days later Jankin arrived at the Great Hall during Evensong, a recent innovation during which Boddi entertained the friars with startlingly moving renditions of popular songs, with his invention in his hands.

His invention was quite possibly the first custom-made pair of orthopaedic shoes in the history of the world.

'Now I feel like a real man,' said Boddi, wearing his shoes. He was also a tall man now, since Jankin had built up the left shoe too much and had to compensate on the right.

'No. You always were a real man. Now you *look* like one,' said Brother Hew.

That night Boddi was dragging his bedroll into a corner of the great hall to the spot where he liked to sleep, and wondering whether you removed shoes when sleeping or not, when Brother Godwhen beckoned him away. He led him up towards the tower where the 'concocting' went on – some kind of brewing, Boddi thought. Some friars claimed that water was an ungodly drink, and only let ale pass their lips.

They were entering a part of the Friary where Boddi had never been. As they climbed up and up the spiral stairs, Boddi skipping a little on his new-found feet, Brother Godwhen spoke.

'It is a cruel world, Boddi, as you are perhaps beginning to understand. And it is not cruel because ordinary people want it to be but because those with power use cruelty to keep their power. I am talking of kings, and barons, tyrants and warlords, even the bishops who mete out cruel punishments for so-called heresy. Jesus had no such power – no tyranny was His. But He has *us*.' Here he turned to Boddi on the stair – they were nearly at the top – 'and it is our duty to do whatever we must to stamp out tyranny on earth, for Him. At this Friary we have our own special way.'

A thick oak door *slid* open. Most of the doors in the building creaked. This one was silent. How? The room inside was brightly lit with oil lamps which were somehow attached to the walls. The walls themselves, on which they shed yellow pools of light, were odd. They were curved of course, this being the tower, but they had a shininess as if they had been whitened by years of scrubbing. A kind of lacquer appeared to have been spread over them. At intervals round the walls were wooden shelves, also lacquered white, with scrolls and bibles upon them. At least Boddi assumed they were bibles, for they were leather-bound tomes with gold filigree lettering on their spines. He had been taught to revere all such manifestations of God – the Written Word.

At a bench on the far side of the room sat a friar, bending over a glass bowl with liquid in it, stirring it from time to time with a glass spoon. Above him, stretching to the full height of the tower room, were narrow shelves full of phials in which were colourless liquids. There might have been, had you time to count them, two thousand such phials.

Brother Godwhen motioned the friar to leave, which he did, sliding the door shut behind him.

'Deadly poisons,' said Brother Godwhen. 'You can't see it, you can't taste it, but it steals into the brain and puts out its light for ever.'

'For the enemies of God,' said Boddi, wonderingly, gazing at the ranks of narrow shelving.

Brother Godwhen smiled, deeply satisfied. Any other man might well have shrunk back disgusted at this display of deliberate murder, but not him, not their own Boddi.

'And of people,' he added. Then Boddi frowned.

'Why are you showing me this?' he asked. Brother Godwhen opened a drawer and took out a small piece of ivory with a shiny and a matt side and gave it to him.

'Because if you ever come across such an enemy, I want you to promise that you will send this slate back to me with his name etched on it clearly. The unshiny side takes an impression. Then he will be dispatched.'

'Am I to leave then?'

'Brother Godric has had one of his visions and in it, he saw you leaving us and heading for great trouble. The dreams of men are but shadows of God's meaning, but we do well to rue them.'

Boddi placed the ivory slate inside his tunic, and kept it lovingly, securely there, patting it from time to time.

20

A Good Night's Sleep

There was an unholy mob swaying at the foot of the spiral staircase in St Boddi's. Not having a small incendiary device or any tear gas to hand with which to scatter them, Krul grabbed Bess by the collar of her anorak and said, 'Let's get rid of Bess.'

'Charming,' she said, being dragged upwards like a puppy by the scruff.

'Sorry,' whispered her mother to her, running behind but taking no action to free her.

'He didn't mean get *rid* of her,' said Addie, lamely.

'Just as,' added Morris, 'Lottie doesn't really mean let's put the children *down* – only to sleep.'

'Still has a nasty veterinary ring to it,' said Bridget, moving very deliberately *away* from anyone under twenty.

The new girl being thus manhandled up the stairs was a magnet for the other children. If there had been a bullfight, they would have watched that. There was a big girl of maybe thirteen, struggling against Krul, her worried mother bleating behind her. Might something horrible ensue?

All Lottie and Morris's kids had voted after all (in the round bathroom, a very democratic place) not to sleep in the TinCan so beds had been hastily improvised for them in Sophie and Toby's bedroom, despite Krul's disapproval. His main worry was that Sophie would not have sufficient oxygen for a good night's sleep. Toby was that much smaller, so he would manage. Lottie had opened windows and smiled sweetly at him. Not even Krul could overturn the sacred workings of family voting.

Krul had released his grip on Bess so suddenly in the dorm,

as Lottie was insisting on calling it now, that she nearly fell
down. When he left, Lottie urged Hugo to siphon the python,
Greta to brush those sneggies, Clare to turn her jammies round
the right way, and asked Toby to nod if he would like a dwink.
He did not. Whatever that was. Sophie did, and tried nodding
and got no response. Then there was a flurry of clothes, breasts,
comics, bears, urgent requests for biscuits, books, Mer-mer
and Num-num and small silky remnants of things without
which certain children had no hope of sleeping. Addie watched
Lottie and Melanie coping with it all. She was astonished at
Lottie's calmness, in such contrast to Melanie's deranged
flitting about, like someone on the verge of a nervous
breakdown.

'Mum. Leave me alone, willya?' said Bess finally.

'I don't know how you do it,' said Melanie to Lottie.

'Easy-peesy-Japanesy,' she was bound to reply.

When all was quiet, Morris appeared and read them a chapter
of *James and the Giant Peach* in a sing-song voice whose
melodious timbre soon had most of them hypnotised. The
mothers crept away. It didn't seem to matter that at least three
children there had read that whole book right through before.
His voice and the words and the darkness worked their magic.

When he re-entered the nave, it was to wonder at what he
saw. Even for a large room, there were too many people doing
nothing and not related. In other words, there was no focus for
them all being there, as there would be if it were a party to
which they had all been invited, or a family celebration. They
simply looked like nine folk stranded in a large sitting room
which had once been a church. Krul was moving between them,
delivering drinks. Mobile, and in control. Morris questioned
again the wisdom of his being there.

Lottie was drinking beer (so good for the milk production) as
if it were water and as a result finding her body movements
considerably slowed and slurred and disobedient. She motioned
lazily to Morris, her hand blurring through the air momentarily,
to come and sit next to her, but he ignored it, thinking the least

he could do was entertain one of Krul's guests – his cousin would be a good start.

So he sat himself down by Zina and began wildly inventing unusual dangers in exotic places he couldn't remember the names of. Confessing she had *never* been abroad, Zina egged him on. The greater his exaggerations, the more likely she found it. Hadn't she always thought that Turkey was full of bandits, India of deadly insects, Russia of spies camped out on hotel corridors?

James was sketching Bernard with a charcoal pencil but finding a halo of pink light kept swinging from behind him where the saint was having his innards kicked out. Also, it was difficult to draw Bernard's actual features. They seemed to slip about indefinitely.

Bernard himself was in a dream, unable to stop watching Bridget stretched out at great length on a couch. She seemed unaware of the picture she made. The skin of her legs was golden. Now and then her hand would travel carelessly down one thigh as she spoke, to scratch an insect bite on her knee.

Neil had finished the dishes but was still discussing with Addie the joys of a dishwasher. Did he think she could install one before the next meal? He didn't seem to appreciate the reasons she had for *not* having one – the Green issue (why use electricity?), the olfactory one (the smell of dishes waiting to be washed sickened her, or the practical one (most of her crockery was handmade pottery, some of it by herself, and would not survive a dishwasher). Still he insisted that no civilised person should be without one. And Krul complained that only women talk trivia! She felt trapped.

She looked across to Zina who was half listening to Morris and stroking her belly lasciviously without realising it. She too used to do that: 'cuddling the foetus' she had called it. When large vehicles screamed past her on busy London roads, she would quickly cover her belly to stop the noise entering, to protect the child. If someone said something awful to her, or something dreadful occurred on the News, she covered the foetus with her cardigan. And in the long evenings when she had sat with her feet up reading six-inch-thick Australian novels to while away the time, her free hand would stroke and stroke the casing of unborn Sophie.

Melanie was telling Bridget all about Colinthebastard and Bridget was encouraging her and (to Melanie's astonishment) calling her 'sister' though she was finding it such a cliché of a story that she wondered whether Melanie was not that one person who kept writing in to women's magazines with this problem, told ten ways. Melanie was relishing the telling because this was someone who hadn't heard any of it before. She could give it the full treatment. Bridget was not slow to point out to Melanie that Colin's main drawback was a) his upbringing and b) his possession of a penis. Melanie was loath to agree, since neither of these was mutable. At least . . .

Morris was right – Krul was enjoying being in control. He felt a fatherly watchfulness towards his guests, counted them, smiled upon them, gave them last drinks, checked on their wellbeing, blessed them and sent them to bed. Addie couldn't believe it when she came back from the toilet (that being her only means of escape from the tedious Neil): they were all wandering away to their beds, wherever that might be. Apparently Krul had assigned everyone somewhere to sleep.

'Where?'

'Bernard and James in the spare room; Bridget in the bath; Neil and Zina in my study, Melanie in the boxroom; and Lottie and Morris on their inflatable bed in the dining room, though they offered to sleep in the TinCan. But I don't want you to have to deal with their kids if they wake in the night. Hence you and I can sleep undisturbed in our own bed.'

There was no reason really why any of this arrangement should strike Addie as sinister. It was all reasonable and sensible, and yet she stood at the bottom of the stairs thinking, worried perhaps at the ease with which he had fitted them all in. As if they had seventeen people to stay every Bank Holiday weekend, or as if he had *planned* it.

'You look worried,' said Krul.

'I can't think why!'

'Bridget *asked* for the bath.'

'It's not that.'

'What then?'

Despite years of training to keep inside what ought to be kept there by sensible people who coped nicely with everything, it would come out.

'Krul – will you sleep yourself?'

He laughed.

'Of course not.'

21

The Purport of his Thoughts

Krul did occasionally surrender himself to sleep. But generally he regarded it as a weakness, acceptable only in women and children, to need more than three hours maximum. He had no difficulty in filling those hours when his hemisphere went blank. He read books, fiddled with programs on the computer (accessing data denied to sleeping employees while their Mainframes danced the night away), listened to the tapes of telephone conversations he had made, made notes on the computer for future reference, and did muscle-building exercises on a T-bar spring he had installed in the tower.

But the best thing about Krul's nocturnal life was the freedom of thought. He had all his best ideas at night; solved all his problems, and even some of Addie's at night. It was as if the darkness and the quiet opened in him channels which were shut in daylight.

Anyone but Krul might have sensed the presence of God on nights such as these.

Well, he did, in his own way. A contest took place, each night, for St Boddi's. Krul always won, of course.

He and Addie lived in a godless world. It was possible to lead their lives from day to day, without ever giving religion a second thought. In this they were not alone in the Western World. But it was not merely the ease of secularity which attracted them to it. They had come to a decision about the part religion would *not* play in family life, from two different directions.

Krul had been brought up in a militaristic version of the Church of England. Duty and conformity had been so stressed, that he imagined God, when he was ten, not as something to be prayed to but to be saluted. As soon as Krul had outgrown the Cadet Corps, he outgrew God. It was simply logical to do away with anything which interfered with his mechanistic view of the universe. He was famous in his family for saying the first Christmas when he refused to attend church, 'Henceforth, if God needs me, He knows where to find me.'

Addie's upbringing had been about as opposite as you could imagine. The nearest her parents had ever come to being religious was a mild flirtation with vegetarianism, ending, quite sensibly, when James developed anaemia. Otherwise they had let the children grow up pagan and free of dogma. It wasn't until Addie reached adolescence and longed for something greater than herself, something to *worship*, that she discovered the Quakers. Sighing, her father had said, 'If you *must* have a religion, I recommend the Friends.' Even James approved, sceptic though he was on every front. The Quakers, his research revealed to her, were unique in that no evil thing (war, famine, usurpation etc.) in the world could be laid at their door. On the contrary, they were responsible for Oxfam!

So Addie became a Quaker. But a few years later, she gave it up and became an Artist, still going to meetings of the Friends from time to time, finding their vague spirituality and freedom from weird beliefs uplifting. Hence she, like Krul, could see no point in sending their children to Sunday School or inculcating in them the *fear of God*. And to her that phrase was loaded with significance: the *fear*. Christianity, seen from the outside in, as she did, though living in a culture informed by it, seemed to be mostly about Fear and Death; hence she was determined that her children would grow up without the lead-heavy deadweight of Christianity.

So, though they both inhabited this secular world, they interpreted it differently. When Sophie asked, as any child who has just learnt to speak and spots a dead something on the lawn will ask, 'What happens when you die?', this dichotomy in their thinking became suddenly, dramatically evident.

'Nothing,' said Krul, 'you rot back down into the soil like cabbage leaves.' Sophie wasn't horrified by this. She would have accepted it if Addie had not leapt in with,

'Don't be silly, that's not *all*!' Your *spirit* goes on.' Of course there followed four thousand specific questions ('Now you've done it,' said Krul, 'we'll never hear the end of this') on the nature of spirits, the geography of the place where they dwell, the decomposition of skin and hair and eyes, what sort of wings you would need, and so on.

How could this happen, thought Addie? How could two people who had lived together for years, had children, talked through a million topics, not know what the other thought about the most important question in the universe? Easy. Courting couples steer off the topic. Come in for a quick drink, won't you – we could talk of death! Ah, lovely, don't mind if I do . . . no, the topic had simply never emerged.

Addie and Krul both live in a godless world, but Addie finds her spiritual outlet in her love for her children, and for Krul, and in Art. Krul has looked hard, with his clever, all-seeing eyes, and not found anything worthy of salute anywhere. Addie sometimes fears he wouldn't recognise the Sublime if it was handed to him through a fax machine. Only the weak need such comfort. Only the weak long for solace.

Krul wasn't the weak at all. He was the strong. His thoughts were big ones, and mostly nocturnal.

So it was a lonely and degenerate world where Krul hatched his night-thoughts. Most of them were designed to vanquish any religious spirit still hanging about St Boddi's uninvited, like a computer virus introduced into the system at its inception, now irrelevant and annoying. One such idea was that he would like to devise a means by which couples could be having sex all over the building virtually at once. Not an orgy as such, but a sort of ubiquitous mating! This idea caught hold of him like fire and rampaged about his brain. He didn't want to take part, merely, somehow to observe it.

He had now in St Boddi's eight possible candidates for this

great Manifestation of Lust. Ten if he counted himself and Addie. Which he did not.

Addie was already naked underneath Krul's robe, and slid into the bed for the second time today. She was full of foreboding. Krul was sitting on his side of the bed thinking. She daren't say, 'What are you thinking dear? as a wife might this late at night, for he would only turn on her and declare the privacy of his own thoughts inviolate, which they were. Also she dreaded to know the purport of his thoughts. For she had suspected, for some time now, that his thoughts were not just thoughts.

Krul once said that the Iran–Iraq war had been wonderful for the birthrate in Iran; they were now seriously overpopulated. There will have to be, he said, some natural disaster, some terrible Act of God like a plague or famine or earthquake, to bring the population down. She could see him imagining upheavals of earth and flattenings of villages. Two days later fifty thousand people lost their lives in an earthquake in Northern Iran. See, said Krul, I was right.

So she became very careful indeed, though it was hard, never never to mention anything which might lead him to imagine the death of their children, or even any small injury to them, so that she could thus prevent it, as if there were some awful, random turbulence operating between his mind and the real world.

Hence now she trembled at what wild thoughts were germinating in his mind. What errant imaginings?

'How will Bridget manage in a *round* bath?' he said, finally.

'Foetal position?'

Krul stood, turned, smiled, and left the room; Addie followed him. Mischief was fizzing in his eyes.

He opened the bathroom door. Bridget, inside a navy blue nylon sleeping bag, was not in the foetal position. She had her knees drawn up, though, and was reading Alice Walker's *You Can't Keep A Good Woman Down* balanced on them, her head on a cushion between the taps. She looked extremely comfortable.

'I suddenly thought this is just a device in movies, no one *really* sleeps in baths, so I was worried about you in here,' said Krul.

'How touching,' said Bridget, unable to believe that Krul had spared her one tenth of a thought. 'I'm fine thanks. Addie there?'

'I'm here, Bridget. You could go down to the sofa.' Addie pushed past Krul, under his arm, to say this. Meanwhile Krul had gone down the three stairs to their left and opened the door behind her into the spare room.

'What's he up to?' said Bridget, suspiciously.

'Heaven knows,' said Addie and followed Krul down the corridor. There she heard him say to James and Bernard, 'Now this isn't good enough. Who is gentleman enough to offer Bridget a real bed? Surely I need hardly tell you chaps that the female body has more pneumatic protrusions and is therefore less suited to sleeping in a hard steel bath?'

'It's acrylic,' Addie heard herself saying, lamely.

From inside came sleepy rumblings, so Addie moved nearer to hear who was saying what.

James was saying that Bernard was too tall for the round bath and therefore it should be him, the shorter, with the reservation that Bridget had every right to opt for the bath, pneumatic bits notwithstanding, and it was up to her.

Addie wasn't daft and realised what Krul was doing. Obviously by putting Bridget in with Bernard he was hoping . . . so she said, from behind him,

'No. There must be some other way. Why don't you take the bath, Krul, if you're so worried about Bridget?'

'And Bridget sleep with you?' How she wished she had not said this the moment he turned on her. 'Let's ask Bridget, I'm sure she'd prefer that,' he said, smiling, 'wouldn't she, darling?' Addie felt herself burning in the face and turned away.

'Krul!' she whispered. 'You promised.'

He turned to address Bernard and James,

'Of course Bridget and Addie go back a long way, you know.'

James, bless him, jumped up at this point and said,

'That's enough, thank you, Krul! I'm going,' and left the room, heading up to the bathroom. Krul was indeed silenced and they all waited rather theatrically for the entrance of Bridget. Bernard showed no expression on his face whatsoever.

When she came, clutching her book and rucksack, blinking and frowning, she said, 'James says he *needs* the bath. What's going on?'

Krul laughed. 'And the little one said, roll over.'

'You can sleep here,' said Bernard, rolling away towards the wall, trying not to giggle.

'Thanks. I wasn't looking forward to a night squirming about on hard steel.'

'Acrylic,' said Addie quietly.

'I'm sure you weren't,' said Krul, shutting the door. He walked back to the bathroom, where James was about to enter the bath.

'Comfy?' asked Krul.

'No. Bloody awful.'

'Come with me. Lift up your bed and walk.'

He led him down the corridor, past the children's room, to the boxroom where he opened the door a few inches. Inside Melanie stirred and said, 'Sorry?'

'Company for you, Melanie.' He walked in and erected a camp bed, really a garden lounger Addie had forgotten to take down to the garden, and James gratefully sidled up to it.

'You don't mind, do you?' he asked.

'Of course not,' said Melanie, straightening her loose hair, rearranging herself in the bed.

Addie was waiting on the landing.

'Go to bed,' said Krul.

'I can't. I could wake up to any combination in the morning . . .'

'Exciting, eh?' Krul put his arm round her shoulder and let his fingers slide under the edge of her nighty for a moment.

'Come to bed, Krul.'

'No,' he edged away from her, 'you're exempt.'

In the tower, where Krul usually spent his nights, were Neil and Zina, on the sofabed, and Fred on a blanket under the radiator, having been rescued from a night outdoors by Bernard who had heard him yowling, all three of them wriggling about trying to get comfortable despite the ungiving nature of floors and thin mattresses and Zina's bump. Krul knocked and entered. Knocking on his own sanctum!

'Bear with me for a moment,' he said, 'I have to make a few adjustments to the computer.'

'Used to it,' said Zina. 'Neil plays twenty-four-hour combat games.'

'Shshsh,' said Neil, 'Krul doesn't want to know about that.'

'Quite right, Neil,' said Krul, slotting a video tape into the front of his video machine and sitting on the edge of the table. He gazed at them too long for comfort, so that Zina said,

'Reminds you of Addie's first?' It was a stupid thing to say but it filled the silence and was all she could think of.

But Krul's eyes lit up, as if she had given him a present.

'Yes, indeed it does. It's a frightening time for men, eh, Neil?'

'Well . . .'

'Thinking about the unknown all the time, worrying.'

'Well . . .'

'They even say that near the end, when the bump is almost bigger than the woman, and the baby moving about so much, that some men stop making love altogether.'

'Well obviously . . .'

'I wonder why that is?' Krul devised a mock-frown. Zina smiled, Neil was flustered and began a long sentence starting with, 'It might be unwise . . .' but Krul stopped him.

'I know actually. I know why. The man thinks, but deep inside himself, not admitting it to anyone, that during love-making the baby will reach down, open the lock of the cervix, grab the penis and *pull it in*!'

Zina laughed hysterically.

'Right, Krul, right!' and slapping the bed and rolling about laughing. In fact, thought Krul, that is the rather explosive, exaggerated laughter of someone who hasn't had a good laugh for a long time.

While Zina composed herself, wiping away tears, and Neil stared into space, Krul activated the video.

'So, in the spirit of undampening your ardour and dispelling such ridiculous qualms, I have here a little entertainment for you.' And he left.

As he closed the door the grey dots on the flat screen before them resolved themselves into black, and red letters sprang up from the bottom of the screen saying:

LUSTY LADS & LOVELY LADIES LIE LOW

'An L-ish alliteration,' said Zina, snuggling up to Neil and laughing.

Krul tripped feather-light downstairs to the bedrooms and down further to the transept dining room where he motioned Morris to stop laying out sleeping bags and come into the nave.

They whispered there together for a few moments and laughed and then Krul handed something to Morris, who saluted him and ducked into the dining room where Lottie was just heaving her deliciously nude bulk into an almost transparent cambric sleeping sheet.

22

An End is Put

Although the lights were out in the spare room, Bridget felt Bernard's eyes were tiptoeing across the carpet, scaling her box-spring, lifting the corner of the duvet and inserting themselves into the bed where they wandered at will over her skin. What had Superman really seen with his X-ray vision – breasts, nipples, or right through to the bones beneath? If so, how disappointing for him; people don't need total X-ray vision, just a few inches of insight.

A rather high-pitched and pompous (almost Prime-Ministerial) voice said, using her own mouth as an amplifier, 'Perhaps I ought to say that I have decided to prefer women.'

There was a definite chortling, which nearly unnerved her.

'That's something you can decide rationally, is it?' came the reply, surprisingly soon and shockingly near. They could almost have been at the far ends of the same huge double bed. Bridget now wished she hadn't spoken at all, hadn't begun what could so easily become an intimacy, and instead had pretended to be exhausted and sleeping. But that never worked. Besides, she had slept once today.

'Why not? I have every right to.'

'I'm not saying you haven't the right; I just doubt anyone has the outright choice.'

'It's not *natural*, you mean?' Of course that's what most men think in the face of *unnatural* lesbianism, and many men had said to her, supposing that she was that way inclined because she didn't fancy their greasy paws on her knee just then, 'I can cure you, darling. A good rodding's what you need.' How it must anger gay people to be offered such a cure! She could feel with them so dearly that indignation, that she had more or less decided to join them. Almost out of solidarity.

'No. I think it's the most natural thing in the world. I lust after women so why shouldn't women?'

'Are you lusting after me?' This was outright flirting, she knew: fanning the fire.

'Of course. And you?'

'Perhaps.'

'Perhaps! See, who is the more honest of us here? Men aren't generally praised for being honest in these matters.'

'You must be the exception.'

'Then *perhaps* you could make an exception to your rule?'

'What rule?'

Bridget felt she could make an exception. Ah, gladly make it, especially in view of the fact that he was a long, lovely, gentle, honest man and only a few inches away and doubtless knew what was what; however something bothered her.

'And flower?'

'You mean Fleur?'

'Yes.' Solidarity again. Bridget would sooner lie there and burn for hours than inflict pain on another woman she had not met but who had obviously chosen so well: chosen someone with sane ideas, or inculcated them herself.

'If she were here, she'd definitely be lusting after you too.'

Well it *was* only a few inches and soon traversed, by Bridget, and an end was put, if 'put' be the word, (yes put is the word) to all the lusting going on in the most natural way possible, given that it was late in the twentieth century and even the quiet reaches of St Boddi's were not immune to the stalking of that killer, AIDS. The only slight regret, on Bridget's part, was that they had thus fulfilled Krul's stratagem despite themselves.

Returning to her own bed, Bridget noticed that the wall against which it rested was not solid. Part of it was an ornamental roodscreen with eye-sized holes at intervals.

23

Dear Faces

More than most people, James had learnt just how true it was that beauty is an entirely transient and imaginary perception. As an exercise in proving this he had taken photographs of cinema stars, male and female, and caricatured them grossly. The more beautiful the subject, the easier it was to draw something which was hideous and also recognisable as them. No one had unassailably perfect features, and with age people became their own caricatures quite naturally, without the intervention of his wicked pen. Thus he had grown to admire older people, those whose features spoke of tragedy, of experience, whose faces were not smooth soft palettes waiting for life to surprise or amuse them. The vapid young he left alone. It was crumpled, twisted, asymmetrical faces like Melanie's which caught his eye.

Hence he was rather pleased Krul had insinuated him into the boxroom, though he knew Krul to be so perverse in his nature and so hostile to him (simply because Krul hated anyone and everyone who had pre-dated himself in Addie's affections, witness his insinuations about Bridget) that it was not beyond the bounds of possibility that Krul knew something about Melanie (like her being a Carmelite nun or dying of AIDS) which would preclude any frolics between them whatsoever.

Still he was, like his sister Addie, essentially an optimist.

Obviously someone who said 'sorry' all the time must have a well-developed sense of pity.

'I hate the dark,' he began, sitting up.

'Oh dear,' said Melanie. 'I'm sorry. We could have the door open.'

James arose and opened the door to let in a slice of light. Returning to the campbed, he said, 'I think it's really loneliness. As a child . . .'

Gradually it became obvious that it would be easier to continue his story sitting next to Melanie in the bed, which he did. Since the bed was very narrow, and neither of them very narrow, it became obvious that he needed to put an arm around her to anchor himself, which he did. Then the proximity of their bodies, together with the sad tale of loneliness and childhood terrors, and the heat, combined together to entwine them still nearer in a most comforting embrace. Which they did.

Melanie had not yet encountered any challenge to her fidelity to Colin. This was partly circumstance and partly her nature. She didn't regard herself as at all attractive. She assumed that to be attractive, a woman had to be well groomed, well dressed, well educated, and have much leisure to spend on keeping fit. Or, in other words: look like Addie.

Even if Melanie had had some or all of these elements at her disposal, she still would probably *not* be attractive because she would feel too guilty to spend all that money on her appearance. She would have to give it away to charity or someone more deserving.

And that's what she was doing now, really. If you think about it; just giving it away to someone more deserving. James was a nice man. A lonely bachelor. Addie's brother. Seeking solace.

Also, serve Colin bloody right!

The door quietly swung on its own oiled hinges and closed itself then, and, curiously, James didn't even notice the ensuing dark at all.

24

The Bank Holiday Condom Conundrum

It was one of Lottie and Morris's adages that You Always Run Out of Condoms on a Bank Holiday. Most such sayings owe their longevity to the fact that there is a scientific explanation: the buttered bread always falls that side down because that side is heavier, buses arrive together at long intervals because of traffic patterns, you come down with a cold on the first day of your annual holiday because the germs have been waiting for your immune system to let down its guard for weeks, and so on ... but no explanation presented itself to Morris why the Condom Law came into operation every Bank Holiday.

Could it be that the shareholders in those few shops which opened on Bank Holidays and sold the items went secretly from house to house (or in his case, van to van) removing and destroying condoms so that the need to visit their shop (a lucrative one, for who would dare to buy *just* condoms? – no really, I needed this packet of processed cheese slices with a medieval datestamp and thought, while I was here I might as well just buy some) would be an almost universal need.

'I suppose you've run out of johnnies?' said Lottie wearily, settling down for a long sleep.

'As a matter of fact, no.' He squeezed in beside her and dive-bombed his right arm into her line of vision. In his hand was a small oblong packet. Which reminded him of a time in Morocco when ...

'Good heavens. Where did you get that?'

'Krul.'

'Oh, how sweet. The host with the most! You didn't *ask* him, did you?'

'No, he guessed.'

'Good for him.'

Good for them too. For despite her endless breastfeeding of any pre-pubescent child who happened her way, Lottie was apt to ovulate at random, possibly because she was so well nourished, in every sense, so there was never a safe time and all their children had been a surprise. Neither of them felt they could handle any more surprises.

Morris wasn't used to making love in the open like this. Usually they managed to secrete themselves, despite Lottie's bulk, somewhere in or about the van. However, there always *was* a problem associated with all living in the same room/van. Lottie often wondered that Victorian couples in families where seventeen of them shared a bedroom managed to make love at all. She and Morris had been reduced to some ridiculous stratagems in bad weather, involving innocent garden sheds and bus shelters.

In the safety of this stuffy dining room they each fantasised in their own way about more exotic places they might be, had been, would be again.

That dining room was simply one end of the transept and anyone sitting at the bottom of the stairs up to the bedroom floor would have had a splendid view of their goings on.

25

Taking Advantage

'Ridiculous!' said Neil, deactivating the video equipment. 'As if women lie around naked in offices, murmuring and just longing for any old bloke to come along.'

'Yes, ridiculous,' murmured Zina, lying naked in Krul's office, just longing for any old . . . 'Entertaining, though.'

'It's an insult to intelligent, well-educated people,' he added, bitterly, giving the dozing Fred a nudge with the foot (to see if he was still alive) and climbing into bed.

'Like us?'

'Yes. I can't think why Krul thought we might want to see it.'

'Can't you?'

'No. And in the morning I'll tell him so.'

'Will you?'

'Well, not in so many words.' Zina thought he was going to sleep then and sighed, loudly. But he wasn't.

'Those women!'

'Yes.'

'I mean, for example, breasts aren't really *that* big in real life, are they?' Zina switched on the lamp and pulled down the cover, revealing, due entirely to the overproduction of hormones associated with her pregnancy, two enormous breasts.

'Gosh,' said Neil in what Zina liked to think of as his Beano voice, 'good heavens.' Obviously he must have seen them recently, must have caught glimpses of them when she was undressing or dressing, or bathing. He must have. But somehow, until now, he had not really taken in their enormity. Quite suddenly their enormity was of intense interest to him.

'Amazing?' she said, happily. 'We could take advantage.'

'Yes. You've got something there.'

Twenty-five minutes later Fred noticed a small buzz in the corner of the ceiling cease to buzz. It was that feeling you have when you aren't aware of the ticking of a clock until it stops. But Neil and Zina were already asleep.

Krul switched off his monitor, turned, swaggered along the corridor, now completely quiet, smiling a smile. He could, quite possibly, be the only human being out of a possible seventeen and a half awake in the house. He felt a sort of completeness rising within him. As he came into the room with the stained-glass picture of St Boddi he couldn't help whispering, 'Any objections?'

St Boddi didn't reply.

Addie was fast asleep on her back on the far side of the bed. He went round and sat on her chair, the one she always put her clothes on. Her face was pale, bluewhite, almost transparent, and her alabaster arm lay over her chest, which rose and fell gently. Her red hair, released from clips, spread and sparkled over the blue pillow in ripples. She was an effigy from Atlantis: perfect, unassailable. He could no more have touched her than joined her dream. But no need to touch her: she looked to him to be deep in a dream of his own spellbinding.

He sat for over an hour in silent adoration until sleep claimed even him.

26

From the Feet Upwards

Boddi was learning how to strut with his newfound evenness of leg, and was doing so in the grass aisles between the rows of vegetables in the vegetable garden, where he was noticed by the cook's daughter, the Virgin Mary. Brother Godwiy had begun the habit of calling her this because of her shyness and the fact that though nearly seventeen and fair of face and body, she was not yet courting. In fact her name was Primrol.

Of course Boddi had registered Primrol out of the corner of his eye at meal times, and when hobbling through the kitchen, seen her peeling things, washing things, scraping things, and so on, and he had registered her as *pretty*. But being a cripple had not only meant that girls would not consider him, but also that he, to avoid disappointment, never considered them. Since he had no love for his misshapen body, he assumed no woman could have either.

When that morning Primrol walked out into the garden a few feet from him, nearly bumping into him, he realised, with a jolt like a bar of molten metal forming through his centre, that all that was changed.

'Primrol!' he gasped, like a fool.

'Boddi! Your. Your body!' she blushed. She hadn't witnessed the transformation from shoeless to shod, and could not comprehend. 'Is it a miracle then?' she asked.

'Oh yes, it is.'

She ran away to tell someone about the miracle, leaving Boddi helpless with confusion and lust.

That night, after Evensong, just before the betting began in earnest, for the friars needed entertaining sorely after all their travails with the poor, which were many indeed, and the stakes were only draughts of ale from a communal barrel in the Hall, Boddi spoke.

'I want to place a bet with Brother Hew.' A silence fell on the company. Brother Hew sat up straight.

'Good. What is the nature of the bet?'

'As you all know, I am indebted to Brother Hew in many ways, and am very grateful for all you have done to educate me. But I am still not a free man.' A low moan went around the room and Brother Godwhen spoke up.

'You know that was only a trick to bring you here. Brother Hew would never willingly enslave another man. You are free.'

'No. Sir Piers Maldespeau gave me into slavery to Brother Hew and only he can free me.'

'This is only a temporal law . . .' began another brother, but Boddi went on.

'In any case my proposal is this. I will place a bet with Brother Hew and if I win the bet, he must provide me with a horse and some gold so that I may go back to Wyndcombe and buy my freedom.' Again there was silence.

'What is the bet?' said Hew.

'That I can seduce the cook's daughter, the Virgin Mary, or Primrol, this very night. And to prove it, produce a lock of her hair at breakfast time.' A roar of laughter went round the Hall, every man there, Hew especially, being convinced of the impossibility of the task. It was just a young man's whim.

'And no force to be used?' ventured a friar near him.

'Of course not.'

'I accept the wager!' said Hew, happily.

Only Godric, man of visions, neither laughed nor smiled nor looked in the least relieved. Later, in the solitude of his cell, he wept tears.

Boddi knew he wasn't a comely man – for neither his face nor misshapen limbs had any grace nor his skin any of that bright paleness which men of wealth enjoy. Neither was he witty or gifted with great charm, like some men who, though unlikely to look at, win the favours of surprisingly comely maids through the offices of the tongue alone. However, he had noticed that when he sang, no matter how bawdy the ditty, those listening were melted. They were helpless with reverie and completely entranced.

He intended to use this Gift, as Hew called it, to influence Primrol. It was all he had, that and the cover of darkness to hide his rough brown self.

In the dead of the night, wrapping a borrowed cloak about him, he climbed up an escarpment to position himself by her window, at the back of the Friary, a most secret and dark place. Her window was open about three of Jankin's knots.

And here he began to sing:

> Betwene Mersh and Averil
> When spray beginneth to spring,
> The lutel fowl hath hire will
> On hire lud to sing.
> Ich libbe in love-longinge
> For semlokest of alle thinge –
> He may me blisse bringe;
> Ich am in hire baundoun.

Her window opened further and she leant out to hear

> An hendy hap ich habbe ihent!
> Ichot from Hevene it is me sent.
> From alle wimmen my love is lent,
> And light on my Primrol!

During the next half hour, Boddi sang as he approached her casement, never ceasing first to praise her hair, her brow, her eye, her slender and 'well-imake' waist, threatening to 'feye fallen adoun' if she would not take him. Then climbing in at the window, he sang that at night when he 'wends and wake' with pale cheeks, it is her fault entirely for having the neck of a white swan. As they lay side by side on her narrow bed (she still utterly entranced) his song reached its climax as he told how he was weary as water in a whirling pool but she could easily un-doom him with her dear dear arms.

Which she did, dear girl, and later gave him gladly a lock of her hair as a keepsake for the long journey he must go on that day.

PART TWO

Sunday

27

The Contest Begins

Bess, an only child of twelve, awoke on Sunday morning in St Boddi's in a room containing lots of other children. She counted. In the bunk beds to her left were either two double-headed monsters or four children top-to-tailed in the two beds. Whether boys or girls, it was impossible to tell. She had met them last night, but briefly and at the end of a long, long day.

Next to the bunk on the floor stood a plastic box with handles in which slept a baby and next to it a small inflatable air mattress with a girl (the plaits gave this away) of about four, asleep. This made six children and her.

Having thus reassured herself, like someone who had fainted, as to the nature of her environment, she closed her eyes and listened. She could hear the soft sighing of six children asleep and the sea crashing nearby, nothing else. The quiet made her uneasy at first, partly because she was used to the continual background hum of London traffic, the hourly scream of a nearby locomotive, and the rowing of her parents, and partly because she could not anchor herself in any of these sounds and had no idea where her mother might be in this building.

Perhaps she had died? Could the next world be this over-crowded? Yes, it would be, wouldn't it, considering the numbers of dead people there were to accommodate. But you wouldn't hear the sound of the sea. Or would you, if that was what you wanted to hear for ever?

For ever. Nothing is for ever, hold on to that. Comfort yourself with this: the black bickering, rising to yelling, rising to violence, all that rising is finite, cannot last for ever. Eventually the violence will top-out. One day I will be grown up and leave them. Then they'll be sorry. Why does Bess never visit us, they'll whimper. Well I can't stand to spend one second of my life within these walls with you two, that's why.

Monsters now, they will be old one day, though to Bess, twelve, each day is a century long and the future is beyond imagining, though she strains and strains towards it as towards a saviour. Stranded in the present, save me, the future, save me.

Monstrous, he rises from his chair at a meal. Meals of dynamite dumplings and cordite custard. They haven't horns nor are their eyes really molten steel but ugly as the Devil when they fight and ridiculously they turn to her afterwards, battle-torn, holding ice to damaged faces, diminished, and ask for her allegiance! As if she gives a *damn* about who is right and who is wrong. She would lose an arm to have them stop it. More. More than that.

So enwrapped are they in their own embroilments that they do not realise that under their roof lives a twelve-year-old person who, if she had to make a definite decision in order to go on living, would usually not bother.

So when yesterday morning, returning from ballet lesson, her mother had greeted her with packed suitcase and 'We're leaving now', her heart had jumped for joy – wherever they were going *he* would not be there and so they could not fight, not in person, not within her hearing, and that was all that mattered. Whatever happened in letters, or on the telephone or in divorce courts or at the dole office could no longer affect her now that she was here.

For no apparent reason, the baby began to cry. It was a piercing, almost electronic noise. A large girl rose suddenly, only opening her eyes a fraction, leant over the edge of the bottom bunk, and rummaged around in its box for something. She found a dummy and plugged it in the baby's mouth. The noise stopped. She saw Bess then and jumped.

'Oh, it's you, Beth, or . . .'

'Bess.' Thus began a round of introductions and a flurry of awakenings and names which Bess tried to store systematically in her brain. It was easier for them because all of them knew each other, though not her, thus they all had one name to remember and she had six. She did remember Sophie a little from London and Toby Two Tongues as they had called him at school, on account of his speech defect. But both of them had changed so much: browner and bigger.

The other four were a 'family' – Greta, the girl who had plugged the baby (her brother George, what a silly name for a half metre of flesh!), called the boy on the top bunk with TT, 'my brother Hugo' and the girl with the plaits on the air mattress 'my sister Clare'.

It very soon emerged though that she was the eldest by eighteen months, apparently a very important thing. They had a vote which seemed to decide that she could make them breakfast.

She was quite happy to make them breakfast, lunch, dinner, anything, now that she was free of everything nasty to do with London, which she now knew she must be because she remembered that Sophie and Toby had moved 'miles away down to the South Coast' so that is where she must be.

It never struck her that in agreeing to provide breakfast, she was agreeing to contend for Leader.

Krul, busy in the nave drawing up a rota with the help of his portable lap-top computer, was aware of a file of children passing behind him into the kitchen, but decided to leave them to it. On Sundays his own children often fended for themselves for the first few hours. He had no interest whatsoever in other people's children and it was only six o'clock.

He did have a momentary qualm when Addie's phone rang in the dining room a few minutes later, but heard Morris answering it and returned to his calculations.

It was Colin, Melanie's husband.

'I want to speak to Melanie.'

'Who is Melanie?'

'Who is that – Krul?'

'No, shall I get him?'

'I just want to know if Melanie is there.'

'Calm down. It is six a.m. and lots of people are here, one of whom may, for all I know, be called Melanie, but I can't say just now. Try ringing back later.' He hung up.

In the arch of the transept dining room stood a tall well-developed girl with long curly brown hair and a slightly haunted look. She could be any age at all, but Morris decided she was the one who had arrived late last night. He reached to cover himself, for he was totally naked and she was staring at his groin.

'Do you know where my mother is?'

'Er, no, I don't.' Finding nothing to serve as fig leaf, Morris was using his right hand and found he was waving his other one about conversationally, trying to look casual, pointing into the nave, 'but ask that man over there – he'll know.'

'Thank you.' Bess approached the man who had dragged her upstairs the night before, trying to wipe from her mind the picture of this man with a third, trapped hand pointing at her from between two bushes of hair in his thighs.

'Yes. Go upstairs and to the far end. It's the door on your right.' As she went, Krul laughed out loud. Reconfirming, as if she needed it, that he was *not* a nice person.

She opened the door quietly and saw two people linked together in a narrow bed. There was no mistake – that was Mum, but who was the man with the turnip nose? As she stood there neither one of them woke, which was incredible because something inside Bess exploded and shot parts of her at least two hundred metres into the air, leaving her shaking and about to scream.

But she didn't. All those years of quietly sitting at the table while the two people she loved best in all the world hurled at each other the most dreadful abuse and unimaginably horrible threats had prepared her well for keeping the hurt in. So she shut the door, walked back down the corridor, down the stairs, smiled condescendingly (she hoped) at that dreadful man who was watching her, averted her eyes from the room where the naked three-handed man lived, and entered the kitchen.

Where Sophie had tied an apron around her nightie and was putting Ryvita, Marmite, honey, oranges, apples, knives, plates, margarine, cornflakes, sugar and spoons onto a table around which sat Toby, Hugo, Greta and Clare. The baby they had got rid of somehow.

'Who is that man in the big room?' she asked.

'Krul – their father,' said Greta.

'Where's the baby?' asked Bess then, sounding, Toby thought, like someone's mother.

'We left him up there, to sleep,' said Greta with some self-importance; she would shortly bring him down to re-establish her standing. The contest for Kingperson had begun.

The heat was already rising. As they ate, Hugo was rolling a marble over the table. It was the only good way for a person not possessing a spirit level to test for the horizontal.

'Rollyeyes surrender!' said Toby.

Hugo looked at Sophie, who said, 'Give him the marble.' Hugo gave it to him, astonishingly, without question. Toby held it up to the light and looked at it. It was green glass with a blue iris and yellow flecks. After a few seconds, he dropped it as if it had burnt him.

'Why did you do that?' asked Hugo, fishing for it.

'Lookened straight back,' said Toby, trembling.

Bess shook her curls and laughed hysterically for a few moments. Clare, who could never withstand a giggle, joined her. It was a relief.

They ate in silence, and everything. Their parents would not have believed, had there been anyone to tell them afterwards that their respective children had eaten, without fuss, a most nutritious combination of fibre, vitamin B, powdered skimmed milk with vitamin D, and chopped oranges. Pith and all in

Toby's case (he also favoured the crunchy part of a boiled egg). Bess wielded the knife on the oranges, poured milk over the muesli, spread honey; and as she did so, it seemed to Greta, grew inches taller every moment.

But, thank God, George cried out and the sound poured out of the open window above them and into the kitchen. Greta stood.

'I'll have to get the baby,' she said with mock-weariness.

'Babies are *supposed* to cry,' said Bess, 'it's good for them.'

Greta sat down. He stopped.

'See?' said Bess. 'It develops their lungs so that they can hold their breath under water later in life, and it gives them the information that the world is not here just for their sakes, that they are insignificant.'

'Babies are not insignificant,' said Sophie, 'we were all babies once.'

Except you, thought Toby, who never were, ever. For if you were, where was I?

'Why will he be under water?' asked Clare.

'Wound in down drowning,' said Toby.

'I wonder why he stopped, then,' added Clare.

'Gills by gilliam,' said Toby, quietly, 'better far for under underbubbling.'

'What?' said Clare.

'He won't drown,' said Hugo, 'my big sister would rescue him.'

'Why?'

Oh God, thought Bess, it's like talking to the radio, round and round. She wanted to control the anarchy, to make them all concentrate and make sense, if only to distract her from everything, from the confusion of everything, of naked men and men in beds and houses which felt like churches. How could somewhere in England be so unlike London?

'The boys must do the washing up,' said Bess. It was a simple idea but Greta joined in.

'They'll need chairs in front of the sink.'

'Yes,' said Bess, 'and they must not break anything.'

'They must roll up their pyjama sleeves.'

'They must put the marble *away*.'

'And be careful.'

Bess couldn't let her have the last word so she added, 'And quiet, so as not to wake the grown-ups.'

'Ups up,' corrected Toby, a stickler for grammar.

'That boy's not as stupid as he seems,' announced Bess, and thus got Sophie and Toby's vote for Kingperson without even knowing it.

Toby gasped: he and Hugo were like two men in a nuclear power station with oversized rubber gloves holding contaminated rocks at arm's length in foaming plutonium solution.

'This is good,' said Hugo after a while, having discovered three things about plumbing.

He didn't understand how dangerous it all was, thought Toby.

The girls were milling about in the garden, avoiding the plutonium bubbles everywhere, no doubt.

Lottie, with George under one arm, found the boys. George was drunk. Mother's milk had addled his brain. He was even less capable of sensible thought now than a baby of his age could be expected to be, and drooled drunkenly into the boys. It was as if he wanted to grow his gills now, thought Toby, or join with them in some exquisite wet huggery.

'Sweeties! Chapolatas!' she said. 'Having a wet play? *What* a good idea Where is Greta, love-ums?' They both pointed and half a pint of radon lather swooshed over Lottie, missing George. She was only wearing a shirt of Morris's.

'Oh sugar!' She slopped away, hunting for girls. She found one.

'Greta, darling, Angelface, look after Porgey will you? I've fed and changed his nappy. If he could just mess about with you guys while I snooze a bit more. There's a dear. What would I do without my precious one?' She handed the baby over, kissing Greta sleepily on the ear. 'Poor mite, he was screaming his little head off.'

Greta and Bess and Sophie all thought one thought: I shan't breastfeed, if that's how wet you get. Sophie adding, internally, that she wouldn't adopt either if that's how you had to talk.

Lottie went back indoors and was asleep again in under a minute.

'Show me everything,' said Bess. Sophie had forgotten Bess had that effect on people. Even her teacher in London would sometimes complain that she had spent ten minutes talking to Bess while the class rioted. It was the vivid eyes, the grace, the riveting charm. Stay with me awhile, hear me out. Oh, I will, I will.

So Bess had the tour as no one else had it, of the grounds including the beach and the graves, the Treehouse and the Chalet.

Greta bounced George fiercely on her lap, as she watched them. Having George was not working. George deposited some white fluid on her nighty and looked at it as if to say, did I do that?

She had to admit that Bess was big. Of course size itself means nothing, but the parts must be well acquainted, good friends. In children they seem to have met recently, just been introduced. Only hands and faces and forearms were friends, usually, but Bess's movements said there was only one way of doing everything, she had done them so often, she had found the best, the easiest way, and the most efficient. She had had more practice living in her body, in the world. Now she was stooping, fussing over that dog and asking about him.

'He belongs to my Aunt Zina and Uncle Neil.'

'Dogs belong to God, not people,' Bess said.

'I know. I mean, he obeys them, I guess. Though, if he . . .'

'Sit!' said Bess, touching his back. He sat. He looked up at her, waiting.

'Stand!' He stood.

Toby ran out of the vestry shouting, 'Oh no no.'

Hugo had broken a few thingummies. No he hadn't. Toby had.

'Toby never breaks anything,' said Sophie, and she knew why: he was terrified about setting off some chain reaction in the world in which everything breakable would shatter, including people.

'It really doesn't matter,' said Bess, calmly. She proceeded quietly to clear away all the evidence. She had to. Lottie and Morris and Krul and Addie had all told their children that if they ever saw broken glass to report it, and keep away. But Bess lived in a world where broken glass and crockery were as much a part of the environment as air and dust. Even Greta, determined not to be, was impressed at the efficiency with which she dealt with the breakages, without hurting herself. And what's more, she didn't even seem to *mind*.

'There ought to be a Girl Guides Badge for this,' she said, 'I'd have dozens.'

Riding on the crest of this triumph, Bess led them all down to the Chalet where she asked Greta (still holding George) what she thought was the best way of choosing a leader. Naturally Greta preferred voting, having been raised a Democrat, so while Hugo got busier and busier until his hands were full of Sellotape which he could not flick off, they held a secret election, with pieces of paper (and Sellotape in Hugo's case).

Results of the Election:
Elizabeth, nearly thirteen, Autocrat, good with broken glass,
   3 votes
   (Toby, Sophie, and herself)
Greta, eleven and a half, Democrat, good with crying babies,
   3 votes
   (Hugo, Clare and herself)

The problem was that George had no vote, being too young and unable to write. Also Fred, though he was looking wise, could not cast a vote. Was this discrimination?

'It's a draw then,' said Bess, 'we'll have to have another election. Perhaps someone will change their mind.'

Someone did, but it was impossible to tell who since Bess, the winner, screwed up the ballot papers and put them in her pocket, after they had been counted by Sophie.

Sophie was not surprised: she was used to Little Notes which passed between herself and her father, which Toby called her Daddyfaxing, being secret and destroyed on reading.

So something organised began to take shape and Bess changed it as they went along, naming their queendom Bessarabia with inspiration from an old Philips school atlas, and arming the troops with inspiration from the dressing up basket. Sophie found a crown, and they coronated Queen Bess the Third, there already being a first and second one.

They ran around, sang, whooped, marched, moved furniture, sweated, felt dizzy, fell down, stood up and ran again. From a distance it seemed as if they were playing at full speed, having a party.

Every so often Hugo and Toby met by chalet or grave or buttress and collided. Hugo always fell over in confusion.

Bess did a curious thing soon after the election. She crept indoors and brought out a bundle of clothes from her and Melanie's suitcase. From this she extracted, for Sophie and Greta only, several lovely dresses they could wear. They were truly amazed at the finery, though it was the genteel finery of the very poor who shop at jumble sales: they weren't to know that. Thus adorned, Greta didn't mind being Second-in-Command at all, and Sophie draped the 'precious babe' (all tribes had one she believed – witness the Nativity of Christians) in net curtains and Clare was given a bucket with instructions to 'draw water' which puzzled and delighted her.

The boys made themselves guns (sawn-off kindling) and found each some gull feathers to put in their hair, after Toby had inspected them for fleas.

The precious babe would cry. It was good for him, though. Every now and then Fred, the Guard of Honour, would lick his entire face coated in a rather sweet white substance, with one great suffocating slurp. Toby imagined that George would shortly develop a dreadful disease. Was the spit of dogs antiseptic or poisonous? It was a shame he couldn't ask Hugo, for he could have devised an experiment to find out.

Face paints were found and they were soon masked, all except the precious babe.

The only group they could think of to emulate was Robin Hood who was not only a man, but had mostly men in his gang.

Everyone was considering this and catching their breath on the grass in front of the Chalet and Bess felt they were waiting for her to speak, so she told them about Africa.

About how the rain would not fall because rich people had found a way of making all the rain fall on England, so that the poor dusty black people had to pick grains of wheat off the floor and eat them *raw*.

They were incensed.

She told them how just a few pence could feed a million people for a year, because the money grew as it travelled.

They marvelled.

She told them that if they stole keys it would be even better because they were made of silver and could be melted down and sold for lots of money.

They agreed.

Egged on by nudging from Toby, Hugo asked who the baddies would be. There had to be baddies, apparently, in any game. Who would oppose them? Yes, they would surely have enemies, Queen Bess warned them. It would be Krul. Neither Sophie nor Toby contradicted her. So anything stolen from him for the Third World would be doubly valuable.

Everything was decided. Bess felt a new wholeness invading her spirit, as if she could achieve unlimited things within this limited environment. If only George would stop *crying*.

28

Apartheid

It was past nine o'clock that Sunday morning when the first adult voluntarily stirred from sleep. It was Zina, or rather her bladder, which had expanded during the night to the size of a bungalow. She eased herself gently out of bed so as not to burst the bungalow with the foetus and carried both carefully down the hall and up the stairs to the bathroom. On the bathroom door was a sign saying, in Krul's aggressive copperplate:

GENTLEMEN
To ease the strain on the one lavatory system, the management suggest you use the Great Outdoors whenever possible.

Sitting on the toilet (the world being wonderful again as enough fluid to solve all Ethiopia's problems left her body), she thought that there ought to have been someone *here*. Last night someone had been bedded down in the bath. Who?

Bridget. Bridget was lying, awake, but her eyelids shut tight. She was wondering what to do, whether to get dressed in a matter-of-fact sort of way, as if nothing out of the ordinary had occurred here last night, or to reach a hand over to Bernard and perhaps ... She got up and dressed and left the room before he had stirred.

The moment she had left, Bernard opened both eyes.

Bridget found Lottie and Zina in the bathroom talking about bladders, and waited, trying not to show her impatience. She looked down the corridor to see if Addie's door was open and saw James walk out of the little room at the end, walk past her, read the sign on the bathroom door, and go downstairs, presumably to comply with it. Then Melanie emerged from the same room and walked towards her.

'Sorry,' she said.

'About what?' asked Bridget.

'Adding to the queue,' she explained.

'Oh that. I thought you mean the Other Thing.' Bridget winked at her, thinking, what a shame women don't share the locker room talk tradition of men. Just think, they could go together into the bathroom and swap notes. James *v.* Bernard. They say short men are more sensual. Could she say such a thing to Melanie? Leg over, dear? How was it? Worth the guilt? Did you do it to fuck Colin up later, or just for the hell of it?

'I felt sorry for him. He's a very lonely boy,' Melanie whispered to her, blushing, though no one was there to overhear.

'Well,' she giggled, 'aren't we all?'

Zina came out, then Lottie, who said to Bridget, 'Sleep well?'

'Yes thanks. All sorts of hanky-panky up here last night, I can tell you,' (winking at Melanie who turned white).

'Oh yes, I'm sure.' Lottie laughed. Was she taking the piss with 'hanky-panky' or getting into the mood nicely?

By the time Addie reached the vestry/kitchen at ten o'clock, deliberately waiting until everyone else was up so that she wouldn't have to react to the sleeping arrangements of the previous night, the adult's version of breakfast was well under way.

Anyone who has ever worked in the kitchen of an institution will tell you that breakfast is the most difficult meal to organise on a grand scale on account of the eccentric variety of things people want or need to eat. The trouble is breakfast is a democratic meal. The choice is almost infinite, and up to the eater, whereas most meals have a set pattern which you have to adhere to whether you like it or not. Most meals are autocratic.

Also adults are bloody fussy about eggs, always. No one

would dare tell the chef that they wanted their fish poached for exactly eighteen and a half minutes, on each side, with butter and parsley, and served in an oblong dish warmed previously, and yet the instructions for the cooking of eggs are that precise. The possibility of getting each person's egg right when there are more than six people to cater for, is very slim.

So, the odds being long, Krul had set himself this task and was performing it with *élan*. Addie wondered whether he was engaging one of his Business Precepts: that you need not always *be* right, you simply have to convince people that you *are*. Krul was good at this.

The hubbub rose. In the middle of it children, their faces disorted with paint, and their heads decorated with feathers, came and went, rooting in cupboards and drawers for things. Addie couldn't think what, but noticed that Toby was tailing Hugo, keeping an eye on him. She had noticed him doing this before, as if some children were prone to cause catastrophes and he could prevent it by sticking close to them. Toby seemed to spend his whole life at the moment averting disaster, one way or another.

The hubbub died down. In the gap Krul decided to read out the rota. At first everyone laughed, everyone but Addie, but it soon became clear that this was no joke.

ST BODDI'S ROTA   Cooking and Washing Up

SUNDAY	Breakfast	children	themselves
	Breakfast	adults	Krul
	Lunch	children	Lottie & Addie
	Lunch	adults	Bridget & James
	Dinner	children	Addie & Zina
	Dinner	adults	Bridget & Neil
MONDAY	Breakfast	children	Lottie & Melanie
	Breakfast	adults	Addie & Lottie

Krul had expected a viciously worded critique of his rota from Bridget, since she appeared twice on it. She didn't disappoint him. But it wasn't her own double appearance which sparked off her ire, it was Addie's triple one.

'Obviously, having a dangling reproductive member precludes domestic duties,' she began.

'Are you trying to tell us something about James and Neil we never suspected, then?' he countered.

It went to and fro, Krul fending off all comments with rational explanation, mostly of the sort which allots to everyone what they can best *do*, and only Addie stayed absolutely quiet throughout the discussion.

This was because she thought the whole idea ridiculous and thought it would break down before lunch. No one seemed to realise that the rota covered so little of what was actually required. For example, what with broken crockery and disposable nappies, both dustbins were entirely full, and the kitchen bin overflowing. No one was detailed to do this. Still, she was all for learning by experience. Let Krul find out for once how wrong he could be. However, one thing she had to ask him about. She went and stood by him at the sink as everyone was drifting away.

'And what about tomorrow? Do you expect them all to go?'

'Oh yes, they will all depart tomorrow. Did you think they were here for eternity?'

'Yes, they aren't ever going, any of them. We have become a commune.' Addie grinned at him. 'Just what you always wanted.' He ignored this, handing her the brush and a wet plate.

'I'm not doing this again.'

'Tomorrow is a Bank Holiday,' she continued, beginning the washing up, 'and travelling then is inadvisable, especially from the south coast northwards. The whole of England and its children and dog will be jamming the roads. There aren't even trains.'

'I can guarantee,' he said, not looking at her, 'that some time tomorrow, they will all leave. Trust me.'

Greta appeared at her side, wearing a 1960s ballgown of blue nylon and facepaint. At least it looked slightly like Greta.

'Could we have some biscuits, please?'

Lottie rushed up behind her then and said, 'There you are, my little dumpling. What a frock! Can I have George?'

'No. We need him. Forget it.' Addie gave her a packet of biscuits, and she left.

Lottie smiled a false smile and said to them, 'Such wonderful ideas they have, children. I expect he's a vital part of some game.'

'Yes,' said Krul, laughing, 'probably the sacrificial victim about to have his throat cut with my missing Stanley knife. Children have such wonderful ideas.'

Krul need fear no evil. Sophie has already sent him a note saying, 'nice to have so many children to play with.' She would have told him if anything was going wrong.

'Krul!' said Addie. 'Don't worry Lottie, Sophie is *very* sensible; no harm will come to him I'm sure.'

Notwithstanding this reassurance, Lottie snuck out and tried to spy on the children. It was not hard to discover their whereabouts: George's crying was loud and lusty and coming from an outbuilding about fifty yards from the back door, with 'Bessarabia' chalked over the doors in the centre. A string in front of the outhouse stopped her and Fred set up a bark as she tried to break it, for she was too fat to slither under it or climb over it. Out of the Chalet came Sophie. Remembering her mother's praise of the child, Lottie appealed to her common sense.

'Sophie, I need to feed and change the baby. He must be soggy with wee wee. It will shut him up. Then I'll bring him back, all calm and googley again. Good idea?'

'Excellent,' she said, and went to fetch him. On handing him over she warned, 'But we do need him back.'

'Of course.'

*

Thus Lottie was the first to discover that St Boddi's had become two distinct nations, two tribes. The First World of the adults was a sophisticated, decadent civilisation on the decline, but with a certain expertise and holding all the Ultimate Power. The second world, or developing world of the children, Bessarabia, was a dictatorship (sometimes benevolent, always kind to dogs) with primitive superstitious rites and a strategic importance of the access to the beach. But no Finance – the occasionally benevolent dictator was seeing to a loan. Shall we call it a loan? Why not? Third world loans are, after all, seldom paid back.

The armed forces of Bessarabia fulfilled their allotted tasks of pillage with surprising efficiency, considering that they were so poorly trained and inexperienced in pilfering. On the other hand, like the Mujahadin, they were committed, and therefore would have been a formidable opponent had the first world realised for a moment that it was under attack.

Hugo was especially good, having a natural affinity with all things small, shiny, and easily lost. Also, he had pilfered before. His trousers, like Toby's pulled on over wet pyjamas for the adventure, twinkled delightfully with this and that.

There was a moment when diplomatic relations seemed on the point of complete collapse. Toby was watching Hugo hunt in the kitchen cupboards, surrounded by the first world in the form of two tall men and two ladies. Since they were both boys with no grudge in them, it did not occur to them to be at all furtive.

'Excuse me, but what are you up to? Lost something?' said Melanie.

'Oh, they're playing so nicely,' said Lottie, 'don't be nosey. You might spoil it. I can see behind this that there is a Good Idea somewhere.'

They ignored her. Toby was busy assessing for Hugo in an improvised sign language they had invented, the relative merits of a potato skewer and a hand-held whisk with regard to metal content.

They did well. They found eight things for Ethiopia, not realising that they had effectively sabotaged the kitchen as a machine by so doing.

Toby took the eight things, pocketed them and ran. It's only a game, he told himself, dodging back, hoping to get back to Bessarabia well before the metal objects in his pockets turned molten and bored through to his upper leg bone.

Sophie had no intention of stealing anything. For one thing, if she did, she would have to inform on herself. She would have to send a Little Note to her father. So she had appointed herself Keeper of the Babe rather than rebel openly. While he was gone with Lottie (which was, strictly speaking, against the law), she was uneasy, not knowing what to do. On the other hand if you do nothing, you can do nothing wrong.

Colin phoned. Lottie was passing, coming down from washing George, who had been covered in mud, up in the bathroom. She had only answered the telephone a few times in her life, when she had been separated from her children, and feared it was them. She hesitated. It was a stupid phobia. How could this be bad news, or affect her?

'Hello?'

'Could I speak to Melanie, please?'

'Who, dear?'

'Melanie.'

'Ah, she's the one who's preggers, is she?'

'WHAT?'

'Sorry. Look. I'll find her and get her to phone you. Who are you, by the way?'

'Colin.'

'Right.'

On her way back up to the perimeter, with George dangling from one arm, Lottie said to Zina, 'Know anyone called Colin?'

'No.'

'He wants someone to phone him back.'

*

174

Sophie took the Precious Babe and promised not to put any more mud on him. She was encouraged to go on playing with the baby, especially now he was not crying. Fred barked at Lottie again.

'Someone ought to feed that doggie,' Lottie said into the air, on her way back.

'Not on the rota,' said Zina.

Addie and Melanie were bagging up so much rubbish you'd think a pop concert had happened in the kitchen when Lottie entered.

'Lottie, could you see if the milkman's been?'

'I thought I would phone Fleur,' said Bernard, squeezing under the low doorframe, bumping his head on a gargoyle, the only indoor one, on the doorframe into the vestry.

'Phone Fleur?' said Addie, noting that Fleur was not deaf.

'Only the thing is,' he said, 'I seem to have misplaced my address book with her work number in it.'

At work on a Sunday! Could she be a Beefeater, or a Jewish grocer?'

'Where did you put it?' asked Krul.

'It was with my wallet, along with keys and things up in the spare room.'

'But it's not there now?'

'No. In fact, everything's gone. Or moved, anyway.'

'I'm sorry, Bernard. I'll have a look in a minute. I've just got to find the pressure cooker valve first, it's always here and whoever cooks lunch, which might be James, might need it.'

'Can I help?'

Addie set him, being the tallest in the world, the task of stroking all the inaccessible high places of the kitchen for the valve, explaining her theory that once you start hunting for something where it could *not* be, the gods take pity and sometimes fling it at you. She was in fact surprised to have lost it for this never happened to her – Toby had even called her *psychic* once for always knowing where lost things lived.

'Milkman's been!' said Lottie. 'And left six pints.'

'Good.'

'And a bill.'

'NO! I left the money out in an envelope under the empties.'

'At least the children aren't bothering us,' said Melanie.

'That's right,' said Lottie, 'they're playing so nicely. Even George is included. There's nothing like *lots* of children to make for peace, paradoxically,' she added, noting that Addie was staring at her.

'I find one draining enough,' said Melanie.

But then, her one is Bess, thought Addie, cruelly.

'Oh, no. They have such good ideas if you leave them *alone* enough, for the ideas to flow naturally. Self-initiative, how I encourage it! You'll see, before the weekend is out, they'll have hit on a Really Good One if we give them time.'

Weekend is *out*, thought Addie. Sounds ominous.

'Where's my watch? I left it here,' said James.

'I'm missing my children,' said Addie to Melanie.

'But it will give them such an opportunity for self-initiative,' said Melanie, making sure, by looking around, that Lottie had gone. They giggled.

'Did you know there's a string out there?' said James, coming back from the outdoors, still watchless.

'It's called apartheid,' said Bernard, finishing his search.

Neil was trying to put a stop to the apartheid single-handed. Or rather double-handed, for he had Henrypuppet in one hand, Berthapuppet on the other, and a towel draped over the string to help with the illusion.

The Bessarabians gathered for the entertainment. Zina watched him from her chair, thinking what a good father he was going to be. The only man who had any time for these children.

29

The Wizard of Godnet

Flushed with the applause of six children, Neil and Henry and Bertha climbed up to the tower. Here Neil pocketed the puppets and began to hunt through his luggage for dog food. He had forgotten it. Krul entered.

'Seem to have left Fred's food at home.'

'Oh, we'll have to slaughter a child or two to keep him in meat then, Addie being nearly vegetarian.' Neil smiled, he was used to Krul's humour.

'I blame myself, Krul.'

'You always do. It's a bad habit.' Krul sat at the table in front of his monitor and switched on.

'Enjoy the film last night?' he asked. Neil realised this was not a *real* question, more of a challenge. As usual when challenged to defend himself in some way, he retreated behind a 'yes' and a homely cliché:

'Yes, well, it's not really my cup of tea.'

'Not your cup of tea?' Krul made the simple statement sound ridiculous.

'I prefer foreign films actually.'

'That was foreign. It was partly Swedish, like me.'

'I mean . . .'

'Yes, I know what you mean,' Krul said impatiently, attending to the screen.

'Same model as mine,' Neil said to change the subject.

'And what do you do with it?' asked Krul.

There was an embarrassed silence. Then Neil said,

'This and that. You know.'

'No I don't. Income tax, novels, letters to *The Times*, diary, games?'

'Yes, games actually. Mostly.'

'What kind of games?' Another silence.

'It's called Godnet,' he said. Krul stopped, and froze at the keys.

'Codename?'

Almost automatically Neil responded, 'No Big Dealer.'

Krul turned slowly in the swivel chair and looked at him in such a way that Neil felt as if he had just said something unutterably rude by mistake, so he laughed, which was what he always did when nervous.

'Find it amusing, do you, being in prison?'

'How do you know that?'

Krul turned and typed something on the keyboard and on the screen came a file with the name 'No Big Dealer Profile' in large white letters at the top.

'Because I am the Wizard,' he said.

'You are the Wizard?!' Neil stammered, as if someone he saw every day had suddenly revealed that they were really the Queen of England, or from Mars.

Neil sat on the stool by the monitor and read, his mind racing. It was like secretly reading your own medical records while the doctor wasn't looking – compulsive, horrifying, and all so true. Krul seemed to have pinpointed his weaknesses (no strengths apppeared) and predicted his moves successfully again and again. He compared Neil's threat factor with others and found it minimal. Krul scrolled on down the profile. The number of times in prison and why, all noted. And this last one – 3 August – Fell for it.

'Fell for it?' said Neil. Krul chuckled.

'You attacked your own men – you nuked yourself, for God's sake!'

'But that's not possible. It's in the rules.'

'The rules! What rules?'

'Come on, Krul – the rules of the game. The rules inside the program.'

'Which you think of as inviolable, do you?'

Neil sat up and straightened himself. 'Oh God, you didn't. You couldn't.'

'Of course I did. The rules didn't suit me, so I went in there and changed them. At night.'

'That's cheating! How can anyone play then if you can change the rules at a whim?'

'By constantly monitoring the game, like Sugardaddy does, and everyone who *isn't* often in prison. After all, isn't life like that? All legislation is just changing the rules. All progress is changing the rules, the very flux of life!' A nasty gleam came into his eyes and he stood up, invading Neil's private space with his angular Scandinavian face.

'Poor Neil, you are one of life's victims, aren't you? A loser in every way. Those little piggy eyes of yours – I expect the baby will turn out to have them too and failure on a grand scale will be carried on down the centuries by Neilettes playing every game by the perceivable rules, and losing losing losing.' Now he was so close Neil had to back away and he stumbled and fell against a black metal tube with the disk drive hanging from it. Krul bent over him, his lips parted and for one moment Neil thought he was going to *bite* him, or something worse.

Krul turned and sat down at the computer again.

'You can go now,' he said. Neil got onto all fours and noticed something had fallen out of his pocket – it was Henry. Quickly he stuffed the furry thing back in his pocket and glanced at the screen. At the bottom was a box which had been empty, for 'Objectives' and Krul was typing in 'Extermination'. Neil skirted the circular edges of the room and left, at the double.

He walked into the garden, nearly fell into an open grave, and found Fred alone on the beach, eating a dead seagull.

Well, a dying seagull actually, since it was still jerking.

All his fault, that the beast had been so hungry he had killed another living creature. All his fault. By Neil's digital watch's reckoning it was only ten o'clock – some Pakistani shop must be open in Windmouth to sell dogfood, but by the moon's reckoning it was high tide, so the road was impassable. This Neil discovered after two and one third minutes, and cursed, and blamed himself for even that. The hot lead roof of St Boddi's, now having been subjected to three months of unremitting heat and no rain, was giving off a strong metallic smell and Neil felt apprehensive. He must find Zina and tell her about Fred and the lack of food.

Zina was picking up the baby and putting him in a pushchair in the shadow of the vestry, round the back, the north side of the house.

George seemed to be the only native of both worlds, crawling under the perimeter string, a dribbling, incoherent ambassador. He noticed piles of brightly coloured plastic objects, buckets, spades, inflatables, and piles of soft objects, towels, swimwear. He crawled into all piles to investigate and was picked up, swung into the air and placed somewhere where he could no longer see the pile. He would crawl forwards for a while, on the fringes of understanding something about geography which as yet still eluded his parents, when he was scooped up one last time – the ground gave way completely, arms gripped him, and he was being imprisoned in a pushchair.

Zina was imagining that this was her baby – trying to get the feel of it. Neil approached her.

'Beach,' she said.

'Fred had to eat a seagull,' said Neil, 'and Krul plays Godnet too.'

'Wonderful,' said Zina, 'real food and something in common with him at last.' He noticed she was barefoot. He had *never* seen her barefoot before.

'You don't understand.' Was her optimism entirely hormonal?

'Neil! Shape up!'

'And the road is flooded.'

'Hence the beach. The sea is warmer.'

'Warmer? How could it be warm – it's the bloody Channel for God's sake. People put pig grease on them to swim it.'

'Be scientific. Here is the Gulf Stream and warmed sand quickly warms shallow water.'

'Oh I see. You won't be swimming, though, will you?'

30

Snake in Paradise

Zina hoped to be swimming. Perhaps Neil wouldn't notice. A beach is the sort of place where you don't need to do or be anything. She wouldn't have to be the pregnant one resting. She could simply start a brisk crawl out to sea, and someone could join her without it meaning anything, and then on the hot sand . . . simply the primordial need to stretch out in the sun and read a book or drink something foul from a thermos would assert itself. She could even watch George without seeming to be doing research.

They were nearly ready when Krul appeared in the garden, by one of the open graves. He looked disdainfully at the beach equipment spread on the lawn.

'Seems mad to me to go, in the midst of a drought such as this, to a hotter place where you will doubtless all get skin cancer. I shall stay in the cool.'

'Inside you mean?' asked Morris.

'Actually here are the really cool places, Morris, my own personal tumuli. Every house should have one, or six.' He indicated the open graves.

Toby felt a hot metal strip bisect him: one half of him *wanted* his father to go into one of those dark damp bottomless places for ever, the other half would do anything to prevent him.

'Very funny,' said James, 'you do the Dracula and we'll make the most of the weather. Children need the outdoors anyway.' Then Krul sang to them:

> I know where I'm going
> But the Dear knows who's going with me

'Oh Krul,' said Addie, 'please.' He was about to play a trick on someone: he had that manic gleam in his eyes.

'Neil. Come and see this.' Neil walked over and looked into the grave. Krul pretended to push him in (Addie knew he would) and then pulled him back, laughing. Neil laughed too but it was the laugh of a man who has grown used to insults in his life and Addie felt angry as well as embarrassed.

They escaped to the beach and, as Zina had predicted to herself, it had a calming effect on everyone – even the children's mask wore off, and they became, for a while, just children. Except Toby of course who immediately found evidence of a massacre: the flaked and shattered remains of a family of crabs.

'Crabtastrophe,' he said to Fred.

By this late in August, the sea has warmed up, even this sea. It is not the Mediterranean, admittedly, but nor is it the Atlantic end of the Channel and as Zina had so rightly pointed out, the water was warmed by the Gulf Stream swirling up for the eighteen millionth time from Nova Scotia. On entering the water, the gasping only lasts a minute or two and courage is rewarded. Once the head has flipped in, the air feels less welcoming than the sea.

'I'll have everyone's valuables with me,' said Melanie, making a sand-dent in her outspread handkerchief. Nothing short of Bess's drowning would induce her to let her body come into contact with sea water which she knew to be full of radioactive sewage, oil spills, and worse. Didn't she feel a twinge of guilt every time she flushed a toilet?

No one, not one of them, could find any valuables to put there, and Melanie suspected that they distrusted her. It might have been a comfort to her to know that the Troops of Bessarabia had lifted everything shiny from the bedrooms during their breakfast.

Geographically, a beach is just the place where the sea has met rocky land for so many millions of years that sand has occurred. But psychologically, it has a disproportionate effect on humans. No other stretch of anything, say mud, or volcanic dust, or ice, demands the removal of clothing and such odd behaviour in quite the same way. Also the beach has a democratising effect on people: children of different ages make equal contributions to sandcastle building and adults and children paddle in the sea in the same way. A great leveller is a level beach. It even levels out educational differences. No one talks deeply of Philosophy or Nuclear Physics on a beach: they talk of wet and heat and food.

Thoughts are something else, though, and Addie was deep in thought about Krul's behaviour and their guests.

Bridget was determined to have Fun and so headed out to sea at a crawl, and Zina, James and Morris joined her. The children ran and jumped and splashed and built and destroyed and dug and fell and screamed and swam, all of which distressed Fred, so that Neil had to walk him up and down the beach to calm him. Soon Bernard offered to take the dog from him.

Despite being the world's best-travelled toddler, George had not seen the sea before and was studying it closely before taking any irrevocable steps down the evolutionary scale.

His mother was impersonating a rude seaside postcard on a collapsible stool, impossibly small under her partially exposed bulk pinkening beneath the merciless sun.

George threw caution to the winds and crawled into the first wave which presented itself. Unfortunately it was a large one, which had intended passing him to begin the tide's long turn down the beach towards nightfall. Thus, instead of pattering neatly into it, as into a pile of water, or wetness, George found himself lifted upwards on his inflatable orange armbands and flipped backwards onto his back in the foam which dragged him instantly and incredibly fast out to sea.

By the time James and Bridget had dragged him back to shore, Zina, stepping gingerly out of the shallows, was feeling most unwell. The emergency seemed to have tightened a steel band around her pelvis which was sending out rings of pain down through her lower abdomen in lighthouse-like spasms.

She also found, she who had delivered dead babies without showing emotion, she who had sliced the perineal skin of hundreds of women in labour, herself weeping, moved to tears, by the *possibility* that George might have drowned! Since she couldn't stand straight, everyone agreed to go back to the house now. Neil and Bernard carried Zina on a chair made of their linked arms, and Lottie fed the distressed baby as she walked and chastised her other children for not 'keeping near him', though gently.

'How quickly you found the Snake in Paradise,' said Krul, maddeningly, when they all trooped back into the house. He had seen them approaching from the tower. In fact, he had seen George launch himself out to sea as well, and as usual, not only knew everything they might want to tell him, but had already thought one further: a pithy saying and a rug under which Zina might rest in the nave on the sofa in the cool gloom save for the roseate glow from St Boddi in the window.

31

A Missionary

Shortly after they got back from the beach, Colin phoned. Bernard was making a half-hearted attempt to find his wallet in the transept, and so answered the phone.

'Hello.'

'Look, I don't care who you are, I just want you to put down the phone and go and find my wife, Melanie, and ask her to come and talk to me. It's the least she can do. I have a right to be worried. Just *don't hang up*!'

'I had no intention of hanging up, but I think you may have the wrong number.' Melanie? He was terrible at names.

'Don't give me any bullshit. Just go and get her!'

'Listen, there is no need to be offensive.'

'Do you know how many times I have phoned this number?'

'No. But perhaps she doesn't want to speak to you. I wouldn't be surprised, if your tone is always this abusive.' Suddenly Bernard knew to whom he was speaking. James had told him that morning, after breakfast, the sad tale of Melanie and her travails with a wicked husband. He had only told him to explain his own behaviour.

'That's absolutely none of your business. Just go and get her.'

'No.'

'What?'

'I've decided not to.' Colin was lucky that Bernard was by nature reticent for though he had heard the barest details of Melanie's flight, he had seen the black eye, and there were many things he wished to say. He was sure, at any rate, that

Melanie would not want to speak to him, and also that her reluctance was probably quite reasonable.

Colin tried to phone back immediately, but Bernard was ringing his own home number, since Fleur was back from work by now, and he knew his own home number off by heart, as men do but their women sometimes don't.

Addie grabbed Krul in the morning room.

'There's something else. Something worse.'

'Worse than what? Have you gone mad?'

'No. Someone's nicking things.'

'What sort of things?'

'Watches, wallets, pressure cooker valves, milk money, Zina's bracelet.'

'I'll do a discreet search. There must be some explanation.'

Heading out of the door, Bernard approached them.

'Addie, would you like me to go? You know all these extra . . .'

'No! Absolutely not! Not you, Bernard, not you!' Had Fleur asked him to come back?

'Everything all right with Fleur?' she asked, wishing she had asked Krul to record their call (shamelessly she would have listened) for she knew he could do this. Apparently it was important when conducting business on the telephone to be able to say later that you had a record of the call, just as you would keep a copy of a letter.

'Oh yes, fine. You know, a bit . . .'

'Yes . . .'

As if they really knew what the other one was talking about.

Bridget was starving. She felt faint. When with the Senior Zits recently she had eaten lunch at 11.45 so her stomach was on an early regime. She consulted the rota, discovered that it was down to James and herself and also that there only seemed to be a few tins and packets left in the food cupboard.

'Time for the men to make a contribution,' she said to James and Bernard, together on the bench, drinking coffee. 'Do you need any advice?' Quite as if these two were to make the meal alone.

'Yes,' said Bernard, looking up appreciatively at her, almost lasciviously, James thought, 'your ideas would be most welcome. James? Let us to the kitchen.' He liked the idea of doing what the rota did not ask of him.

Bernard's resolve lacked two ingredients: food and culinary knowledge, for he had not the slightest idea how to make a meal out of the scraps which presented themselves. He could follow a recipe or follow Fleur's instructions, but a meal for seventeen *ad hoc* like this? Still, surely it was not beyond his intelligence to think of something. Bridget handed him a vegetarian cookbook with a particularly unappetising title and a lentil-strewn colour photograph on the front. A quick dip in this book assured him that brown rice in great quantities was called for, and there seemed to be about half a tablespoon in a glass jar. There was custard powder too but hardly any milk powder. But what to have with the custard? Jam tart? One gigantic one!

'Can you make pastry?' he asked Bridget. She laughed. Only servants and those who had read Mrs Beeton cover to cover could make pastry. Bridget didn't even have a clue as to the ingredients.

'Oh God,' said James. 'Let's go for fish and chips.'

'Money and tidal roads notwithstanding,' said Bernard, calculating quickly that fish and chips for seventeen might well be a tall order, financially.

Morris was determined to avoid the kitchen and Bridget's dominance which he found jangled his nerves. She would never let him finish a sentence, and, like someone speaking Latin, his sentences were often constructed so as to leave the crucial aspect until the end. Lottie realised this and never interrupted him except to correct his geography. So, when he had finished amusing the small ones with his story, 'Captain Pugwash travels to the Congo', he left them and wandered off to the chalet to 'tidy it'. His thinking was that it was a playroom really and his son Hugo had *played* in it, therefore, he concluded, correctly on historical bases, it must now be in chaos.

Most of the children were in the treehouse, feeding Fred. They didn't see him snip the string with his penknife. He was struck immediately by the altered state of the room; in fact there was almost nothing which even vaguely reminded him of the room he had seen yesterday.

Pieces of pink cloth had been hung over the side windows, giving the room a dusty pink glow, and a throne had been made out of the old armchair in the centre of the room. In front of the throne was a small box with a plank on it. On this plank were arranged various shiny and leather objects in a pattern.

There was a ball of twine which had been used to make the perimeter boundary, wound around some object like a valve. There was a willow pattern cup without a handle, full of silver coins, and a plastic bucket with water in it, at the bottom of which were about a dozen or more keys, removed from their rings and fobs. There was an antique teddy bear sitting next to the bucket, propped against it, with a pile of wallets and purses in his lap. In front of his feet were arranged unopened packets of Durex, like a string of oblong pearls. The bear was wearing a bracelet around its neck and about seven watches on its various mangy limbs.

When Mary Kingsley explored West Africa in her long Victorian skirts in the 1880s, her subsequent warnings to future travellers give a clue to the dangers she most often encountered. One of them was, quite naturally, water pollution. It was not amoebae and germs which inconvenienced her but 'dead Africans in the water'. The thought of bodies in the system rather puts into the shade the odd piece of raw sewage which so exercises Melanie's imagination. But on the other hand, that mixture of fascination and revulsion was exactly that which Morris now experienced, coming across this primitive display of totems. For what else could it be? Like those explorers who found that their delightful friends the Ivs of Iks, a tribe of beautiful naked savages, score the faces of their women until blood flows, and staunch it with holy ash, Morris felt both a moral indignation and a delight. It was so *interesting*, after all.

Their totems were well ordered. The Master Key represents mistletoe, and wards off nightmares; the cup was there, the lance, sword and stone, and dished objects to represent the female. All the related symbols later distorted into the simplicity of the Tarot: all here in the simple childish putting together of objects of beauty.

Morris glanced behind him. Who had seen him come here?

Colin rang. Bridget heard the phone and gratefully escaped the decision-making in the kitchen to go and answer it.

'Hello there.'

'Hello. Are you having a good day so far?'

'Why yes, in some ways. It has been a day of shall we say, more exercise than food. Screwing and swimming's all very well, but there's no substitute for a good meal. Still, I hope this might change. But who am I talking to?'

'I am Colin. How do you do?'

'Fine, this is nice. Is there anyone you want to speak to, or will I do?'

'Actually there is. Much as I am enjoying speaking to you, er . . .'

'Bridget.'

'Bridget, but there is someone. Do you know someone called Melanie, who is staying there?' Ah, so it's Colinthebastard!

'Melanie? Yes, I do.'

'Great, now we are getting somewhere. Melanie is my wife, and I would be eternally grateful if you could arrange for her to come and speak to me on the phone, if it isn't too much trouble?'

'I'm not too happy about the pronoun, Colin.'

'Sorry, the what?'

'*Your* wife? In what sense is she *yours*?'

'In every sense! Well, no, I see what you mean. Perhaps you could get Melanie for me.'

'That's better, using the name, giving her some personhood. A wife is a different order of thing, to, let's say, a caravan, which you could legitimately say is yours, if you had one.'

'I am the one who brings in the money, who supports her, pays the rent, the father of the child, and so on.'

'I see. It's a financial and biological transaction, this wifedom, is it?'

'I only mean. No, I share that. Everything that's mine . . .'

'Is hers? Hand over the pay packet, do you, so you can sort it out between you?'

'Look, Bridget, I am unemployed at the moment, and perhaps this is between me and Melanie. Maybe we could talk about women's rights some other time. I don't hand over the money because she would only siphon it off for her father, who is rich as Croesus but a miser. I have to have some entertainment.'

'And she has to have some entertainment too. Do you give her money for her entertainment?'

There was silence.

'What do you look like, Bridget?' Bridget sat on the telephone table.

'Want to know what colour they are, do you? This is getting interesting.'

Scratch a pig, and there's a pig underneath!

'No! You've misunderstood me. I only want to know who I'm talking to.'

'Well, here I am, Colin, in the nude in fact. Everyone here is in the nude. It's all so exciting. I myself have long blond hair, about waist length, my fingernails are long and scarlet and caressing my enormous tits, which are, you know, that sort that stand outwards without benefit of bra, and point slightly left and right. Oh, Colin, I wish you were here!'

'Cut it out!'

'You'll never know, will you? If it's true.'

It was Colin who hung up.

James entered with two fistfuls of cutlery, looking sheepish.

'Found some food then?' said Bridget.

'Not really but Bernard thought I ought to lay the table and maybe some sort of voodoo would happen.'

'Doesn't sound like Bernard.'

'Yes it does. Loaves and fishes.'

'You mean he's a *Christian*?'

'Not openly, but I bet he is deep down.' Bridget stood, thinking. It always shook her when anyone she admired even slightly turned out to be a Christian, even slightly.

She walked across to the kitchen to see for herself whether, despite having slept with him, she had failed to notice some rather obvious outward sign of this weakness, like stigmata on the hands, or wing buds on the shoulder blades.

Through the kitchen door's glazed upper half she spotted Morris, making his way towards the house with a wicker basket before him.

Morris marched purposefully down the path from the Chalet end of the garden with the basket cradled in his arms. He had put everything in it except the Durex, which he thought no one would be pleased to own up to in mixed company, and besides, he needed them.

He put the box on the picnic table, most dramatically. 'The solution to many mysteries is at hand,' he said.

'That's ours!' said Sophie. Greta and Bess backed off towards the apple tree they had only just left, Bess pulling at Fred's collar. The guards and Clare were peering into the basket. Inside were the wallets, purses, jewellery, the magic valve and the bucket of silver keys and watches.

Morris lifted out the bucket. Everyone was looking in astonishment.

'So, it was the children,' said Melanie, trying to spread the blame, but knowing, deep down, that it was Bess. Only she of all the adults had nothing to retrieve. Bess knew she was so poor that the loss of a watch would mean the end of time for them both.

'What the hell did you think you were up to?' said Krul to all the children, collectively. However, it was Sophie who was wrenching his heart. How could this have happened and no Little Note? Had she turned traitor?

So this was the catastrophe predicted by the crab, and his own premonition. Bess had said Krul would be the enemy. Toby had noticed that whenever you did anything which turned out to be wrong, and this could be almost anything, Father was always, magically there. Like God at school (not God at St Boddi's who was a different person) perhaps he spied on your thoughts with the Secret Police of his Brain, all the time to make easier deciding when what you had done would turn out to be wrong: to save time.

'It was for Africa,' said Sophie, which was right and proper because since she *never* did anything which turned out to be wrong, she was an ideal spokesperson, 'for the starving people – scratching in the dirt. We are sending it to them – from the rich to the poor. The keys are melting down – for silver – in the bucket.'

Morris was a bazaar hippy, with his box of tricks, and the dozens of hands groping in among his wares for their property. That's my watch. Ah, my address book. The little rascals! My bracelet.

'Do you realise this is stealing?' Addie said it half-heartedly. Toby knew that Sosij often told them off to prevent Father having to, even though she didn't regard something as quite so wrong as he did. Then all he had to say was, listen to your mother, which wasn't half so bad as a full dressing down.

'I didn't steal anything.' Sophie was true, as usual. 'And it was robbing, not stealing.' A good distinction. Adults were keen on this type of thing – though she should have explained about Robin-robbing.

Melanie, who had nothing to claim from the treasure, gazed into the treehouse, where her daughter was cowering with Greta and the dog.

'Bess! Come here. I want a word with you,' Krul said. Obviously she had no idea how awful were Father's dressings down or she wouldn't have leapt so lightly from the tree, or followed him so willingly to the chalet. Here he shut the door behind them, and the assembled group didn't hear another word.

Dressing Down

On the subject of child discipline Krul was an extremist. He believed in a despotic sort of guidance. All for the child's own good of course. No child could feel secure when the adult strata supposedly in charge of the world showed any weakness, any bending or compromise. More firmness than kindness was called for. After all, the kindness could be dished out later by mothers, preferably swiftly and in the background. The important thing was to lay down the law. Especially since Krul suspected that this child, Bess, had been brought up so far in that namby-pamby child-centred way which can only be an invitation to delinquency. He felt sure she required only a firm hand to set her on the right path. He couldn't have been more wrong.

He stood with his back to the glass of the doors, blackening his shape into a silhouette which only gradually resolved itself, from Bess's point of view, into individual features. She stood at the other end of the Chalet, with the sun in her eyes, at every disadvantage.

'How old are you, Elizabeth?'

'Twelve and a half,' she replied. He let his eyes travel slowly up and down her as if examining her uniform for inconsistencies. As if a twelve-year-old ought to be wearing certain things, look a certain way.

'Twelve and a half. You're a big girl for your age, aren't you?'

She didn't know whether the question was to be answered or not. After some time she said, 'Yes.' But instantly felt that had been the wrong reply, for he *smiled*, as if he had already made a victory and she felt as if her body was swelling. As if her breasts, only small buds, had burst obscenely through her T-shirt to wink naked at him.

'Big enough to know better, perhaps, than to incite younger children to criminal acts? Eh?' Now she had definitely to reply, for the 'eh?' was high-pitched, rolling out of him like something to be pitched back before it knocked her over, so that he could say the next, unfair, thing. She wasn't sure about 'incite', either.

'I didn't realise . . .'

'Oh, you *didn't realise*! I wonder, Elizabeth, if you have heard at all about the difference between Right and Wrong. Have you?'

'Yes, of course.'

'What is it then?' Bess wasn't to know that this was a question vexing grown-up philosophers the world over. She thought it was a simple question of supreme importance that a twelve-year-old ought to be able to answer. So she tried.

'Right is what you ought to do, and Wrong is what you must not.'

'Good. And where does stealing come in this balance?' He held out his hands in the air, cupped upwards, as if to trap drips, and moved them up and down alternately. 'Right or Wrong?'

'Wrong.' While he was thus leading her, she knew, though only twelve, into a trap, he was staring at a fixed point behind her so rigidly, she turned briefly to see what was there. Surely there was a rude word written on the wall in huge red letters? A momentary glance told her: nothing.

'I need your attention here, Elizabeth. Don't let your mind wander. So stealing is wrong. We have established that.'

Oh why doesn't he just wallop her and get on with it? The heat in this shed has risen in the few minutes they have been in it. She felt sick. She felt hungry. She wanted to run away. She wanted to scream.

Panic lent her inspiration. 'I'm *sorry*!' she said, loudly. He laughed.

'Oh that's all right, then. Everything's all right then. Elizabeth is sorry. Just imagine it: a man steals someone else's car and crashes it. He says, I'm sorry, so everything's all right. I could set fire to the house and just say afterwards that I'm sorry. Murder your mother and turn round with the knife still dripping in my hand and say, I'm so sorry! and everyone would be happy, would they?'

'No.' She felt tears coming but didn't allow them. The effort of not allowing them stung her eyes.

'Why not?'

'There must be . . .' she thought hard for the word. It wouldn't come. Only the word 'prison' floated there.

'Punishment?' he said. That was the word.

'Yes,' she said, brightening, thinking a smack would soon put an end to all this torture, 'punishment.'

'What sort of punishment do you think would be appropriate? I mean for encouraging young children to steal valuable things.'

'I don't know.' Surely he didn't mean her to request the smack?

'Prison,' he said, as if he had, as she suspected he could, read her mind. She felt slightly relieved because he couldn't send her to prison. She was too young. So the whole discussion had been *in theory*, not real.

Then he took out of his pocket a fob of keys, selected one, and turned to try it in the lock of the chalet door. It worked. She began to understand. He was going to imprison her inside here.

'Oh, and I've got something for you,' he said, fishing in his pocket again. This time he pulled out a small book the size of a pocket diary with a picture of a surfer on the front. '*Tidal Predictions Year Book Windmouth 1990*, it said. He handed it to her. 'Tidal times. Memorise any three pages to get out.'

She took the book from him. Her hands were shaking. She suddenly needed to pee. Where was Melanie?

Krul left the chalet, after one sweep of his eyes hard enough to rivet nails, being sure to lock the doors tight. Krul felt a glow inside him. He had stamped out a first spark of rebellion, most efficiently too.

Addie caught up with him well before he reached the table, where a meal was waiting. She read his face, and asked, 'Does she get any lunch?'

'No.'

'But Krul, she's a guest.'

'Guest! She's not a guest. She's a refugee. Refugees ought to be grateful for whatever they get.'

'She's only a child, for God's sake. We all make mistakes.'

'Look around you, Addie. Try observing the *real* world for a change. See if you can work out what is actually going on here. They are *all* refugees. Except Bernard of course. Don't be so stubbornly naive: it doesn't suit you.'

For a moment the world span around her. It was as if she had woken up to find twenty years had passed, or that she was on another planet. What could he mean? Then the world stopped and returned to normal.

Krul gained the table. Melanie was pale.

'Sorry,' she said.

'What, you too?' asked Krul, laughing. 'You don't want a young criminal on your hands as well as all your other trouble, do you, Melanie?'

'No. Thank you for dealing with it, Krul.' He sat there and ate his meal as if he had not just sentenced a twelve-year-old child to prison and hunger for the whole afternoon.

'The chalet is out of bounds,' he told the children, his mouth full.

Then everyone started to eat. At least they tried. Despite hunger everyone but Krul had lost their appetite.

After a few moments of stolid munching, Neil stood, grabbing his throat. He was completely silent, clawing at his own neck.

'He's choking,' said Zina and rose. Several others stood and James, who was next to him, gave him a heftly slap on the back. He staggered forwards into the table, but still made no sound. His face was drained and terrified. Zina grabbed his shoulders, making him sit, and pushed his head down between his knees so that his head was lower than his back, and James bashed again. This time they saw a piece of something about the size of a large tablet come spinning out of his mouth and onto the sand.

Neil gasped and started to suck in air noisily, then he fell off his chair to the ground. He may have fainted briefly, because by the time Zina said, 'panic over,' he could hear her, but didn't know where he was.

This emergency seemed to eclipse the child in the shed in their imaginations and they all started to eat, between tales of choking, near choking, and jokes about things 'sticking in the gullet' and macabre stories, including now gruesomely funny anecdotes about perfectly healthy people choking to death on seemingly innocent cabbage leaves.

Only Toby found it hard to eat now. How could he now let past his tongue any morsel not chewed fifty times or until it felt like a purée, whichever was the sooner?

'Do get a move on, Toby. We haven't got all night.'

But naturally everyone's first thought, when the meal was over, was for Bess. And yet no one dared to mention her. To make the afternoon pass quickly, because of the heat, and so that Bess wouldn't miss anything, Addie suggested that all the children have a siesta.

She was surprised at how readily they agreed. Krul could see that a little firm discipline was already having its desired effect on the lower ranks, who had only witnessed it. *Pour encourager les autres!*

But even he was surprised when the adults too joined in. First Zina said she ought to rest, and Neil confessed that his emergency had drained him. They colonised the morning room. Bernard thought that now England had this Sahara-like weather, we should soon all be on a siesta rhythm, and why not start now? Bridget, whose bed was in the same room, simply followed him up, a little vaguely, not knowing how to interpret his wink. Lottie and Morris went to settle the children and never returned, simply snuggling down with them in the coolth of the sunless bedroom. Hence Addie found herself left with James and Melanie in the kitchen. Krul had already gone up to his study to see to something. When they had washed up, Melanie and James disappeared, and Addie went quietly towards the Chalet with a glass of water.

She knew Krul would be watching her from the tower, but she didn't care. When she got there, she was surprised to realise that she had expected simply to open the door and hand in the drink. Of course it was locked! It would be. She could see Bess, sitting in the far corner of the room, her knees drawn up. She had been crying. Addie smiled at her. No response. Addie walked round the building. No chink big enough for a glass.

'Sorry,' she mouthed through the glass of the front doors.

'PISS OFF!' screamed the inhabitant, and rolled into a ball, a small book in one hand. At least she was reading to pass the time.

Addie went up to bed, the only one in the house with too much room.

All afternoon the heat rose and the tide receded. The road linking St Boddi's with the mainland shrugged out of the sea and dried instantly in the hot sun's scorching, but nobody used it. Shops which might have sold dog food were shut anyway, and nearly all those in or around St Boddi's were well into dreaming. Nearly all.

33

Predictions

Adjustments for British Summer Time have already been incorporated in the predictions contained within this book.

At first Bess, a gentle person who abhorred violence but had been shamed into a corner, had thought to destroy the room by emptying the shelves and throwing things at the windows. She could rip the curtains and shred books and break and smash everything. But none of these things were Krul's. They were Sophie's and Toby's. They were the throne room of Bessarabia. Besides, he would return and see the heap of broken things and prolong her punishment. No.

Windmouth Harbour. Navigational Light Characters. Swash channel and approaches. L. Fl. 10s Adjustments for other areas: At Christchurch Quay, 1st HW is 20 min. after Windmouth Harbour; 2nd HW and LW are 20 min. later. Rise and fall the same. [for St. Boddi's split the difference – KB]

Then she had thought to destroy herself. Then he'd be a murderer. The dripping knife. They'd all see how cruel he was. She punched herself hard in the stomach and doubled over with the pain. No.

Windmouth Harbour is situated near the middle of the degenerate amphidromic system halfway along the south coast just north westward of the Isle of Wight. Predicting tide times and heights for this area is extremely complex, due to the distortion of the normal tide curve, and the large open expanse of shallow water, together with the meteorological influence. Double high and low waters occur in the vicinity of nodal points of the main tide (a nodal point being where the size of the tide is very small and sometimes nil), eg. at Windcombe. Beware also Neap Tides (lowest point of High Water).

Then, fifteen minutes into her punishment, she ceased to have thoughts, as thoughts, and primitive instincts took over. First she walked the perimeter of her cell. Then she emptied a Lego tin and weed in it and placed it in a corner of the room with a lid on. Then she sat in the corner opposite it and said a string of the worst words she could think of. She had heard her father shout them at her mother. After this she felt doubly relieved.

TIDAL ROADS in the area: the flood stream commences 4 and a half hours before the first HW, and the Ebb three quarters of an hour after the first HW, although the level of the water may not fall. The stream may be rotary.

So she cried. At first it was delicious to cry. Toby would have called it Kreening. Then her hunger and her thirst rose up in her and said, don't waste your bodily fluids, don't waste your energy, lie low, recite the tidal times.

Windmouth Harbour covers an area of a hundred miles, with a wide range of winding channels to explore, favoured with double high water. The tide stands at HW for more than 12 hours a day, small draught vessels can run in and out freely. The mouth of the River Frome can be reached, just below Wareham. Smaller channels: Wych, Middle etc can be explored at leisure, pref. in dinghies on rising tide. Take great care walking ashore should you run aground: the mud is soft and very deep.

I have seen deep into the heart of the enemy now and it made me powerless and sick. I had no strength to answer back. No one came to save me. The sun is an enemy too. It leans into this room through the magnifying glass of the doors and finds out every last inch of this timber-hot place. There is a sweet smell of cedar burning. The air is hotter than my throat. The only shade is a moving oblong sail behind the throne. I have to scuttle around the throne like a dog, following the shade. All the time my sore eyes are scanning the hot print of this damned book about the ocean.

I could drink an ocean.

Sophie's mum came with a drink to torment me. She prowled around the shed and made a face at me through the window. I'll get my own back. They'll be sorry. When I'm out of here, I shall be a different person. I shall be ruthless. I shall do such things.

I must be clever though. What does Krul most value? Where will he hurt most when punched?

Nothing else matters now like revenge matters. It would be as sweet as drinking a long cold glass of white milk, slowly. Satisfying both hunger and thirst in one continuous gulp.

August 27 1990. Bank Holiday. Ist HW 0126. Ist LW 0609. 2nd HW 0908, etc.

Concentrate on this. The tide turns continually but not regularly like a clock. The marine year follows the moon and folds in half in August, on the Neap. The Neap. The index sprouts eight facts about the Neap. Bess sniffs them all out and discovers something mariners spend their lives pondering and discussing; that the Neap is only a theoretical moment. Bess does not even possess the vocabulary or the underlying concepts to express it to herself. But understanding dawns: she is a very clever girl.

The Neap is an idea only. Since there is a low tide and a high tide and one turns into the other, there must be a moment when the turn occurs, the very lowest point of the high tide, which is also the highest point of the low tide. Of course no one could film or measure this moment. No scientist could put it under a slide. It is like gravity and Heaven – invisible but there. And something different occurs to the Neap in August. It is happening now fifty yards from this shed.

Oh Krul, don't think I won't use this knowledge you have given me somehow.

34

Insurrection

Bridget woke sweating from a nightmare in which she had been attempting to swim to the mainland, over the flooded road, when she had looked down and seen a child floating below her, face up, dead. It was Bess.

She looked at her watch: she had been asleep for an hour and a half! She sat up and pulled on her shorts. Somehow, if that child was still there, and still alive, she would rescue her. Now.

The wonder was that they had all watched without comment when Krul had incarcerated her. Some spell he had over people. Well he wasn't here now, and Bridget would not be alone.

She looked at the sleeping Bernard. A desirable man, but no ally against Krul. He was the real guest after all, and an old friend, whatever that meant. She couldn't ask him to help her to break the Law of Krul, but she could ask James. She had noticed that James, while male, was an anarchist where Krul Law was concerned. He should welcome an opportunity to frustrate the loathsome turd, his brother-in-law.

James was with Melanie. He had reassured Bess's mother that no child could die of a few hours in a shed, and they had lain together in the small boxroom on the one bed like dear friends, like two old tramps under newspaper, or, indeed, refugees. At first. The trouble is that desire, once inflamed, has a way of flaring up again, so that they weren't altogether innocent in their siestering.

Bridget was quite surprised to find them thus – looking a

little dishevelled, like people who often sleep together. She had rather labelled Melanie as repressed as well as oppressed partly because of her reaction this morning to questioning, and partly because she had imagined her as that one woman whose outlet was to write whingeing letters to women's magazines complaining, quite rightly but rather drearily, about the men in her life. How would this letter go?

> *Dear Margery,*
> *I recently left my husband, who, as I pointed out in my last letter, treated me with all the respect due to a farmyard animal, and, taking my daughter with me, went down to stay with a friend in Dorset. That night I slept with the brother of my friend, and the following day, the husband of my friend shut my daughter in a shed for a minor misdemeanour, so, when taking a nap . . .*

All this went through her head in the moment before she stooped and shook them, tenderly.

'What?' said James, blinking.

'Wake up, James. Melanie, wake up.' They both looked frightened. Perhaps they were embarrassed?

'I've decided Krul's treatment of your daughter is nothing less than child abuse, and we ought to rescue her from that shed,' she said, to Melanie.

'But she did such an awful thing. It's only for a while, and . . .' Melanie sounded on the brink of tears.

'Would *you* have punished her like this?' asked Bridget.

'No, of course not.' Melanie swung her legs out of the bed and reached for her dungarees on the floor. 'Her father would have hit her, once, very hard, on the bottom. Is that preferable?'

'I don't believe in assaulting children, but in some ways yes. At least it would now be all over.'

James decided he would like to be a part of anything which would madden Krul, and said, 'Let's go for it, girls.'

Bridget smiled at him. 'Meet in the morning room in five minutes,' said Bridget, on fire now with the thought of rescue.

She left them to dress and quietly padded down past the children's room. She knew Morris and Lottie must be in there, but waking them would entail waking the children too, and she didn't want a mass of people, just a few daring conspirators. Past the spare room. She was especially quiet going by Addie and Krul's room, since it was open to the stairs down. Krul would be a light sleeper. His couldn't be a clear conscience. Have nightmares, Krul.

Zina and Neil were already in the morning room, both fast asleep. Neil had made a bed on a rug with a cushion and Zina had taken the couch. Their dog was curled at Neil's shoulder and stirred when she entered. They hadn't undressed.

'Neil. Neil.'

He woke suddenly, looking like a fat, old man.

'Who is that?'

'It's me. Bridget. I'm worried about that little girl locked in the shed. I think we ought to let her out now. I wouldn't leave a dog to suffer in this heat in a locked shed.' She thought a reference to dogs might alarm him.

Zina stirred at the sound of whispering and heaved herself upright on the sofa. Melanie and James arrived then.

'Oh, it's a revolution,' said Neil, smiling.

'Krul's sodding cruelty has driven us to it,' said Bridget. Seeing Zina's eyebrows rise, she added, 'Sorry, but it's true,' remembering that she was referring to Zina's cousin.

'Krul has the key,' said Zina. It was the first practical comment anyone had made.

'I don't think that bothered them when they stormed the Bastille,' said James. They all laughed nervously, as Neil and Zina arose and straightened themselves up, ready to join in.

They all walked out into the surprisingly bright sunshine of the garden. The heat had multiplied as they slept, and, if possible, it was even hotter than they all remembered.

As they walked out, the telephone rang. They all ignored it of course: the answering machine was on.

It was Colin.

'Okay, here's my message. It's Colin here. Remember me? I don't believe this. Adeline Boyd, how many people are there in your house? Is it a commune, or what? I'm beginning to wonder whether I have gone mad. This is not the first time I've phoned. I think I must have got to know quite a few of the inmates by now. What's happening? Is it about what happened on Friday night? I admit I might have been a bit over the eight, but a man's entitled to a bit of relaxation now and then, surely. I'm sure you didn't mean to do something so stupid, certainly it's no reason to run off without telling me. What do you think I'll do to you? You took the rent money out of the satchel! How am I going to pay the rent tomorrow? I realise there are two sides to everything but I can't bear it all on my own in the flat. I can't live without you two. I'll go mad. I could die here and nobody would know. That's it then. All is forgiven, even the things you haven't done yet. Just so I don't ever have to be on my own again.'

Having listened, Krul wiped the tape and reset it, and turned his attention to the scene outside. He could see below a slovenly little band of five adults: Bridget in the front, then James, then Melanie, then Neil and Zina, and the dog following. They were heading for the Chalet.

He chuckled. Such fun. Such fun at last.

35

The Storming

Both knobs were too hot to touch. Each tongue-and-groove slat of cedar was welded to its neighbour with gluey, melted preservative. The panels of slats were bolted together with tight, hot nuts. There seemed no way in.

'Jesus! It's like an oven with a padlock on it.'

'We need a gun to shoot away the lock,' said James. Bridget looked at him fiercely. 'I haven't got one,' he added.

'Got a penknife?' asked Zina of him. He had. It was a Swiss Army one with eight devices. One of them was like a screwdriver. He began work on the screws holding one of the doors in place

Bess watched them without moving from the other end of the chalet, behind the throne, where there was a whole ten centimetres of shade.

When one screw was out, Bridget pulled at the door and there was a sharp creaking sound. Bess flinched. What were they *doing*? Had *all* the adults gone mad?

Two out and the door came away by a few inches. It began to split.

Krul walked quietly down from his office to the dormitory where he woke the children with, 'Come and watch something.' Lottie and Morris woke too.

The children were sticky-eyed and confused. Lottie brought George too, though Krul hadn't meant her to.

'What is it?' Morris asked him as they shepherded the children down the stairs, all barefoot.

'Some moral education, Morris. The sort of thing you love. Learning by observation.'

They tiptoed through the morning room and out into the angry heat of the garden. A few yards away were Bridget and James, trying to wrench a door off the chalet, and Melanie, Zina and Neil were watching, their backs to them.

'Look, children. This is called vandalism. What I can't understand is why they didn't just ask me for the key.' Krul had stopped whispering.

James stopped what he was doing. Bridget stopped. They all looked round at Krul and his small crowd. Only Bridget found her tongue.

'Because you aren't reasonable, Krul. You are the worst kind of tyrant. This child could suffocate in the heat because she played Robin Hood with all the others, that's all. And you think that's reasonable, do you?'

'Let's ask *her*,' said Krul, approaching the half-broken door of the chalet. He fitted the key and opened it.

'Ready to come out?' he asked Bess.

'No,' she said. She said this for two reasons: first, she had not quite finished the memorising, and second, she did not want to make her exit so observed because she needed to dispose of the tin of wee privately.

Morris spoke up.

'This often happens with Time Out, Bridget. The child him or herself decides how long the punishment will last. It is the seed of self-discipline.'

'It's very different when you're a parent,' added Lottie. Bridget could have killed her, had she been armed. Didn't the woman understand anything?

'In future, Bridget, and James, feel free to consult me first, *before* you start destroying property.' Bridget felt he had won some terrible victory and was about to leave, even if it meant swimming the channel, when James, surprisingly, said, 'Only if you consult *us* when you are next planning to imprison someone. Okay?'

But his fearlessness was lost in the air because Krul had

already turned and was calling to Addie, who had just arrived, to put on the kettle.

At six o'clock Bess was allowed out of her confinement. Krul gave her five minutes off for the toilet before summoning her into the morning room for the recitation. The rest of the children stood watching her with awe and wonder. No one crowed. Even Greta wouldn't now challenge her leadership ever again. She had suffered for their sins. They worshipped quietly while she recited to Krul. He was impressed. Elizabeth had not just memorised the tidal variations, she had worked out how to predict the Highs and Lows intelligently. She gave a brief summary of the patterns involved. It was the sort of one-upmanship he would have devised himself.

Silly Krul! He, of all people, should have realised that a little knowledge can confer a lot of power.

The rota for the preparation of meals had ceased to have any meaning by six-fifteen that afternoon when it was discovered that there was barely enough food in either the food cupboard, refrigerator or TinCan to provide a snack for someone on a strict diet, let alone seventeen very hungry people. It was decided to feed what there was to the children, put them to bed and then send a search party out for fish and chips.

Bess was the hungriest.

They ate semolina and tapioca made with the last of the powdered milk, and Lottie drank two pints of water, Zina informing her that this would help her produce more milk for George. Not only that, she secretly collected some in a cup (Mer-mer always leaked when Num-num was in action) for her own tea: she wasn't daft and she wasn't squeamish. No doubt Krul would have said this constituted auto-cannibalism or something, but she thought it only sensible.

Krul should have killed Bess.

It was a mistake to allow the crushed victim to reamass her troops in the bedroom after lights out. Crushed minorities should be divided, sent to camps, starved to death, utterly wiped out. Otherwise they will simply regroup and wreak terrible vengeance on their oppressors, which is just what happened.

As soon as the lights were out and Addie had blown everyone kisses and Lottie had buttoned her blouse and they had sidled out of the door, Bess switched on a torch, shone it on her face, and in the eerie uplight it cast over her emergent features and flame-red tresses, quietly outlined her plan in great detail. There was not a murmur of dissent.

After all, she had, as it were, come back from the grave for a purpose, and some people almost without knowing it have a natural authority over others. It is an attractive, warm, beautiful feeling which stays with you in the darkness of a bedroom full of strange children in a house which is really a church and is full of strange adults, stays with you in the warm sheets under the quilts of warmth in the womblike darkness, knowing you are safe because someone is in charge of the darkness.

36

Krul's Game

By early evening all the adults had something in common other than being at St Boddi's: they were all starving hungry. Hunger is relative of course and we couldn't say they were really hungry in a global sense. After all there is always someone in the world, as Bess told the children that morning, who has eaten nothing for *weeks* and is still, barely, alive. The inhabitants of St Boddi's have a long way to go before we could class them with The Hungry then – they have first to use up *all* their bodies' reserves of fat and fluid, then they have to pass through the cramps stage and then on to the acceptance stage where the stomach ceases to request food and the brain can't work out any reason why life is preferable to death.

But enough of this. It's too depressing, and there's a party going on; Krul is in high spirits. He is informing everyone of the joys of fasting and distributing the contents of his wine cellar, pointing out that its effect will be greatly heightened by 'abstinence' from food.

'Abstinence implies a choice,' said Bridget, who was never at her best without food. In fact food and sleep were all she regularly asked from life, these being her only real requirements, but lack of them rendered her almost incapable of civilised human contact.,

'You have a choice,' said Krul. 'You can borrow my wetsuit, swim to the mainland, hitchhike to, let us say Exeter, where you might find a fast-food restaurant run by someone who doesn't realise it's a Sunday before a bank holiday.'

'Some sodding choice.'

Addie was beckoning him from the other end of the nave. He went. She was looking more worried than usual. Krul assumed it was the Bess incident still upsetting her. Discipline was not her strong point, even self-discipline. There were two tapestries half finished in the Morning Room to his knowledge.

'Krul, don't they need you – your network of people?'

'*What?*'

'Haven't you put some people behind bars for the weekend?'

Krul rested his hand above her on a protruding buttress of stone and said, 'Fancy your knowing that, remembering that.'

Truth was, she was not concerned for those unreal people coded into binary on the circuits upstairs, but concerned for the real people sitting downstairs in the nave, and wished to save them from his next move. Only the computer might successfully compete for his attention.

'Usually at the end of the weekend . . .'

'Ah, but this weekend isn't over yet, is it? And besides, these guests take precedence.'

So, he isn't to be duped – he would rather sheriff the real souls.

'You said they weren't guests.' She knew it was stupid thus to bandy with him, but she was playing for time. The reference made no sense. It only prolonged the discussion.

'Exactly,' he said. 'I thought we might all play a game. You included.'

'Krul – you know I hate games. Charades and so on. I'm no good at anything competitive. And everyone is so hungry.'

'I'll amuse them. It'll distract them from the hunger. I have a game all worked out. "Roads." It's not competitive. You'll love it.'

Addie feared that light in his eyes. Invulnerable, wicked Krul, cooking up something she would have to eat, and serve to others.

'Please don't,' she said, meaning whatever it is you have planned, don't do it. If she had known what he had planned, she would have been in a better position to try to scupper it. But she didn't.

'Pull yourself together, Addie. Don't let me down. Don't go to pieces on me.'

'I don't know what you mean.'

'Then don't interfere!' He swept off then into the seated mass by the altar end of the nave, purposefully.

The light fell suddenly, the way it does in late August when the hot days are so humid and exhausted they want to hurry into autumn, to fall suddenly into fall. St Boddi, under the boot, disappeared momentarily behind the unlit altar, until Krul moved an anglepoise lamp into a position where it shone a spotlight onto the pulpit, illuminating just the pulpit, a small area around it, and the backdrop of bloodstained sand St Boddi struggled upon.

'What are you doing, Krul?' asked Morris. 'Is it charades?'

'No.' He started to switch off all the other lights, hushing the assembled company as he did so, without having to tell them to be quiet, and into the silence said, 'This diversion I have invented is called "Roads" and in it, we shall Network to God, via this pulpit.' They laughed, most of them. Krul stood in front of the pulpit with on his face the vacuous grin of a gameshow host. He held up a handful of white index filecards and said, 'I'll shuffle these so that the order is totally random.' He did this.

They couldn't see the cards so James asked, 'What's on the cards?'

'Depictions. A cup, a book, a barrier, a crowd, water, and a wild animal – the animal of your choice. The idea is to stand here,' he went round and stood in the light, 'imagine a road and start to travel down it. Out loud of course. Unexpurgated and continuous.'

No one laughed at this.

'You will come across these universal symbols in your travels. When you have all completed, I will explain the significance of the symbols.'

'So who wins?' asked Bridget, unable to believe that Krul could invent any game where there would not be winners, and, by definition, therefore also losers. Of course there were such games in the universe, games where people co-operated and solved problems. Games women play. Krul wouldn't know one single one, or if he did, wouldn't see the point of it.

'That's irrelevant,' he replied.

'The one who sets the rules declares the winner,' said Bernard, from somewhere in the gloom. Was it a quotation? No one could see him. Bridget wished she were nearer him. She wanted to tell him about the attempted insurrection, how no one could ever win against that bastard: a man who abused other people's children. His voice sounded far off and had bounced about the rafters above them.

'Will you commence, Bernard?' asked Krul, peering into the dark.

'No. You start. I'll follow.' Good, thought Bridget, he might gain some advantage by this: there is something she has heard about in business called 'leading from behind'.

In the spotlight of the anglepoise, Addie saw a flicker of doubt pass over Krul's face, but it was so slight, could so easily have been a cursory glance down at the order of the cards, and so soon gave way again to that smile, that only she could possibly have detected it.

1. *Krul's road*

Perhaps Addie had misjudged him. After all, this was just entertainment: Krul standing there in the pool of light, his large hands spread over Egor's wings, an alar lectern seldom used in real life, about to swoop on the quarry of his imagination and create, who knows what?

Not as threatening as parlour games like that one where you have to tell about your most embarrassing moment or answer truthfully questions about masturbation. Surely if you wanted to create a road exotic enough to be indetectable in, you could?

Or boring enough to circumvent all your neuroses? Knowing spiders are nightmare-weavers, you could travel down insect-free zones. So they were thinking, as Krul began, all in their different ways, of subterfuges they could employ.

Krul himself, of course, was employing a double subterfuge, so that the road he described was the road Addie would have predicted, only since he was saying it out loud, she was not so sure.

'Mine is a Roman road, straight and wide and stone-flagged. I am on horseback, leading the crowd, my hordes. My hordes are about to rape and pillage a small hamlet in the south of Britain called Piddle on Pissing.'

'Exactly whom will they rape?' asked Bridget.

'Primitive maidens milking cows in the field, hoeing and contributing to the agricultural economy. Raw, Saxon maidens.'

'I bet they'll love that.'

'Well, they do say women have mixed feelings about these crises of life. I won't be doing any rape and pillage personally, you understand. Too busy directing the hordes, drawing maps, sending messages to Caesar and so forth. Ah – a gold chalice for my wine. Many centuries later archaeologists will unearth this. The leader drinks first, then the others can.'

'And get drunk?' asked Melanie.

'Ah, no. I can hold the liquor. Only the lower ranks get drunk. I am too busy in any case writing my diary: "...got up, conquered Dorset ..." In the gap between two of our tents a bear fight is going on. A bear versus a griffin. The sound of the ripping of flesh assails my ears. I may disapprove of this, but it keeps the hordes occupied for a bit in the evening after supper. Really it's uncivilised, but the lower ranks enjoy it.'

'Uncivilised?' asked James, puzzled.

'Yes, they might run amok, get overexcited.'

'Don't you call rape and pillage uncivilised, then?' he asked.

'No, that's a means to an end. We are conquering, you see.'

'So political violence is okay, but not entertaining violence?'

James pursued. Krul laughed and consulted his cards before him.

'A barrier. What obstacle could there be to an invading Roman Legion? The local populace. They are a bit unwilling to accept the might of Caesar in these parts. Nothing a bit of rape and pillage won't ameliorate.' He looked at James and smiled. James smiled back and lit a cigarette. Would Krul interrupt his flow to tell him to smoke elsewhere?

'Of course Ancient Britain, unlike Modern Britain, is renowned for its rain. It is pouring torrential rain, making a mudpath of the road. The troops are getting restless. There's no shelter save tents. I am thinking of ways to harness the rain. Perhaps I shall invent the aqueduct soon. The water makes the road impassable: *AQUA VINCIT OMNES!* Perhaps I shall have this inscribed over the baths I am having erected nearby.'

That was it. His road came to an end. There was to be no time to reflect on it as they entered the vortex of the game, for Krul said, quite clearly, as he stepped out of the light, 'There will be no break between turns,' meaning, no discussion.

'Right. I'll go next,' said Zina.

2. *Zina's road*

Krul offered her a stool to sit on, but she declined, preferring to stand in the light the way he had, smiling.

The smile drained quickly from her face.

Standing in the strong light, she could not *see* anyone. She hadn't anticipated this. The feeling of panic, of pure stagefright, is a common one, and many's the extrovert who dries up under the lights despite themselves. What was uncommon was, first, a slight buzzing feeling which swept through her (had she stood up too quickly, confusing her blood pressure? severe hunger? foetus at risk?) and second, the vision in front of her of an autumnal hilly moorland. It was a place from childhood, the scene of a trauma which still troubled her dreams swelling before her dazzled eyes in perfect and vivid colour.

'Oh no.'

'What's wrong?' Neil asked.

'She thought she could make up a road,' said Krul.

'Been here before. Pendle Hill, Yorkshire.'

Little Zina asked for a horse. Not one of her own. Poor people didn't have those. Only rich girls in books. She wanted to take Olwyn's milk round pony for a ride.

Uncle Olwyn was a giant. Seven-foot-four. Who says there are no giants left? It is a genetic defect. When he stands at table, he hits the roof.

Crash!

'Tha shalt 'ave pony for t'afternoon.' Out the back past tipple toilet shed, on cobbles and downhill.

'Be back be five and beware the witches o' Pendle Hill,' calls Aunty.

Ages ago. There are now no such things. Even the cats, their familiars, have gone. The witches of Pendle who dwelt in the caves dwell there no more.

Though she is eleven, walks two miles alone to school, and goes to Skipton with a friend, there is still the small voice. It says, if there are giants, why not witches? She can't get lost on Pendle Hill. It is visible from the Colne Valley. Just a smooth mound of Northern moor, dotted with black potholes.

'Scenery's nowt wi-out 'ills.' Meaning, the rest of England: flat streets, flat voices.

Walking down the familiar streets with the giant, Zina muffles the small voice. They have rituals, her mother and grandmother. Rituals which keep them safe.

Even the blunt knives for eating are spiked with danger. Laying the table you must never let one knife lie across another. It means death. If a knife is given as a present, a farthing must be paid. Otherwise it means the death of love.

Which could creep up on you, like the death of a baby inside the woman. Stretch up for that daddy-long-legs and you'll twist the cord around its neck. Drink wine and the baby will be cleftpalated. Touch a dead cat and death will enter the bump as a jump of electricity to electrocute the insides.

Should Grandmother and Mummy say a word at the exact same moment one gives the other a number between one and twenty-six. Straight away, without thinking. The other then counts up the numbers on an alphabet. So 'ten' is 'J'. Then the other would say a name beginning with the letter. John. John was conjured up: he must be *thinking* about them.

It was so easy, to become, without knowing it, the centre of a criss-cross of psychic evil. You had to be so careful.

They never forgot. It must have kept them safe.

Every full moon, Zina's father gave her a coin to turn over in its beam. This kept her safe from poverty.

Every morning Granny mixed reddle in a bowl and went to spread it on the front door step. Redding the stoop. This kept ghosts away.

'Tell me about the witches of Pendle, Uncle.'

'No. There are no witches.'

So cobbly downhill, she and Olwyn. He whistles, keys chink. Happy. Dangled from the neverending length of his arm.

'Can tha rayde?' asked Olwyn.

'Yes. Two lessons.' He laughed.

'Were that i' Sheffield?'

'Yes, they have ponies there, truly.'

'Shame,' he said, 'tisn't rayte.'

Then they turned into the yard. Men were carrying great metal churns and dragging leather harnesses and sweeping.

He talks now, dressing the horse. He first had the milk round when a lad of fourteen. Too young but so big and so bad at schoolwork, he was put to the pony. He and the pony, this same one, would trot round the streets at five-thirty and deliver cupfuls of milk to the women who came out to fetch it from the street. The man who made ice-cream always had his last: he had what was left over, all of it. He lived at the top of the hill, at the end of the valley. The churns empty, the cart light, Olwyn would turn the pony and cart round, mount up and say, 'Home

Boy!' It was daft really, he could see that now, it wasn't 'rayte', but the streets were empty that early, and the route all downhill. So hardly anyone witnessed the galloping pony rocketing home out of control on the cobbles with the massive fourteen-year-old astride the wooden cart, reins in one hand, balancing churns with the other, yelling, 'Faster!'

The nameless pony had an old saddle. No kneerolls. Olwyn plopped her on his bony back like an empty milkchurn. Now level with Olwyn's head. He pointed to Pendle Hill and said, 'That's where he laykes.'

'Thank you, Uncle.'

She had been alone on buses. Alone once on Ecclesall Road weaving. But alone with a horse and the turf and the sky and the empty Yorkshire moors? No, never. Had Olwyn realised? Should she have told him? Would he have let her go?

Up Pendle Hill. Almost into the clouds. The pony walks steadily. Now and then he stops to rub his nose in the gorse and wrench off grass to chew. At the top she looks down at the valley: mill and pit and railway and rows of blackened houses. Which one is Aunty's? The hill is not small and near. It is really huge and far away.

Smoke rises from a large chimney stack. The picture wobbles and drifts. She can just make out the dip of the valley. There is the mill chimney stack. The rest is just a darker and a lighter area and then, nothing. She turns the pony round to see the other side of the hill. Mist. Or has she gone blind? A misty barrier has risen up. Or a cloud has fallen onto them. She turns again. This way was the town. Surely. Or that way? Like the North Pole, all directions are equal.

Wait for the mists to clear. This happens: sudden weather changes in the Pennine winds. She dismounts and sits. She keeps hold of the pony's reins. He grazes.

Time passes. The mist thickens. She is wet now. Soaked through. And the pony. Once damp enters the bones, there's no curing it. To the left is a darker patch of mist. Perhaps the entrance to a pothole?

On all fours, she creeps in. Holding the reins. Here is a flat, dry, stony place where she can sit. Cold though. A breeze comes out from the back. She looks into the darkness of the cave. Less mist. She sees a shape moving towards her. Then a growling, like the growling of a dog.

The pony jumps back. She jumps up. Two bright eyes look out at her. She screams. It is a witch's dog!

She must have scaled the side of the pony from a rock because she never remembered remounting properly but she remembers now, time and time again that then, and in the nightmare she says, 'Home Boy,' like Uncle Olwyn used to all those years ago and the pony rears and puts himself in top gear and *gallops* so fast through the mist that she flattens herself onto the back of his neck, face buried in his mane, to avoid being decapitated by low-flying trees, as the world, just a dark wet invisible backdrop, speeds by. The painful jolting lasts an eternity and she *knows* that she will fall.

Only by ear can she tell that they have left the hill, reached the road and then the cobbled alleyways of the streets near home. Only the drumming of his fast-forward hoofs on the ground. One last sudden twist and she is off, but fortunately she slides slowly to the ground and finds she is in the milk yard when she opens her eyes, for they had been tightly closed since the cave, and the mist is gone.

'Uncle Olwyn!' she cries, 'I got lost and the witch's dog growled at me.'

He approaches, carrying a blanket for the pony.

'On this pony, tha's nivver lost, lass. And I tol thee there are no such things as witches,' he says, picking her up from the ground where she is almost sobbing. 'Thar't afeard o' life itsel'. T'ony witch tha've to mind is Aunty and she's rayte mithered wi thee for being layte.'

Zina runs all the way home and into the back door and to the fire, where a crowd of elderly relatives are smoking pipes and Aunty strips off her wet clothes. In the background is the crying of a baby coming out from the dark recesses of the cottage.

Did her grandmother know that at the age of ninety-one she would die redding the stoop? If she had *failed* to do it one day, what *worse* thing might have happened? Eternal life?

And now, Zina, nurse of geriatric nights, participates in that most serious of mass redding – the curtaining. When someone dies on the ward, first she crosses herself, not because she is a Catholic (she doesn't even whisper, 'in the name of the Father . . .') but because it would be silly not to. Then she draws the curtain and this keeps herself, and the rest of the ward, and the rest of the world safe from the encroaching of death. Otherwise it would surely seep down the ward, from bed to bed, and out the window and out along the highways of the world full now of unreddled stoops and crossed knives and things unsaid swirling like mists trapped for ever in the dark interiors of caves.

3. *Addie's road*

Addie stood there in what media people call 'dead air'. Except that despite her silence, it was not dead: it was alive with sounds. The sounds of a ferry docking after a short voyage, great oily ropes as thick as whole people banging across the dark water, men shouting to each other in Finnish, and replying in Estonian. Long grey buildings squatted into the docks, a customs shed with 'Passport' in Cyrillic script scrawled in blue paint.

Addie rehearsed her few words of Russian, her 'nothing to declare', her 'tourist for one day, returning to Helsinki'. Her companion said that she had hurled her *Time Magazine* into the Baltic Sea (it had opened like a bird clutched tight whose wings are caught and splayed by an updraft) just now and that was the only concession a Canadian need make to the Russian bastards.

Well they may be bastards, from a global point of view, but Addie was open-minded about this and held judgement. She would see for herself whether Russians were any more bastardly than, say, Americans. Addie thought of herself then as a Human not a British Person.

She hardly had time. There on the dock were a crowd of blond people, of Onu this and Onu that and Taddi this and Taddi that and some cousins with names like Kriin and Rain, all tallking fast in the forbidden tongue, grabbing them, kissing them, walking them away into Tallin. Not speaking any Estonian, save rather odd phrases learnt from her companion, Addie tried her primitive Russian. This met with a shocked silence, a drawing back. She tried German. They smiled.

'*Wir sind nicht frei, du verstehst.*' We are not free, you see. The older generation had learnt German as their second language before Stalin gobbled them up and were happy to speak it to her. Addie's friend spoke fluent Estonian.

They walked down drab streets of wooden buildings where the street signs had all been forcibly changed to Russian some years ago but as a gesture of protest, the Estonians had translated the streets wrongly so that only fellow Estonians with good memories could now understand an address. They were entertained in a small flat where everything doubled as something else and invited to eat a plate of smoked salmon and drink home-brewed something from a cup.

You live well, Addie said, in German. They all laughed. Fish caught in Tallin, the greatest fishing port in the Baltic, was sent to Moscow and only on the black market could any real fish be purchased. They had paid a week's wages for that salmon. Addie choked.

Addie began to feel the oppression, in her throat. The salmon would not go down. Would not go down her Human throat.

'*Wir sind nicht frei,*' Hile said. So she sat near Hile Taddi clutching her pocket dictionaries, her Key to Pronunciation proving less than useful since the Estonians had their own way of speaking German, and listened.

Hile described how her country house had been turned into a museum now, full of her brother's paintings. She had brought some of the paintings she had saved, secretly of course, for Addie to see, knowing that Addie was an artist herself. She was appalled. What if these pictures were dreadful dreary oil paintings, not worth the risk she had taken? Addie would have to dissemble, praise them sincerely. It wouldn't be the first time she had thus dissembled, for who wants to risk losing a friend for the sake of a sketch, but it would be the first in German.

There was no need to dissemble. They were startlingly good. Landscapes. Romantic depictions of an idyllic countryside well before any invasions, Nazi or communist, but without sentimentality. The colours were pure and still bright, the figures of people and animals enviable still and peaceful. Addie was dazzled by their beauty. *Wann wir werden frei*, said Hile: when we were free.

Yes, they spoke of freedom, even Addie, brought up in a free world by ridiculously liberal parents who let her draw on the walls, could see that. A beautiful and natural disorder of colour and form.

By the time it was the hour of re-embarkation, Addie and her friend had been asked to smuggle those paintings out of the country, and make sure they reached Canada, as if there were no such thing as the Gulag.

Addie's friend agreed. Addie felt faint. Perhaps she didn't mean it. They could simply *pretend*, take the paintings to the ship and when the relatives weren't looking, abandon them? She didn't like the idea of leaving them, but could see that it was more important to humour the Estonians. It meant such a lot to them.

Naturally, there are ways to smuggle things out of the Soviet Union, some of which have succeeded: Addie's friend at Oxford had sewn an ikon into the lining of his donkey jacket, switched jackets with another friend at the last minute, sweated through a fruitless body search while his friend sailed through, unwittingly carrying a twelfth-century ikon under his left arm. But there was no time for such trickery, for any finesse, so it was out of the question.

When they reached the dockside, Addie whispered to her friend, 'Where you going to leave them?'

'*Leave* them?' she shouted, loudly. 'Nowhere. They're coming with us. Haven't you understood? My uncle did these paintings. They are my inheritance. They belong in Canada, with me. I promised.'

'We can't do that. It's against the law. They'll shoot us, or worse. Don't be silly. How could we do it anyway?'

'We'll brazen it out. You're an artist. We'll say you did them.'

'But the paint is so old it's *cracked*! Please, let's go and talk about this.' But there was no time to do that. Onu Rain had rushed forward with chocolates. Goodbyes were being said. The ship was sounding its embarkation hooter. The customs men were standing stiffly by the barrier.

'*Shto etta?*' What is it, asked the customs guard, armed, pointing his finger.

Addie's friend unrolled the canvases and pointed to Addie.

'She is a painter,' she said. 'She did them.' But the pictures were so obviously thirty years old, this could not be true. The border policeman laughed. She began to speak in Estonian, no doubt outlining a theory of International Friendship being Consolidated via Art which she had instantly invented. They pretended not to understand her, though they were able to say, in Estonian, that they did not speak Estonian. Any more. The Estonian-born guards were not *allowed* to speak Estonian. Addie felt sorry for them, until they led her friend into a cabin on stilts above the gangplank, suspended by steel ropes.

Then Addie panicked. All her life she had been safe. There had never been any question of being safe. She had done some daring things, but always within the boundaries of security. Now she was standing at the land end of a gangplank leading to a ship she was not allowed to board, being stared at by an armed man with whom she could not communicate. And she had broken the law of the land she stood on.

She could hear raised voices in the cabin above her. Angry voices. She moved near the roped edge of the gangplank and looked down. The water was a good fifty feet down. She didn't really intend to kill herself: she knew she was too good a diver and too good a swimmer to risk that, but she knew how to dissemble. She might not have the impulsive courage of her friend, but she was a better actor. She wound up a spring inside her and made as if to jump into the swirling Baltic below, and the guard stopped her.

Then there was running and shouting and Addie's friend appeared by her side and they were allowed to board the ship without the paintings and sail back to Helsinki. There, in the Youth Hostel, they opened the chocolates that Rain had given them and found no chocolates – only a neatly folded oil painting of exquisite beauty.

4. *Morris' road*

Morris was reminded, instantly, of a thousand thousand journeys. Not for nothing was he a professional traveller, the globe his village, the roads upon it his roads, its inhabitants his neighbours, his nationality spanning the planet. He thought it would be amusing to design a road to nowhere: a journey with no beginning and no end, a kind of open-ended and philosophical unwinding. A rubber band of tarmac approaching from the horizon rather than any movement towards a real place. Like the man on the bridge who tells a story about the man on the bridge who tells a story about the man on the bridge who tells a story . . .

But he too was hooked. Instead of this, the ringing in his ears of the *muezzin* calling the faithful over an amplifier at four a.m. would not stop until he allowed himself to be taken back down onto that hard marble floor in the cool of a room in the middle of a house in Teheran where he was lying on a thin bedroll trying and failing to steal a few more minutes of sleep from the dawn.

It was years ago in the time of the Peacock Shah, Mohammed Reza, and Morris was a guest of relatives of the Shah in the privileged sector on high ground to the north, the Caspian Sea side of Teheran. This was an embarrassment for him. He would rather be roughing it in the British Council hostel on the other side of town, but he was not so invited. He had stayed a week to see the bazaars and the beggars and the wealth, and was about to go. Those moments before a journey are precious. It is when his spirits are at their most expansive and he could sing for joy. Not like the muezzin for duty, but for sheer joy, for the flight into the unknown, the desert between there and Shiraz to the south, about to be undertaken.

He shall not be going, like the devotees at Persepolis, on camelback, horseback, caravan, but by air-conditioned bus. He is not suicidal. This is high summer and white men do not venture into that desert without the twentieth century firmly with them. It has taken almost a week to obtain the bus tickets (first class, with air conditioning), for many officials exist entirely for the collection of bribes associated with bus travel. More such officials will dot the route, he feels sure. Though only nineteen, he is wise in the ways of bribes. He is pleased to be wise in the ways of bribes, for it gives him a colonial pleasure to assess the underlying meanings to surreal gestures, and statements. The common ground is human nature.

The bus stands in a square near a mosque, the one he entered to admire the blue glass but found he could not: the art was too mathematical and scrawled over with artless spirals of Arabic writing, the inevitable quotations from the Koran. A woman in a black chadore, only her eyes and one gnarled hand visible, begs from him.

You'd think Morris, of all people, himself a freeloader on life, would give to a beggar. But no, he knows better. You give to one, and ten more appear, desperate. There's no end to it then.

All you have to do is shut down the imagination. You must not imagine that this woman has lost her husband, has eight children to feed, no shelter, no hope. It is an easy matter so to do. The mind is accustomed to it, the western mind. Has not Morris sat through a thousand sermons in the draughty halls of school chapel on the subject of charity and, like the hundreds of others identically clad, given his sixpence and left with a light heart, his duty done? What is this woman wound in black to do with him? Nothing.

To avoid her stare, he brushes her away with his shoulder. She gets the message.

He inspects the bus. There are large black boxes hanging from each plate glass window, betokening air conditioning. Allah be thanked!

About four hundred people had been sold tickets on this bus and it was up to the driver to decide which forty would enter and ride to Shiraz. Tumani (or dollari) did some of the persuading but, curiously, there were obviously other factors. An American with a rucksack who had just parted with many dollars explained that he thought women with children were being turned away because of 'toilet difficulties' and any Turks or Arabs because they were 'scum'. Morris tried not to think about this latter and hoped that his Tumani had been his entrance qualification rather than the colour of his skin, but human nature being what it is . . .

After two hours of wrangling, the bus was full. It was more than full, for there were people in the aisles and some standing by the driver. Perhaps their entrance requirement had been that they would amuse the driver with stories, like Sheherazade, for the duration of the journey.

Morris was expecting the air conditioning to come on with the engine of the bus. It did not. By the time they had reached the outskirts of Teheran the air inside the bus was fetid and at least gas mark 9. He called down to the American, two seats further along, who shouted back, and Morris's heart sank at the sound of it.

'Broken. It always is.'

So this overcrowded, unconditioned ancient bus entered the desert abruptly (there being no polite winding-down of the city, simply a last tower block on the last road, a building site and then flat sand for ever) to begin its eight-hour journey south to Shiraz, home of the poets and a university, and Morris wanted more than anything to get out and run away.

One would simply have to sleep. Morris worked this out before his brain softened with the heat. To conserve his supply of water (one thermos with self-screwing cup) and make the awful time pass through the inferno, he would have to sleep. This was going to be hard. The man next to him took up two thirds of the available space they shared, and was eating his way through melon after melon. If things get very bad, thought Morris, I shall buy a melon from him.

Morris allowed the hot air to scorch his throat, enter his lungs and fry him to sleep. Nightmares assailed him. The man next to him split open like a melon and the sticky sweet seeds crashed down onto Morris until he awoke crying out and there was a man in uniform standing over him saying, 'Papers! Give me papers!' This was not a dream. The bus had stopped on the road beside a barrier guarded by armed, uniformed men.

'What border is this?' asked Morris. He stood up, a difficult achievement in so confined a space, and hunted through his jacket breast pockets for his passport. He found only keys: stupid keys to a flat in London, to a van left in Cambridge, to a left luggage box at Waterloo. The soldier misunderstood his gesture and misinterpreted the metallic sounds and drew a gun on him. It was a small black pistol. Morris sat. This much he knew: when threatened, lie down, get down, submit. It's the only safe reaction to a gun.

'Don't shoot me. Please. Here passport and tumani for you. Enjoy. God is good.' He was trembling, despite the heat, from fear. This man could simply shoot him, drag him outside and leave him on the sand for the heat to melt him or the vultures to eat him and no one would ever know. Melonhead beside him would simply expand gratefully like a custard tipped out, to fill the two seats.

'I am tourist here. English. Not American,' he said.

'Good,' said the guard, looking at the passport. 'This Inglis?' he asked.

'Yes, sorry.' Sorry? thought Morris, I am apologising that my

English passport is in English! As if it were some dreadful novel in an infidel tongue! Sorry.

'What country is this then?' he asked. Presumably the bus driver had got lost and they had encountered a border crossing by mistake. Maybe the driver, distracted by the jabbering of the passengers standing near him, had turned right at Qum and landed them all in Iraq. The soldier looked at him for a long time as if he were an idiot, and laughed in his face.

'Isfahan,' he said, then added, 'Iran, Persia.' Morris sat. So they were still in Iran. He took back his passport, looked out the window and saw the most staggering array of tanks, heavy weapons and barracks *almost as far as the eye could see*. The bus started up and they passed through the raised red and white barrier pole, and on into the desert.

As night fell, the air cooled a little, Morris watched the desert pass and his hatred for Melonhead abated. Inside Morris was an instinct almost stronger than the survival one: the need to be loved. So far in his life this had involved him in hours and hours of getting to know people so well they told him all their secrets. Melonhead looked like a man who had many secrets. The trick was to confide something awful about yourself first, to disarm them.

'The people I'm going to visit in Shiraz don't know I'm coming,' he confided.

Melonhead said something savage in Farsi and stabbed another melon.

At regular intervals through the hours he saw one encampment after another, each holding acres of tanks, armoured cars and lorries and marching groups of men. By the time the bus drove into Shiraz down the avenues of almond trees and squares of fountains and ice-blue mosques, he had formed the inescapable conclusion that either Iran was about to go to war or it was armed against its own people. Either possibility was devastating. What did the Shah so fear? Why were these men searching every vehicle for spies or weapons? Why were they all so nervous? Persia has been here with those worshippers walking up that staircase on the frieze at Persepolis, carrying sacrificial lambs as offerings, ever since there were first Shahs of Persia, so what could there be to fear?

Six months later when Morris was wooing Lottie in Paris, the Ayatolla had returned from there to Iran, the Shah was dying somewhere else, revolution was underway and a war was brewing between Iran and Iraq. Some journeys are just in time, completely discreet, and there's no going back, ever.

5. *Bridget's road*

Krul shuffled and laid out the cards on the lectern. Bridget looked at them, determinedly casual. She was *not* going to feel intimidated. Shit! She was a guest here. A guest of Addie's.

Unfortunately she was so bloody hungry she was fantasising about eating toothpaste or cooking Filet of Fred. Food was the one thing she could not have, so it filled her mind. What a friend the mind is, that it does this, harps on so despite the outward reality of things.

'Ah, a book: a recipe book telling us how to make edible the furniture we sit upon or how to find the secret horde of food somewhere in this building which you, Krul, are hiding for your own amusement. A cup: which could hold say a thick home-made potato and leek soup partially made with those squiggly lines of the water. An animal: obviously the hapless beast who had supplied the meat. The barrier: now this could be just a knife and fork leaning together, waiting for me to tuck in. A crowd of stickmen: all us folk who have obviously just eaten or are just about to eat. I see this as an exposition on food. I can think of nothing else.' It sounded pathetic.

'Neither could the others, but they tried,' said Krul. 'Think of somewhere you've been recently. You've been on the road, haven't you, Bridget?'

That was no good of course. Did Krul realise this? The Senior Zits in Brugge! Christ! Now she wanted to drop out of this game.

'Think I'll just . . .'

'NO!' said Krul. 'Europe. A barrier. Come on.'

Europe. A barrier. Come on. Europe. A barrier. Dizzy and spinning, she put out her hands to steady her on the smooth carving of the eagle's wings and it gave way, the barrier opened onto a train station in Munster.

A Gothic structure dwarfing you. Only the trains are in scale. Guards walk down the long platforms in pairs. They are not marching. Not quite. But their faces are set.

She and Addie have no money but they have a deadline: they must reach Sweden by the next day. The Paris–Stockholm Express is due in any minute. If only they could board it.

'We need a miracle,' says Bridget.

'Right. Let's organise one then.' Addie's ridiculous trust in people, even, or especially, in men in uniform (the sort of men who populate Bridget's nightmares) leads her down the platform towards the guards. Oh no, Bridget almost shuts her eyes. What will she ask them?

Fortunately Bridget's German is so hazy that she doesn't gather the content of Addie's speech, only the tone. The tone is humorous, questioning. Her eyebrows arch deliciously. The younger guard says something to the older and they both laugh and the older one says, '*Man kann immer versuchen.*' Addie translates – one can always try.

'Does he mean jump train?'

'Yes, he must do.'

Addie has done it – organised a miracle. And with such ease. Don't look a gift horse, as her father used to say (twice daily), so while the guards looked the other way as the Express pulled in to Munster, they jumped on through a door left open by a businessman barely breaking step as he marched out.

'I can't believe this,' says Bridget, 'it almost makes up for the war.'

Addie can believe it though. It confirms her faith in people, the improvability of everyone, the redeemable world. Even men! She sees only the good in everyone, until they bite her. Then she finds excuses for the bites. There's always a reason. No such thing as evil: just good gone wrong – deep deep down she is still a Quaker.

She even chatters away now in German to people who can doubtless speak English better than she can German, but undaunted she says, when in doubt, make it up, no one minds. Not only do they not mind, they all fall in love with her. On a train where fare-paying passengers have to stand in the luggage room, Addie, a hobo, is offered a seat by a young man in uniform. Bridget, of course, stands. She stands from Bremen to Copenhagen, walking onto the ferry from Elsinor to Malmö with Addie, simply passing by the ticket checking person without looking up. They both stand from there until a small town just south of Stockholm, which she often thinks of as Forgottenburg, when a ticket collector began his trek down the train and about thirty young people with rucksacks decided they had reached their destination suddenly. Many people had decided you could *immer versuchen*!

There was a sort of solidarity as the recipients of various miracles flooded off the train at that small central Swedish town in the middle of nowhere.

Perhaps the fact that there was a pop concert going on in Forgottenburg on that day had something to do with it. At that time in the western world there was always a pop concert going on somewhere. Groups of people with tattered clothes, long hair, and plenty of money to spend on dope and time to spare doing nothing, sat around on grassy knolls all over Europe and North America unable to make out a single word of the songs someone was bashing out a few hundred yards away, and not caring in the least. God Almighty! Bridget could think of nothing worse. Addie's eyes lit up. Lover of humanity in all its forms, she rushed forward to embrace the first group of humans she came across on the first grassy knoll in Forgottenburg. Bridget sat and scowled. What sodding bad luck!

Addie was without Krul in those days (a wondrous mercy which Bridget didn't appreciate at the time) but she was never without admirers. She never had very long hair, never went barefoot or wore strings of beads, and yet she *fitted in*. Of course Bridget was there to protect her, to hoik her out the moment some arsehole seemed about to take advantage of her naivety. And Addie was grateful:

'What did I ever do before you came along, Bridget?'

No irony. She was without irony, in those days, the days before Krul, the days when she had many companions of both sexes, travelling ones and other ones.

The night was hot, and drink and hash were plentiful, so as soon as dark fell, late here in Scandinavia and short-lived for it would be light again in a couple of hours, everyone lay down randomly to sleep. Mostly on tartan rugs with fringes. Nothing had real edges in those days: everything was fringed or deliberately frayed. Especially the people.

How wonderful the Pill is for Men! No more restraint, no more I'll Stand By You If The Worst Happens. It's a free-for-all now, and Bridget has to hear, so modern an insult, that if she were a real woman she'd be on the Pill: she'd be universally available, for every turd who took it into his pea-brain to grope her. It was a terrible lack of imagination and foresight that she was not available to these intoxicated, inarticulate, rat-arsed humanoids lolling on knolls in Forgottenburg. How mean of her. How mean of her to be a woman and not on the Pill.

Men always want the Quick Hit: the goal before half time, the two-minute orgasm with no nine-month result, the slug of whisky in one gulp, that moment of triumph at the tape, the encapsulating photograph. They need a bigger, better bomb. Whereas women desire evolution, the long result, the full forty weeks' gestation, the childhoods of children to be memorable and as slow as possible, generations of loving family rituals, street upon street of neighbours on down the years, a happy town, a long culture in a big metropolis, a cheerful nation, a sorted out world, a thriving planet, a cool universe . . . women want things to last. It's a shame men run the world: the poor world, victim of a million quick hits. It stands to reason: planting the seed is a one-off; carrying it is millennial.

She longed to communicate these (and other) thoughts to Addie, that's all, but Addie was busy. Addie had a right to be busy. So she zipped up her sleeping bag aggressively hoping the rain would come in the short night and dampen all their animal ardour, and tried to sleep, tried not to imagine she could hear . . . anything at all.

She tried to read her book by torchlight.

It wasn't jealousy, of course it wasn't. She didn't want Addie for herself, not in that way, but the *waste* hurt her. The waste of everything, of spiritual energy, of time, of Addie. It was a waste of Addie.

Then she stopped reading her sodding book and rolled up her sodding sleeping bag and zipped up every damn thing and went. If she needed her, Addie could frigging well search and find her the next morning. Enough is enough!

A few hours later, the next morning, Bridget woke alone. She didn't panic. She often had woken alone after all. And this was Sweden, not the equatorial jungle.

People were making their breakfasts in between the knolls, out of the breeze. Bridget left off her shoes, to help with acceptability, and roamed the site looking for a lift to Stockholm. Not having Addie's facility with language, she was reduced to sign language and loud English for her query – 'Room for one more to Stockholm?'

It took her half an hour to arrange a ride, and even then she was not sure of it. Only that a van would leave at noon and there *might* be room. This gave her three hours to kill, not looking for Addie.

It was hard not to look for her. Everyone who passed might be her, but wasn't.

At ten o'clock she had recourse to her book again. By eleven o'clock she had recourse to a bicycle she found leaning against a tent, and by eleven-thirty she was brave enough to use the mike and amplifier lying on the grass by some boxes to say:

'ADELINE, COME TO THE BARRIER FOR A LIFT TO STOCKHOLM NOW.'

Addie made it. Bridget asked no questions, in the van, or later in a café in Stockholm where they feasted on bread and chocolate and, finances being short, one cup of coffee. But gradually Addie swam back up into her world and they reinvented the scale of points for men, laughed about the sons of bitches who thought they were God's gift, laughed and laughed and re-established that intellectual superiority over men which had been the hallmark of their travels so far. It was cosy again. Not the bread or the chocolate, but they nourished each other in a special way and the bond was nutritious.

'I knew you'd find me,' said Addie, smiling.

Nutritious as milk and eggs and cereal and meat, not those glazed pastry triangles each with a shiny peach winking under aspic.

Food again. Oh Hell.

6. *Lottie's road*

Somewhere in England Lottie was scrambling on all fours in a gooseberry bush trying to trap two runaway guinea pigs and calming her terrified children. The small pigs, her face among the large thorns, her hands on the dark wet slippery earth and the screaming, it was bound to happen. Her eye stung like a splinter of barbed wire and blinked blood. Morris was somewhere else; he always was when disaster struck. In the TinCan with the four of them suddenly silent in the back, Greta shushing them and hushing them, Lottie prayed Please God give me enough sight to get to the hospital, wherever it is.

'Quiet, kiddiewinks, Mumsie's peeper's . . .' what? finished?

Usually when Lottie needs a campsite, there are signs for the railway, when she needs Paris, there are signs for Switzerland, but the gods are with her and a small blue sign says 'Hospital'. She follows it. There is a barrier. Since she is not an ambulance,

the guard there tells her, she cannot pass. She takes her hand
from her eye. He is frightened and raises the barrier.

By the time she has unloaded the three children and the
baby, the eye has stopped bleeding and is clotted shut. A nurse
on reception in Casualty says they don't do eyes here. She must
go to the Eye Hospital four miles away. She reloads the van.
Single-peepered, she drives the four miles as instructed and
repeats the whole process.

Hell must be this: eternally unloading four frightened kiddies
at institutions which reject you, and the pain increases until you
go blind. Sorry we don't do blind here, but four miles away . . .

The Outpatients clinic is deserted. An Asian doctor leaves as
they arrive. Lottie hopes he is only one of two. Alas no. A nurse
sits her down by some rows of chairs (which Hugo manages to
be destroying) and asks her for a complete medical history.
Lottie begins at her deliveries, scoots back to her own birth,
gets to age two (tonsillitis) and stops.

Just as she is in need of some comfort and love and pain
relief and a 'there, there' or two, she is asked, here in this
aseptic hall, by a stranger, for an oral biography.

'Who are you?' If only she could just give her name, rank and
serial number! That's all a captured soldier has to do. She feels
like a captured, wounded soldier. The war has, for her,
temporarily ended. The real world has gone into a truce.

Though she is not sure what the war is about, who the
participants are, or whether she is winning. Perhaps eleven
years ago, before the birth of Greta, she could have more easily
answered the question, who are you, but now she is thoroughly
submerged in the day-to-day business of keeping four children
alive while moving about the world and this gives her, fortunately perhaps, no time to contemplate the Meaning of Life or
the nature of her identity. And the more often she finds herself
not at home anywhere, the easier it is not to question anything.
Survival is uppermost, is her religion now, and to maintain its
importance, she and Morris keep on the move. To stop
travelling would mean having to decide on their own colour

scheme, their own routine, their own neighbourhood. Lottie dreads it. But this nurse has asked her to stop running and give a resumé.

'Must I go on? The pain is killing me.'

'Do you work outside?' Outside? A farm worker, road repairer?

'No.'

'Housewife then?'

'House? Wife? No. I mean, yes.' Greta interrupted the interrogation at this point in order to clarify one or two things.

'You see we do have a house usually to ourselves, but when we aren't there, which is nearly always, someone else has it, though it isn't theirs, though when we come home, though home is really the TinCan if you ask me, the people living in that house have to go and live somewhere else, or if they haven't got anywhere to go, they could stay in the TinCan. You see?' The nurse hadn't been listening. She had been staring into the middle distance, to which she now drew Lottie's attention.

She asked Lottie to read some letters at the far end of the room which she couldn't do with the left eye since it was shut. She hurried on and showed her some fingers. Lottie realised she was seeing double because she saw her forefinger twice: no two fingers are that alike.

'Ringman and Pinkie,' said Clare.

'No, it's Foreman,' said Hugo.

The nurse asked for an account of the accident and Lottie told her she scratched the eye on a fruit bush while rescuing a guinea pig. She appeared to write this down and took Lottie into another room.

'Greta – mind the children.' Here she handed Lottie over to another nurse who had just come on duty. This nurse told her to put her chin on a rest and keep the head still. Lottie couldn't. She got cross.

'Why are you shaking?'

'I don't know. Sorry.'

'Move your chair round so I can see into your eye.' Lottie moved her chair at random, a few inches 'round'.

'Not *that* way.' Either the nurse didn't know her left from her right since she was unable to transpose them and say 'move to your left' for she had to come round the machine and move the chair herself, or she thought Lottie didn't speak English well enough.

'I have the same problem with maps.'

After looking at the wrong eye for a while she said she couldn't see anything because the head was moving and the doctor would have to see it.

'But the doctor isn't here so you'll have to wait outside.'

Lottie waited. George had Mer-mer. Clare was enraged and went off to the toilet. They waited. George wailed. Clare locked herself in the toilet, and Lottie had to feed George again. Hugo rescued Clare and asked if he could keep the lock. What lock, dear? This one here.

Another man arrived and another, each giving his medical history out loud at the side of the room. Lottie and her children got to know much about these men as the time passed and Lottie had to explain 'Vasectomy' to Greta and Hugo, after which Hugo announced, loudly, that he didn't want a snipped willy ever.

Later that day, the doctor arrived (the same Asian one) and the nurse showed one of the other men into the room to see him first. Greta was so angry at this that she said, 'Hey! It's not fair!' to the closed door. Lottie was on the point of fainting, and told Greta that if she should, she must phone Morris and ask for help. Greta said she had never used a public telephone, but Hugo reassured her that he had once played with one for hours and there was nothing to it.

'Nothing to it once you'd played with it.' Oh God, where was Morris?

After a while the nurse who examined Lottie went off and came back with a plate of food and went to eat in a side room. Lottie would have given all she possessed (a spare nappy and a set of car keys) for a cup of tea. Or any drink at all. Another nurse was wandering about aimlessly and then came up to Lottie and asked her when she had last had a tetanus injection.

'As a child. Why?' You aren't supposed to say 'Why?' in clinics. It annoys them. It is a direct challenge to their omniscience.

'Oh, it's just . . . You'll have to have one.'

'Why?'

'Well what *sort* of an animal was it scratched you?'

'Animal?'

'It says here a guinea pig scratched you.'

'No, a *bush*. Just a *bush*.'

'Oh, that's all right then. You won't need a tetanus.'

George cried again. Lottie handed him to Greta. The doctor called her in. He prized open the injured eye, by means of a piece of lint soaked in water (obviously a skill only trained doctors can perform) and told her to put her chin there and keep her head still. He found a scratch across the cornea, not serious, and advised antiseptic cream and a patch. He sounded bored. He looked down at the notes, by now a small cardboard book of half-truths, misunderstandings and misrepresentations. Lottie could hear George screaming in the waiting room.

'Look at this, nurse,' he said, 'each child born in a different country. That's *very* unusual.'

'The eye is all right then?'

'Yes, it's fine. Just a scratch and you did the letters and fingers all right.' Lottie didn't tell him that she couldn't read a letter and had seen two Pinkies. It would just have delayed things, and George and Clare were having a decibel competition now next door.

Then, just as she thought it was all over, the doctor said, 'Now tell me all about this globetrotting of yours. I'm interested in that.'

'Sorry,' she said, 'it would take hours. Do you mind?'

'Well, could you just tell me how you travel?'

'By van.'

'I see and is that a Landrover type, long wheel base, or one of those people-carriers, designed with children in mind?'

'Please, I just . . .'

'Don't you have trouble finding parts in say, Oman?' It was a jolly good thing that Lottie did not have about her person a weapon, say a .22 pistol, or a sawn-off shotgun, for she would definitely have aimed it carefully (allowing for monocular vision) at the grinning head of this beautiful young doctor and shot him dead.

Instead, she closed her eyes and said, go on, faint now, to her body, go on, you deserve it. But the gods wouldn't oblige, and she just slid down the chair ever so slightly so that the nurse jumped forward and put cream and a huge patch on her eye and asked her to come back tomorrow afternoon.

Wouldn't that be an even more perfect Hell? Yes, just when you think you can go now, they tell you you have to come back tomorrow.

Lottie can imagine it:

The Review Clinic is from two to four p.m. and at one-thirty a small crowd of two hundred people all wearing patches arrives and starts camping in the clinic. The doctor arrives at two-forty p.m. and sees the first five in thirty minutes. The other hundred and ninety-five get seen up until five-thirty by which time each person is being given eight seconds and is on the verge of a nervous collapse.

'I'll be there,' lied Lottie.

'*Now* can we rescue the guinea pigs?' asked Hugo.

7. *James's road*

Niagara Falls was full of liars. James's companion was lying about the place in a commissioned article of two thousand words. The waiter in their hotel was lying about everything to increase his tip revenue on which he pretended not to survive. The hotel manager had lied about the rooms, and the reasons for the heart-shaped Jacuzzis. The honeymooners themselves, faces pale and hair limp from too many trips on the Maid of the Mist, lied in their very demeanour – no, their body language tried to say, we have not been bonking away for hours in the daytime on the heart-shaped bed upstairs, we have been reading serious literary fiction and we are ravenously hungry because of the negative ions given off by the Falls, not because of the unusual amount of physical exercise we have been subjecting each other to.

It should have suited James to be here (doing the cartoon to accompany the article) – for if he wasn't himself an habitual liar it was only because he never let it become a *habit*. He rationalised every untruth in terms of a higher truth, which was his art.

But he hated it here. He hated it because he was with a male colleague and not his bride. In fact so vast was the amount of dissembling going on around the vicinity of the Falls that he sometimes had the impression that the other people staying at the hotel thought his companion was his bride – that they were a couple! To counteract this supposition both of them affected unnatural macho swaggers in the lobby.

But nothing could make up for not having your own bride in this town. James had lied so often to so many about why he had never married that he almost believed his own lies. He had said that he didn't want children; that marriage would restrict his freedom to travel; that he couldn't *afford* it. All these things had an element of truth in them – they were in the shadow of a truth at least. But the whole truth was elsewhere.

James's colleague announced that he was walking up to the hydro plant that morning, and was James coming? No, he would go his own way.

James wanted to get right out of this kissy place, this Toothsome Twosomes' Town, this sugary heart-shaped Once in a Lifetime Place and go somewhere *else*. He consulted the map.

Two miles away was something huge called Marineland. He asked the girl on Reception for a brochure. Here there is a

brochure on everything. Even one on 'Suggestions for Newly
Weds in Niagara'. She handed him a full-colour one:

> Marineland where all things majestic and marine appear for
> your pleasure. A four-ton submarine of living flesh, a killer
> shark from another world, trampolines in air over the aquatic
> plastic of a concrete pool. Also folks, we have deer you may
> feed and real bears in their natural environment.

The brochure was surreal in the extreme. There was a photograph of a woman being kissed (or eaten?) by a killer whale.
The possibility of finding an image which might sum up the
unreality of Niagara for his cartoon seemed a large one.

He went.

The fact that he had been warned by the commissioning
editor to *concentrate* on Niagara didn't come into it. You can't
restrict art with petty rules.

Driving down a long straight road between completely iden-
tical fir trees for two miles, James amused himself as usual by
captioning himself – interviewing himself for a television docu-
mentary on famous cartoonists. The voice-over was lyrical:
'Reality passes beyond his windscreen; he is sailing close to the
wind. Life is Art' and so on.

MARINELAND AT NIAGARA WELCOMES YOU.

So does the girl who takes his five dollars. He sits with a crowd
in a small amphitheatre and watches the pool for signs of life.
The show is about to begin. The pool blackens and shudders.
The crowd cheers. Men in wetsuits jump out of mock plastic
submarines suspended over the pool. One of them stirs the
water with a fluorescent paddle and a giant fish appears, flies
over it and plunges back into the pool. The spray of its wake
wets the audience. Disney was here.

James is bored. He scans the audience. The man with the
microphone is calling for a volunteer. She is a middle-aged

woman from Pennsylvania. James knows this because the human announces it and the audience cheer her on at the information. She is kissed by the killer shark. The crowd 'ooh' and 'aah'.

James leaves. He passes the outdoor restaurant where the tables are fin-shaped and the cups have sharks' teeth on them. He can feel an anger boiling up inside him. Unspecified as yet, without caption.

The long road winds into the distance promising 'Grizzly Bears in Their Natural State'. This road is so long, it winds through fairground rides, each set in its own acre of tree-shorn ground, a dollar a ride; an entire mock-medieval castle with a deer park where 'feeding the deer is allowed'; a building site where 'exciting future developments' are under way.

What is this anger, this aloneness? James is feeling desolate. He spots, at the turn of the road, a gaggle of thirty tourists standing at the edge of a jutting platform gazing down at eight black bears below lounging on wet rocks protruding from the shallow waters of their 'natural' concrete setting.

With unerring accuracy and very little effort (his eyes are only half open) one gorgeous creature summons a few languorous muscles of an arm, merely a creasing of the fur, and swipes out at the falling pellet, popping it into his jaws. Another swivels his head, opens his mouth, and lets a pellet fall into it.

These creatures move him. He hadn't expected that. They have taken his breath away. They are *not* in their natural state – they are in a concrete mock-up of it, but their *power* is present and is preternatural, supernatural, awesome. He never imagined they would be so *big*, so prehistoric or that each paw would be the size of a small brown sheep, or that they would expose two gruesome rows of shiny white knifeblades with a sinister sort of yawn. He had thought, as English people do, that they would be a cross between a cuddly panda and a teddy bear. Instead it was obvious, looking down at these beasts, that one swipe with their clawed paws would put out your light for ever.

And he is put in mind of Krul, his brother-in-law. There is

only one human in the whole world who frightens him, and he is married to the only person in the whole world he really loves. This contradiction, this schism in the very heart of him is the reason, the real one, why he is single. He had to watch his sister enter the bear pit and he now has to fraternise with the bear though he knows it will one day prove fatal. To him, not his sister.

For Addie is that girl in the fairy tales who has a magic power over the Beast: she enters the woods and it senses her goodness and knows she will never give it away and is gentle. But let the woodsman – her father or brother – come near it and it will sever head from body with one sideways fling of its powerful claws. Without even looking up from the forest floor.

The only consolation there is for the woodsmen is that Addie is safe. She is safe from all danger by virtue of the bear's quiet vigilance, his very possessiveness.

James finds he is shaking. He, a grown man, is afraid of the bears. There are children here, laughing, feeding the bears with the small white pellets. Their innocence and twenty yards of concrete protect them. James buys pellets from the hut there for the purpose. He examines them. They are soft and white and powdery outside. What can they be? Presumably some clever combination of vitamins and minerals essential to bears. James wishes for the millionth time in his life that he had not given up science so young and could understand this.

A child next to him pops one into his mouth. James nudges her mother.

'Oh – your child has just eaten one!' he says, alarmed.

'It's okay – they're just marshmallows.'

Of course they're marshmallows. What else? The girl in the hut confirms this. James cannot bring himself to send one down. Even here in the soft sticky-sweet capital city of honeymooners where it would be sort of apt and fitting, unlike the cartoon which that week graced a serious article in a national newspaper on Canada's world-famous hydro-electric system at Niagara depicting:

Loudly dressed tourists about to drop giant marshmallows on a group of bears with Niagara Falls behind them. Underneath was the first verse-caption he ever wrote:

Their home is concrete, no caves or hollows –
And from the sky rain (yes!) marshmallows!

8. *Melanie's road*

Melanie sits in a corner of her flat on a hard plastic chair foot-cuffed to the floor. Imaginary steel manacles are biting into her ankles. Around her are cardboard boxes full of dusty objects she could no longer name. The carpet is red with orange swirls, mercifully faded and worn to tracklike threads under the table with its stained and cracked pale blue formica top. Light streams along the dustlines above it from the early summer evening outside.

Bess is in the next room watching television. Colin is out drinking. Using air for money, for he had none on him. She had checked. Mock-frisking him for a gun, she had giggled and checked for coins. He had not been amused. Piss off, he'd said, just piss off.

If only there was someone out there – someone to go to. Then she wouldn't be manacled to this floor in this block of flats. She might not be stuck in this life.

Bess opens the door and peeps in. She is a beautiful child – a budding adult almost at budburst. So beautiful that she looks as out of place here as a ballerina in a farmyard. Momentarily, her brightness, her loveliness, angers her mother.

'Mum – it's *Blind Date*. Come and watch with me?'

'No.'

Instead Melanie rises, takes a key off its hook and leaves the flat.

She is wearing a pair of dungarees gone at the knees and plimsolls gone entirely. To collect her coat she'd have to disturb Bess. She creeps out.

Outside the familiar London streets are unnaturally quiet.

Perhaps she is never out at this time? Perhaps something sinister has happened and because she did not have the radio on, she alone does not know. Perhaps war has been declared, or the Bomb is imminent? Was the ambulance she thought she heard half an hour ago really the four-minute warning? And if so, shouldn't she run home and spend the last few moments with Bess?

A car passes by. Then a bus. So normality is going on somewhere. She knows now that she has come out to find Colin. To surprise him. It angers him that she will never go to the pub with him, especially now Bess is old enough to be left on her own for a few hours.

No sign of him in the first pub. Nor the second. She walks on. Over the river. Now people are running towards something and she can hear trouble up ahead. Odd sounds which she does not associate with the outdoors – the sounds of a huge audience gasping and shouting at something. A football match in central London?

She turns a corner and gasps herself. She is standing near the very heart of London, near the river and Houses of Parliament. To her right are some of the most expensive shopfronts in the world – places of such opulence they no longer even excite her bitterness (merely her inter-galactic curiosity), and yet *here* in this place there are running crowds under cardboard banners and broken glass and burning litter and fire, fire, fire.

London's burning. Or at least some upturned cars are ablaze. Perhaps there has been a bomb? Something is seriously out of hand even in these incendiary times. But what?

Melanie has never seen horses charge before. Only on television. A line of mounted policemen charge down the streets normally packed with cars as if the tarmac were suddenly a polo field and all theirs. She feels a swelling and vibrating of the pavement under her.

She can hear screaming.

Now the mass of people turn, like a field of high grass and

moves in her direction. She stifles her own scream and starts to run back the way she came.

A row of giant navy helmets behind perspex shields snakes down the wide avenue like the end of a whip and Melanie finds she is already the end of the crowd, and is winded slightly. All around her are bodies moving and shouting. One banner is now legible: No Poll Tax.

So this is the peaceful demonstration against the Poll Tax, thinks Melanie, her feet now leaving the pavement as she is carried sideways towards the bridge.

The crowd are moving downhill then, towards the river under the pressure of the police – so obviously it was their idea not the mob's.

An hour later Melanie turned the key in her own front door and *fell* into the house, her arms bloody and a black eye already forming.

When she came round Bess was bandaging her arm lovingly and dabbing something astringent on her face. Colin stood a few feet away, leaning on the wall. Behind him was the black bare pane of a cracked window.

'Well you're a pretty sight,' he said. 'Not only leaving Bess all alone but getting yourself roughed up into the bargain!'

'Dad! Leave her alone. She's not up to it, is she? Not now.'

'I'll be the judge of *that*, my girl, and don't you be cheeky.' He aimed a swipe at her but she ducked expertly and smiled down at her mother.

'He's drunk,' she mouthed. They could lipread each other. Colin could not: he felt as excluded as a hearing person living with two deaf signers.

'I was in a riot,' Melanie began.

'I know *that*,' said Colin. 'How could you be so bloody stupid? To go getting yourself involved in something like that when it's the last damn thing we need. Can't you get it through your thick skull how dangerous it is living as we do on the say-so of the petty Hitler down at the Social? Do you really think no one *saw* you, with fifty thousand people and four television channels on the streets? Do you think no one will rat on you? Do you think there weren't photographers hired by the police to snap people in the act for arrest later?'

'Oh, Colin, I just went out . . .'

'Answer me, woman – *did you think at all*?' Now he was screaming and raging about the room, staggering like someone drugged and incapable. Bess started to cry and Colin sent her to her room.

When she had gone he pounded the wall until his own fist was bleeding.

Hours ago, Melanie should have stood and crossed the faded carpet in the evening light to go and watch with Bess Cilla Black doling out fate to star-struck couples for two reasons: first because what could be more important than choosing the right person in the first place (always a blind date with the future), and secondly because life is short and all that really matters is spending time with the child you love, who nowadays can be sent to her room but one day will not come back.

9. *Neil's road*

Neil's was one of the widest roads in the world: the twelve-laned highway leading from Santa Barbara to Los Angeles in California. He was on a bus with forty teenagers, going to a zoo.

He could hear insults about him behind him. He was used to this. They hinged on a comparison of him with the exchange teacher who had left their school to teach in England for a term. The comparison was unfavourable in the extreme. Unfortunately Neil's predecessor had been a Cool Dude with Charisma. Many people would have been stung and shrivelled. Not Neil. Instead he reached in his bag for Doctor Beaver.

Doctor Beaver was Canadian of course. Hence he was neither British (like Neil) nor American (like his pupils) and so could be neutral on many issues which might have caused strife in the classroom. Neil had made him with this in mind. This class had not met him yet.

They fell silent as Neil stood (the bus driver jumped), Doctor Beaver aloft on his right arm. At one time these fourteen-year-olds might have considered themselves too old for puppets, but Jim Henson has done much to counteract that prejudice. A puppet is now acceptable everywhere and always.

Unlike short fat English teachers with a thick chubby face, sparse eyebrows beneath a sparser head, which shone like the dome of a robot.

Doctor Beaver was life-sized, had feet and a tail and large brown eyes (stuck on with velcro but very expressive somehow). Neil was a ventriloquist and when the beaver's lips moved, the words issued directly from them.

This was the first thing which held their attention – it didn't matter what he said at first, the fact that *he* really didn't seem to be saying it was riveting.

Doctor Beaver commented on his surroundings and on the passengers of the bus. He even whispered and gesticulated (no mean feat for an animal with arms like furry paddles) some fantastic information about the bus driver – he was definitely an alien from outer space – the coin holder at his waist was really his batteries which kept him going.

After only a few minutes those who had earlier been denigrating Neil himself were calling out replies to Doctor Beaver as if he was a long-lost friend they had just met up with again.

'Do you agree that no one is wiser than me?'

'We agree! We agree!'

'Am I to be obeyed above all others?'

'You are! You are!'

'Well, Doctor Beaver, I that is, has decided that brown eyes are best.' They fell quiet. A few laughs washed around the bus.

'Well I myself have brown eyes, do I not?'

'You do!'

'Stand up all those who have blue or green or grey eyes. Any colour not brown.' They stood, the laughter dying down. The driver grumbled something about the danger of standing on buses.

'I want these people to leave the bus in a moment, when we stop at the lights.'

He should have warned the driver: the poor man was panicking: 'Whatthehell?' he mumbled.

Obviously they didn't want to go. There were a few dissenting shouts of, 'Steady there, doctor!'

'Okay, okay. I'm a reasonable beaver. You can stay, but you must stand over by the windows at the back, with your backs to us.' They went, sniggering.

Then Doctor Beaver made some brown-eyed pupils erect a barrier of bags between the two groups.

Addressing only the remaining Brown Eyes, Doctor Beaver said, 'I'm sorry to have to tell you that people with blue eyes have been found, in experiments done at universities all over the world, to have a *lower* IQ, a greater tendency to commit crimes. Most murderers and child molesters do not have brown eyes. Hitler had blue eyes. Jesus was brown-eyed. Most people with AIDS have blue eyes, most homosexuals are blue-eyed. In the animal kingdom only the killers have blue eyes. There is a tribe of Indians in the rainforest who kill all babies born with blue eyes at birth, because they know this, and they have a zero crime rate in that tribe. Under the circumstances, should we educate these people, give them all the advantages our society can confer, even take them on outings, in the sure and certain knowledge that they will seek only to undermine our civilisation?' Doctor Beaver's paddle-arms were outspread in a questioning stance.

At this point, there was silence.

The silence was broken by a girl saying, 'This might be true, someone in my family with blue eyes is in jail.'

Someone standing against the window with blue eyes wailed into the quiet of the bus, 'Well why did God give me blue eyes then?'

Doctor Beaver suddenly had an idea: 'Shall we vote on it?'

'Yes!' Yes, everyone agreed that will be fair. The majority decide.

'But, Doctor Beaver,' spoke up someone from the Blue Eyes at the back, 'it isn't fair: most people have brown eyes. It must just be a fact of nature. A coincidence.'

'No such thing as a coincidence,' said Doctor Beaver. 'Also it's worse than you think because I shall not allow you to vote for the reasons already stated.'

Then mayhem ensued. Doctor Beaver seemed to glory in it. They only just stopped short of physical violence.

The driver did *not* glory in it. He was furious and honked his horn.

Then Doctor Beaver began to howl, 'Oooooooo, my eyes!' and covered his face with his paddle-arms. When he removed his paws there was the sound of ripping velcro and he revealed a startlingly large pair of blue eyes.

The trick dawned on them and gradually laughter trickled among them, spilling between them like water from an overfilled cup, as they re-established alliances, broke down the wall of rucksacks, though there were three or four who didn't laugh at all: the Jewish children, the Black children, those with sad, colourless eyes, all the outgroup.

'You fucking commie prick, call yourself a teacher?' said the driver, pulling the coach to a halt outside the zoo.

10. *Bernard's road*

Finally, there was only Bernard left, and he took his time approaching the pulpit. When he did appear, he had Fred in his arms. He sat on the stool with Fred on his lap and hoisted the dog's top half onto the bottom edge of the pulpit's desktop. He then wrapped his arms round the dog and buried his face in the back of his furry head so that when he spoke and gesticulated, it seemed to the onlookers that a dog with human arms was speaking.

'I come to you representing, as you might expect, the

Underdog. But what is this here? Pictures! A crowd? That's you lot, who didn't feed me.' Here Fred/Bernard flicked the card into the audience. 'A fierce animal! Ugh I hate competition!' Flicked again, this time towards the altar. ' A book! But we underdogs never learnt to read.' Flick. 'Cup! Water! The cup I don't need: I lap directly at puddles nowadays.' He flicked away the cup and the water. 'A barrier! Haven't you seen me leap all barriers?' Flick. When the laughter had died down, and the last card spun through the air into the darkness, the Dogman began.

'Our road is in the sky. In a small aeroplane I wing my way over the world, looking down from time to time. There are muddy goings on below. Roman Britain by the looks of it. A representative of Caesar thinks he is conquering Britain for all time, doesn't realise his days are numbered, that the Invasion of Britain was Rome's most notable failure. He'll see in time, though. North I go to Pendle Hill where I see through the fog a little girl on horseback, who thinks she is lost, but isn't. East to the Soviet Union where someone is lying to a customs official about a painting, though there is no need to risk anything. Then I go south to Iran where I follow for a while the route of a bus travelling safely through a desert bristling with weapons. Then I turn north again to Sweden where I fly over a pop concert where thousands of bored people are trying to find the Meaning of Life. Nearby someone else is scratching her eye on a gooseberry bush: perhaps *that* is how her many children were conceived? West to Canada, to the great Falls, where the bears are being doubly exploited: first by marshmallows and then by a cartoonist. Back east to London, where there are Poll Tax riots and where, happily, repressed anger is uniting otherwise dissonant groups of people, and finally, I fly west again to the west coast of America where I salute that coach of American Youth finding out about prejudice the easy way.

'Weary of all this self-discovery I head south, fuel low and engine distressed by so much backtracking. Down over the continent of Africa I go, through the deserts and the famine areas where hunger is a dear friend, almost a family member. Like it is here.

'Heading for the Gold Coast, Ivory Coast: ending up in the little known West African Republic of Yffy-yf. I only have a short time to spend here. There isn't long to achieve anything and I have come with the dual mission of designing them adequate bridges and the roads leading to them. I'm not sure which is more important. I was going to be swayed by the inhabitants themselves.'

Fred had rested his head on the pulpit a few moments before and now seemed to be asleep, so Bernard gently lifted him down and resumed his story without him.

'Let sleeping dogs, eh? Actually, Fred found it a bit tiresome in Africa. The heat and humidity of those parts of Iffy-yf where they most needed bridges, not to mention roads, the innermost swathes of the equatorial jungle, were trying for him. The problem, as I understand it, is that the heat, just like extreme cold, is a sort of mental trap. The mind is obliged to devote such a high percentage of its attention span to coping with the temperature, that there is insufficient left to cope with day-to-day reality. Hence Fred became, it must be admitted, somewhat less than astute in his dealings with the natives, the Yfs. In fact there were times, early on, when they regarded him merely as a pet.

'I had no such difficulty though. I found the heat invigorating and the Yfs were hospitable in the extreme. Having fed Fred his early morning dish of chopped paw-paw with lemon juice squeezed over it, and woken the small government interpreter who slept at the end of my yard, I would sally forth into the village and knock on the ornate door of the village Headman's compound. Each day this was a different door, of course, since the post of Headman was tenable from sunrise to sunset on each day, so that by the end of one year, all men over sixteen dwelling in the village had been Headman for at least one day. This may sound sexist since no women were allowed to be Headperson, but in fact the women voted frequently as to whether they wished to be Head and consistently voted not to be. The reason I soon found out.

'One of my tasks while there was to investigate the hunting patterns of the hunters in the village, to see where they most needed bridges. Each day I would extend, with the help of that day's Headman, the map of the area. When it came to the important decision as to whether the bridge should be of local materials (felled equatorial trees) or imported, reinforced concrete, the Headman declared himself to be unable to make that decision.

'Why not?' I asked.

'It is beyond me. I am not good at making decisions,' he said, through the interpreter.

'Then what are you good at?' I asked, hoping to reframe the question.

'Catching monkeys, and fishing,' he said, proudly. He could see that I wasn't happy with this. 'It is not given to everyone to be good at decisions,' he said, 'and sometimes people who think they are good at decisions jump to the wrong one and make a mistake. And then we are in need of a great Forgiving Ceremony.'

'Then who will decide?' I asked.

'Someone else. I will find someone suitable. Probably it will be my wife, or any other woman she thinks capable of making the decision. Women are often better at making the right decision, don't you know that?'

'I thought that a rather dubious opinion until he pointed out that the mere sight of a woman taking out her breast for the feeding of a baby was enough to produce, in most men, an unplanned erection, so that it was obvious, even visible, that men could not control their feelings so well as women.

'So the reason for the reluctance of women to accept the post of Headman became clear: the post held no power. On the contrary, by not being Head, the women held more real power. Of course they also held all the babies and all the food and sometimes Fred, which they considered a great honour because

Yffy-yf in their language means "the tribe who is looking for God". They had been looking for many thousands of years, from each sunup to each sunset, and since they knew that they were not necessarily the rulers of the earth nor its servants, but neither was any other animal, they were completely open-minded about what God might be, and since they had never encountered a dog before, thought that he *might* fit the bill. After all he did no work, but was fed, spoke no words but was easily understood by white man and Yf alike, communed with the Other World much (sleeping we call it), was good with children and was extraordinarily beautiful.

'At the end of my visit there, the roads and bridge planned and drawn, I was sorry to leave. And they were so sorry to see me leave that they begged me to leave Fred with them as a memento. Such total acceptance I have not had elsewhere, though my visit there may have been in vain for somehow the vision of a future Yffy-yf linked by a network of main roads and steel bridges and highway codes evades the imagination.'

37

Exposure

Bernard stepped over Fred, and left. Krul put the lights back on and sat in front of the pulpit, now simply a wooden tower with a bird's wings peeping out from it, and everyone adjusted themselves as you do when the lights come back on, even if you have not been doing anything disgraceful during the blackout, squirming a little and blinking. The general feeling was not one of comradeliness as it might have been after some games but rather of alienation: as if they were simply nine adults who had just travelled from somewhere exotic (Tallin, Yffy-yf, California) and were somehow stranded in this place temporarily, without a common language.

Krul looked from one to another of them, like a teacher who is about to announce the results of some crucial test and wants first to set the tone by making it absolutely clear that they have *not* done well, not at all well.

'Well hasn't that been enlightening? Nothing remains obscure. Are you still in any doubt as to the significance of the symbols?'

'Yes, I am. You can't get away with that, Krul. Were they totally arbitrary then?' asked James.

'No, indeed not. I had the advantage over the rest of you in that I knew what the symbols represented *while* I was hearing the roads, like a historian reading the newspaper who knows the first signs of revolution so well. The cup represents love, the book knowledge, the animal fear, the barrier a current problem, and water is sex.' No one moved. They were all thinking, so vital is the self-image, of their own roads, and their significance in the light of this revelation.

'I always felt reluctant to accept that any symbol could be universal, myself,' said Krul, 'the Jungian symbols strike me as a bit superstitious in their exactitude. Still, educated people put great faith in them. But this is not a governing consideration, because I've found out everything I need to know.'

'What did you need to know?' asked Bridget.

'Why you all came here.' Krul smiled.

'Coincidence,' said Morris, 'surely.'

'No such thing exists,' said Krul. 'I will now demonstrate how the miscellaneous information you all let slip in your roads has illuminated, for me, the truth you have all tried, and failed, to hide from me. I knew most of it before you all commenced your expositions, but I needed confirmation. The game was my confirmation. Before I begin, Neil, extinguish that pipe or leave.

'Lottie and Morris, did you actually invent the cousin who had gone abroad? Neither of you have a very firm hold on reality unless it is slipping past you outside a moving vehicle. Didn't you simply run out of money as you always do, due to mismanagement and the inability of Morris to settle down to a decent job anywhere, and decided to rent out your house for the Bank Holiday weekend, and sponge off Krul and Addie? Best not to forewarn them because that would be admitting your own stupidity, and they might say *no*. Addie is so odd about visitors. Perhaps it's time to cash in those shares?

'James, the paperboy seldom makes the effort to wade through the inch of water on our tidal road, but he did this morning, and left the paper: your one. Strange that a paper came out despite the strike. I suppose it was one of those lies which justify themselves in the long run somehow? To put it charitably, since you are a relative of mine after all, you are like the cobbler's son who asks his father to cover the world with leather because his feet are sore. Let the whole world conform to James – he will never conform to it. No doubt you have finally annoyed the editor sufficiently with some cartoon in such poor taste, or so politically out of keeping with the paper, that he has given you the push. About time too – you've gone downhill since Niagara, but you might have told us.

'Bridget, your father phoned yesterday desperate to know if you were alive. He wasn't angry that you had deserted two dozen elderly folk in a country where they could not communicate, but he was worried sick that you were ill or dead. Could you not even have sent him a postcard? You, who count yourself so *reasonable*? Didn't like being deserted yourself in Sweden, did you? No one else has a right to their ideas, just Bridget.

'Zina and Neil, thank you for breaking the news to us, the news we have been waiting for, for so long. But you need not have come. You could have sent a letter, made a phone call, couldn't you? Well, no, not quite, because there is the question of Fred. What to do with the dog, now that you don't need him any more? And Krul and Addie live by the seaside and could easily take the dog. Well sorry, folks, we don't need one either, and you are just going to have to face up to the fact that the animal you once doted on, who had the body of an Olympic athlete, the brain of a nuclear physicist, has ceased to have a meaning in your lives, and will have to be destroyed before he licks germs all over the new baby's face or blinds the child by messing himself in the hall just before he falls in it. Your story was so touching, Zina – the wicked witch's dog, the crying baby at the end. Ah well, it's all a question of priorities now. And Neil, you'd better abandon hiding behind those puppets of yours and have the courage to come out as yourself for once. No wooden doll is going to put Fred down for you.

'Melanie, you did deceive everyone as to what really happens in that flat. Which is normally your own business – you chose the delightful Colin, who I am sure does have a redeeming feature though it's hard to imagine what. But when you come here expecting refuge, you owe it to us to be honest. Colin wouldn't give you a black eye, would he? The wall, the furniture perhaps – but not *you*. By the way I think I've guessed his redeeming quality – it's his telephone manner: Colin has phoned here innumerable times, but one time in particular.

'Now, finally, Bernard, the guest. We did invite you, by letter, in advance. The way things are normally done. And you arrived. Not alone. We had invited Fleur too, as we always do. But she wasn't the one accompanying you. She never is. And now I know that the only reason Fleur doesn't accompany you is the colour of her skin. She is as black as the Yfs. You called them that, not me. I expect it was a joke. What does she think to suffer here *if* she should come? Be eaten alive? This is a curious and painful insult, Bernard.'

Krul stood as if to leave but Zina, first taking a breath to aerate the foetus, said, 'Your cruelty is boundless. You made us bare our souls and then you sliced them up.'

'Yes. Amusing, though. The sermon is now over. The congregation are hereby warned that each of them will receive punishment in a manner suitable to their sins tomorrow morning. Perhaps *atonement* is a better word.'

'I'm so sorry,' wailed Melanie.

It wasn't Krul who left, it was all the others. No one stood their ground, no one argued their innocence or denied his accusations. So it was with feelings of disappointment and then horror that Addie watched them all troop off to bed, up the open tread stairs, with, as it were, their tails between their legs. Every one of them!

She was in the unique position of both feeling angry at having been so duped (for at least some of what Krul had said must be right) and feeling frightened at the turn of events in which Krul seemed to have been in complete control.

So she sat still, thinking hard, while Krul collected up the cards Bernard had flicked, all the glasses and bottles and took them into the vestry. She watched him closely, trying to ascertain from his movements alone whether they were allies or not. She watched while he rearranged the furniture so that it was just how it always was, with the cushions at sixty degrees to the chairs, and the side tables at right angles to each other. Soon the room looked as if nothing had happened there, nothing at all.

The main light went off. Addie continued sitting. Where was Krul? Only the anglepoise shone on St Boddi in glass. Fingers tightened on her throat. She jumped.

'Krul! Stop it! That's not funny!'

He released his hands a little and said, 'First of all, don't think I didn't understand your little diatribe. I did. Frustrating your creativity, am I? Standing customs officer at the gate of your self-expression? It's not true, Addie. If you'd only organise yourself better, you'd find you could achieve anything. You're too scatty, that's all.'

'You've misunderstood everything.'

'Oh, have I? I doubt it. And the other thing: Bridget's story was interesting. Interesting for me, I mean. Rutting away like a little rabbit on the knolls of Forgottenburg were you? I didn't know about *that*! Rutting away. Rutting rutting!' One of his hands shot down between her legs and grabbed her.

'Don't be silly. That was ages ago. I was an adolescent then. It was before I met you.' She removed his hand and straightened her skirt. He was mock-panting.

'Huh-huh ahuh-huh. It'll all come out now, Addie. Nothing can be hidden from me.'

'I wasn't trying to hide anything from you, Krul.'

'Wise of you,' he said, removing the skirt altogether.

38

Altar Cation

Addie knew what was coming, she always did. It wasn't mystical foresight or premonition or telepathy. It was a deep, if unsympathetic understanding of Krul's character, his needs and desires. Nothing turned him on like humiliating others.

'Not here, Krul.'

'Yes, here.' By *here* he meant the altar itself, the long flat wooden stage in front of the depiction of poor St Boddi in what seemed to be his final throes.

Only weak, stupid, inadequate men rape their wives, and Krul is none of these. His hands know the topography of Addie's body, the ins and outs: the power lies in seduction, not rape. She is unwilling, which makes seduction all the more challenging.

Challenging, but not out of the question. Addie has noticed with alarm that Krul is freer than most people from the constraints of reality. Reality could take off all its clothes, stand naked in a telling spotlight and shout, here I am – look at me, but Krul would still be convinced of the glorious rightness of his own point of view. Reality could jump down from the sky and grab him by the neck, shaking him violently and say, for God's sake take notice! and Krul would simply pick himself off the ground and say, see what I have to go through just to prove my point? Somehow the word 'stubborn' is as inadequate a word as 'damp' is for 'flood'.

So despite Addie's obvious unwillingness, Krul was determined to have sex with her on the altar now, and he was determined that she would *join in*. Short of arranging to die instantly, there was nothing on earth Addie could do to prevent it.

And then, there was the unspoken bargain they seem to have struck at the dawn of their marriage, though neither of them would have put it so crassly: that it was not unreasonable for a husband to require a sort of servicing from his wife. Krul had that sort of appearance which turns heads, always female heads, and no wife can be so confident of her charms that she deliberately gives him cause to encourage that attention. All this went quietly through their interactions unacknowledged, invisible but present like the Ph of soil.

'Not *now*, Krul.'

'Is your chief objection the location or the timing? Make up your mind.'

Addie's head, her mind within it, lay now on the altar.

'When you have calmed down.' She shouldn't have said that! She was referring to something against which Krul's mind was always closed. Only scatty, fizzy people need ever calm down.

'I am quite calm. I am deadly calm. Watch out for my calmness, Addie.'

There followed the very deliberate unslotting of buttons, unsliding of zips, unpeeling of sleeve and ruche and unlooping of bead belt. He did nothing fast. He pinned her gently while he shrugged off his own shirt, swam effortlessly out of his jeans with one deft backward arching of arm and torso.

His wise hands knew where to go. Not one cupping or flicking or plunging was wasted. Deft. Homing on the triggers. His other hand locked under her chin to direct her face to him. He liked her to have her eyes open. Legs open. He rocked himself against her. He teased. He reeled in her concentration stage by stage until she could think of nothing else. She was caught and he dangled her over warm water. Wait while I hover here. Hover and plunge.

And plunging he can be in many directions at once so that Addie is helplessly rising in two parts. Two charged wires of her afire with electricity, which finally intersect and send the fused charge back down into her middle, making her shudder in spasm. Spasm one notch from pain.

'Close now. Keep still,' he says, for when she has come, then she must shut her eyes. He only takes his pleasure then and quickly, as if it is of no account, and only an afterthought. Hence his loss of control is minimal and fleeting and Addie only feels it under the dark red of her shut lids and as a faraway slight addition of wet to wet.

Neither is he ever changed by making love in any way. Some people after all, men in Addie's past, have melted and been full of love just afterwards, as if the body and its requirements had now been dealt with and could be dismissed, in favour of a dual and waking dream. Not Krul. He simply gathers up what needs gathering, his face blank, like someone who had downed four stiff drinks but had no difficulty holding them.

Beside the scooping and gathering of the naked Krul is the image of St Boddi. Addie now regards him as an intimate. Sorry you're having to see this, Boddi. Not fitting, you in such trouble and all. Though maybe it cheers you up, the stupidity of the living, humping away like animals when they ought to be worshipping, or *where* they ought to be worshipping.

With my Boddi, I thee worship.

39

St Boddi's Road

It was with utter sadness and nigh on weeping that the Brothers one by one came into the Hall for breakfast and contemplated briefly the small lock of hair on the middle of Boddi's platter. A token of dolour if ever there was one.

Hew, having lost the bet so obviously, provided him with the best horse he could find, the drought having meant that several were put out of their misery recently, a bag of gold coins, and a set of decent clothes. Boddi could not understand the silence and sorrow of this parting.

'I'll be back, brothers. This is my home now. Boddi of Bodiam will return a free man!'

'You will always remain in our hearts,' said Brother Godric, having to be supported by two younger friars, so weak did he seem.

Boddi had discussed the route with Hew that morning, reversing the stages of the journey they had undertaken only three months before. For his protection, Godric had insisted that Boddi be given the cloak of a novice friar and a large rosary, to frighten bandits on the road. Boddi laughed at this but ceased to laugh when Hew pointed out that when they made the journey before they appeared to be a holy man and a cripple, whereas now Boddi might appear to be a young squire carrying gold, with two good legs and a horse.

Boddi agreed, though he would not take any arms with him, because they might be 'used against him' if he was captured.

Jankin gave him a rabbit's paw to ward off 'the evil eye', though he did so when no friar was watching.

Primrol gave him a twisted cloth of biscuits, blushed and ran away.

So equipped with his talisman and his rosary and biscuits and his disguise and his horse, Boddi set off in the direction of Dorset.

Boddi had no map; there were no road signs and very few other travellers, but he had a good memory and boundless optimism, and the drought was in his favour for he never had to shelter from the rain.

By the time Wyndcombe Manor came into view, with the fields surrounding it empty and yellow and dry, some of Boddi's optimism had begun to fade. Where were the workers on this ordinary weekday? Where was the steward, reeve, hayward checking the hedges, cowherd, dairymaid, foreman of mowers, smoke from the bakery? Where was the bailiff on his horse, treading the boundaries to check the fences? Where were the children sliding down the cliff paths and paddling in the sea? Boddi saw his home village now with different eyes. It was a small, dead place without even the church which, by rights, Sir Piers ought to have built.

A terrible quiet hung over the village as if plague had visited. But he would have heard tell if such a thing had happened. Someone would have travelled to Sussex to report it, to warn people of the coming of Death.

He stopped his horse outside his mother's cottage, by the edge of the village green, now a swathe of dry earth with tufts of grey grass dying all over it, like the beard of a very old man. He called out, 'Mother!' Nothing. He waited. There was a scuffling from inside and she appeared, slowly, in the door and looked up at him, shading her eyes from the hot sun.

'Boddi, is it you?' He slid down from the horse and stood, now head and shoulders taller than the small woman, and embraced her.

'What is this miracle?' she asked, looking down at his legs, now straight and even, the folds of his novice's cloak hiding the built-up shoe.

'I have been with the friars, Mother, and am a new man!' was all he said, but she hobbled indoors to find a handbell and started ringing it so that after a few minutes villagers started to emerge from their dwellings, blinking in the noonday sun and coming to see what was happening.

They all looked years older and muddled, as if having just risen from a long daytime sleep.

Despite the drought, and the lack of food or water, and despite there being no longer any work, there was a secret supply of ale in the village under the floor of the granary. Boddi's return and the miraculous nature of his cure, which he didn't feel about to explain, occasioned the collecting of this hidden manna and soon the entire village was engaged in drunken reverie under the pitiless sun, aided by Boddi's sweet singing (the miracle had also conferred on him the voice of a god), and, ale being what it is, eventually, his dancing also.

Boddi tried to make his old mother dance with him. She refused, saying when last she 'danced merrily' it was with his father and led to 'many an unforeseen thynge'. Boddi had never seen her so tipped up with ale before and pressed her to explain.

Laughynge, she toold of dallyinge wyth a yong friar passynge thru the vilage who had daunced and mad boold with hire so that come the Sprynge time she boore frute and yt was a boy and what to calle hym but Boddi after the home of that Fryre, Bodiam in Sussex? To whych he had mad returne alredy.

'What was his name, Mother?' asked Boddi, agog with wondering.

Hys name was God-somewhat for all tho Fryres callen themselves by a holy name and it meaneth nothynge. But he was a sweet man and shulden he come agayne, she wold luv him also.

Reeling, in more ways than one, Boddi joined the dance. Having been a cripple, Boddi had never even tried to dance. How he had longed to though. More than marriage, which was to him as complete an impossibility as returning from the dead, he had longed to hold a girl in his arms and whirl her round the maypole. Now he danced like a demon, swirling on his own, throwing his arms up like a madman and wildly aping children throwing a fit.

'Dance, Boddi, dance!' they shouted. Boddi thought, in so far as thought was available to his spinning brain, this is like the last throes of a sick animal, this village dancing when the drought has almost killed it. But he danced even harder, and the sweat mounting made him start to throw off his clothes. A chill wind (it must be in his mind) suddenly caressed his hot skin, then his sweat was leaping off him as he whirled and twirled and then a loud crack like thunder crashed above him and the air was instantly dark overhead.

It began to rain.

'Keep dancing, Boddi. Dance!' they were yelling. No one ran for shelter. They simply held out their hands, opened their mouths and tried to catch the drops. Crack after crack of thunder and flashes of lightning sundered the air, now dark grey-blue with water.

Boddi did stop. He had to. He was exhausted and the ground had turned to mud so that he could no longer dance. He felt himself falling through the mud.

He must have fainted. When he awoke he was in the great Hall at Wyndcombe Manor and Sir Piers was sitting beside him, on an upholstered oak chair, eating a lime.

'Well well, Boddi, you are *de retour*. Back in the land of the living. We thought God had taken you unto His bosom.' He laughed. Boddi sat up.

'Interesting shoes you have there,' said Sir Piers.

Behind him stood the bailiff who now said, 'My Lord, Boddi returned. He danced. It rained.'

'And the villagers think it is a miracle, Boddi. What do you think?' Boddi thought very carefully. He had been taught how to argue effectively, and how not to fall into traps.

'No mortal man can perform miracles: only God can do it. Perhaps He chose me as the device.'

'Oh I like the word "device", Boddi. I see you have been learning to think while away.'

Now Boddi sat right up and looked about him. The Hall was full! It was full of villagers, men, women and children, sitting cross-legged or squatting on the stone floor, quiet and still as statues. Outside was the steady drumming of heavy rain. For the first time in his life Boddi felt responsible: as if all these people were counting on him for something and he must not let them down.

'Now everyone can get back to work,' he said, indicating them.

'Well, perhaps. But perhaps this storm is a sudden freak and will not happen again.'

'No, the weather has broken now.' Boddi didn't know what gave him the courage to say this, to disagree with Sir Piers, but a murmur of approval from the villagers spurred him on. 'And flooding must be avoided. Rocks placed at the edges of fields, barrels placed to catch the water, trenches for irrigation. You know what needs doing, Bailiff.'

'Yes. Have I your permission, Sir Piers, to set them to work?'

'Wait!' said Sir Piers. 'I need confirmation first.'

Only Boddi knew the word, and his heart sank. Hadn't Brother Godric once told him that only tyrants with a weak hold on their own feelings need to control the behaviour of others, to have confirmation? They can have no faith, neither in themselves nor in others, and so they must have confirmation. Boddi knew then that his hours were numbered.

'Boddi will perform another miracle, and that will be the proof,' he said.

'What miracle?' said Boddi.

'You have until tomorrow morning to turn this water into wine,' and he handed an earthenware flask to Boddi. 'I'm sure you won't have any difficulty. But if you do,' here he turned to the sitting multitude, 'your life will be forfeit for daring to take His name in vain.'

Of course Boddi knew all the clever ways he could get out of this one. He could say that God does not perform miracles to order, that since there is no *need* for the wine, it will not happen, and so on. But the villagers did not seem at all dismayed by the challenge and would not have understood these quibbles. To them he was the Saviour, the bringer of rain, and he didn't want to disappoint them. But he was afraid of death and during the night offered a nightwatchman gold to let him out of the Manor. Unfortunately, the gold had been seized already, presumably while he was fainting on Sir Piers's couch, so the nightwatchman was unable to help. In any case, the nightwatchman had faith in the water-to-wine miracle, saying it was 'ony a smal thinge to aske Hym' compared to an end to drought. This man has more faith than I, thought Boddi.

Prayer has its uses, said Godwhen once, when pressed by Boddi. Especially to those in sorrow and trouble. Boddi tried to pray from within himself, but only the Prayer of Bodiam came to mind:

> O Lord bless al tho livyng under the bote, al tho who swepe up the skitterynges of otheres, who malgre so tyred thei wolde slepe, mak merrynesse for the hospitalite of the Gueste amonge them, as yf they were noten at ende theyre wittes, who, withoughten hope of Hevven, struggle myghtily ayaynest opressiaun here on erthe until nis one drop of strengthe lefte withinne ande they dye. And plese Yow to sende, Fader ov usse al, unto Eternall Damnynge al tho who abuse theyre swaye, who mak unneeden controllynge, bullyinge, tho Despott wyth ony armye hys owne, who werke and swinke thro the nichte longe to fynd outen sinnes of otheres, al tho who wythen rod of iron smelt wyth harden handes, mak virtu of harshnesse, tho of cruel kind, who see untolleraunce and hire clowse cousin Bigott as strengthe. Wracke wyth paynynge al Pedauntes, tho who can mak no halfway thynge to sayve bludde, al Maistery of Unebendynge, the fulle wayte of the Lawe, who Persecewtrixes, Extreemystes, and Tyrauntes. Yiv them yn the warlde no ynfluence, no swaye, no sovraynty, no supremasye, no Domynyon, over us. Yiv lavyshe and terrible dysees to al tho who sette themselves ovver otheres – be thei

man or womanne, mak thus an ende to Malevolaunce, for other it wille that the ruthlesse shall inheritt the pastures where the human spirite dwelleth forever seekyng Peas, and thys verry skye be yn outrage.

Heer endeth the Creed of BODIAM.

PART THREE

Monday

40

Close Call

Dawn tips into the edge of night as Krul's three hours' sleep
come to a close, the cool cloudless night on the French Channel
spiralling up and away as the heat of the day approaches. Out
in the Atlantic are opposing swirls of wild weather playfully
challenging each other to attack Nova Scotia, or Normandy, or
Dorset but they are as yet too far out to mean anything on the
southernmost coast of England, though informing the air with a
heavy electric current which humans awaking will call *closeness*.

In England, it is the August Bank Holiday: that pleat in the
year when real life is suspended, deactivated, decommissioned,
when the whole country is having a day-long siesta. When you
can't get a dentist to extract a nuclear bomb from your mouth,
when you can't buy a typewriter ribbon for ready money, when
the doctor will see you when he has gone through his list which
will be next year, when if there is a power cut, or water cut, or
gas leak, or floods or hurricanes or disaster, you had better pray
to God, for only He is unaware of His statutory rights this Bank
Holiday. No one else will turn out for you.

On the south coast of England, rows of Forestry Commis-
sion's next year's Christmas trees, small and grey with the
drought, lean their tired shoulders against the sky and wish for
no walker to drop sunglasses or glass bottles or lit matches this
incendiary day.

On such a day as this Things could land from Mars and go
unnoticed down behind the backs of the fronts of the rows of
slumbering England.

If you were thinking of declaring war on them, do it now.

This hot morning, Krul listens to Addie breathing the close air, and hears the sound of a large person's naked foot on his wooden stair, the opening of doors, the sound of frantic running, a gap, another set of urgent steps on stairs and then a definite piercing, adult scream. It is Lottie.

'KRUL! WHAT HAVE YOU DONE?' She bursts in on Addie and Krul and almost falls upon him, shouting, 'Where are all the children? Is this my punishment? Has it begun? Are you some kind of devil?'

'Calm down, Lottie. Go and get the others up and dressed.'

Quickly Krul's eyes scan the allotted place for Little Notes. His fifth column has collapsed.

It didn't take the adults long to discover that the children were not in St Boddi's, not in the outbuildings, not on the island at all.

'Even the baby!' as Lottie kept wailing.

'Even the dog,' thought Zina, despite herself.

As soon as Addie's brain cleared and she realised what had happened, that all seven children had left, possibly in the night, she felt herself panicking. It never crossed her mind, as it had Lottie's, that this could have anything to do with Krul, for Sophie was missing, and she was the Apple. He would destroy the whole world to have her safe and happy.

'Krul – the Coast Guard, the Police, what shall we do?'

He looked so calm. He would take control. He would find them. You could rely on Krul in an emergency. Small things enraged him, the big things sent him into a deep calm. He said, 'Get dressed. Tell Bernard to get his car out of the garage and facing the spur road. Ask everyone to assemble by the car.' Addie dressed in three seconds and went to obey him.

Rather fastidiously, Krul pulled on his hardiest jeans, strong walking shoes, sweatshirt with the five-sided star with shoulder straps in which he placed the loose end of a length of nylon rope from his middle drawer. He also wound a green belt around his waist on which was a money belt into which he placed two cards, and a fifty pound note from the dressing table.

Into the other side of this belt he fastened the holster for his cellphone. He leant out of the window to check on the boat which was adrift in the middle of the drying road.

Only it wasn't drying. The road was submerged. Krul reached for his Tidal Predictions and turned to 27 August Bank Holiday and read the High Water times.

'Oh Shit,' he said. August is when the tide turns. The Neap alters. Did the children *know* this? Bess!

He phoned the Coast Guard.

'Seven children and a dog,' he told them, 'up to two hours ago. I can't be sure of the time.' Then he phoned the police and discovered that cuts in the service meant that, it being a Bank Holiday, one man on a motorbike was all they could spare. The duty sergeant did point out that surely there was 'safety in numbers' working here.

'I've always thought that a stupid maxim,' said Krul, 'witness those crushed in football stadia,' and rang off. So the Dorset police would not be sending a hundred men with sticks to beat the New Forest inch by inch.

As he suspected. When it comes to the crunch, you are on your own. You and yours, that is. He clipped the phone into his belt and went downstairs to assemble his private army.

The drawbridge was up: the road a good three inches under the surrounding sea, and Bernard sat in his car, the roof down and the engine firing. Neil's mini was on the mainland, but Bernard's car had better visibility.

'We'll risk it,' said Bernard, 'it's not too deep.'

Krul stood and surveyed his army, a breathless and worried-looking crew whose faces betrayed nothing but complete panic.

'This is England,' he began, 'there may be madmen and eccentrics abounding, but they are unarmed, and there are not bandits and kidnapping is rare. Neither are there really any natural dangers other than the sea and the cliffs which are obvious. There are no snakes or quicksand around here, so it is just a question of locating them as quickly as possible.'

Addie was wondering whether he realised his own children

were a part of 'them', so cool did he seem. Somewhere out there is your darling Sophie: take care to get it right.

'Bernard and Morris and I will take the car and search the Windcombe area, leaving the TinCan here so that we can summon it if we need it.'

'How?' said Lottie.

'By phone. James, my bike is in the barn. You do the bridlepaths through the woods where we can't go. The women stay here in case they come home and as a contact for police. Lottie – you can drive the TinCan, I take it?'

Lottie squeaked in reply. Obviously words were failing her.

Bridget had no intention of following his orders and was already planning her own route.

'What about me?' asked Neil.

Krul had forgotten him entirely and said, on the spur of the moment, 'Are you up to a bit of tracking?'

'What?'

'Go on foot and try to track them. Like Fred would if he were here. Surely you did animal footprints with your classes?' Under the circumstances it would have been churlish of Neil to take this as an insult, which it was certainly intended to be, rather than seriously.

41

Human Lighthouse

Krul and Bernard and Morris squashed into the Morgan were the first over the water, sending up two arced wings of water on either side of them. They were followed by James on the bike, who veered left into the woods as soon as he reached the shore. Then Neil stumbled after them on foot, wishing he had something more substantial than sandals on, for the road was not just waterlogged, it was mudlogged too. He also wished that he was fitter, and that he hadn't parked his car so near what might well be their first footfalls on solid ground.

Bridget didn't wait to explain herself to anyone. It was no time for words. She fled upstairs on the double and rooted in her rucksack for the ancient map of South Dorset she had used to get here. Brilliant! Every path, however small, noted. Then she went into the children's room and looked at the mural. She thought it best to try to put herself in their shoes, imaginatively. Sheep, a cave, dunes, the sea. What had Toby said in his story? If anything had happened to Toby . . . that sodding boat should have been *padlocked*!

She ran out the main door and splashed through the road and onto the shore, passing Neil on all fours in the sand and his small yellow mini parked at a rakish angle, like an insect which had dive-bombed to its death. Up the road she went until she came to a footpath to her right. She plunged in and found herself in virtual darkness, the air hot with heavy pine and rot scent.

Back at St Boddi's, the women were all in the dining room around the telephone. As if it might ring any moment.

'Lottie,' said Zina, already, miraculously, dressed in a maternity jumpsuit of delicate peach, 'get dressed. Wash. Be reasonable.'

'Reasonable!' screamed Lottie, clutching at her hair, 'I can tell you're no mother yet. I have lost *four* children not a fucking dog. *All* my children, and you want me to be reasonable. George will be *starving to death* without me.'

'No he *won't*. No baby *needs* breastmilk to survive. Even if he's had nothing, he could survive for days. Newborns are abandoned all night in the snow. They survive earthquakes and ten-hour operations!'

'Melanie! Tell her! Tell her!'

'Sorry, but you really should get dressed, Lottie, and pull yourself together. Supposing the police arrive?' said Melanie.

'Oh, the two of you. Of course your bloody daughter is the one. She's the one who's led them off. The big bully. I'll kill her, if any hair of their heads . . . I'll kill that child of yours.' How quickly had the death sentence replaced Time Out as punishment!

Lottie stepped closer to Melanie and raised an arm. Melanie flinched but did not move. Zina stepped between them and steered Melanie away through the arch. Why did Melanie attract violence?

'Get dressed, Lottie. They may need you.'

Lottie went, sobbing, towards the van, and her clothes. Zina and Melanie sat down to guard the telephone, in case it should jump up and run away.

'How old is she?' asked Zina. Melanie hesitated.

'She's twelve, but . . .'

'What?'

'In some ways she's older. I sometimes think she's very old, because of the way we live.' How could Melanie begin to explain to this woman that her only daughter had to stand referee to traumas all day every day, that her childhood was surrounded not by laughter and love, but by anger and recriminations? That she could hardly be expected to behave like a real child any more?

'Then sensible? Maternal?' Zina smiled wanly. Her own child was kicking her, sensing her distress.

'Oh, she isn't. Trouble is her natural environment. She will have planned something to avenge Krul's treatment of her.'

Zina put her hands protectively over the peach expanse of her bulge and said, 'Surely not.'

Melanie started to weep. 'It's all my fault.'

'No it isn't,' said Zina automatically, thinking, yes it sounds as if it is.

Lottie's problems were not all emotional. The skirt was no problem, for it was elasticated, but she could not make the buttons of her blouse meet over her breasts. They had swollen and filled during the night efficiently for George's seven o'clock feed, and now they were full and sore and leaking. She sat down and wept. Soon small rivers of saline joined the milk over her ribs, which made her sob all the more, as if the life blood of her children were dripping away.

Up on the main Windmouth to London road, PC Reynolds turned his head, seeing a black dog disappear round an alleyway between two trees and a gleaming old-fashioned sports car. Bernard saw the motorbike on the wrong side of the empty road and applied his brakes. His *wet* brakes. The car skidded into the motorbike and came to a halt by virtue of the impact and a rise in the ground, not the brakes.

PC Reynolds found himself flying upwards and forward. So forceful was the thrust which propelled him through the air, that he had no time for thoughts or to readjust his body. Like a person taking his first high dive, he shut his eyes and hoped for the best. He landed inside the car on the back shelf next to a man with long hair. It was a painful but cushioned thump.

On landing, he passed out for a few seconds and when he came to, thought, if this is death, it's not so bad. Not so very different from being alive.

'Are you all right?' asked the man with the long hair, and of course, thinking it was a question from some kind of guardian of the Underworld, he replied, 'Fine. Wonderful,' so as not to miss out on anything being offered.

As soon as the car had stopped, Krul jumped out and ran for the skidding bike, travelling sideways down the road under its own steam. He caught it, and as he righted it, the throttle on the handlebar returned to position and the wheel stopped. He looked back for a moment at the car. The man who had been hurtled in was now struggling out, and Bernard was helping him. Morris looked more stunned than the victim. He knew that Morris, despite more man hours at the wheel than most long-distance lorry drivers, had never had an accident. Krul got on the bike and rode off, downhill towards the farm.

'Ah, that man has inherited my bike!' said the PC.

'He's looking for his children; he's distraught,' said Bernard, examining the policeman with care, with the eyes of a man who fears prosecution. 'Inherited' must be the new police jargon for 'stolen'.

'I too was looking for his children. Seven of them and a dog. That was when it happened.'

'Is there anything I can do for you?' asked Bernard.

'Oh no. I'm fine.'

'Let's go, then. Get in.' Bernard said a small prayer to the God of Evaporation, asking him to work a small miracle on his brakes, and started the car, driving far too fast. Then he stopped (the brakes making a half-hearted attempt) and reversed. It was barred, for pedestrians only. Krul must have cut through between two trees and headed west.

Now the going was hard, Bridget was finding. The path had narrowed and darkened, and she wondered for the first time whether her intuition had misled her.

Then she found a dummy. At first she thought it was a gleaming mushroom nosing out of the pine needles, then she saw the yellow handle of it. Nothing in nature is that yellow. She put it in her pocket and walked on, faster, more confident.

Addie was not so confident. She had known something would go wrong, and so this was it. She found the company of Melanie and Zina who was trying to help the forlorn Lottie to express some milk into a cup, too much to bear and went off to the tower, where she stationed herself, surveying the surrounding coastline regularly like a human lighthouse.

The Coast Guard helicopter was circling the bay to the north, its whirring reaching her, and then not, according to the acoustic bounce of the cliffs' edges. It was not a comforting sound. On the local radio station recently she had heard a woman's account of losing a six-year-old daughter to the sea and the woman had said, and these words now echoed in her mind, 'I heard the sound of a helicopter buzzing and the next thing I saw was the body of my daughter being lifted out of the Solent.'

Oh Saint Boddi, you know I don't really believe in you, except that maybe one day centuries ago you walked around these parts and did something remarkable, and you know I'm not devout or saintly, though I acknowledge the possibility of another world, with which I have tried to make friends, only I am at the end of the line here. I have a hot dangerous feeling as if the world is about to split apart and I lose the only thing that matters to me, my children, and I need some intercession between myself, so small a lighthouse without light and the cruel Almighty who has let this happen. I have heard it is possible that in moments when the world seems on the point of splitting open, not to ask God directly, for he will not hear you, but ask a saint to go personally for you to Him and ask for this little thing, this little assistance and God might bend His ear and might render the glue to keep your world together.

Well that is what I am doing now. Please go and do something, Boddi.

When Addie opened her eyes, she was looking down the

coast, southwards, and she could see two things: first that clouds were gathering in a sky which had been white-hot and empty for three months, and second a shining bullet-shaped object seemed to be lying on the very edge of the cliff, just below the bottom edge of Windcombe Farm. Why had she not seen this before?

'I am not praying for rain,' she said, out loud, 'not now.'

Neil had found a pattern of small footprints in the sand together with a set of doll's pram wheel tracks and dog prints. These were real, literal clues to the fact that they had all been there. Seven, count them. But somehow it did not impress him. This was not what *mattered*. An idea was forming in his mind that what was needed was not tracking, as Krul had called it, but some leap of the imagination. He felt as if he might be able to find them by the power of thought alone, but tried to shake this idea away. Breathlessly, he cursed his overweightness and started to climb the zigzag path to the top.

Bernard and Morris didn't know where they are going without Krul, and had to ask PC Reynolds. At least that was the name on his ID card though he seemed reluctant to admit to it. He also seemed unwilling to give them any directional advice, without giving also its opposite, for the 'sake of fairness'. Both Bernard and Morris found this infuriating but were too polite, and both feared that they might be in breach of some law or other simply by having a policeman with them, to say anything.

'You don't get a lot of children missing in these parts,' he informed them, 'people hereabouts are close with everything – they keep their kids on a tight rein, they save tin foil and those plastic tubs ice-cream comes in. The sea has a reputation for cruelty – quite unfair I think. The sea is just the sea. There it is. Swarming with blooming plankton at this time of year – you can't *see* plankton of course, not even in the Atlantic out there where whales farm it, keeping the planet oxygenated – but it's there all right. You and I, and even him back there with the long hair, prove it. We wouldn't have lived at all if the plankton weren't photosynthesising away merrily out in the briny deeps.'

'Yes, officer,' said Bernard. 'I wonder if there is a playground or something like that, where the children might have headed?'

'Playground?' The man frowned.

'You know, swings, and a roundabout, that sort of thing?' said Morris.

'I can't quite see what you mean, in my mind's eye like.' Morris leant over the front bucket seat from the back and looked the man closely in the eye.

'Stop the car,' he said. Bernard did. PC Reynolds had a faraway, dreamy look on his face and was very, very pale.

'Oh no,' said Bernard, 'he's concussed.'

'Or worse,' said Morris. 'Drop me here and take him to the nearest hospital. I'll go on searching on foot.' He climbed out of the car, saying, 'Interesting it took us so long to work out he was incoherent.'

'I've thought of a joke about playgrounds. This will amuse you, honestly. A policeman approached a man in a dirty raincoat . . .' Bernard started, at great speed, in the direction he thought – oh so hoped – Windmouth might be. If only he *had* persuaded Fleur to come. Then, he would at least have had access to a doctor!

42

Waking Dream

Bess woke powerful before dawn that day, stifling the small bleep of a quartz watch alarm with one swift, sure bat. The full swell of the tide just in, the road submarine, pursuit impossible, the whole world asleep.

One by one she whispered the children awake, save George. Stroke their ears and they come up from dreams like newts from a dark pool, rapid but silent.

The plan is afoot, the adventure begins. No more noise than a cat rolling in feathers do they make, gathering and dressing and swaddling the sleeping George.

The dog is awake by the back door. Toby attaches a leather belt to his collar, stilling his thumping tail on the doorpost. Greta fetches the doll's pram from the chalet, the light from the tower fading as the sun rises over its roof. Only Sophie knows how to unhook the boat. Father showed her in case she was ever trapped. Slip the knot, reloop the clamp and buckle up the one oar. You only need one oar, for the pull of the sea is constant. I am ten years old and I can do these things. Bess also has told us what to do. She even forbade me to send a Little Note. Not this time, she said. It must be a surprise.

'I'm hungry,' whispers Clare.

'Shshsh!' Climbing in is twofold – the foot offered first must give way to the second quickly to avoid slanting the boat into the water. The pram sits too high for the balance of a boat – eight hands brace it, keeping George's dreams afloat. The dog with its damp nudgey nose lies down flat in the space at Toby's feet. He is not the only one ducky-footy, is he?

286

As the sun rises high and fast, the small crew of seven and dog bob landwards and Bess dares to tell them, kneeling at the prow with the oar, that they will find food, a feasting place, where they are going.

One quick glance back – does that man ever sleep? Have faith, she tells herself, have faith.

Everyone feels hungry at dawn – the sun finds out your empty middle and dries crisp your slime of watery dreams. I am not really starving, thinks Toby – not really. I could just do with a sandwich, that's all.

Greta sees Hugo pinch himself and wonders if she is in his dream, or he in hers, and whether that warmth of the sun, that close red dawn of a beginning of a sun is quite right. Or is this how it would be in a dream – slow and quiet and the red stripes on the wake of the small boat too regular and too silent, and the land approaching as in a picture where you have made the perspective absolutely correct?

'Take the oar, Greta,' said Bess. Even the way the pearls of white water slide down the edge of the oar and join the flat water below is unnatural, like a dream.

Sophie knew that the boat ought to have been refastened after they had left it, but she didn't want to speak in case her words might carry, amplified, over the water, to Father's ears.

So the boat pulled out against its restraining rope into the middle of the channel and stayed there while they climbed up, skirting the small yellow car sinking into the sand, pushing the pram and pulling the dog and following Bess into the woods.

The woods were full of witches, of bats and wolves and half-men, creatures who could find no rest, harps made of pine cones which sang of murder, those who were lost at sea and come home to roam the pinekernel darkness and banquet on children. The long brown pillars their fingers, the green speckled twining above their hair, the blackberry barbed wire their bushed eyebrows. Something was always watching the seven and dog as they trooped down the bridlepath over the brow of the hill, or, if you were a giant and the whole of Dorset just an elbow-rest shaped like an ear, the bit of the ear just above the earlobe where an earring would pierce.

Toby had never been so frightened in all his life. If I am allowed to live, he prayed, I shall never do another bad thing in all my whole life. Oh, let me be allowed.

Something invisible in the woods reached down and shook George, who cried out and spat his dummy into the air, thick with swarms of midges. Greta, who was pushing, looked around for it, but whatever it was had gobbled up the rubber-sucker, handle and all.

After a lifetime, after a millennium, after the last moment when Toby thought he could bear no more had passed three times, a light carved a slice into the row of trunks in front, and Bess turned and smiled at them all. As they sped up, half-trotting now, turning with the last bend of the path, narrow, in single file, the darkness splayed out, fell back, and they were in the light.

A field with sheep stretched out before them.

Fred made a deep gulping noise and lay down on the ground. Then he slipped his collar and pulled away from Toby who stood there with empty leathers, terrified. Did sheep eat dogs, or dogs sheep?

Fred danced among the quadruped clouds. He scattered them and banked them up and drew them out into one thin long line. Then he lost his legs: shrank down on his belly and swam across licking the dry grass with a long pink tongue. Nearer and nearer he came.

'Farmers shoot dogs for doing that!' said Greta.

The farmer would miss, Toby foresees, and down they would go like tenpins.

Bess scans the world. Behind them, downhill a small road, already off-white grey with the heat, sloped down to the cliff's edge and on towards – towards the rest of the world. But before the rest of the world lay a wondrous object, a sort of metal spaceship, rusted, with its wheels up like a mechanical dead fish in a cemented dry mudfield. It lay, this rusty castle, on its side between the road and the edge of the world.

'Quick!' shouted Bess, running towards it. She would save them from the farmer's gun.

Toby grabbed Fred by his thick fur neck before he dived into the spaceship, perhaps transport to another world where there might be – Toby hesitated, the mastiff pulling him downhill – sandwiches?

Inside was spidery, but cool and damp and a smell of old fork and spoon rusted the air. The door in was sprung upon them and creaked shut when Hugo tested it to see if it would.

'Now you've done it,' said Greta. Normal to Hugo that all the world said this every time he touched something. He wasn't even sure what it meant. Good or bad?

'It's all right,' said Bess, 'what goes up must come down.'

And *down* was right. Sophie and Greta, the oldest of the young, scanned the edges of their environment and found that the craft where they were was *hanging* over the cliff, for to look out of the windows on the far side was to look straight down a mile long tunnel at the end of which was a small beach the size of a blond giant's eyelash.

'Oh shit,' said Bess, 'locked up again.'

The shut bus was short of air, and rocked as they tried smashing the door with the pram. George cried. Clare cried. Bess shouted that they must sit still and wait. Wait for what? For rescue. They sat. The heat rose inside the bus, the air thickened. George passed out. One by one they all fell asleep, on the outer side of the bus, the sea side. Only the dried runnels of mud, cement-hard with drought, held the wheels of the bus where they were, preventing it from falling over the edge of the world.

It was the very spot where seven centuries earlier Boddi, setting out on a journey, had looked down and seen his mother and feared that he would never pass that spot again. If there are unstable places on earth where the past might seep up into the present, this is surely one of them.

The hinged door of the bus folded in half and a man stepped

through. Toby awoke with the stroking of Fred's tail on his leg and looked at him. He was not very tall, with bushy brown hair and a beard, a long brown cloak or tunic, and those shoes people wear whose legs are uneven lengths.

'Hello,' said Toby.

'Wake the others,' said the man in a thick country voice Toby hadn't heard before, 'we will have a party.'

'With food?' asked Toby, amazed that the right words had come out together, just as he'd thought them.

'Whatever you want.'

'I want egg and cress sandwiches, and fishfingers and baked beans and a large tub of chocolate milkshake! And singing and dancing too! I said it!'

'There's a man after my own heart!' sang out the stranger.

Toby could see the others waking now and stretching. The man walked down the middle between the seats and gave something to Greta, who started to feed George with it. It was a banana-shaped glass bottle with a rubber teat on the end, full of milk.

Then in the bus with no music to go by, the small man sang mightily some ancient tunes. The children soon learned to join in with 'terly terlow' and other nonsenses, and danced in the confined space with the fellow with two odd legs and the bushiness and lumpishness of a human beaver, his long cloak catching under their heels. Bess announced that she had been right all along, her mouth stuffed with sweetmeats provided by the entertainer, and the bus rocked with merriment.

Until, apparently outside the bus, but very near, was the sound of an engine, as if, thought Toby, the engine of the craft were starting up independently, and the man said something like (for they still had trouble understanding his accent):

'Here cometh Sir Piers and I must be gone' – at which he vanished through the door as suddenly as he had arrived. Toby had the feeling that the poor man had made a mistake, but there was no time to tell him so.

As he left, the first drops of rain fell on the roof, the first drops fell to loosen the mud-hard runnels, and the bus seemed to be spinning.

43

Catapult

By the time Krul and motorbike entered the top of the field below Windcombe Farm, the rain was bucketing down. Where it had come from was a mystery. The rain loosened dust everywhere, so that clouds of yellow mist hung along the edge of the field, though the bus was clearly visible at the bottom. He hoped to God they had not gone in there. He would check anyway.

As he skidded downhill on the now greasy dead grass, the radio, which he had not yet learned how to deactivate, kept asking Reynolds to respond, and asking him whether he required assistance or ambulance back-up. Though he could (and did) shout back at it, Krul assumed that the disembodied voice could not hear him unless some switch was depressed.

At least the sheep responded: they scattered on hearing him.

Before he reached the bus, Krul noticed Bridget enter the field from the east, running along the narrow asphalt road, map in hand, Morris trotting up from the woods, James on his bike. They were all converging on the wreck on the cliff's edge.

Krul was there first, and saw all seven children, and the dog, lying asleep on the floor on the far side of the bus, and the door was rusted shut.

Without speaking, they all tried to prise off some piece of the bus to let in air without unbalancing its precarious hold on the loosening earth, and all failed. Krul phoned Addie and told her to bring everyone, and the van and more rope. Then he clamped the end of his nylon rope to the back axle of the police motorbike and, seeing what he meant, Bridget and Morris and James all stationed themselves along the rope, paying it up from the back wheel of the bus where James had tied it, so that Krul could pull the bus free from the cliff's edge.

When the women arrived minutes later and added their weight to the rope and even another rope to the front wheels, it made no difference, and the bus stayed swaying perilously close to the edge of the cliff and Lottie started weeping again as the Coast Guard hovered, undecided. The farmer arrived, swearing, with useless block and tackle and the rain so shot down that now it was obvious that should anyone let go, the bus and the rope and all the holders of the rope could sail over the cliff to the bottom in a matter of seconds. Or rather, Krul and the children would.

If a catapult is just a wooden 'Y' with a rubber band stretched from its two arms, the bus was the split leg of the catapult and Krul on the revving motorbike was in the middle of the rubber band, a hundred yards uphill from it. As the wheels of the bus loosened their grip on the runnels they were lodged in, the tension on the rubber band, Krul's nylon rope, increased.

Until this moment in his life, Krul had never felt the need for other people. He had not been connected to others. Now he was, and so literally. Should one of them, Lottie, or Bridget or James, or Addie or Zina or Melanie or Morris, or any of them, loosen their grip for a moment, he and the bus would shoot back over the cliff. His own children were in that bus. And Lottie's.

He wrenched his neck round and looked down the two lines of the rope, taut and hissing in the rain. He had offended every one of them. Even Addie. Too late to ask forgiveness. He had to trust his life, and the lives of his children, to these seven people he had humiliated. It was not a position he had ever thought to be in.

Stuck. Absolutely stuck. There is an eternity of time, and no one must move. A helicopter will sort it out. Won't it? Hold tight. Listen to the 'copters. Listen to the rain. There is time to think. Or is it time to pray?

No, think. Think well. These may be my last thoughts. I never thought I would fail. I am now the stone in the catapult and I would happily have the thumb lifted from me and fly upwards towards death now if it would save the children. Even those children not my own. But it won't. There must be something I missed. Omitted to do. Some mistake I made. I am not winning. I must win. Surely life is more than just these random throws of the dice?

'*Help!*' shouted Krul.

No one moved.

44

Heart Full of Fur

Neil heard this cry for help just as he entered this scene of mud and rain and ropes and helicopter. He was already breathing hard, his bare knees scarred like a small fat schoolboy on an unwise hike, his whole lower half muddy from traversing the spur road.

It took one half minute for him to understand the physics of the situation. He was the only person *loose* and mobile. At the moment when he decided what to do, he also bade farewell to this life, knowing that he most probably could not survive it. He looked towards Zina briefly, who was, like everyone else, looking hard at him through the rain, and the surreal thought passed through his mind that she was carrying in her bump his afterlife.

He approached the bus, stepping rather gingerly over the ropes and into the lane defined by them. Standing by the glass door, he tapped on the window. There was no response from inside. The bus moved away from him.

With one hand he banged even harder, with the other he reached into his pocket for Henry.

'*Move away from the vehicle!*' said a tannoy from the spinning blades above.

Neil ignored it. Inside the little girl with plaits had opened her eyes. Henry slid up into the middle panel of the door and beckoned her towards him.

At this point, mercifully, the helicopter must have flown away, for it became quiet, apart from the rain. Neil put his lips to the hinge, a small rusty gap, and threw his voice, or rather, Henry's, into the bus.

'Help me! I am just a small furry creature and the wolf is coming to get me!' Clare woke and stood up, wobbling, a frown on her face. He thought he saw her lips saying, 'Oh no.'

'I need lots of friends. Wake up your friends for me. Quickly!' Clare started to prod the others awake. Gradually they all blinked and staggered towards the door. When most of them had moved, the bus began to slide towards Neil. He didn't dare lose his hold on them, didn't dare move away. He turned slightly then and shouted '*Pull!*' behind him and tried to jump out of the way of the bus, now sliding uphill towards the tug of war, at the apex of which was Krul revving the motorcycle, which moved forwards at last.

Neil almost jumped free. Only his left foot was crushed by the axle of the bus, but it was severed almost entirely. Never had pain been so sweet to him as he lay there, fully conscious, watching the crowd freeing the children from the crumpled bus. Zina was stumbling towards him, her dress stuck tight to her tight bulge in the rain.

'It's only a foot, you lucky bugger!' It was a Coast Guard, the one who had tried to get him to move away from the bus. 'If they can't sew it back on, you can have a wooden foot, or a built-up shoe, no one will know. It's not like losing a hand or your wedding tackle. The things we've fished out of the sea, things propellers have spewed out, let me tell you . . .'

By the time his stretcher was in the helicopter, Neil felt almost *lucky*, and Zina, beside him smiling and radiant and adoring, told the pilot proudly that not *one* of those children was theirs, though the dog was, as if that meant anything.

45

Wyndcombe Manor Farm

Windcombe Farm, built in and on the ruins of the ancient Wyndcombe Manor House, took on, for a time, the atmosphere of a First World War Field Dressing Station, for into it poured gratefully the battle-torn, the weary, the starving hungry, and the official helpers, all seeking solace, escape from the mud and rain, and a hot cup of tea.

The inhabitants of Windcombe Farm were only too pleased to dispense this hospitality for two reasons: first, they felt responsible for the fact that they had allowed the bus to be dumped on their land in the first place, although James pointed out to them that this was the fault of the present government, which had so impoverished them that they felt more in need of a few pounds sterling than a clear sea view. Second, they were both very shy people, and had no friends of their own and yet here, pouring past their sagging front door, were a lifetime's friends, greeting them like long-lost cousins, telling them their life stories, eating their food, drinking their tea, and generally behaving as if they had arrived not on a run-down farm, but in Paradise.

To Krul, it was not quite Paradise. Just as the helicopter with Neil and Zina on board had lifted off the field, he had reached it, running. The desire to say something to Neil, or even to touch him had been overwhelming and been frustrated. As the helicopter flew off, he found himself making a salute of sorts with both hands. Ten minutes later Addie had suggested, noting his agitation, that he use his cellphone to phone the nearest hospital, which he did. He had been told that Neil was 'expected in theatre'. To get this information, he had said when asked 'Are you a member of his family?' that he was. Then, with a jolt, he realised he was. They were cousins by marriage.

So now Krul's money belt yielded up money, some of which he gave the farmer's wife so that she might later replenish any stores used to feed the multitude. She was not too proud to take it, the dear woman, since so badly was the farm doing, what with salmonella in the hens and mad cow disease in the cattle that they had been obliged to seek assistance from the government for the first time ever. With the fifty pound note safely in her inner apron pocket, the farmer's wife was happy to fry all the eggs she possessed, all the bacon, open every tin of corned beef, empty her milkchurns into the children. Since it was a Bank Holiday and what with the Incident, the milk had not yet been sent off to Windmouth. Let the Windmouthians drink powdered, she had a small army to feed here.

They were all in what she called the kitchen annexe: a huge room they could never afford to heat in the winter, but which now, with the addition of refectory tables, card tables, milk-crates and so on, made an excellent dining room for the twenty or so people thronging it.

Why so many? Apart from the seven-and-dog rescued from the bus, there was Krul, sitting with Sophie on his lap looking like an ordinary dad, though rumoured to be the rich man who had desecrated St Boddi's with newfangled ideas, Addie with Toby next to her, who was telling her, in perfectly ordinary English which he seemed to have picked up during the ordeal all about a man he had dreamt of who came and sang and danced for them in the bus. Melanie was telling the Coast Guard whose place in the helicopter Zina had taken all about the behaviour of London police at riots.

Bridget was personfully opening tins of peaches in the vast larder with Bess. She felt light of heart. Bess wanted, more than anything, to be forgiven. Bridget forgave her immediately because she saw the whole incident as 'Paying Krul Back' for his inhuman treatment of her. Every particle of her congratulated Bess on her getting even with the bastard. Thus Bess clung to Bridget until Krul came to the edge of the larder, which was the size of a small garage, and said, 'Bess.'

'Yes?' She wanted to scuttle behind Bridget, but didn't dare move. What could the punishment be for attempted murder on such a scale? Life imprisonment in the larder? Decapitation?

'You worked out the tides, didn't you?' Bridget was surprised. This wasn't what she thought he'd say.

'Yes.'

'That was very clever. You understood about the Neap. It's a shame the expedition went wrong. It could have been such an adventure.'

Then Bess couldn't stand it and blurted out, 'I did it to punish you!' and did place herself behind Bridget for protection, where she added, too softly, alas thought Bridget, for Krul to hear, 'You pig.'

'Oh I know that, and I don't blame you. That's what I'm saying. That I don't *blame* you.'

Bridget could see that Krul was in difficulties to say what he meant, for once. For once in his life he was stymied. All he needed to say was 'sorry' but he hadn't ever said it, and was struggling. Bridget could have triumphed at his distress now, could refer somehow to the years of torment, of struggle over who loved Addie best, who would win her. That's what a man would do. Instead, she put an arm around the girl cowering beside her and said, 'It's all over now, Krul.' She smiled at him, and he smiled at Bess, and they all smiled at the farmer's wife who came into the larder just then and asked whether their daughter was very fond of cling peaches then.

Bess found her mother with James. Again. He was making Melanie a promise. It was to do with a 'Safe Harbour'. Bess asked him what that meant. He gave her a key.

With the key went a piece of doggerel he had instantly invented just for them.

Girls! Let me be your safe harbour –
Your tin of sardines in the back of the larder,
When life is rough and getting harder.

Morris and Addie were arguing about the ancientness of the place where they were.

'Surely St Boddi's is medieval?' said Morris.

'No,' said Addie, 'no more medieval than we are. A Victorian fake. But this place feels like the original Manor House. The real thing, though built over a bit. Can't you feel it?'

Morris could. He could also now feel how father birds must feel at the end of a long hunt when the chicks take everything, for whatever was laid in front of him, two of his children, Greta and Hugo, were snitching playfully from his plate, as if to stake a claim on him. His other two children were guzzling from Lottie's nipples. Clare and George had fought for breastmilk and both won. To the company at large, Lottie said, 'This mineral water tastes like wine!' for she was drunk with the pleasure of seven safe children, as if artesian water had somehow turned to wine!

And besides these folk, there was the farmer himself distributing largesse as he had never hoped to do again, especially when he was able, having ascertained his name from Addie, to propose a toast to the hero of the hour, Neil, and to hope with all his might that a miracle might happen and his foot be sewn back onto his leg. Aptly perhaps, they drank his health in milk, beer, bottled and tap water, and orange juice, but every adult there made a small, superstitious rite of their own to back up the toast.

There were also two off-duty policemen, a farm worker, two ambulance men on double pay, Addie's Domestic Maintenance Operative in mufti, and Bernard, who had returned and was somewhere among them explaining how he had been arrested.

It was a good story and the off-duty policemen found it such a hoot, they *both* spilt substances down their fronts. Arriving at Windmouth in the middle of a Bank Holiday, Bernard had found the streets deserted so he had called in at the police station to ask where the hospital was. PC Reynolds was by this time slumped over the dashboard (soberly for once in his life, quipped one of his friends). When Bernard had run in to ask, their man was spotted there and Bernard arrested as a suspected hit and run, though he had not 'run'. His car keys were confiscated and he was put in Windmouth's only cell. Meanwhile Reynolds was rushed to the nearby cottage hospital while the Sergeant quizzed Bernard about the missing motorcycle. Bernard didn't feel he wanted to say that Krul had stolen it, so he asked if he could make one phone call, which he did, to St Boddi's. Naturally there was no one there, but Krul's answering machine told him a number where Krul could be reached. But Bernard was not allowed to make another call. Windcombe was not the jungle, you know, they knew that *one* phone call was all he was allowed. Did he think he could run up a massive bill chatting to all his friends? Where would it end? Bernard sat in his cell, praying that Reynolds would not wake up with total amnesia and he be in court, the flashy Londoner with the fast car mowing down the local constabulary. Life imprisonment for sure.

Fortunately Reynolds lost no time in recovering and though a little confused ('How could they tell?' asked his other friend), exonerated Bernard entirely, at which point Bernard did phone Krul's cellphone, paying for the call when his wallet was returned, and discovered that all adventures were over, the children safe, and everyone at the farmhouse.

'I seem to have missed all the fun,' he said. So moments after a near-tragedy, it is 'fun'. The time lapse between tragedy and humour is shortening, isn't it? Time was when a century had to pass before the tyrannies of one regime gave way to the mockery of the next, now animated rubber caricatures mock politicians the same day, sarcastic comments flower in the newspapers that night if a famous person makes a *faux pas*. We have no time to wait. Mock now while the sun shines.

So they all giggled, not so much about the stupidity of

entering a rusted bus on a cliff's edge, for some of them still trembled internally at the danger, but, gradually, about the coincidence, for the farmers did ask about this, of their all being there. So there began a round of explanations at Windcombe Farm for the benefit of the farmers, who were told of Bernard's invited girlfriend being too shy to accompany him, James being sacked, Bridget throwing up a job in Belgium, Lottie and Morris running out of money (don't we know, they said – we can barely feed those hens), the absent but heroic Neil and his wife Zina trying to dispose of their dog ('I'll take Fred – Fleur wants a dog'), and Melanie leaving her brute of a husband ('That'll shake him – he'll behave hisself now, be'nt it?').

Toby tugged at the farmer's trousers. He looked down. There was one of those hushes which happen by chance when massive numbers of people all talking together momentarily run out of things to say, or just need to draw breath.

'Yes?'

'Sorry we rustled your sheep. Don't shoot us.'

Everyone laughed at this. The laughter rang and rang until Krul found he needed some air and some quiet and slipped out the side door onto the hill's edge and looked over towards St Boddi's, the rain now abating slightly.

Addie had seen him go. So had Sophie and Toby.

'Where's Father going?' asked Sophie.

'Gone home to think,' said Addie.

St Boddi's was empty, the front door swinging, no one in the tower. The open graves were one by one being filled by mud sliding over their cut edges in the rain. Reclaimed. Desecularised. One day soon, perhaps in ten years or fifty or a hundred – who knows how long we have? – the earlobe of land will be entirely severed from the mainland, which is itself, in reality, only a larger island. The tidal road will no longer be high or wide enough to rise up again, so that the sea will sneak in from the Atlantic, stealthily along the Gulf Stream channels, in the night, or those few moments before the dawn, and cover St Boddi's for ever, the earlobe falling into the Channel like a tear.

Krul remembered Sugardaddy, SantaKlaws, Great Wolf, Yogi and especially No Big Dealer and started down the zigzag path on the slippery cliff's edge, to free them. He kicked off his shoes to run faster. Suddenly it was a matter of some urgency.

Vision of St Boddi

In the night Boddi dreamt of feasting and banquets, such as the Lord would put on perhaps to welcome him to Heaven later that day. He woke feeling refreshed, for all the guests at the banquet had been children, dressed in colours as bright as birds of the air in a metal ship with wheels, as if dying really did entail being lifted up and born again. In the morning the Bailiff came to bring Boddi and the flask from the cell under the massive kitchen. The Bailiff took Boddi to one side first and said, 'Sir Piers bid me search you for anything valuable, when you were resting after the miracle, and I did. But have no fear – I gave the gold to your mother to dispose of and the rabbit's paw I gave to Mad Awdlay to help him. A few groats I gave to Sir Piers, to prove I had searched you. Nothing else did I take. Forgive me.'

'Thank you,' said Boddi.

'Aren't you afraid?'

'No, I dreamt well.'

In the hall Sir Piers had gathered his women and household servants together and laid out tankards on the table for the tasting. Some representatives from the village were also there, including Boddi's mother, but the rest had been told to wait outside.

Boddi approached the table and put the flask on it. Without speaking, Sir Piers poured out three tankards and passed one to the bailiff, one to his wife, and took one for himself.

The bailiff would not drink.

'Taste it!' shouted Sir Piers. Slowly the man lifted the pewter to his lips and sipped at it.

'Wine,' he said. Boddi felt a cold hand squeeze his chest. Surely the man had condemned himself to death. Sir Piers drank quickly and smiled.

'Mine is water,' he said, and looked at his wife. She drank.

'Oh,' she seemed to say.

'That is French for water,' said Sir Piers. She nodded her head, and said, 'yes.' One by one Sir Piers made the villagers come in and sip from the bailiff's drink and one by one they all agreed it was water.

Boddi spoke up for the bailiff. 'But the faithful might taste wine.'

The bailiff smiled at him, carelessly it seemed.

'Clever,' said Sir Piers. 'Bailiff, fetch the whip.'

Boddi was relieved that the bailiff's punishment was only to be beating him to death, and not anything worse, though to look at his face you would think he would have preferred his own instant death.

The villagers watched the beating, not because they enjoyed the spectacle but because they were ordered to and were all wondering whether Boddi might, miraculously, somehow survive it, and wanted to be present at the miracle if there were to be one.

Only Boddi's mother and Awdlay wept outright and by the time the bailiff had pronounced him dead and the rain had started to fall again, only about ten people remained to see Sir Piers place his boot on Boddi's neck.

Boddi's mother demanded the body and six men helped her to drag him down to the cliff's edge, where they propped him up for a 'last look at the sea' as they always did for Wyndcombe-born people: their spirits needed this last glance to give them direction.

Boddi opened his eyes.

'I'm dying,' he said. They all gasped with astonishment. 'Take me down to the spur.' They carried him, though blood was pouring from the wounds on his back and his head lolled sideways dreadfully. His breathing too was loud and crackling.

'Is Harden here?' he asked when they had arrived.

'I'm here, Boddi.'

'Where's your horse?'

'Still living. In Far Field now. Why?' Boddi reached inside his tattered tunic and brought out a piece of what looked like white bone. For a moment his mother thought he had wrenched away his own breastbone, and shrieked.

'It is only ivory,' explained Boddi, 'give me a knife.' With Will's knife he scored a name on the matt side of the ivory. SIR PIERS MALDESPO, he wrote, and handed it to Harden.

'Ride with this to the Friary at Bodiam and they will welcome you. They will know what to do.' And then he spoke no more and his mother began to keen, knowing the end was soon.

No magic sword rose from the sea, no angel came to collect him, nor were the skies rent asunder for his passage, but quietly, to himself, Boddi had a vision at the moment of his death.

Where he lay on the then wide spur of land pointing out to the edge of the world, at Wyndcombe, he saw rise up a small church with a modern shape and stained glass, and it was his church. The Church of St Boddi.

But something was wrong. The church looked desolate. The door swung forlornly, as if the people of the future had not made their way there. He heard overhead the beating of giant wings and looked round. There, beyond the crooked arm of his old mother, he saw a wizard running down the cliffside towards the church. He had colourful, close garments on and a pentangle on the chest. Various sorts of armour and magic devices clustered on his belt. He was sodden with rain, like Boddi, and running barefoot. When he reached the church, and before entering the open door, the Wizard looked straight at Boddi as if he recognised him.

Death came to Boddi gently as a slight turn in the tide, a slight swell, warmed by the Gulf Stream, sliding back down the smooth wet sand. His spirit kicked off its unequal shoes and all its dreams and entered the flightpath of the neap tide, even at last.

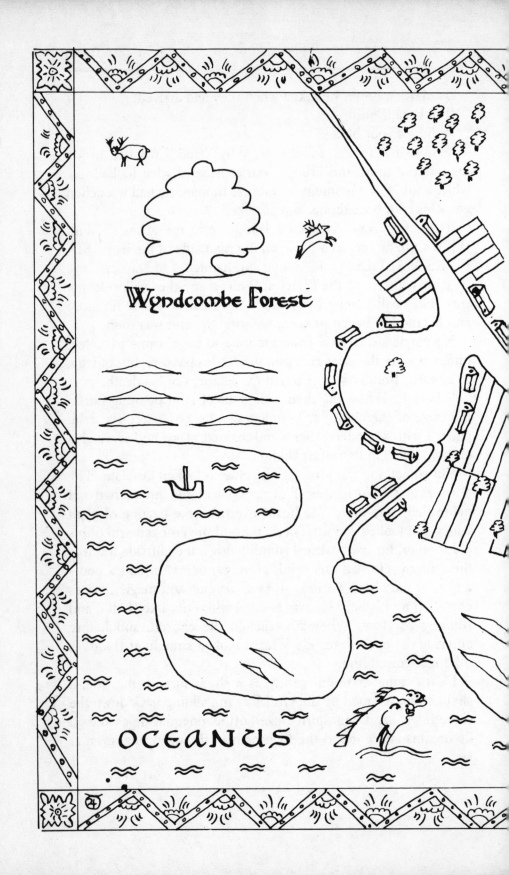

Wyndcombe Forest

OCEANUS

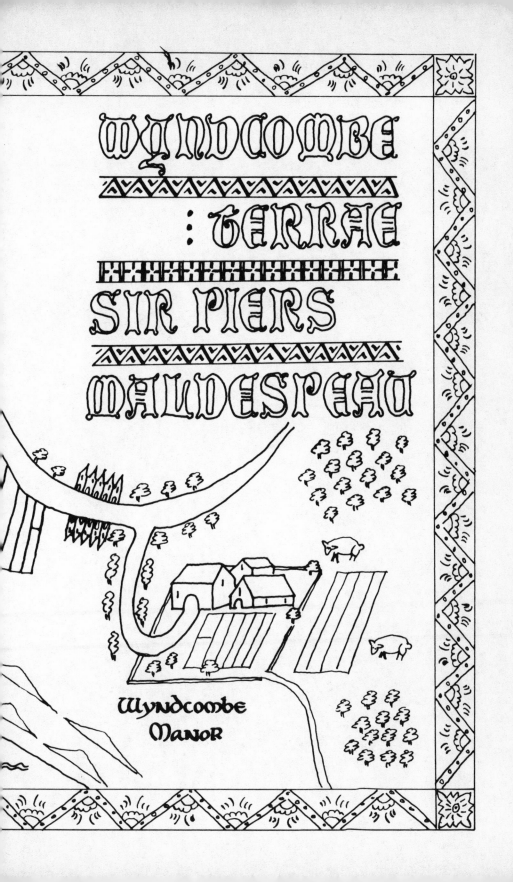

WYNDCOMBE

: TERRAE

SIR PIERS

MALDESPEAU

Wyndcombe
Manor